Leeds Library and Information Service
24 hour renewals
http://librarycatalogue.leedslearning.net
or phone 0845 1207271
Overdue charges may apply

AF

A LITTLE BIT ON

THE SIDE

John W O'Sullivan

Matador
9 Priory Business Park
Kibworth Beauchamp
Leicester LE8 0BX UK
Tel: (+44) 0116 279 2299
Fax: (+44) 0116 279 2277
Email: books@troubador.co.uk
Web: www.troubador.co.uk/matador

ISBN 978 178088 1591

British Library Cataloguing in Publication Data.
A catalogue record for this book is available from the British Library.

Printed and bound in the UK by TJ International, Padstow, Cornwall

Matador is an imprint of Troubador Publishing Ltd

CONTENTS

'My dear sir, you have but one complaint, and it is the worst of all complaints; and that is having a conscience. Do get rid of it with all speed; few people have health or strength enough to keep such a luxury, for utility I cannot call it.'

Dr Erasmus Darwin.

1

Half Ox, Half Fox

'I suppose you realise that all the locals knew what you did for a living before you even moved into the place?'

Jack looked up in surprise at his questioner. About half-an-hour earlier Jimmy Gillan had asked him how he and Kate were settling in to country life on Barton Hill, and Jack had expanded at some length on the problems they both seemed to be having in making anything other than arm's length contact with their immediate neighbours, let alone the wider community.

Kate had been received and civilly served in the local shops whenever she went into the village, but had been puzzled when the butcher asked her if she would like a receipt when she paid cash for an unusually large order of meat for their week-end visitors. She'd also found it strangely difficult to get beyond anything other than trivial day-to-day exchanges in her conversations with the women. It had all been rather unsettling.

Jack's experience in the local pub mirrored Kate's: everyone polite, but distant and reluctant to engage. So much so that eventually he'd taken to having the paper with him, and sitting for a read while he enjoyed his solitary pint. It had been much the same when they went together to the Christmas Gala evening in the village hall: not cold-shouldered exactly, but not warmly welcomed either. They'd eventually assumed that that was how it was with all incomers to Barton Hill, and that things would in time get better. Now it all made sense.

Barton Hill - they'd chosen the place for its remoteness. For almost forty centuries its inhabitants had lived out their lives and gone to their graves in isolation and obscurity. To its dreary, treeless heights few ventured even in summer, and there were no permanent settlements, just a scattering of tumble-down huts to provide a temporary shelter from the bleak winter fogs or scouring winds for those few unfortunates whose business called them there from time to time to oversee the unhappy flocks of sheep that roamed the barren heathland pulling hopelessly at its thin grasses or, overwhelmed by the futility of it all, as a thinking sheep might perhaps express it, slumping down in sickness to die alone beside one of the bronze-age burial mounds. They were poor benighted creatures, long-shanked, shallow-chested, wild of eye and short of breath: the sheep were little better.

A few hundred feet below the heights, where the heathland ended and the topsoil thickened a little, the settlements began: just a few makeshift homesteads here and there at first, and then, a little lower down the hill, the hamlets and villages. But even here, hemmed in by a maze of deep lanes, narrow roads and rough and rutted byways, the age-long isolation and remoteness had nurtured a close-knit, inward-looking and determined people in whom self-reliance and suspicion of the unfamiliar was bred in the bone: the communities of the hill were not such as extended the hand of friendship readily to strangers, as Jack had cause to know.

The slaughter of the Great War may have thinned out the ranks of their working men, but little else happened to change the old ways of life on the hill until 1939 and the coming of a new war, when the outside world began increasingly to intrude.

New roads arrived, and old ones were improved to carry men and machinery to the hill's 1700 foot summit, and within months its age-old silhouette, unchanged since the last ice-age glacier melted away to the north, was broken by the elaborate structures and latticed masts of a radar station and the straggling buildings of an anti-aircraft battery. And with access improved, more contractors arrived to scrape away the thin topsoil and quarry the ancient underlying rock for yet more roads and airfield runways in other parts of the county.

With the introduction of conscription and direction of labour that came with war many of the Barton men, and in due course the women, felt the full impact of the demands of the state for the first time in their lives. And when the war was over they returned to find that much of the old isolation had gone, and other radical changes were not long in following.

Barton village had always been the highest point on the hill where life could be lived with a tolerable degree of comfort, but even there life had been demanding and hard until the years following the war brought the introduction of many basic services that had previously been missing. One after another they arrived within a relatively short space of time: piped water first, then electricity, and finally main drainage and the domestic comfort of a flushing water-closet.

Not that the latter was embraced with the same whole-hearted enthusiasm by everyone. There were, it is true, a few who were considered to have gone too far when they had their WC installed inside the house. The majority, however, evincing a degree of fastidiousness remarkable in folk who lived so close to the basics of nature in so many other ways, thought such intimacy with the natural bodily functions was carrying things a little too far. It wasn't natural or healthy, they said, to have all those smells and stuff inside where folks were living, and for such as these a Gerry-built annex tacked on to the house was the preferred option.

And inevitably there were a few stout individualists who condemned all such innovations out-of-hand as the self-indulgent excesses of a modern world of which they wanted no part. For them the water from their own well was sweeter than mains, the light from their oil or gas lamps softer than electric, and their earth closet in a well -ventilated garden privy a true place of easement by comparison with the cramped and noisome boxes that most of the village now endured.

'Expensive and wasteful,' thundered old Tom Sutton, their spokesman. 'Just paying to flush away good muck for the garden. I've used it, me Dad used it, and his Dad too, and we none of us come to harm. Bit draughty in winter, but in summer I can sit with the door open, have a bit of a smoke and a think, and just watch the veg grow. Who could ask for more?'

Eventually most of the community did, but not Tom, who persisted to the very end, and so entered into legend when one bright morning of early summer, some ten years after the end of the war, he failed to return from his post-breakfast regular, as he called it. At first Ada, his wife, thought that he was just having his usual early morning potter around the veg plot, but when he wasn't back by eleven for his tea and second bite she began to worry. Tom never missed that, so she left her housework and set out to find him.

Ada always said afterwards that when she saw the door to the privy standing wide open she knew right away what she would find: and there Tom was, still sitting four-square on the scrubbed deal seat that he'd sat on since he was a boy. With his shoulders resting easily against the back timbers of the privy and his head dropped down on to his chest he might just have been asleep, but Ada knew otherwise, and from little signs and his few comments had indeed been half-expecting to lose Tom for a year or two.

If the Barton women felt deeply, they had been brought up not to show it: excessive displays of emotion were in general frowned upon. Folk were expected to 'bear up' in such circumstances, and true to the Barton code Ada bore up well. She stood for some moments shedding a few quiet tears, and then bent to pick up Tom's pipe, long since cold like Tom himself, and tidy up his trousers, still crumpled round his ankles. By herself, however, she could do nothing more, and so leaving Tom undisturbed she set off to break the news to her neighbours and seek assistance.

With more than half-a-dozen helpers assembled in her kitchen Ada's first thought had been to fetch Tom back to the house, but now she was a little more composed she changed her mind.

'No, let's leave him where he is for a bit,' she said. 'He looked so comfortable and sort of happy out there, and this will be his last time. We'll leave him till after dinner. . . But don't go just yet.'

Turning to the cupboard she reached in and brought out a couple of bottles of parsnip wine and an assorted selection of glasses.

'Year before last,' she said. 'A really good drop.'

Nobody left. 'To Tom,' said one of the men, and they all echoed the toast and sipped appreciatively. The second bottle was opened, and a third placed on the table. Then for half-an-hour or more they sat reflecting on the strange ways of life and death, and rehearsing all those comforting platitudes that help to ease the strain of such occasions.

'Lovely way to go though, if it has to come. Just what old Tom would have wanted I'll be bound.'

'Hard on those who find you though.'

'Always is though, always is – nothing changes that. Don't matter how ready you are, it's a blow.'

'A pretty good life all-in-all. Saw a bit more of the world too than most of us when he was young.'

'How old was he now Ada?'

'Eighty-four last March.'

'Eighty-four eh! He didn't look it you know.....always came up with the best of the caulis at the village show too.'

This non-sequitur was more than enough to silence their routine exchanges of solicitudes, and so they sat in reflective silence for a moment or two before George expressed the thought that must have been in the minds of all the men.

'Ada,' he said. 'Would you mind if. . . .'

He nodded towards the door, and Ada had no difficulty understanding.

'No, course not George. You're his oldest friend. You pop out and see him if you want to, he'd like that.'

And so, one by one, the men popped out to have a final word with Tom, and then they all left: the women to cook their bit of dinner and the men for a quick visit to the local, from where the news soon spread. The understanding was that they'd be back about two-ish to bring him in, but before then more than half of the immediate neighbours must have been down to gaze through the bottom hedge at old Tom sitting there gazing out over two flourishing rows of caulis which would surely have taken the prize once again.

When three of the men had returned, Ada went down with them to the privy where with all proper respect they sorted Tom out, gently pulled up his trousers, and prepared to bring him back to the house. By that time, however, Tom had stiffened up a bit and wasn't exactly willing to cooperate. His passage along the path, through the door, and finally up the stairs and into his bed was an awkward, angular affair with arms and legs

6

getting in the way however they turned, but they did it with as much dignity as they could muster, and eventually Tom was back and at rest. Ada could then turn to the formalities which she had known all along had to be observed, but she wasn't going to have anyone mucking Tom about, she said, until she got him back and laid out comfortably.

If the doctor was surprised at the somewhat irregular disposition of Tom's limbs for a man who had supposedly died peacefully in his bed he said nothing, and as both he and the local representative of the law had known Tom and Ada for many long years, neither was inclined to be a stickler about the finer points of the legislation. A death certificate was issued without question: Tom had died from natural causes, and was ready to proceed to his final rest without any interference from the coroner's office.

At the highest point of the village stood The Barton Shepherd, generally known as the Sheepshagger, or more briefly the Shagger, to the exclusively male customers who gathered in its public bar to enjoy, or as some said endure, the somewhat unusual bitter and mild that flowed from the nearby Stanton brewery. An eccentric brew, as a visitor once described it, but at least it was well kept by Albert who knew his customers and how to keep them satisfied, which he did far into the small hours when they gathered that evening to celebrate the life, times and passing of Tom Sutton. The last of his generation and the end of an era, said the vicar, who was never averse to spending a convivial hour or so with his flock.

That, as his flock would certainly have noted, was not an original thought from the Rev Breakwell, who had used it at the passing of every one of the old brigade for the last five or six years. On this occasion however it embodied what all of them knew well to be true. Old times and ways were passing fast, with the post-war world increasingly breaking in to disturb Barton's long isolation.

Within two years or so of Tom's death the first incomers arrived when two of the smaller holdings on the sheltered side of the hill were sold. One to a businessman from Wolverton who visited the property only occasionally, and possessed of more money than sense, taste or decency, allowed the land to revert to scrub, and turned the house and out-buildings into a rural gin-palace with a conversion that spat in the eye of local convention and building styles. The other to the Gillans, a youngish couple in their thirties who by dint of hard work, common sense and a fund of practical knowledge earned the respect and acceptance of the local community astonishingly quickly by the way in which they applied themselves with some success to achieving self-sufficiency on a worn-out and run-down small-holding. They would be followed by many who tried to do the same and failed.

Traditionalists and conservative to the soles of their muck-encrusted boots, the men of Barton Hill, for it was still only the men whose opinions carried any weight, looked on these local developments with a jaundiced eye, as they looked on all change, both locally and in the world at large. Contented and at ease with the old Tory paternalism that they had known for so long, they condemned all post-war nationalisation out of hand. Surreptitious use of the NHS was, however, tolerated by the patrons of the Shagger, but when 'gummy' Alcock of the sunken chops and lisping speech startled them all by returning after a short absence with a gleaming set of dentures and perfect enunciation, he received few congratulations, and was henceforth marked down as a Labour man.

Comfortable once again with the return of 'Winnie' and the urbane MacMillan, their loyalty was subsequently severely and doubly tested. First when the Beeching cuts brought the loss of Barton Halt at the foot of the hill, and then when the Profumo affair burst like a bomb in the bar of the Shagger, where it silenced all talk of improvement grants, the pool price of milk and a local outbreak of liver fluke, as the regulars eagerly devoured each succeeding instalment of the Cliveden scandal.

A few grey heads may have been shaken with token disapproval, but for the most part they soaked it up with the same eagerness as they soaked up their beer, and the publication in the Sunday Mirror of 'that photo of that Keeler woman' was the event of the year. It stopped them mid-pint as their libidinous imaginations ran wild on the sensual delights enjoyed by those they still considered as their masters and betters. But if it sowed any seeds of political doubt it didn't stop them voting en masse against Wilson and all he stood for.

Any socialist or liberal concepts were anathema to them. Staunch supporters to the last of the death penalty they inveighed against the relaxation of laws on homosexuality and abortion. It wasn't right was it? It wasn't natural. No good would come of it all! And with an inbuilt rustic stubbornness and a reluctance to allow to their wives a freedom they themselves enjoyed, they objected to the use of the pill. At home they sired their wives' children, and away they occasionally sired one they couldn't acknowledge, and that was an end of it. From then on it was up to the women.

Such was the reactionary, bigoted, narrow-minded and insular community into which Jack Manning was to blunder as he, increasingly restless in his job and of his lot in life, decided like many before him, to opt out of city or town living and go in search of the rural idyll. He hadn't set his sights on Barton Hill from the outset, but the remoteness appealed to him. It was at the heart of an area he loved, and he knew the surrounding country-side well.

A visit from an old friend provided the excuse, and a fine summer weekend the opportunity, to get out the car and potter off to the west with no particular object in mind other than that of ending up for lunch in Barlow, a handsome old country town that in many ways still seemed to be living in the thirties, having avoided the excesses of re-development that blighted so many towns in the south. It also had the attraction of The Parish Pump, a rambling sixteenth century building which over the years had lived many lives as blacksmith, drapers, barber-surgeon and others until, when Barlow bloomed for a few decades as a fashionable regency resort, it finally settled down to life as an inn, and so remained.

For those who had the good sense and taste to choose The Pump for their eating and drinking there was the reward of a cook who provided traditional food that was as good as its range was limited, and a landlord who was fussy about the way he kept his traditional beers, and pulled a pint of freezing lager with ill-disguised contempt. Such was Jack's anticipation that he could almost taste his favourite bitter on his tongue as he set off with Kate, his wife, and Roger, an old friend from their early days in London.

Turning immediately on to the minor roads and country lanes he loved, Jack meandered along with no particular object in mind other than to travel west and chat as they went. They reminisced over old times, caught up with the news (mainly Roger's), and then just talked. Or rather Roger talked: a cold, methodical dissection of Jack's naive vision of the smallholding life, in which he drew upon the unattractive reality of his own far from romantic country childhood, but by then it was clear that Jack had got the bit between his teeth and wasn't listening.

Forty minutes of motoring found them waiting impatiently in a narrow lane leading to Barton Hill, while a flock of sheep squeezed by on either side, filling the car with the greasy, malodorous stink of soiled fleeces drying out after an overnight shower.

'If you're thinking of taking on something like this you must be bloody raving,' said Roger, nodding at two pathetic old ewes limping towards them who, despite their condition, insisted on disputing the narrow passageway alongside the car, and in the course of their bumping and boring exhibited a pair of revolting, stinking rumps on which the wool was matted into a foul and tangled mass by their diarrhetic discharges.

'That's about the measure of what you can expect if you meddle with sheep,' said Roger, 'Foot-rot, scours and hour after hour of hard graft for no return with God's most stupid creation.'

Jack's response was cut short as the last of the sheep passed by, and the young boy who was driving them bent towards the window and offered what might have been a few words of thanks, or just as easily a mouthful of abuse.

'Bloody hell,' said Jack. 'I'd always heard that the Barton Hill dialect was a strong one, but that was utterly incomprehensible.'

A little further along, where the lane widened, Jack pulled off to the side, and they set out to stretch their legs as far as the top of Midden Hill, Barton's lower neighbour. Initially it was comfortable walking over turf close-cropped by the sheep, but on the final stretch it became a steep climb, and they were breathing hard by the time they got to the Iron Age camp at the top and dropped down onto the grass behind the ridge of the old defences, where they were out of the wind that blew on both the hills even when it was calm below.

'God it's so shaming Jack,' said Roger when he had caught his breath. 'Clapped out and not yet forty. Fifteen years ago we'd have done that at the jog-trot and still had breath for a seven-a-side. Too many fags, and too much bitter.'

'And in your case too many loose women I suspect, but don't let's go into that.'

'Ah well, we can't all have your luck of a happy marriage with a good woman,' said Roger blowing Kate a kiss.

Kate, very genteelly, held up two fingers in response, and then they stretched out in the sun, content to lie there quietly while they smoked a cigarette, and watched the broken clouds scudding across the sky towards the east.

Once again on their feet they could see, far away where the clouds were heading and almost lost in a haze of city pollution, the cluster of high-rise flats that marked out the centre of Wolverton, to which Jack commuted daily from his 'executive' style house on the outskirts of the city. Close by to the west was Barton Hill, and further off the spire of the old parish church of Barlow, marking their lunchtime destination and the pint for which Jack was now more than ready after his exertions.

Once back in the car, the snug bar at The Pump was little more than half-an-hour's drive away, but their journey was interrupted once again as they dropped down to the lower slopes on the western side of Barton Hill where Kate spotted a 'For Sale' sign pointing off into one of the side roads.

'Oh do turn off Jack and let's have a look. We've seen nothing we fancy so far, perhaps Roger will bring us luck.'

With his lunchtime pint and meal so near and yet so far, Jack turned off the main road reluctantly, but when they stopped and stepped out to look around, he wondered whether Kate might perhaps be right.

Sheltered on the north-east by the bulk of the hill and a long copse of trees, the property stood on a little plateau with an open prospect to the south and west across the richer pastures and arable land of the lower levels. The house itself was unexceptional in appearance, but the location was outstanding, with uninterrupted views across the valley to Barlow and beyond, where under a blue haze in the far distance the Welsh hills marked the horizon.

To the side of the short drive leading up to the house a large barn serving either as a garage or stables carried a sign providing further information, 'House and nine acre smallholding of mixed pasture and woodland.'

'Don't even think about it,' said Roger, when he saw the look in Jack's eyes. 'You really weren't born for the clodhopping life. It wouldn't suit you. Take it from me: I saw enough of it as a kid. Nine acres is either too little or too much, and with hill farming it'll be all hard slog, sheep shit and disappointment. Hang on to the day job however pissed off with it you feel, and leave this game for the mugs.'

'Oh don't be such a bloody Jonah,' snapped Kate. 'You stick to your city life if you want to. We're looking for some change and a little adventure.'

Roger just sighed heavily. 'I'd like my lunch and beer now please.'

'Sybarite!'

Noting the agent's name and phone number, they turned away and dropped down the long incline towards Barlow which lay about six miles off, basking in the warmth of the early afternoon sun. Spread out around All Saints', a church already centuries old before The Parish Pump was thought of, the town showed little trace of the twentieth century apart from a small estate that lay half-hidden in a valley to the west.

In the narrow alley leading to the main bar of The Pump the flaps to the cellar stood open awaiting a delivery, and the two men paused to gaze down at the stone-flagged floor and the ancient brickwork receding into the gloom, where half-a-dozen chocked-up barrels stood in their cool recesses, their beers just waiting for the summons from the pumps in the bar above.

'They're strange, aren't they, the pleasures of civilisation?' said Roger reflectively. 'We come all this way to fill ourselves up from the barrels down there, only to piss it all out at the back before we leave. Remember that bit in Hamlet about the dust of Alexander stopping a bunghole? How many bladders do you think our beer will have passed through over the centuries before it came to our turn?'

'God, I do wish you'd keep your literary and anatomical speculations to yourself, or at least save them for some other time.'

With that Kate walked on into the bar and they followed her quietly.

The bitter, as usual, was sweet, cool and moreish, and Mrs Arscott, the landlord's wife and cook, had excelled herself. Steak and kidney puddings that melted in the mouth (all local beef) and with fresh vegetables harvested the day before and brought in from the nearby market earlier that morning. That at least was what Mr

Arscott reported when Roger went back to the bar for their third pint. Delicious and satisfying, the puddings left precious little room for an apple pie with goats' milk custard that left Roger speechless. He simply lapped it up and beamed.

Replete, but comfortable, they lingered over a coffee and cigarette, while Roger picked his teeth with the wooden toothpick he carried in his wallet for such occasions, and conducted his survey of the bar.

'Just about perfect for an old-fashioned county town inn,' he said. 'Inglenook with logs set ready for lighting. Comfy seats. Papers in the racks. Four or five well-kept draught ales. Hops over the bar, and the buzz of locals conversing. You're a lucky old lad Jack.'

'And thank God it's not just up the road,' said Kate, 'or he'd never be out of it . . . and that toothpick's a disgusting habit.'

Odd the way Roger and Kate always keep up these sniping exchanges when we're together thought Jack. He suspected, a self-flattering thought, that each harboured a little jealousy over the other's close relationship with himself.

'Ah well. Mustn't be greedy and keep it all to myself. Got to think of generations yet unborn.' And with that parting shot at Kate, Roger left them in search of the gents.

From The Pump they returned to the alley, still in shade between its high walls, and walked through into sunshine and the square where the local market was busy under the arcades of the old market hall and on the stalls that had spilled out across the open area around the war memorial.

'Handsome old building,' said Jack as they passed under one of the arches and into the shade again. 'Late Georgian, rather solid. A bit smug and self-satisfied like the Georgians themselves despite their kick up the arse from the States, but a damned sight better than the replacement planned to celebrate Victoria's jubilee. A bloody monstrosity that would have been. There's a sketch of what was proposed upstairs in the Assembly Room as was: when it's open. Luckily wiser heads prevailed, and they restored this one.'

Too stuffed from lunch to try one of the many tearooms they set off for home, with Kate and Roger snoring in the back while Jack, at the wheel, battled to keep his eyes open. Finally at the highest point of their return over Barton Hill he gave up the struggle, pulled off to the side, lowered the window and closed his eyes. It was more than half-an-hour before he opened them again to the gentle breathing of a rheumy-eyed old ewe reaching up to the window for the tit-bit they had all come to expect from the day-trippers who stopped off on the hill for the view.

Late on the Sunday Roger left them for the fleshpots of London, and on the Monday Jack phoned the agents for further details of the property, and to arrange a viewing.

They met with Dawkins, the owner, a week later. They hadn't been long at the place, he said. Thought they might enjoy the country life, but the wife hadn't taken to the isolation, and now spent more time at her mother's than on the hill – he made little attempt to hide his own dissatisfaction at the turn of events.

Having already looked at more properties than enough, Jack and Kate had devised a little formula to use if the owners insisted in keeping them company while they made their viewing. If either remarked that anything was 'like Aunt Elsie's' it was a signal to cut it short without offending. Neither did, and having finished their tour of the house they went outside to walk the boundaries, have a look at the land, and take in the views.

'There are just a couple of other things I think I should mention at the outset,' said Dawkins. 'You'll see as we move on a bit that a couple of footpaths cross the land which are still used from time to time by the locals, and up at the north east corner there's an old quarry – quite deep, and could be dangerous if you aren't careful. If we go a bit further on you'll see the long gully that runs up to it from the road where they used to take out the stone by horse and cart, but that all finished at the end of the last century. Not been touched since then – full of wildlife, and there's a badger sett at the bottom end of the gully.'

That alone was enough for Kate to determine that other things being equal they would have the place, and so they moved back towards the house to look over the one large barn.

'Useful sized outbuilding' said Jack, as they sat drinking tea with Dawkins before they left. 'Room for a couple of cars and some livestock if divided.'

'There's a bit of a story about that and the house, if you've time' said Dawkins.

'Oh yes please. I love to know the local gossip,' said Kate.

'Apparently some years ago the land, no buildings on it then, was inherited by a Mr Bates who already farmed a couple of hundred acres about fifteen miles the other side of Barlow. He'd got absolutely no use for another nine acres this far away of course, but with a house on the site he reckoned he could sell it and turn a nice little profit. He knew though that as things stood the prospect of getting planning permission was zero.

Now Bates must have been a pretty sharp customer well versed in the dark art of manipulating planning regulations, for he keeps stum about the house, and applies instead for planning permission for a milking parlour on the site. This went through on the nod of course. Agricultural building: no questions asked. Approval received almost by return, and within six months the parlour's in place. Then he puts half-a-dozen cows on the land, makes an arrangement with a local to attend to them, and sits tight for six months.'

Here Dawkins paused, as much for effect it seems as to refresh himself from his cup of tea, but Kate was impatient for the end of his story.

'Oh do go on – the suspense is killing me.'

'Well, having set the scene for the rest of this rustic farce, he then puts in his application to build accommodation on the site, pleading the case that commuting that far is proving too difficult in winter, and that his son now wishes to move on to the land and start up on his own. It seemed a likely enough story, but was initially refused, probably because the committee suspected what was going on.

All this was standard procedure as far as Bates was concerned, so he bangs in an appeal, and engages the wiles of a local solicitor who specialised in that sort of thing, and played golf with the chairman of the planning committee. At that point the planning department seemed to throw in the towel and approved the first set of plans that had been put in. The rest you see around you.'

'Fascinating,' said Jack. 'A wonderfully devious plan of campaign.'

'Ah well, you know what they say about the old countrymen – half ox, half fox. They know what's what alright when it comes to their own interest.'

Story, tea and biscuits over they left, and before the day was out had decided that they had to go ahead. After a little haggling over price the deal was closed, and as they already had a buyer waiting patiently for their town house the legal processes all moved along quite smoothly. Some four months later, as the first signs of autumn began to colour the landscape before them, Jack and Kate were enjoying their first evening in residence.

2

The Gauleiter

Several months had passed and they were in the depth of winter when Jack got to hear from Jimmy of his neighbours' apparent intimate knowledge of his professional activities.

'But how the hell did they get to know? How the hell did you get to know? I've said nothing to you or to anyone else, and I'm commuting more than twenty miles to work each day.'

'Who did your legals? Was it local or in town?'

'Bayley, Bayley and Bedgood, in Barlow. Had them recommended to me by the seller, who'd used them when he came in.'

'Ah! That would explain it. Wouldn't touch them with a bargepole for anything I needed. I'm sure they're fine on the legal side, but Charlie Genner's daughter Hilda works there. She passes on any titbits to her mum, and that's as good as giving them to the town crier.'

'But I don't even deal with the tax for this area, and if I did I'm sure none of their stuff would come to me. I don't normally talk much about the work, but to be honest I don't see any of the farms or businesses around here being in my league. I play with the big boys, if I can put it that way. Serious taxation fraud, criminal prosecutions: that sort of stuff. None of them are at it in that way are they?'

'I wouldn't think so, and they wouldn't tell me if they were, but you know what countrymen, farmers especially, are like: suspicious of anything with even a whiff of authority. Anyway they wouldn't have the faintest idea of the scope of your work. You're a taxman:

that's enough, and I imagine most of them are on the fiddle to a lesser or greater extent . . . . You're known jokingly as The Gauleiter, by the way, and they call the place Colditz.'

'Oh bloody hell, that's marvellous. OK Gauleiter I can see, but why Colditz.'

'It's their idea of a joke: all that fencing you've had done, and the six foot high fruit cage. Remember the scene in the film where the prisoner vaults over the fence?'

'Oh yes . . . Very funny, but I can see now why old Bickley wouldn't take cash when I was paying him for his fencing work: insisted on having a cheque. Suspicion and lack of trust, that's all the appreciation we get for protecting the national flock from the gathering predators. Ah well it's a cross we have to bear. Pity they don't know just how pissed off I am with the whole business anyway. We're just bloody window-dressing: a little bit of diversionary entertainment while the real plunder takes place elsewhere. If only they knew.'

Jack's meeting with Jimmy Gillan and its gradual maturing beyond acquaintance into friendship, at that time the only one with any of his neighbours, had been an accidental affair in every sense of the word.

From his first days on the hill Jack had frequently seen Jimmy passing and re-passing on the field track to his isolated cottage at Gollins Croft about half-a-mile away. Their paths didn't cross for some time, however, until Jack, out for a stroll across his few acres as dusk was falling, thought he caught the sound of a distant shout. He stopped and listened, but heard no more until he drew a little closer to the quarry, when the call was repeated quite distinctly. It was a cry for help, loud, and long-drawn-out in the hope of attracting attention, and it came from the quarry.

When he got to the edge he had no difficulty, even in the closing gloom, in recognising the figure at the bottom as the man who regularly crossed and re-crossed the land. That part of the quarry wasn't steep-sided or deep, and he didn't look to be in too much trouble, but his problem became clear when he called up from below.

'My God am I glad to see you: thought I was going to be stuck here into the night. I got too close to the edge trying to follow the track of a badger. Slipped and took a tumble, ending up here. Not much damage, but I've twisted my ankle, and can't get myself back up the slope without help.'

'OK. I'll be down with you in a minute.'

'Jimmy Gillan,' said the man, holding out his hand as Jack arrived at the bottom.

'Jack Manning,' said Jack, shaking it.

'I know,' said Jimmy with a smile.

With Jack to help, Jimmy managed to claw his way up to the top, and then, leaning heavily on Jack, back to the Croft where Celia his wife, used to Jimmy's long wanderings around the countryside, was getting on with her weaving quite untroubled by his extended absence.

Faint as it had been, Jack had heard more than enough of Jimmy's accent during their walk back to identify him as a Scouser, and hadn't expected to be received by a wife with such impeccable received pronunciation: almost cut-glass, he thought, as he made his way back home, having accepted an invitation to go over with Kate and join them for a meal two evenings later.

By then several months had passed since they moved on to the hill, and all around the countryside was locked fast into one of the hardest winters for many years. With no road access to the Croft it was by footpaths and the light of a good lantern that they left for their first visit in the early evening of a day when a deep frost had gripped the countryside without relenting from the previous bitterly cold night. If anything the cold had intensified during the day, and the first haze of a hoar frost was starting to show in the hedgerows as they made their way across the field track.

They had already passed the cottage a number of times on their own country walks. Well maintained, but unimproved and totally original, it probably dated from the late fifthteenth century. Timber-framed in unpainted oak it was two-storied, but long and low, with upper rooms that would have been a torment for anyone above modest height. Only the roof looked as though it might have been a modern eighteenth century alteration in tiles now multi-coloured with the growth of lichen and algae.

The door at which they knocked looked ancient and original: massive as though to withstand a siege. Hanging from three black metal hinges wider than Jack's wrists, its thick oak planks were heavily studded with black iron nails, and darkened and pitted by weather and the wear and tear of centuries.

It was opened by Jim to a narrow, oil-lit passageway that ran through from front to back with doors off either side. Even when they were inside with the door shut, their breath still hung in the air, and Jack could see that on the inside of the door the clenched iron of the nails was white with the penetrating frost.

'Don't hang your coats out here,' said Jimmy. 'They'll be frozen solid when you leave if you do. Bring them through.'

He opened one of the inner doors, and Celia welcomed them in to a good-sized living room, still oil-lit, but warm with the glow of a wood-burning stove supplemented by a long radiator on the back wall.

'Something to warm you after the walk,' said Celia, holding out two large glasses of wine.

'Vintage parsnip from Ada Sutton,' said Jimmy. 'Almost the last of the Barton originals up in the village – a quid pro quo for a little electrical work I did for her.'

It was as they sat sipping Ada's wine and warming themselves before the glowing log-burner that Jimmy made his original disclosure to Jack, and over the course of the meal he had a little bit more to say about the parallel economy that flourished on and around the hill.

'It's all fairly low-level stuff by your standards I suppose, but it's everywhere. Cash with nothing recorded is preferable of course, but barter's almost a way of life, not only with the farmers but with the traders. Everyone's ready to do a deal. The ladies' hairdressers used to have a sign pinned up: *This establishment will negotiate payment in any form of exchange cash, goods, services etc – just have a word with Peggy.* It was taken down when you arrived . . . . Felt sure I could trust you,' he added with a smile.

'I only wish the rest could,' said Jack, 'And as far as we're concerned they can put the notice back up as soon as they like. Kate won't shop them, will you love?'

He took a long pull at the glass of elderberry wine that wound up the meal before continuing.

'Look,' he said. 'I couldn't do this job if I didn't wear two hats. What comes across my desk is business, just business – nothing personal, as the Mafia used to say. But despite popular misconception we aren't the Stasi, and outside the office I'm one of the boys, so to speak. Wouldn't do to play the game myself of course, but apart from that . . .'

He left the sentence unfinished, but then added, 'Although I often wondered what I'd do if I had a really good offer.'

'Well I'll noise the good news abroad,' said Jimmy, 'I mean about the two hats, not you waiting for a good offer, but they're a suspicious and cautious bunch, and it might take quite a while.'

He topped up the stove with a few more logs, handed them each a glass of what Jack took to be Calvados, and through an increasing booze-induced haze Jack and Kate learned a little of their hosts' time on the hill.

'We bought this place in the late fifties with a little unexpected help from Celia's father,' said Jimmy.

'Family and friends thought I'd gone bush when I went off with Jimmy just after the war,' said Celia. 'Roedean girls weren't supposed to do that sort of thing were they? But Miss Tanner, our headmistress, wasn't snobbish and didn't encourage the girls to be; although I'm not altogether sure she would have approved of Jimmy – bit too radical for her. Anyway the school's evacuation to Keswick broadened my horizons, and as soon as I was eighteen I volunteered for the Wrens, and that really knocked off the rough edges. Even so at first none of them could see the bargain I saw. Could they my big, bold hero? But they came round.'

Jimmy gave her a smile and took up the story, 'This place was sound when we came in, but a bit run down. Since then I've altered the inside to install a few comforts of modern living, without detracting from the charms of the old. The wood burner runs the few radiators we need, and I had the phone and power lines laid on at some expense after a year or so, but we'd got used to the lamplight by then and still prefer it down here. Use the electric upstairs though. As for other basic needs, our water comes sweet and cool from our own well, and my own variation of the earth closet provides for calls of nature. Ever heard of Henry Moule?'

Jack shook his head.

'Wonderful man – sadly neglected. Invented the first earth closet: deserved a Nobel prize for service to humanity. Very efficient, no water wasted, and an end product that goes straight into the veg plot. Everything recycled and fully self-sustaining. Never properly developed though. I've got a copy of his pamphlet somewhere, *Manure for the Millions – A Letter to the Cottage Gardeners of England.* I'll dig it out and you must come over some time in daylight and read it. Then I'll give you a tour of the place, and you can try the thunderbox for yourself – very relaxing.'

Jack smiled at Jimmy's enthusiastic presentation of his idiosyncratic sanitary arrangements, and then as it was well past mid-night, they thanked them both for an enjoyable evening, put on their coats, and by the hard and frosty light of a moon now out from behind the clouds, walked back home across the meadows.

The sense of affinity that Jack felt for Jimmy was clearly mutual, and as the two wives also enjoyed each other's company the four ended up getting together at least a couple of times a month, and in the course of their meetings with the Gillans, they learned a lot more of the background of their seemingly ill-assorted neighbours.

Born in the twenties Jimmy was the third son in an Irish Catholic family swollen by the arrival of yet another young gift of God every couple of years. Home had been a cramped, narrow three-storied house just a few streets away from the docks on the east of the Mersey in the heart of a predominantly Catholic community, and he talked of his life there as one that fell rather disappointingly short of genteel poverty. The house would survive the war, but disappear soon after in the subsequent slum clearances.

His father, the fourth child of seven, five of them boys, had left home and come over from Ireland in 1919 having fallen out with his brothers following a bitter argument over politics.

'When do they ever argue about anything else in Ireland?' said Jimmy, 'And at that time it was particularly bad in the County Cork. Brother against brother, "with us or against us" in many cases, though I don't think it was that bad for the old man. By the time I was aware of that sort of thing they were in touch again.'

'Have you ever been over to meet the family?' asked Jack.

'Not as an adult, but when the two of them went over in the summer of '39 they took me with them. A couple of months earlier Dad got news that his father had died. . . . It was the only time I saw him cry. But he couldn't get over in time for the funeral, and so we went a couple of months later, and met up with almost all of them.'

'Was that back to the farm?'

'No, not at first. By then most of them had moved to Dublin or Cork city for the work. It was just Michael left running the farm with his sons, and my grandfather living in Dublin with Seamus until he died. So that was where we went.'

'Your grandmother was dead then?'

'Gone before I was born. Worn out by hard work and ill health Dad said. We had a run down to see Michael though. Meant it to be just a day trip from Dublin, but when we got to Millstreet we were told that the train we arrived on would be the only one back in about an hour's time. Michael insisted we stay over. Wouldn't take no for an answer, and so one night eventually became three. No phones on the farm of course in those days, nor with Seamus in Dublin, but Michael managed to get a message back to Seamus via the guard on the train. It was a bit like that in Ireland in those years.'

'Sounds rather attractively old-fashioned and informal,' said Jack.

'You wouldn't say that if you'd seen the rural poverty,' said Jimmy. 'But I won't go into that. . . .Learned a little about an Irish family get-together though after Michael got the message out to a few cousins and neighbours. My God they put some stuff away during those three nights: got to sneak a drop or two myself: the first of many to follow.' Before continuing he topped them up with some more of the Calvados.

In Liverpool his father had met Kathleen, from another Irish family, and married her after a courtship that would have been thought indecently short in the old country, but occasioned no comment in Liverpool. Good Catholics that they were the union was soon blessed with a son, followed promptly by another: then a hiatus of almost three years before Jimmy arrived.

Jimmy talked lovingly of his father as a sentimental, quiet and unassuming man seldom in really good health, but who managed nevertheless to hang on to his job when all around were losing theirs, and bring home enough to keep them off the breadline with just a little to spare. Of his mother he spoke with a total lack of affection.

'She was the worst sort of canting hypocrite. Kept up all the Catholic appearances in church and with the neighbours, but was a hard-hearted, scolding bitch at home and a secret drinker. Boozed away what little spare Dad brought back that would otherwise have given us a bit extra. Poor bugger scarcely had enough left to buy his few fags.'

When old enough to leave the maternal nest, Jimmy attended the local Catholic school during the week and the local Catholic church on Sunday.

'Religion dominated our lives spiritually and physically then,' he said, 'Couldn't get away from it even at home, as the bloody church loomed over the wall at the back of the yard.'

He grew up in the thirties to see his two older brothers pass seamlessly from school to unemployment, with no apparent hope of anything to come in the future, and then despite his youth, for reasons he could never seem to articulate precisely to Jack, he began gradually to question the very basis of his religious indoctrination.

'I could never quite understand why I changed,' he said, 'As the rest of the family stuck with the faith through thick and thin. Dad seemed quite untroubled by the way I was going, but that was the end of it with my mother, and whenever Dad wasn't around she'd find any excuse to knock me about a bit.'

The advent of war, and an early raid on Liverpool in which a younger brother and others died when a bomb fell on the junior school shelter, brought about Jim's final severance with formal religion, when he walked out of the requiem mass for his brother.

'Couldn't stand all that Catholic cant, but I knew there was no going back after that,' he said, 'And by the time she got back home from the mass I'd put together my few bits and pieces and left. I was too young to enlist, but I went along to the shipping office, lied about my age, and got a berth on a ship leaving for the States. They weren't asking too many questions about age for the merchant fleet, and that's where I stayed for the rest of the war.'

'That must have been a hell of a culture shock for a teenager,' said Jack. 'How old were you then sixteen, seventeen?'

'There or there abouts,' said Jimmy. 'And yes it was. I went in just in time to catch the U-boats' happy time on the North Atlantic. At first I was scared witless, frightened to sleep at night, but after a while you get to accept it, though it's always there as a nagging thought when you're not busy. I was lucky though in bunking up and messing with a pretty good crowd. I learned a lot from one or two of them. Introduced me to a few books the Catholic fathers wouldn't approve. Politics and social comment I mean, not smut.'

Celia was serving in Bristol when Jimmy's ship put in there in 1944. They met at a dance and enjoyed each other's company, met again the following evening, and kept in touch afterwards, meeting whenever they could when Jimmy's ship was back in the UK.

'We realised early on that we were two of a kind,' Celia told them, 'And eventually he had his wicked way with me . . . You probably know what it was like in war-time.'

'Only by report,' said Kate. 'We were both a touch too young, but it all sounds eminently sensible to me. Not sure it was all that different when our time came though. . . But not so intense perhaps.' Celia had the feeling that there was a note of regret there, but the moment was soon gone, and she couldn't be sure.

With the war over, they said, they snuggled down together like every conventional couple, apart from tying the knot formally. Jim got a job that gave him some training and good experience with electrical work, plumbing and carpentry. Celia went on a secretarial course, and studied weaving and painting at evening classes, but that phase of their life only lasted a little over three years. After all the stresses and noise of the war both felt they wanted to get completely away from it all and try something out of the ordinary.

'Ended up going over the top rather, and taking on a croft in North Uist,' said Celia.

'We must have been raving,' said Jim. 'It was a ravishing spot we found though. Wildly beautiful when the weather was right: fantastic bird life and good trout and salmon fishing. But in the long run all we ended up doing was wasting away what little money we'd saved, and with the best will in the world there was a limit to the one pleasant way of getting through those interminable northern nights.'

'We'd got no phone of course,' said Celia, 'And without being able to speak to me from time to time Mummy got so worried she wrote in the spring to say that she was coming up to satisfy herself that we were OK. Wouldn't take no for an answer, but it turned out to be a complete farce. I went to meet her at the ferry hoping I could persuade her to stay at the hotel, but she wouldn't have it.'

'Farce? It was an absolutely bloody disaster,' said Jim, with a laugh at the memory of it. 'They were able to get a car from Lochmaddy to within a quarter-mile of the place, but then it was all on foot across land that was absolutely sodden. It was raining when they arrived. It was always bloody raining, and I looked out of the window to see them get out of the car, Celia togged up for the weather and her mother in a tailored suit, high heels and a fancy hat. By the time they got to the house she was soaking, practically knee-deep in mud, and almost in tears.'

'The next two days hardly bare thinking about,' said Celia. 'Jim slept on the floor on cushions, Mummy shared the bed with me, and it rained incessantly. By the third morning she was ready to go home, and by the end of the second winter I was ready to follow her.'

'So we fled back south to Celia's parents in Rottingdean while we took stock,' said Jimmy. 'From the gorblimey to the sublime, so to speak. Many late nights, a little emotional at times, but at the end of it all they saw that we were determined to have another go at smallholding, and a family compromise was reached. We agreed to make things legal – registry office only though. In return Celia's Dad agreed to set us up on a smallholding of choice on the understanding that if after three years it hadn't worked out, we'd return to something more conventional. That was over fifteen years ago, and we're still here.'

By comparison with the Gillans the Mannings backgrounds could hardly have been more conventional. Kate, like Jimmy, was from a working-class family, but one untroubled by drink or the financial stringencies that afflicted the Gillans, and blessed with a loving and close bond between parents and children. Staunchly supportive of King, Country and Empire, they offered up their prayers in the established church once a week, and contrary to their own best interests, unthinkingly voted Tory, apart from one rogue branch of the family where the aunt was known to be tainted with liberalism.

Courtesy of her own sharp intelligence and a history master of an independent turn of mind, Kate had been able to free herself from most of her family's prejudices. Some vestigial allegiance to the superstitious mysteries of religion survived even the battering of her university days, but finally wilted and died in the face of Jack's bred-in-the-bone atheism. As the first member of her family to have progressed to university, however, Kate's heretical views were received with a tolerance denied the aunt.

Jack, by contrast, sprang from an extended family of the metropolitan middle class, who liked to see themselves as in direct line of descent from Keir Hardie, and had been chattering away in the suburbs of Hampstead long before their likes had become the butt of political satirists. His mother taught history and economics in a flagship comprehensive school, his father lectured in politics at the LSE. Most of his aunts and uncles, if not similarly engaged, were active in local politics or employed within the GLC.

Daily life for Jack could not have been less homely if he'd been living in the offices of Transport House, and family gatherings in mourning or celebration took on the air of the hustings as wine or whisky took hold, and subtle distinctions of policy and meaning were debated ad nauseam. Such was his force-fed diet of politics and working-class solidarity that Jack spewed it all up when he went to university, where he devoted himself to the arts, and eschewed all political associations. His sceptical atheism, which was there by default so to speak, he retained and gradually over-laid it with a thick skin of misanthropy.

The loving and close relationships that Kate had enjoyed within the family were not something of which Jack had much experience, but he would not have said that there was any coldness or lack of feeling, as between Jimmy and his mother. It was just that it was all rather remote: a family of semi-detached relationships was the way Jack would frequently describe it.

Kate returned to hearth, home and family with pleasure, often with Jack who enjoyed the visits to what he called a normal family life as much as she did, but sometimes by herself when school holidays permitted and Jack was committed to the office.

Jack, by contrast, returned to what he called the political bosom of his family only for those special occasions when he could not decently decline an invitation: weddings, funerals, and more recently a family party to celebrate his father's selection as Prospective Parliamentary Candidate in a by-election for what was considered to be a winnable constituency. Jack's celebration when it turned out to be losable was, however, a very private affair.

'Thank God for that,' he said to Kate. 'He's bad enough as it is. Had he taken the seat he'd have been completely unliveable with.'

If pressed further on his political roots and allegiances, he was inclined to entertain his audience with a falsetto RP version of Alex Glasgow's *Oh My Daddy is a Left-Wing Intellectual,* and maintain that his own views were much too far to the left to bear categorising. 'So far,' he would say, 'That I'm in danger of going full circle, and then Christ knows where I'd end up.'

A week or so after their evening with the Gillans, as the frosts eased towards the end of February, the snow arrived, driven in by a biting easterly that sucked the heat from the house, rattled the tiles on the roof, and then roared its way westward towards Barlow and the Welsh hills beyond. Across the common on the exposed heights the road was the one clear feature, a black scar scoured clear of snow by an unrelenting wind which piled it high in grotesque mounds around the stands of gorse, or dumped it waist-high in the deep and narrow lanes that led to and from the hill.

From early afternoon, and throughout the night snow had fallen heavily, and in the morning, as Jack forced open the doors of the barn he had little expectation of getting very far on his daily journey to work. But even in the half-light before dawn the local farmers had been out and at work with their tractor ploughs. They had flocks out on the hill that needed feed and attention, and cutting a passage through the drifts that lay deep in the narrow lanes they carried the hay to their beleaguered livestock. It proved to be the hazards on the main roads, not the by-ways of the hill, that delayed Jack's arrival at his desk.

The beginning of April marked the start of the thaw and the first of two events which began to allay the locals' suspicions of Jack's trade, and ease them into a comfortable working relationship with the village community.

A bright spring day with blustery squalls racing in from the west spilling shower after shower on the upper reaches of the hill was just beginning to fade when Kate gave Jack a shout from the kitchen, which looked out to the road.

'I think we're going to get a visit from the vicar. He's stopped at the gate, and I can see him struggling with that catch I've been asking you to fix for a couple of months. Do pop out and give him a hand . . . . No, it's OK he's made it and heading for the front door.'

'What the hell would the vicar want with me, if that's not an inappropriate association of ideas?' replied Jack.

'Never mind that. Go to the door and let him in. I've got my hands full at the moment.....and be civil; he looks a nice old chap.'

Anticipating the ring on the bell, Jack had the door open just as the Rev Breakwell lifted his hand, which Jack took the opportunity to grasp and shake. Hearing their conversation at the door extending beyond the mere formalities, Kate called through from the kitchen.

'Don't stand talking in the hall. Come into the kitchen where it's cosy.'

They both soon realised that the vicar's mission was purely social and not proselytising. Offered the choice of a cup of tea or whisky he chose the latter, and they settled down around the table to hear what he had to say.

He'd seen Jack from time to time in the Barton Shepherd and out on the fields, he said, and understood from Mr Gillan that they hadn't exactly been welcomed into the community with open arms. He was unhappy about that, and felt that as they were within his parish he should remedy things with his own welcome, whatever their beliefs might be.

'So you know Jimmy and Celia then?' asked Jack, rather puzzled that there should have been any intimacy between Jimmy and the local representative of any church.

'Indeed I do: wonderful couple. Very interesting life they've had. I went there first of all to take painting lessons from Celia, and inevitably got talking to Jimmy. We've had some very stimulating discussions.'

'I can imagine,' said Jack with a smile, wondering just which variety of the Church of England's eclectic range of vicars he had on his hands.

'Well, as I said, I simply wanted to extend to you the welcome in which my parishioners appear to have been rather deficient. As far as I know you are the first professional commuter to venture out here into the sticks, if I can put it that way, but I don't suppose you will be the last, and as we are both specialists in our own way I thought we should make contact.'

'You heard from Jimmy I suppose?'

'Oh no! I knew who you were and your occupation long before you moved in.'

'Hilda Genner?' asked Jack.

'No names, no pack-drill, as they say.'

'Secrets of the confessional perhaps – well I have them too, so I know what it's like.'

'So I imagine, but changing the subject, have you decided what you are going to do with the land? The grass is already beginning to green up a little, and on this side of the hill it will soon need grazing.'

'Well I've got my veg plot going and fruit cage up, and I'll probably fence off an acre or so around the quarry as a wild life reserve, but we can't quite make up our minds about the rest. We don't want to start something in complete ignorance, so we went to basic husbandry evening classes during the winter, but we're not sure whether to run some livestock of our own, or ask the neighbours if they would like to use the land: if only I can get a chance to have a few words with them, that is.'

Half-an-hour, another glass of whisky and much desultory chat later, the vicar at last decided it was time to leave. At the door he paused for a moment before speaking.

'Would it be rude of me to ask whether despite your beliefs, or rather lack of them, you sometimes attend a church service?'

'Not at all, and we do, but only as social occasions: family weddings, funerals – that sort of thing.'

'May I ask then that you do a little socialising this coming Sunday and slip in at the back for the morning service at St Matthew's. I'll say no more now..... Lovely moon coming up. Thanks for the whisky.'

'Well that was a rum affair,' said Jack, pouring himself a final whisky, and propping his backside up against the bar on the Aga.

'Intriguing though,' said Kate. 'Are you going?'

'Absolutely. Wouldn't miss it for worlds, far too mysterious.'

3

Ian Hamilton's March

St Matthew's in Barton, a plain and undistinguished early Victorian structure, had not featured in the Mannings' early Borders excursions, but the view from its churchyard more than compensated for the building's failings. They didn't hurry to get to the church on the Sunday following the visit from the vicar. Jack thought it best to leave their arrival until the last possible minute, and so the churchyard was deserted when they walked up the drive and pushed open the door just as the last notes of an organ voluntary faded away and died.

Despite their best efforts to slip in quietly in the ensuing silence, Jack could not prevent a perverse door latch from snapping to with a loud metallic 'clack' that turned the heads of half the congregation, to be followed by the rest when their names were whispered around. Surprised to find themselves in a church almost full to capacity, they slipped into the end of the pew nearest to the door, only to find themselves sitting alongside Jimmy and Celia.

'You too!' whispered Jimmy. 'Any idea what this is about? Larry Breakwell called in for a chat last night and suggested I should come, but said no more. Most of the hill seems to be here. What on earth is the old boy up to?'

They sat in silent non-participation through a hymn, a prayer, another hymn and a reading, before the Rev Breakwell made his way into the low pulpit and faced his flock. He made no comment and expressed no surprise at the unique sight of his church full to the back pew, but throughout his address directed himself to the rows towards the front, as though the rest were empty, which they frequently were. It was unfortunate perhaps that he looked a little too often at poor old Ada Sutton, who left the church feeling distinctly uncomfortable with the thought that his remarks had been aimed particularly at her.

'This morning, in a departure from the usual pattern of my sermons I will be taking not one, but three texts, my first being from the Weymouth New Testament, the Gospel of St Luke Chapter 18 Verse 13:

"But the tax-gatherer, standing far back . . ."'

Here he paused as the heads of the curious turned once again to sneak a look at the late arrivals, and there was a restrained murmur of surprise from his audience.

'But the tax-gatherer, standing far back would not so much as lift his eyes to Heaven, but kept beating his breast and saying, "O God, be reconciled to me, sinner that I am."'

Here he paused again briefly as a few smiles were suppressed and the whispers died away.

'My second is from Weymouth, Book of Romans Chapter 13, Verse 6:

"Why, this is really the reason you pay taxes; for tax-gatherers are ministers of God, devoting their energies to this very work."'

He paused again, but this time there was no response as his congregation waited silently for the third text.

'Finally from the Revised Standard Version of the Gospel of St Matthew Chapter 9, Verses 9 to 13, I turn to the Lord's calling of St Matthew, a tax collector, to be one of his disciples:

"And as He sat at table in the house, behold, many tax collectors and sinners came and sat down with Jesus and his disciples. And when the Pharisees saw this, they said to his disciples, 'Why does your teacher eat with tax

39

collectors and sinners?' But when He heard it, He said, 'Those who are well have no need of a physician, but those who are sick. Go and learn what this means, I desire mercy, and not sacrifice.'"

Here the vicar paused, and looking for a focus for what was to follow, unfortunately found it in the up-turned face of Ada Sutton.

'And don't we all of us desire mercy, and tolerance, and understanding? And do we reflect often enough, as we should, on the great mercy the Lord has shown to us, and treat our neighbours with like mercy and kindness?'

They hardly needed to stay to hear the rest of his sermon, an extended meditation on the same theme, on the contradictions and uncertainties of life, and the need to look beyond the surface of things before rushing to judgment. As the sermon concluded the organ sounded again, and before the service had resumed all four of them slipped quietly out of the south door, and headed for the Shagger.

'Well what on earth are we supposed to make of that?' asked Jack. 'Was it true Christian commitment on behalf of one lost and outcast lamb in his flock, or some strange private joke?'

'Oh I don't think it's a joke,' said Jimmy. 'I realised from the talks we've had that Larry's a bit of a one-off and very much his own man. In fact I sometimes wonder just how much he subscribes to some of the basic tenets of the Church, but he wouldn't joke in the pulpit, and if you mean what I think you mean by Christian, then Larry's a Christian. . . . No, I think he really wants to make a patently obvious point to a very conservative and innately suspicious community. He's giving you a clean bill of health.'

'All very puzzling. Though I must say I quite took to him when he called in the other evening. As far as this morning goes though, we'll just have to wait and see, and as far as the locals are concerned, well I can take them or leave them alone without being troubled, but it would be nice if they weren't so cool to Kate.'

Unusually for the Shagger on a Sunday morning the public bar was empty, apart from Albert standing disconsolate behind the counter.

'All very quiet today Albert. Where's your usual *News of the World* brigade?'

'Very odd Mr Gillan. Word seemed to get round that a church visit might be interesting this morning. Haven't had it this quiet on a Sunday for years.'

Picking up their pints, Kate and Celia included, they settled at a table by the door to await the arrival of Albert's regulars.

They weren't long in coming, and within minutes it seemed that most of the men and many of the women in the congregation were cramming in, eager to put Albert in the picture, and buy themselves a drink to stimulate the gossip. Jimmy, whose plumbing and electrical skills had taken him far and wide across the hill, got a few words of greeting from most of them, when he was always Jim or Jimmy, but more than a few now gave Jack a nod and a circumspect 'Morning Mr Manning.'

Before the end of the month came the second event which finally led to their gradual and cautious acceptance by the community. Acceptance as incomers that is: even Jimmy and Celia were not seen by the locals as 'one of us.'

Kate had given notice from her teaching post in Wolverton as soon as they started their search for a home in the country, and had been out of work for a couple of terms before they arrived on the hill. When an unexpected vacancy arose in the Barlow junior school that served the children of Barton Hill a supply teacher was needed, with the near certainty that the post would become permanent. Kate applied and was accepted, and for the first time this brought her into regular and close contact with the Barton mothers who carried favourable reports back to the Barton fathers, leading to the gradual acceptance that, despite the whiff of sulphur about Jack's professional activities, he was not after all the Devil incarnate.

In the weeks following that most unusual of Sunday services, however, Ada Sutton found herself constantly tormented by those ex-cathedra precepts of her priest, and of all the village Ada was without doubt the most faithful and devoted of the Rev Breakwells's parishioners. She realised well enough when she thought things over that his sermon had not really been directed specifically at her, but his words had wrought powerfully upon her Christian heart, and as a village elder and the oldest member of the vicar's congregation she now felt it incumbent upon her to act upon those words. And if Ada was looking only for her reward in heaven, she was eventually to be very pleasantly surprised.

With no man about the house to help her with those occasional practical difficulties that require a young man's strength, dexterity, or technical skill, Ada had increasingly availed herself of Jimmy's jobbing services in preference to her sons, who were always going to pop round to fix it, whatever 'it' was but, constantly succumbing to the demands of their own families, never did.

Jimmy, in return for the chores that he performed, which were neither onerous nor frequent, was rewarded with home-brew, cakes, pies from the best pastry cook in the village, and his pick of the choicest items from the veg plot, which the sons still gardened, but principally for their own benefit.

And as Jim came to know Ada better he increasingly popped in from time to time to see how she was, and gradually came to realise that in some small way she was filling the gap in his life that should have been occupied by his mother.

It was during one of these visits, as Jimmy sat enjoying tea and one of Ada's buttered scones, that she raised with him the matter of his immediate neighbours.

'Jimmy. I've been thinking over what the vicar had to say in church a few weeks ago. You know a bit about that Mr and Mrs Manning don't you?'

Jim confirmed that he knew them well, and added that he had found them to be a very pleasant and friendly couple.

'And do you think they would mind calling in to see an old woman like me some time?'

'I'm sure they'd love to Ada, especially as I've told them a little about you and Tom, and the way things were in the old days. They're Jack and Kate, by the way.'

'Well you ask Jack and Kate if they could call in with yourself and Celia next Sunday afternoon for a bit of cake and tea. About half-three would be lovely.'

The invitation proffered and accepted, the four of them set off the following Sunday to stroll the half-mile or so to Ada's house which stood apart from the village at the end of Goosey Lane, a roughly surfaced track off the Barlow Road.

Despite the attractions of a fine Sunday mid-afternoon in early May, few were to be seen as they passed through the village. One or two men, engaged in some leisurely hoeing on their veg plots, took a few moments off for a word of greeting with Jimmy and a nod to Jack (in conformity with Barton hill convention the ladies were ignored) before returning to their undemanding labours. In the centre of the village all the shops were tightly closed, as was the Shagger, the Sunday lunchtime regulars having returned home for their dinner (nobody 'lunched' on the hill) before turning, some to the *News of the World*, others to international football or county cricket on the box, but the majority to sleeping their way through to a late tea, and then a return to the Shagger to forget for an hour or two the coming Monday and the following week of hard graft.

Putting the vicar's precepts into practice with a zeal that would have delighted him, Ada had been waiting impatiently for her visitors, and was out of the house to greet them before the garden gate had clicked shut. Intimate already with Jim and Celia from many earlier meetings, she spared them a quick smile, but making straight for Kate surprised her with a hug and a kiss on the cheek before a word had been spoken.

'Hello my dear. Lovely to meet you both after all this while, though I've seen you about quite a bit. Should have asked you up to see me earlier.'

Jack clasped Ada's outstretched hand warmly, but ignorant of the Barton conventions in such matters, hesitated in the matter of a kiss on first meeting. His uncertainty was resolved when Ada quite clearly offered up her cheek.

Despite being occupied with the warmth of Ada's welcome, none of them had been unaware of the two shadowy figures shuffling about awkwardly in the gloom of the passage who were now called out by Ada to meet her visitors.

'This is Ted, my eldest, and this Charlie, my baby. When I told them you was coming up to tea they both said they just had to pop round to say hello while you were here.'

Her 'baby', all six-foot-three of him, still not inured to his mother's loving mockery, grimaced as he shook their hands and muttered an embarrassed welcome. Ted went through the formalities with no more than a silent nod of his head. Neither showed any sign of the impatience to meet the Mannings that Ada's introduction had suggested.

Indeed, if their mother had summoned them out and instructed them to 'Say hello nicely,' it couldn't have been more obvious to the visitors that here were a couple of pressed men conscripted to the vicar's cause by their mother's missionary fervour.

Scrubbed, washed, shaved, and dressed in a 'Sunday best' that normally saw the light of day every couple of years, their polished weather-beaten faces struggled hard to express a welcome, but it was clear that their hearts were not in it, and when Ada led them all through to her living room they stood in the background for five minutes or so, silent unless spoken to. When a decent interval had expired they mumbled the best excuses they could devise, and then hurried away to throw off their coats and ties, and make the most of what little was left to them of their Sunday afternoon.

With the conversation proceeding easily amongst the others, Jack had allowed his attention to drift to the family photographs on the wall, and he scarcely looked at the thickly buttered slice of Ada's teacake as he bit into it. But Jack was fond of his food, and he knew a good thing when he tasted it.

'What gorgeous butter Ada,' he said. 'Where on earth do you buy it?'

'There, that's what you've been waiting for isn't it Ada?' said Jimmy, but gave her no time to reply.

'There's no "buy" about it Jack. She churns it all with her own fair hands, don't you my love?'

'Don't you be cheeky, and not so much of the "my love." But yes, that's right. That's how Tom told me he liked it when we got married, and I've made it that way ever since. I can't bear that boughten tack. But with the screws in me hands it's getting harder and harder, and I think this year might be the last.'

'That's Tom is it?' asked Jack, nodding towards one of the photographs on the wall.

'That's right. Taken a couple of years after the war just before we got married.'

'Childhood sweethearts was it Ada?' asked Jimmy, who was now exploring new territory with Ada.

'I spose it was for me, but not for Tom. He was almost ten years older than me, but I knew him when I was nothing but a little thing, and I think I must have been in love with him then. But there were older ones who had their eyes on Tom, and I'm sure he had his fling with a few of them before he noticed me. That would have been when I was about sixteen. But the lads didn't marry young in them days, and I thought as I grew up that I might be in with a chance – but you don't want to waste your time listening to all my tales.'

'Oh but we do Ada,' said Jimmy. 'I can't resist a rural romance, and I reckon we should sit and listen to the old folk talking a lot more than we do. What about you Jack?'

'Absolutely. Wish I'd listened more when I was younger. Too late now for many of them.'

'Well it was the time of the old Queen's Jubilee. A crowd of us youngsters were being taken into Barlow the day before on farmer Watkins' hay wagon, and Tom was sitting up front driving, along with Mr Addison from the school and Miss Bailey from the post. There was beef and mutton sandwiches and fizzy drink to keep us going in the back till we got there, but I couldn't take my eyes off Tom. Oh he did look handsome in his fancy ganzie, top coat and hat, and every once in a while he'd give a flourish of the whip. Not that he'd dare to let it touch Mr Watkins' two lovely Clydesdales.

For many of us youngsters from up on the hill that was our first trip to Barlow, and on that day it looked just like a fairy land. There was bunting, streamers, flags and coloured lights in all the streets, with flowers and pictures of the Queen in all the shop windows, and a big brass band playing under the market hall.

I looked around for Tom after we arrived, but didn't see him again until we set off for home. I think he was more interested in the pubs, and the chance for a change from the Shepherd's brew.

It wasn't until we set off for home that Tom seemed to notice me for the first time. "Hello Ada," he said, giving me a helping hand up into the back. "I didn't notice you on the way out. You're quite the lovely young lady now aren't you?" And I spent all the way back to the village hoping it wasn't just the beer talking.

Then when we got back home we all trooped off down the hill to Mr Watkins' big wagon shed, where Mr Addison and some of the men had got up that old piece St George and the Dragon. I think it was when I saw Tom as St George that I really knew I was in love with him. His brother William played the Turkish knight. He was another lovely lad too, but he never came back from the war.

When it got dark and we saw the beacon fire lit up on Merton hill away in the distance, we lit ours up too, and then things got a bit larky with fun and games around the fire, and a bit of dancing. That was when Tom first got his arms around my waist, and then slipped us away into the shadows, and gave me a kiss. Bit of a cheek that, considering my age.'

'When you talk about the war Ada, which one do you mean?' asked Jack.

'South Africa. The one that was still going on when the old Queen died. Both Tom and William had been in the reserves for years, and were soon called in to the local barracks. Then they were on their way out there within a couple of months. Tom kept a few bits and pieces about the war which I've still got upstairs if you'd like to see them.'

'Well if that's alright with you Ada, I'd be very interested,' said Jimmy.

'They're all in the back room at the top of the stairs, but my legs are so bad I don't go up there now unless I really have to. Pop up yourself. You too Jack if you'd be interested. There's still a few bits of his uniform in the old wardrobe, and some papers and other pieces on the table.'

Jimmy and Jack left the ladies to it and climbed the stairs to the top floor.

'Must have been their room when they were first married,' said Jimmy, walking across to the window which looked out over the garden to the south. 'She's still using the same old privy too, by the look of it. Probably end up slipping away there just like Tom. I think she'd probably like that.'

Jack, his attention caught by a group of photographs on the wall, was too absorbed to answer. It was the centrepiece that first caught his eye – a young Churchill as war correspondent wearing slouch hat and military jacket. An unusual choice from the many popular portraits that were available, thought Jack. Around it was a cluster of photographs, all of them of the King's Shropshire Light Infantry: in barracks, marching for embarkation, or posed outside a tent in South Africa. There was also one of two fine-looking young men wearing what looked like dress uniform and probably taken in barracks: Tom and his brother William, Jack assumed.

On a table below the photographs, in a little glass-topped box, were a few mementos: a Queen's South Africa medal with four clasps, a regimental badge, a glass-beaded heart pincushion with the regimental arms and a sentimental verse, a collection of newspaper cuttings, and a book which Jack took out to examine more closely.

'There's a book here by Churchill. Seems to be about the Boer War, *Ian Hamilton's March*. Know anything about that Jimmy.'

'Absolutely bugger all. Sounds like water under the bridge to me. Who'd be interested now?'

'Some might be in the book. The cover's a bit faded on the front, but otherwise it's in good condition, and as it's dated 1900 I reckon it must be a first edition.'

Jack could see that towards the back of the book a slip of paper had been inserted, and turning to the page he found that a paragraph had been underlined in pencil:

At dawn on May-day fighting recommenced, and soon after six-o'clock parties of the Gordons and Canadians succeeded in gaining possession of the two peaks of Thoba Mountain. Besides this, half a company of the Shropshires under Colour-Sergeant Sconse, managed to seize the nek between them, and though subjected to a severe cross-fire, which caused in this small party ten casualties out of forty, maintained themselves stubbornly for four hours. The points which dominate the flat top of the mountain were thus gained.

Alongside the paragraph was written, presumably by Tom, 'This is where we lost poor William.'

Flipping back again to the front Jack saw that the front flyleaf carried a brief inscription, 'To Thomas Sutton from Winston S Churchill.'

'Well I'll be damned,' said Jack. 'Jimmy come and have a look at this, and tell me now if you think anyone might be interested.'

Jimmy clucked as he looked at Jack's discovery. 'Oh dear, it's a sad reflection on this wicked world that that reactionary old bugger's signature should be worth some money, but I imagine it is.'

They didn't spend much time looking at any of the other bits and pieces, but went down to have a word with Ada.

'Ada, did Tom ever talk to you at all about this and the Boer War,' said Jack, handing the book to her.

'Not a word. Never talked to me about the war at all. He'd been back almost four years before we got married, and he brought all that stuff with him. I saw it in the case of course, but never thought to look at it. Why, is it important?'

'Did he never talk to you about William's death?'

'No. I'd heard all about that from his family long before he came back over. Tom never talked about it to me direct.'

'Did he ever mention that he'd met Churchill out there?'

'You mean the old Prime Minister?'

'Yes, but this was year's earlier: before the First World War.'

'Not a word. Never talked about Churchill other than to say what a great man he was, and how he'd helped to win the war, but he didn't mean the Boer War.'

Jack opened the book towards the back.

'So you've never seen this,' he said, pointing out Tom's entry in the margin.

'Never. Oh poor William. Tom never talked to me about it, but looking at this it makes me feel so sad that he never thought to show me.'

'Or this,' said Jack, turning to the front flyleaf.

Ada looked at the inscription in disbelief. 'Is that really his signature: genuine I mean.'

'Well it's in a good firm hand. Looks good to me, but it would have to be checked out. You didn't realise that it was worth some money then?'

Ada shook her head. 'I don't think Tom did either. I never saw the book out of the box, and he may well have completely forgotten that it was signed.'

There followed an hour or more of excited speculation, while the book was examined more closely page by page. But there were no further inscriptions to throw any light on the matter, or anything in the old newspaper cuttings to enlighten them. Jack and Jimmy meanwhile had been talking the matter over, and before they left Jimmy had a final word with Ada.

'Ada, Jack and I think this needs to be done properly and with care. The book should be professionally valued, and it needs to be done by an expert, someone who knows what he's about. That means London and not one of the local auctioneers. Jack said he'll find out what he can about any specialists in this sort of thing, and then we'll call again, and put together a letter for you to send telling them what you have. If they're interested, and I'm sure they will be, wrap the book up carefully and get one of the boys to go up on the train and see them. If the boys aren't keen to do that, then if it's OK with you, I'll pop up for you.'

Ada was quite happy with that, and the rest of their time together was spent, without all that much encouragement being needed from her visitors, in listening to Ada reminiscing about her childhood and early married life on the hill. And always it was the hill's isolation in those early days that was the underlying theme. It forced on them a self-sufficiency and spirit of mutual support and cooperation that was being lost elsewhere, and in winter in particular it brought with it a fair share of emergencies and tragedies.

Ada, newly pregnant herself for the first time, had been called on to assist when heavy snowfalls had prevented either doctor or midwife getting to the village, and Albert, the current publican, was showing a distinct unwillingness to assume a personal existence independent of his mother's womb.

'But we got him out in the end,' said Ada, 'although he did look a sight. All blotched, scratched and ugly.'

'Not much change there then,' said Jimmy.

'Maybe not, but he's always kept an eye on me since Tom died.'

The tragedy was the loss of David, Ada's young cousin, who cycling home late one night when winter ice lay thick across the hill, had skidded and fallen. His injury itself had not been severe, nothing more than a broken ankle, but none other was to pass that way during the night, and long before anyone was moving the following morning young David had frozen to death.

There were of course many happy times to be recalled, but as always it was the tragedies that left their mark on her visitors.

Unsurprisingly, as they had turned from tea to parsnip wine following the sensational discovery in the book, more than three hours had slipped away before they set off down the hill for home. Despite the excitement of the book's discovery, the dying light of day and the thought of youth and life lost by war or accident had left them all in a reflective mood, Jack in particular.

'Strange isn't it how we can be so affected by the faraway deaths of those we have never even known. I felt like that when I read Tom's few words about William's death. Do you know that Hardy poem *Drummer Hodge* Jim?'

'No Jack; can't say that I do. Remember, you're the man of letters. I'm just a pragmatic revolutionary and man of action.'

'You're a soulless bugger too, but I'm not deterred. Borrow my book some time and read it. Fine piece: only a few stanzas on poor young Hodge dead and buried on an African kopje to spend eternity under an alien sky. Can't remember the exact lines, but there's a bit about Hodge becoming part of that unknown plain and growing to become some Southern tree. A few years and a war later Brooke had much the same idea with his "foreign field" piece. Prefer the Hardy though – not so self-indulgent.'

'Now you've got that out of your system, can we get home please, open a bottle and get stuck into a cold collation,' said Kate.

'God, you're two of a kind. Bloody philistines.'

A specialist identified and Ada's letter sent, there was little more than a week's delay before a reply was received. There was great interest, they learned, and it would be the writer's pleasure to examine the book and signature if they would telephone him for an appointment to call as soon as it was convenient.

Contrary to Jimmy's expectations, both of Ada's sons had shown themselves to be not only willing, but eager to carry the book to London. In fact having seen and heard so much about London in the swinging sixties they went right away, and allowed themselves three nights to explore its delights.

On the Saturday evening following their departure Jack answered a knock at the door to find the two of them fairly bursting in their eagerness to be friendly and make amends for their behaviour earlier in the month, nor had they had to be instructed by Ada to do so.

'Sorry to disturb your evening Mr Manning, but we wondered if you could spare a little time to have a look at what we've brought back: Mr & Mrs Gillan too if you could give them a ring.'

'Can't wait to see it. Come on through and grab a seat. Kate would you give Jimmy a quick ring please, and ask them both if they could pop up right away. Tell them Ted and Charlie have called. . . .and by the way it's Jack and Kate, Jimmy and Celia from now on. OK'

They nodded and then fell into the chairs Jack offered them, trying to balance between them two bouquets of flowers, two packets and one envelope, while maintaining their composure.

'If you don't mind Mr . . . . Sorry Jack, we'll hang on a bit for Jimmy and Celia before . . . I mean . . .'

'No that's fine Ted,' said Jack. 'How's Ada?'

'Oh she keeps marvellous for her age. Looking forward to summer like the rest of us . . .'

And so they kept up a desultory conversation until Jim and Celia arrived, breathless from their dash over the fields.

'Well,' said Ted, who had clearly been designated spokesman, 'We and Mum would like first to say thank you to you all for what's turned up.'

Saying no more he proffered a bouquet to Kate and a box to Jack, while Charlie did the same to Celia and Jimmy, each receiving a kiss of thanks from his lady.

'Oh dear,' said Jimmy, who first had his box open, 'It's going to be a long evening Jack. Where are the

54

glasses?' He held up a bottle of single malt Scotch as Jack opened his box to find its twin.

With all six comfortably settled with well-charged glasses, the men taking it neat, the ladies with a little water, Ted got down to essentials.

'Well, as you know, our appointment was with a Mr Longman, but he'd got another chap with him by the name of Castlebar. We told them a little bit more about how the book had come to light, and then handed it over for them to have a look.

Mr Longman had it first. He looked over the cover, turned to Dad's little note about poor Uncle William, then turned to the front and the signature, before passing it over to the other gentleman. He seemed to compare it with some other papers that he had, and then simply said, "No doubt about it."'

'Oh that's bloody marvellous,' said Jack.

'Crudely put,' said Jimmy, 'But I think it expresses the view of us all.'

Ted then continued with his story.

'Mr Longman said he understood we were going to be in town for a couple more days, and thought it would be safer if we left the book with him rather than in our hotel room. He would give us a proper receipt, and then we could pick the book up when we were ready to come home. In the meantime he would prepare a note for us to bring back for Mum and anyone else she wanted to see it.'

With this he opened the envelope he had been holding, and held up two sheets of closely typed A4.

'I think this is your province Jack,' said Jimmy. 'You spend your days on this sort of thing. I'll top up the drinks while you look at it.'

Jack read and then re-read the papers while the others talked quietly together.

'OK. Do you want the full SP, or just the gist?'

The gist being chosen by all, he gave it to them as follows.

'Right. The book is rare. Only 5,000 were printed in this first edition. Bound in red cloth the book is prone both to wear and to fading. Ada's copy is in good condition, however, apart from the cover which is faded. The spine and back cover are fine. The signature is undoubtedly genuine. The book will certainly be worth thousands, but exactly how much is uncertain because nothing like it has come on to the market before. The effect of Tom's pencil note is felt to be uncertain. It may or may not affect the price one way or the other, but if it were possible by any means to establish with certainty that there was a meeting, and where and when, then that would certainly increase the value significantly.'

Jimmy emptied his glass with an emphatic gulp.

'I take back all I said Jack. There's no other way of putting it. That's absolutely bloody marvellous'

'But what's Ada going to do?' asked Celia. 'Is she going to put it up for auction?'

'Says she wouldn't hear of it,' said Charlie. 'Told us it's our nest-egg when she's gone, and we can do what we like with it then. She wants us to see if we can find out anything more about Dad's time in South Africa. Do you think that's possible Jack?'

'Well if you're hoping to prove that there was a meeting you're going to be hoeing a hard row, and I think with little prospect of success. It would probably need the talents of an expert researcher too. But if all you want to do is find out a little more about your Dad's part in the campaign, then the best place for you to start would be in the Regimental Archive.'

'There you are,' exclaimed Jimmy. 'QED: the practical advantages of having a literary taxman as a neighbour.'

'Oh do belt up Jim,' said Celia.

It was past two in the morning when Ted and Charlie took their leave to stagger off home, and by the time their version of events had mutated two or three times Jack's reputation as a literary expert and authority on rare books was established throughout the county.

'Think Celia could doss down here somewhere Jack?' said Jimmy walking to the window and gazing out. 'I feel like killing the bottle off and seeing the sun up. Are you game?'

'Well I haven't done this for years,' said Jack, 'But as it's Sunday tomorrow, why not. You'll sort Celia out with a bed won't you Kate?'

Jimmy topped up the two glasses, and wishing the ladies goodnight they wandered out together into the night air, and as Kate led Celia up to the spare bedroom she could hear Jack saying, 'Drummer Hodge, Jimmy. I've got it off by heart now. Gaze up into our friendly, old night sky. Listen, and learn.

They throw in drummer Hodge, to rest

Uncoffined – just as found:

His landmark is . . . .'

'God he can be a pompous ass sometimes,' said Kate as they passed out of hearing.

4

Add a Pair of Dagging Shears

Within three years of his arrival on the hill Jack's inept performance as a countryman, and the entertainment it provided to the locals, who watched it all from a distance with ill-concealed amusement, had done as much to endear him to the community as anything else might have. When he turned to them for advice and assistance his acceptance was finally assured.

The fate of Colditz, his fruit cage, in the January of their third winter had been the first act in his rural comedy. Determined not to share the fruit of his labours with the birds and other assorted wildlife, Jack had constructed the cage in the autumn of their arrival. With a stoicism and faith born more of love than common-sense and self-preservation, Kate stood below him holding each eight-foot support post upright while Jack, from the top of a step-ladder, swung a seven pound sledgehammer to drive it in. She survived to see their planting done and the nets in place.

Their plants flourished, and throughout the spring and early summer of the following year they watched their blackcurrants, raspberries and gooseberries swell and ripen with a satisfaction that was only a little dampened as the squirrels bit holes in the netting through which the birds could always find a way in, but never a way out, leading to anguished excursions by Kate to rescue them.

By the end of the season their losses were relatively modest, however, and with their harvest home, they had not only enough for their own pickling, jamming and freezing, but also a tidy surplus, which they offered to their cage-less neighbours, only to find that they too had their own surpluses by the simple expedient of planting an extra row or two for the birds.

At the end of the second season, with all crops gathered and the autumn pruning done, they forgot about the cage and turned to other things, which in mid-December included their first visit to the local pantomime in the village hall. This was an irregular not annual event, as it seemed to take the writers a couple of years or more to assemble the catalogue of salacious, scurrilous and near-libellous references that formed their theme.

Copulation, flatulence, defecation and various close encounters of the physical kind all featured in the script, but two items in particular marked a deviation from the usual rustic programme: the company's own rural version of George Harrison's *Cos I'm The Taxman*, and an obscene sketch of the seduction and subversion from duty of a taxman (unsubtly named Mr Mannering to hammer home the point) by the sexual wiles of the village tart. It was a rude, crude script, but it was played out with verve and gusto. Both items went down to great applause which Jack took as marking his final acceptance into the fold.

A mild, almost balmy, Christmas was followed, as is so often the case, by a dramatic change in the weather which made life on the hill, even on the sheltered western slope, a testing ordeal. For two days an arctic wind scoured the countryside driving the sheep to such shelter as they could find, and burning the last life from any vegetation that had clung on into the winter. Early on New Year's Eve the wind fell away to an ominous calm, as a sullen, grey overcast slowly thickened around the hill, shrouding the heights and leaving the valleys in a threatening half-light.

Two hours or so before midnight, at Jimmy's request, and having fortified themselves with a hot whisky, Jack and Kate set off to meet him at the Shagger for their first visit to the village New Year celebrations. As they passed the church they noticed with surprise that it was in darkness, and so it would remain. No Watch Night Service in St Matthew's explained Jimmy when they met in the bar: the village kept to another, older tradition that no vicar had been able to usurp.

The bar was crowded, noisy and steamy-hot with the physical presence of its many 'well-oiled' customers; the atmosphere smoky, and heavy with an odour redolent of ladies' Christmas perfumes subtly blended with the scent of cheap cigars and the body odours of men who make their living on the land, and may not long have left the milking parlour or pig-pen.

A call from the vicar took them over to the far corner of the bar where he was standing with a whisky and tempting Ada Sutton to her third Advocaat.

'Thought I had to pop in to wish the mother of the village a Happy New Year, but I won't stay long. Don't want to spoil the party.'

Before he could say any more, he was interrupted by a younger group in what passed for the saloon bar, starting up with one of the latest pop songs, but in the public the older regulars were having none of that.

'Come on Ted, give us one of your Dad's songs with Charlie and show those youngsters what it's all about,' came a call from somewhere in the crush.

Ada's two sons were well known in the village for keeping up the tradition of their father, and his father before him, in having at their disposal a repertoire of rustic songs, risqué or sentimental, that never failed to please an audience. Taking one long pull at their pints, which almost emptied the glasses, they moved out to a vantage point beside the fire, called for a bit of hush, put one hand to an ear, and began with *The Maid of Barton Hill*, one of Old Tom's own compositions, with its lusty lads, mossy mounds and the raising up and laying down of 'spirits.' In those that followed there was much sowing of meadows, ploughing of furrows, thrashing of flails and clapping of hands on cuckoo's nests, in which all the men and some of the ladies joined heartily, while those of a more reticent disposition sipped their port and simpered.

But when they turned to *The Chandler's Wife* it was not so well received. It came with a repeating 'knock, knock, knock' in the last line of each increasingly suggestive chorus, which was taken up enthusiastically by the younger men who sang, clapped or hammered out the phrase on the bar or table top. But a few of the older men frowned their disapproval, and many of the women sat po-faced, for as midnight was fast approaching the audience was looking for a little nostalgia, and the singers scarcely had time to finish before some of the older folk were calling for Jimmy and *The Miner's Dream of Home*.

Jimmy's rich baritone came as a surprise to Jack, and he listened with admiration to a song the verse of which meant nothing to him until Jim got to the end, when every voice in the bar joined with him in with the chorus:

'I saw the old homestead and faces I love,

I saw England's valleys and dells,

And I listened with joy as I did when a boy....'

Only then did Jack recognise it as a favourite from the family Christmas gatherings of his early childhood, and he too joined in until he stalled on the final lines, when his eyes misted over and a lump rose in his throat, as it always did on such nostalgic occasions despite his best endeavours.

'Oh my God,' whispered Kate who knew him of old. 'Don't you dare let me down and have a cry. Think of your image, taxman.'

A few moments later, at a word from Albert, the bustle and chatter subsided, and they stood together in silence till the last stroke of the chimes at midnight faded away in the dark tower of St Matthew's. But the New Year's greetings and *Auld Lang Syne* that followed did not, as Jack had expected, mark an end to the evening's proceedings.

'Come on Ada, my love, your turn to lead the way this year. Get your coat on, Tom will be waiting,' called Albert from behind the bar. At this Jack looked at Jimmy with surprise, but Jimmy simply motioned to him to stay silent and wait.

With their coats on, and with three or four picking up lanterns as they went, the whole of the Shagger's company, lead by Ada on Albert's arm, moved out of the bar and into the night, and the bar stood empty apart from the four incomers.

'Give them a few more minutes, and then follow me,' said Jimmy, and leaving a note and a handful of coins on the bar, he stepped behind it to pour them each another fortifying drink, before they too moved out into the darkness.

As they drew away from the lights of the Shagger towards the church, they could feel the gentle touch of snowflakes on their faces and the softness of settled snow beneath their feet, and Jack and Kate wondered where on earth they were being led, and why. Then, not many yards ahead of them, they saw the darker bulk of St Matthew's looming against the gloom of the sky, and the gentle illumination of lanterns in the churchyard.

Heeding Jimmy's caution to move quietly, they stole towards the low wall of the churchyard, and strained their eyes to follow the faint illumination of the lamps carried by the six or seven clusters of villagers as they separated and moved between the tombstones in the darkness, while those without any family connection (surprisingly few) stood quietly just inside the lych-gate.

Focussing on Ada, who was there with Albert, her two sons and four or five others they took to be family, they saw the group stop, and stand in silence for a few moments at what Jimmy said was old Tom's grave, before Ted produced a bottle from his coat pocket, unscrewed the cap, and held it out to fill the little shot glasses the others had been carrying.

As they stood together, ready with glasses charged, Ted splashed a few drops from the bottle over the grave, said a few words which the listeners could not hear clearly, and then as one, they drank their New Year's toast to the old boy.

At the other graves the same quiet ritual had taken place, but as the groups turned and came together again the solemnity of the visit was over, and as the lookers-on stole away towards their homes they could hear louder conversation and soft laughter.

'That was fascinating,' said Jack. 'I've read about similar customs in other countries, but had no idea it existed here.'

Jimmy smiled, 'Oh you'd be surprised what goes on. You'll see them out on the fields with the latest equipment they can afford, or soaking their sheep in God knows what appalling modern chemicals, but at certain times of the year they're still back in the Middle Ages. There's well dressing every September down at Holly-well on the spring line. Some of the older ladies like Ada still talk to the bees, and I'm told that a few of the old boys sneak up to the top of the hill for sunset on Midsummer's Eve. They have a quiet drink together, and then they each leave behind a twist of tobacco and a pipe. For the old spirits of the hill I was told, and they swear the tobacco has always gone when they return next day to pick up their pipes.'

'Good story,' said Jack. 'I wonder who enjoys the smoke.'

When they returned home the snow was still falling, and more heavily: soft, fat flakes now that swirled around them like a blizzard of white autumn leaves, and already the telephone wires to the house were thickening as the flakes stuck, and accumulated.

They slept late the following morning, and when Jack drew back the curtains that opened to the west, it was to a clear blue sky and brilliant winter sunshine glistening on a snow-covered landscape stretching away beyond the spires of Barlow, and white against the horizon on the distant tops of the Black Mountains. It looked like being the perfect start to the New Year

They breakfasted leisurely, and late in the morning were still at the table listening to reports of heavy snowfalls across the whole of the West Midlands when Jimmy rapped on the window and beckoned them to open the door.

'Good to see you out and about so early Jim,' said Jack. 'What a gorgeous start to the year.'

'Breathtaking, and I don't want to dampen your early enthusiasm Jack,' said Jimmy. 'But I think you should both get your gear on and come and have a look at your fruit cage. You've got a bit of a problem: spotted it on my walk. I'll wait out here: don't want to spread snow everywhere.'

Within a couple of minutes, booted and well wrapped up, they had joined Jimmy outside, and together they trod their way through the drifts of the night across the lawn, past the herbaceous border and hedge to the fruit and vegetable garden.

'Oh Christ,' was Jack's only comment. Kate stood in stunned silence.

Where their fruit cage, so laboriously constructed, had formerly stood, was now a scene of utter devastation. Fat, heavy snowflakes, falling hour after hour throughout the night, had stuck and clung to the super-strong top mesh, which Jack in his ignorance had failed to draw back. Layer upon layer, snow upon snow, the load had gradually increased, until not even Jack's three-inch supports had been able to withstand the strain. Scarcely one remained unmoved. Most were slumped many degrees from the vertical, and here and there a post had broken and splintered, allowing the snow-laden netting to sag even further and flatten the bushes it was intended to protect.

'Silly boy,' said Jim. 'If I'd noticed I'd have told you, but from a distance the netting wasn't obvious: until it had the snow on it that is.'

By mid-day the news had been carried back to the village by other early risers out with their snow ploughs, and formed a tit-bit of conversation and entertainment among the regulars, who had gathered in the bar of the Shagger for a New Year's hair of the dog.

Jack's closer inspection of the damage to the cage was enough to convince him that the only sensible course was to bring the whole thing down and forget about it. From now on the birds could have their share, as they did from all his neighbours' crops. He was hoping for better things though from their pregnant ewes, and turned back to inspect them where they had gathered for shelter under the extension built at the end of the barn.

Despite the doubts they had expressed to the vicar on their first meeting, the temptation to run some of their own stock had proved to be irresistible to Kate. At a local farm auction the previous summer, taking expert advice and guidance from Davey Bache, their immediate farming neighbour, who accompanied them and inspected the ewes, Jack put in his bids at Kate's continuous urging, and they returned home with seven clean and healthy-looking ewes tucked into Davey's stock trailer.

Looking back at the evening courses they had attended almost two years earlier, they felt quite adequately prepared for their undertaking, and had no doubt about their ability to cope with any of the problems that might be thrown at them. During the sheep handling exercises Jack had turned and manipulated his sheep with ease, and Kate, who was chosen as being conveniently small-boned, had excelled herself in the practical experiment of shoving her hand up the back end of a mock-up, in-lamb ewe, to identify and deal with any presentation problems that might be encountered at birth.

With the ewes grazing contentedly on his meadow, Jack had set off at once to Jackson's Agricultural with a short list from Davey of the few bits and pieces he might need to see him through his first winter and spring as a shepherd: hurdles, troughs, sheep netting and a run of electric fencing.

'Make sure to ask for Charlie, and mention my name when you give him your order . . . Oh and I nearly forgot: add a pair of dagging shears to the list. You might find you need them later.'

The one man working in the stock yard at the suppliers responded silently to Jack's enquiry for Charlie by pointing towards a door in the buildings marked Trade Desk – Please Enter.

Inside, having established that the man behind the counter answered to the name of Charlie, Jack handed over his list, and said that he had been told particularly to mention that he had been recommended to them by Davey Bache.

Charlie took the list and looked Jack over doubtfully.

'No account with us have you?'

Jack shook his head.

'And Davey told you that it would be cash not cheque, did he?'

No he bloody didn't, thought Jack, and realised at once that he ought to call it a day there and then and leave, but he didn't.

'That's OK if you're happy with COD.'

That brought another doubtful look and a request for his address.

'That's just above Davey's place isn't it?'

'Adjoining,' said Jack. 'We've just taken over a few acres up there, and Davey's giving us a hand with the sheep.'

'Right then, well let me price this lot up for you.'

With that he disappeared into the back of the office to return a few minutes later with the prices marked up alongside each item on the list, but even before he spoke Jack had no doubt what he was going to hear.

'I've listed everything at full price, but the usual arrangement with Davey is 20% off for cash, and I'll look after the VAT. That OK with you?'

Davey knew bloody well that this would happen, thought Jack. Knew it was a tax scam, and pointed me right towards it: the cheeky bugger. A couple of days and the story would be all round the village. He could have stopped right there: knew very well that he should

67

have stopped right there, but he didn't. He nodded his head in agreement with the amount, plus a small addition to cover the cost of delivery the following evening.

Unable to resist his taxman's instinct he nosed around the shop and yard before he left, trying to make some rough assessment of the nature and size of the business. Lovely little arrangement they've got going here, he thought. Wonder how long it will be before they get rumbled.

So that's how easy it is to slip over the line is it? And that's how they all start, the tax dodgers. A little bit here and a little bit there, and then they start to get greedy. Well what the hell. They're all at it – join the bloody club. Why not? He thought he'd keep it to himself though: best all round if Kate didn't get to know.

The following evening the goods arrived spot on time, and he handed over the agreed sum in cash: no receipt offered or asked for. That would be standard practice – no paper trail.

It was soon clear that Davey's belated mention of the dagging shears had been made in anticipation of an earlier need for them than Jack himself might have hoped for.

Their ewes had arrived from leaner grazing than Jack's lush pasture, and he in his ignorance had simply released them onto his meadow and left them to it. Inevitably they overindulged and within days, as the scours overtook them, what had been seven snow-white rumps were turning into a foul, slimy, evil-smelling, pea-green disgrace.

On Davey's advice Jack immediately restricted their grazing, and was rewarded as the ewes' revoltingly liquid discharges slowly reverted to the neat little raisins that he had been expecting. But the filthy back-ends remained, gradually caking hard in the late summer heat, and Jack simply could not summon up the courage to put his shears to work.

And so they remained until October when a ram borrowed from Davey was due to come in to do his stuff. But when Davey saw the state of the ewes' back-sides he left Jack with no option but to buckle down to the job if he wanted to have any lambs.

'You'll have to clean them up before Norman gets at them Jack. In the state they're in he'll smell nothing but shit when he sniffs around them to see if they're ready.'

By midday the following Saturday Jack and Kate, with some difficulty, had the ewes hurdled up inside the barn and ready for Jack to do his stuff.

As he stood, legs astride, across the back of the first, and bent to his task over the stinking, tangled mass of wool and shit, the stench that assaulted his nose was almost too much. His gorge rose, and it was only with the greatest difficulty that he mastered an urge to throw up. Then, for the first time, Roger's warning words came back to haunt him: 'Foot-rot, scours and a lot of hard work for no return with God's most stupid creation.'

Unfortunately their evening course had included no practical tuition on the use of dagging shears, and despite his best efforts Jack found them a difficult, demanding device. He was clumsy and awkward with them, which meant that each ewe was taking him almost fifteen minutes to clean up. Finally, however, the job was done and Jack, who by then felt that he had been defiled, sought relief in a long, hot shower and a stiff whisky.

In due course Davey delivered Norman to them, raddle harness in place, and all ready for action.

'My God, he's a big beast,' said Jack.

'Tops 125kg when he's really in condition,' said Davey with pride.

Opening the gate, they released Norman into the paddock with the ewes, and left him to it, but a week later the ewes showed no sign that he'd been active, and Jack noticed that he was starting to limp.

The limp soon became worse, and as it seemed to be diverting Norman from his ladies and the task in hand, Jack, still full of the confidence his course had given him despite his dagging setback, identified foot rot, and decided to do something about it. At least he'd had instruction in that, if not with dagging.

Norman, although he was built like a tank (and exceptionally well endowed for his job) was a docile, almost affectionate young chap. Enticed by Jack with a few sheep nuts in a bucket, he readily followed him into the back end of the barn where Jack had his trimming knife, clippers and spray ready to hand, and Kate to assist. Now all he had to do was turn Norman to get at his feet.

'Doing a bit of foot trimming then Mr Manning?'

Jack groaned. The voice was that of young Martin Ellis, son of another of Jimmy's neighbours, who had a habit of wandering around the local farms in his free time. Once he had met Jack he seemed to identify him as one who was an innocent in the ways of the countryman, and he now frequently appeared to oversee Jack's smallholding activities and occasionally offer advice. This irritated Jack, but Martin was a pleasant young lad, and he didn't like to chase him away: not good for public relations anyway.

Resigned to having an audience, Jack turned his attention to Norman, and casting his mind back almost two years, strove to recall the technique which had been so successful when he was turning the ewes, the light and delicate little ewes, at the evening course.

'Standing at the sheep's left shoulder, restrain its head with your left arm': no problem with that, Norman was a nice, steady chap.

'Reaching over, grab right front leg with right hand, lift foot firmly up until foreleg is parallel with ground. Release head and switch hands on foot.' OK. . . Done; and Norman barely showing any interest in proceedings.

'Grasp sheep's right hind leg with right hand, lift and turn.'

Nothing! Norman didn't struggle. He didn't even offer sullen resistance. He just stood there, rooted to the ground like a rock, and showing what Jack considered to be a contemptuous indifference to the whole proceeding.

Jack tried again. He might as well have been trying to turn the Sphinx. Norman was utterly unmoved, an interested observer now, it seemed, of an activity that had absolutely nothing to do with him.

'Won't he go then Mr Manning?' asked Martin.

'We shall not, we shall not be moved,' sang Kate with a giggle.

Jack ignored them both. Releasing his hold on Norman, and standing back to consider the problem, he noticed several lengths of rope hanging in neat coils from hooks on the wall. He thought his difficulty through again, and decided that with the help of the rope he might have an answer.

He chose two lengths of rope, soft but thick, gave Norman a reassuring scratch on his head, and put the bucket with the nuts on the floor to occupy him. Then kneeling by his side, he slipped one length of rope around his back legs about six inches above the ground and gently tightened the noose until he felt pressure against the legs, when he knotted it.

Moving to the front feet he made a running noose at the same height, and then gently tightening it, he stood up alongside Norman, still happily nibbling at his nuts. Handing the end of the running noose to Kate, Jack gave her his instructions.

'When I give you the word, pull the noose tight.'

Reaching across Norman's back, Jack grasped the top of his right leg firmly, reached down for his left side and called, 'Now.'

The noose tightened as Jack took a deep breath, heaved and pulled. Restrained by the ropes, Norman's attempts to retain his balance were futile: so were Jack's, and both subsided to the floor in an undignified collapse which left Norman cradled between Jack's legs.

'Just as well the neighbours can't see this Jack,' said Kate. 'It looks for all the world as though you're screwing the poor beast.'

From then on Norman offered no real protest at the proceedings, and even when Jack set to work on his feet merely turned his sad, grey-green eyes on him with a look of deep reproach at man's duplicity.

When Kate had released the ropes, Jack turned to dealing with Norman's feet. Three needed little more than trimming, but the one at the front that he had scarcely been putting to the ground was a stinking mess that Jack cleaned out with distaste before spraying with a proprietary mix. Allowed to regain his feet Norman showed no malice, and looked for no revenge beyond giving Jack a friendly butt when his back was turned that sent him staggering against the wall.

Jack had almost forgotten Martin who had been watching all this, until he heard his comment.

'Dad don't turn'um that way, Mr Manning.'

'Maybe not,' said Jack, 'But there's more than one way to skin a cat.'

Martin clearly didn't know the expression, and turned for home with a puzzled look on his face, and as Jack had realised, another good story for the village to enjoy when he passed on his account of proceedings to his father. Davey, who like the rest would have got to hear it, said nothing, but Jack was left with the feeling that he did not approve of the unorthodox methods adopted with a ram that was his pride and joy.

Back in the paddock, and no longer in discomfort, Norman showed renewed interest in the ladies, and by the time he had to leave them it looked from the ewes' markings as though he might have earned his keep, and enjoyed himself a little in the process.

Although there were no further falls of snow after the destruction of the fruit cage, the New Year's drifts lingered on under the hedgerows until early February, when the cold weather left as rapidly as it had arrived as a warm front swept in from the west bringing wind and rain with it.

Through late February and into March, Jack and Kate cosseted their ewes and watched them swell as the lambs grew inside them: as they believed. Working from the date when Norman had departed in mid-November they were expecting to see some of the lambing signs they had been told to watch for from early April onwards.

But a week passed, then two, and then three with no signs of restlessness from their seven ewes, until eventually Jack asked Davey to pop over and have a look at them.

With the ewes confined in the lambing area prepared for them at the end of the barn, Davey set about his methodical examination. He squeezed and prodded the rump and back, ran his hands down the sides and belly, gently felt around in front of the udders, lifted the docks and examined the vulva. Eventually, satisfied with his examination, he stood up and turned to Jack.

'What have you been feeding them?'

'Hay ad lib, and a daily ration of nuts and supplements. They've always had plenty.'

'And when did you start?'

'Well I've always let them have a few nuts, but upped their rations about six weeks before the ram came in and added a little sugar-beet pulp.'

Davey's analysis was brutal.

'You've been over-feeding them. They were and are too fat, and they aren't pregnant.

That fiasco, and the entertainment it provided far and wide, was more than enough for Jack and Kate. Stock rearing was abandoned for less demanding pursuits, and Davey had the run of the land for whatever stock he chose.

5

There's Something Funny Going On

From his seventh floor office at the heart of Wolverton's vibrant commercial centre, as the council's PR department liked to describe the undistinguished cluster of buildings, Jack lit his first cigarette of the day, and cast a jaded eye across the urban sprawl that lay between him and the distant flush of autumn colour through which he had just driven from Barton Hill.

His early-start, early-finish routine suited him fine when he was able to get down to a little work at his desk before the interruptions of the day began, but this morning it meant that he had time to kill as he awaited the arrival of Tony Bewley, his companion for the day, who kept more conventional hours.

In the street below the morning traffic was beginning to build towards the town's modest rush hour, and a few other early birds like Jack were making their way towards the entrance to the building. Tony was not amongst them, and would not be for almost another half-hour, and so turning from the window to his chair, Jack settled himself as comfortably as the official issue permitted, put his feet on the desk and drew deeply on his cigarette while he considered his position.

Despite more than four years on the hill, the move from town to country which he had hoped might relieve his restlessness had achieved nothing, less than nothing, as the restlessness had grown with the years, and he now had the sense to see that the problem lay not with his private life, but with his job and nowhere else. Almost twenty years in taxes, much of it on investigation work, had corroded his soul and left him with a cynical distrust not only of the people with whom he had to deal, but the nature of the work itself and the world in general.

His boil of discontent had finally burst the previous Saturday evening when what started as a quiet pint with Jimmy had turned into two when they were joined by Larry Breakwell, and then three or more when Ada's two sons and two or three others joined in as the session proceeded.

Neither Jack nor Jimmy could remember afterwards how tax dodging came to be mentioned in the first place, but by the time the topic came up Jack was well-oiled, fully primed and ready to run, as Jimmy described things afterwards. It was perhaps unfortunate though that Jack's little diatribe was triggered by an innocent remark from the well-intentioned but naive Rev Larry Breakwell.

Ted Sutton had been going on at some length about the tax fiddles enjoyed by a pal of his who was on the lump in the building trade. Larry, presumably simply repeating something that he had recently read in his newspaper, said that things surely couldn't be as bad as Ted said, and that historically the British were a nation of relatively compliant taxpayers.

'Oh Father, Father,' said Jack with a groan, 'I forgive you for you are not of this world, and speak out of deep ignorance, but that is complete and utter bull-shit.'

He got a dig in the ribs for this from Jimmy.

'That's all right Jimmy,' said Larry. 'Let him get it out of his system. I think this could be quite interesting.'

'Relatively compliant?' said Jack. 'Relatively compliant? Relative to a banana republic perhaps. Christ everyone who can is at it. Have been for more than a century, except for the poor bloody wage-slave of course, and he gets his pocket picked by the Chancellor before he even gets his money. Clever stuff that PAYE – beats the Artful Dodger.'

Jack had by nature a big voice, indeed he was often accused of shouting when in what he would have described as normal conversational mode. Now, fuelled by the beer, he could be heard throughout the bar, and in no time Albert was hanging over the counter earwigging, as were most of the other customers standing nearby, and Jimmy, who initially had felt inclined to try and check Jack, had changed his mind and decided to enjoy himself. He'd heard most of what he guessed was to come at home over a few glasses of his home brew, and thought it might not be a bad thing if it had a broader audience.

'Oh come on Jack,' he said. 'You're not telling me that our Albert here or Bill there in the grocers is at it, as you say.'

Deep as Jack was in his cups, he wasn't going to fall for that one.

'No, course not. Not our Albert, not our Bill naturally. Not even Jackson's Agricultural eh Davey?'

That earned him a laugh.

'What, skim a little cash off the top – never. Forget to pay for those choice little items taken from stock and the three-hundred mile holiday in the business car. Pay wages to a wife who does sod all: I mention just three for starters. Perish the thought eh boys. But Barton Hill men excepted, God-fearing, law-abiding taxpayers to the last, they're all at it: John O'Groats to Land's End. They might not call it fiddling. Some might not even know it's fiddling, but fiddling it is, and it builds up, it builds up.'

'Venial sins, venial sins surely,' said Jimmy, stirring the pot a little. 'Wouldn't you agree Larry? You know about these things. Sins I mean.'

Larry just shook his head with a smile, and waited for Jack's response, which was a little slow in coming as he was sipping a whisky and soda Albert had brought round.

'On the house Mr Manning,' he said. 'To whet your whistle.'

'Well you're bloody forgiving Jimmy for someone who pays no tax,' continued Jack, after a nod of thanks to Albert, 'But the rest of us pick up the tab for what you call venial sins, and I've only touched on the all-pervasive, low-level stuff. I won't addle your heads with the more inventive frauds the pros in the big league get up to: millions, hundreds of millions, billions in fact if the truth about avoidance was known, and bugger all gets done about it.'

'But I thought that was what you did Jack: something about it I mean. Not on your own of course, but your department,' said Larry.

'Window dressing, window dressing: pea-shooters against an elephant, just scratching the surface, nothing more. Short on powers, short of staff. Many of the best get the experience they need and then sod off and join the opposition. Better money, good fringe benefits, and a chance to fiddle a bit for themselves. Now that must be very satisfying. I mean if they don't know how to do it who does?'

With that he fell abruptly silent.

'Have a pint on me Jack. We've just about got time.'

Jack cast a bleary eye up at the speaker.

'Ah! Mr just-mention-my-name Davey. Very civil of you. Many thanks, but make it a Scotch again will you?'

Davey nodded to Albert to bring the same again, and pulled up a chair to join the group around the table. Jack, however, was now sitting in silence, gazing vacantly at the empty glass in his hand. Nor did he seem inclined to return to his theme when another Scotch arrived.

'What about avoidance Jack,' said Jimmy responding to a mute plea from the others to prime the pump again. 'Tell them about avoidance.'

'What's to tell?' said Jack. 'Anyway my game's fraud and evasion. You tell them Jimmy, you've heard me often enough – must know it all off by heart.'

'Can't do that Jack. I'm the soulless bugger: you're the man of letters. Remember?'

Jack emptied half his scotch and soda and embarked on a dissertation for his audience which as Jimmy later reported, was somewhat rambling, but had an underlying coherence.

'Avoidance: born 1908, unnatural offspring of supertax. A fecund, libidinous little sod eagerly adopted and nurtured by the rich and super-rich. Spawned a whole generation of weasily, devious little bastards all duly legitimised by the judiciary, with Law Lord Clyde leading the charge.

Ten thousand pounds to spare? Wash a few bonds boys: keeps it clean, and it's money in the bank. Strip a few dividends instead perhaps. Sounds dodgy, but it pays well. Spread your wings lads, try a bit of hobby farming and live like a lord while the rest of us pay for it. Not difficult, just ask the experts. Need a bit of cash to start with though. Oh there's no bloody end to their devices: on and on and on . . . . . to the last bloody syllable of recorded time. Ooops sorry . . . too many bloodies there.'

Here Jack fell silent again and it looked as though the Shagger's seminar on taxation might have come to an end until one of the youngsters at the back of Jack's audience chipped in.

'Can't they pass a law against it then?'

Jack cast a long and compassionate look of pity at his young questioner before turning back to his intimates at the table, and continuing in the unduly slow and measured tones of one who knows he has drunk not wisely, but too well.

'I assume that by "they" our young swabber means Parliament. All our honourable members at Westminster. . . . And Brutus was an honourable man . . . Oh they can pass laws alright. They pass them almost as frequently as they pass water, and to about as much purpose. Or to quote one celebrated Right Honourable, and I think I've got this right, "Advisors find new loopholes as soon as Parliament has closed the old ones." QED. Here endeth the lesson.'

Jack's heckler was not deterred.

'But surely they could do something if they really wanted to.'

'Ah, now we've got there,' said Jack. 'Well of course they bloody could if they wanted, but they don't want to do they, and I'm a bit too befuddled at the moment to go into the detail. Vested interests. Old boys' networks. Blind trusts. Wheels within wheels. Powerful interests in the city. Party funding and favours not forgot. All that sort of thing. Friends and families. Their sisters and their cousins whom they reckon up by dozens. That vast, self-serving, self-preserving, monied establishment with far too much to gain from preserving the status quo which serves them so well.'

He paused to light a cigarette, and seeing his own glass empty took a long swig from Jimmy's with every intention of proceeding, but Jimmy, responding to a meaningful look from Larry, intervened.

'Don't you think that's enough for tonight Jack?'

'Enough? Enough? I haven't bloody got started yet. People don't know the half of what goes on.'

'I know,' said Jimmy, 'but some other time eh?' and with Larry to assist him they ushered Jack from his chair and towards the exit.

'Goodnight Mr Manning, and sleep well,' said Albert. 'I think we all really enjoyed that. Not sure we understood much of the tax stuff, but it certainly made a change from Saturday dominoes.'

It was with the memory of those Saturday night's excesses fresh in his mind that Jack turned to the business of the day. Some eighteen months earlier he had opened up an investigation into the operations of a Wolverton travel agency whose proprietors had been less than frank and forthcoming about the true level of their profits for taxation purposes.

Unlike most travel agents who tend to favour a reference to the nature of their business in their trading name, the company whose affairs Jack had in hand traded under the curiously bland and uninformative title of Scott Stevens (Wolverton) Ltd. While this may have been purely a matter of chance in the first instance, it had clearly been found to provide a convenient anonymity as the business flourished, and the eccentric but highly illegal services it offered became known both within and beyond the bounds of Wolverton.

In the early stages the case seemed to promise nothing more than a routine cash settlement, and the investigation followed what Jack would have described as a bog-standard approach. The directors were called in to an interview when the company's accounts were formally challenged and the directors shown the instruments of persuasion, or the Hansard Extract to give it its formal revenue title.

They responded with the traditional, 'It's a fair cop guv, you've got us bang to rights,' or words to that effect, and instructed their accountants (a national firm with international affiliates and therefore of impeccable probity) to conduct an investigation, and in due course submit to Jack a full and comprehensive report into the affairs of the company and its directors.

After a delay of six months or so the reports had been received. They were, as is traditional, constructed in such a way as to employ every conceivable device to minimise the extent of the fraud and diminish the character of the offence whilst staying (just) on the windy side of the law. It was all part of the game.

Once the many inevitable but unwarranted assumptions made in the directors' favour had been reversed, agreement had been reached on a hefty figure of understated profits representing business takings siphoned off over many years to feather the directors' nests with a variety of private investments and assets. A few supplementary enquiries were dealt with, and then it was time for the usual revenue examination of the books and records of the business. As was customary revenue practice, this would in the first instance be carried out at the business premises.

In addition to the relatively simple and attractive proceeding of putting a hand in the till, there were also a whole range of other inventive frauds and imaginative devices that businesses could employ to reduce liability to tax, all of them illegal. The nature of Scott Stevens' activities, however, did not seem to be such as to lend themselves readily to such machinations, and Jack did not expect the examination to take up much of his time. In the event that would prove to be far from the case, and by the time Jack left at the end of the day he would have embarked on an entirely new path in his life that professionally and privately would be challenging, personally rewarding and downright criminal.

As was usual on such occasions, Jack was to take with him a fully qualified accountant to deal with any of those esoteric aspects of accountancy in which he was not fully versed. He'd chosen Tony Bewley, a senior accountant of long standing and up to all the dodges: all those that were detectable, that is. Neither Jack nor anyone in the department was in any doubt that there were dodges that weren't. Indeed most of them could have designed one to order, if that had not been illegal.

Throughout the morning and into the afternoon they devilled away searching through those areas of the books and records most likely to reveal further fiddles. Apart from a few minor adjustments they found nothing, however, until Tony, who was casting an eye over a selection of copy sales invoices while Jack ferreted away elsewhere, called him over.

'I think there's something funny going on here Jack, but I can't for the life of me make out what it is.'

On the desk in front of Jack he spread out copies of invoices issued to customers over a period of six months. These he had divided into two piles, one large and one smaller, but still containing a good many invoices.

'If you look at these,' he said, indicating the larger pile, 'You'll see that on all of them there is a description, sometimes summarised but more generally in detail, of the holiday or travel facilities that have been provided.'

Jack flipped through the invoices in the larger pile. All included some reference to rail, train or flight travel, to the nature and cost of hotel accommodation at the destination, or perhaps gave cruise details. A few were for holidays at run-of-the-mill destinations on one of the Costas or a similar resort, but most seemed to be long-haul holidays to pretty classy, up-market destinations and hotels. Jack noted in passing references to 'no expense spared' individually guided safaris in South Africa, a ten-week Canberra cruise in stateroom accommodation, and a Sherpa-guided climbing expedition in the Himalayas.

'Do themselves proud, don't they Jack?' said Tony. 'Got to be pretty well breeched to book your holidays with this outfit. But now have a look at these invoices.'

Jack turned to the smaller pile and quickly flipped through them. Not a reference anywhere on the invoices to flights, cruises, hotels, safaris or indeed to holiday travel of any sort, just a few bland and totally uninformative lines. 'Consultation and advice on improving business model,' and 'provision of administrative and advisory service' were two favourites amongst the various phrases adopted, none of which were services the company actually provided.

'Well they must have some other documents of their own for whatever these really relate to,' said Jack. 'So let's have a rake around.'

From a reference number on one of the invoices they soon found their way to a rank of box files containing not only the documents they were looking for, but all the correspondence between the firm and its clients. With the information from the box files it took them only a few moments to establish that all the invoices were for precisely the same sort of holiday or travel arrangements, only on the invoices in the small pile those arrangements had been deliberately misdescribed.

'Time for a natter with the boss do you think?' said Tony.

Jack nodded, and asked one of the clerks to see if Stevens, one of the two directors, could come in and spare them a few moments. When he arrived Jack referred him to the two piles of copy invoices, and pointed out the differences in the descriptions of the services provided.

'From what we have seen in your own documents and correspondence, it seems that the only thing distinguishing the two piles is what I would call the calculated ambiguity, or rather misdescription, of the wording on the smaller pile of invoices. Can you tell us what that is all about?'

'It was done if a client requested it.'

'Didn't that seem odd to you?'

'It did, but if that was what the client wanted I wasn't going to turn away good business.'

'Did any of your clients say why they wanted their holiday arrangements to be described in such misleading and ambiguous terms on the invoices – without any reference to the holiday arrangements at all?'

'No.'

'Did you not think to ask them, or wonder why?'

'No. That was their business. It didn't seem to me that there was anything particularly wrong in obliging them. If I didn't, then probably someone else would.'

'And can you say when you were first asked to provide an invoice in this form.'

'I would say not more than four, perhaps five years ago.'

When they were again alone Tony looked at Jack with a wry smile.

'Well I've been at this game almost thirty years, but it's the first time I've met a scam like this. The bugger's lying of course. He knows as well as you and I why his clients want them like this, and it looks as though there must be scores of them. I'm not surprised they get plenty of business.'

Jack couldn't have agreed more. Most accountants who came across such invoices would have absolutely no immediate reason to suspect that they were for anything other than proper business expenditure, and the few who queried them would almost certainly quite readily accept whatever codged-up explanation was offered to them. It was, as Tony said, 'A very nice little scam: half-price holidays subsidised by you, me and the bloke next door.'

As the company kept its records for six years before disposing of them, they began at once to examine and extract all the dodgy invoices for those six years. This they would normally have continued to do together, but Tony had another appointment which meant that he had to leave by early afternoon.

Left to himself Jack carried on alone for almost three hours, with the work taking longer than expected, and he was just winding up and getting together the books, invoices and papers that he intended to take away to complete the analysis at leisure when Stevens put his head round the door.

'I wonder if you could spare me a few moments before you leave Mr Manning.'

'Surely,' said Jack. 'Just let me finish strapping this pile of documents together . . . Right, fire away.'

'This is an unusual situation for me as you can imagine Mr Manning, and I think I now understand why it is that you are so interested in those particular invoices.'

He paused, but as Jack said nothing was obliged to speak again.

'I find it rather difficult to know how to proceed . . . I wonder if I could ask you, do you have any sort of scope for compromise in your proceedings?'

'I'm not sure I understand you Mr Stevens. What exactly do you mean by compromise?'

Stevens had clearly been hoping for something a little more helpful than that, and paused again as though casting about for the right form of words.

'Well the truth of the matter is that among the invoices that interest you there are several for just one concern where I would rather things didn't go any further, and I wondered if there was any way in which that might be achieved. I am ignorant in such matters of course, and wondered if you could assist . . . It would be worth quite a lot to me.'

By now Jack had absolutely no doubt what was going on. The bugger was propositioning him, but was nervous about coming right out with it. It was something the group occasionally talked about when they got together for a beer or two, and no one could recall having ever received even the faintest hint of a proposal to buy them off with a generous quid pro quo. A tribute to the known incorruptibility of the service it would seem: always assuming that they were all honest in their replies.

A week earlier and Jack would have had no doubt about his response, but his drink-fuelled tirade in the Shagger had driven the thin end of a wedge of insurrection into his soul. He hesitated, and then decided to let Stevens run on just a little further.

'And which invoices in particular are you interested in?'

'If I can just run through those you have extracted I will pull them out for you,' said Stevens.

After a few moments sorting through the invoices he'd selected those he wanted, and handed them to Jack who looked through them.

'All for Campion Holdings and Investments,' said Jack. 'What's so special about them?'

'If you don't mind, I'd rather not say. It's a personal connection and I don't want to betray any confidences. I

can, however, give you an assurance, if that means anything to you, that it does not impinge in any way on my
own taxation affairs or those of my company.'

Jack knew that he was already treading a very fine
line. His response so far left him uncommitted, just an
investigator's natural curiosity: unwise perhaps, but
nothing more. Any further, however, and it might be
difficult to draw back. He knew nothing of the mysterious Campion connection, and didn't trust Stevens to tell
him the truth even if he questioned him further. It was
something he needed to investigate himself. Until he
had done so, and considered his own position more
carefully Stevens would have to wait.

'I've nothing further to say at this time Mr Stevens,
and you might be wise to say nothing more yourself.
When I have had the opportunity to examine in more
detail the documents and records that I am taking away
with me I will telephone you. We will then meet again
and talk further. Do you understand?'

Stevens thought he understood correctly what was
being said, and realised that in any event he had little
option but to go along with the proposal. To be ob-
structive at that stage would simply be to throw away
any chance of ultimate success.

'I'll wait to hear from you then Mr Manning, and
hope that it won't take too long to bring this whole matter to a conclusion that is beneficial to both of us.'

Now you're getting a bit bolder thought Jack, and
then, assisted by a couple of Stevens' clerks, he carried
out to his car the documents and box files that he
needed to examine further, before driving away, first to
drop them off at the office, and then to make what
would be a late return to Barton.

As he left the city and headed west on the country
roads to home Jack was in an unusually reflective mood.

He realised with some surprise that he had felt no sense of moral outrage that Stevens should have seen him as a man who might readily be suborned.

And why not? Weren't they all at it? It just depended on your weapon of choice. Tax fraud here, insider dealing there. Dividend stripping for Jack, money laundering for Jill. Blind trusts, revolving doors: all at arm's length of course, no undue or improper influence. Or good, honest, down-to-earth corruption like Poulson and Maudling. Just a little bit of greasing here and there to keep the wheels of commerce turning. If the Chancellor's at it, why not me? Just need to be careful and not too greedy.

A malefactor's creed, he thought, surprised at how readily he justified his actions to himself – and all without a twinge of conscience. Was it really that easy to slip over the line? To smile and be a villain, and having done it once, do it again, and again? For the moment it was no more than an interesting academic exercise, but he mulled the idea over many times before he arrived home, and comforted himself with a whisky and the thought that he hadn't committed himself finally. There was no rush, wait till he'd dug a little further into the Campion business, and then make up his mind. He said, and would say, nothing to Kate.

Back in his office the following morning, with no weakening in his resolve to carry the matter a little further, Jack assembled the Stevens' records on his desk and side table, and then stopped to consider how he should best proceed. Although not yet committed to what would be a seriously criminal act (he was realistic enough to see it plainly in those terms), it seemed to him prudent to proceed as though he were, but what in practical terms did that mean? In his official activities it had been his practice always to work with half-an-eye on the worst possible scenario.

It took no imagination to see what that might be in the case of his little bit of private enterprise, and with that in mind it seemed to him that the one prerequisite was that he should, as far as he possibly could, be able to disclaim all knowledge of, or connection with, the Campion side of the equation. That meant avoiding paper trails, and keeping all personal contact to a minimum and to such as could, wherever possible, be justified as being on legitimate official business.

This presented him with a problem. If he was going to burn his bridges then he needed to know as much about the Campion connection as he could. The only way to do so with any certainty would be to ask the district to let him have the Campion tax file on loan, and that would mean that there would be a record of his request. It would establish a connection of sorts, but he felt that he had no option. Unless things went seriously awry it would mean nothing to anyone.

Turning to the Scott Stevens' records he had brought away with him, Jack's first step was to extract from them every invoice, document or piece of correspondence relating to the Campion connection. These he placed in a folder and locked in a drawer of his desk. Apart from himself these had also been seen by Tony, but only in passing and as part of a larger collection, so he was unlikely to remember them.

Next he called in Charlie Thomas his clerical assistant, passed over to him the remaining copy sales invoices and other records covering six years, and told him to sort out all those invoices that contained no reference to travel or holidays, link them with the documents and correspondence he would find in the box files, and then assemble them in chronological order. Thomas returned the work to him a few days later.

'Bloody marvellous scam they've got going here Mr Manning. Almost a pity to spoil it. Old boys' network I suppose: Masons, Rotary Club, Round Table, something like that. You scratch my back; I'll fix your holiday expenses. Oh we do see life.'

'God you're more of a bloody cynic than I am Charlie. Where on earth were you brought up? More respect for your masters and betters please.'

When Thomas spread out on Jack's desk the papers he'd been working on, the full extent to which Stevens would go to please his customers could be clearly seen.

For the first two of the six years all the invoices seemed on the face of it to be in order, and not until shortly after the start of the third year did the first suspect one appear. From then on the numbers grew steadily as the news of the very special service Stevens was willing to provide filtered through the chosen in the business community.

When the final sort had been completed Jack found that he was left with two hundred and forty seven invoices, covering almost four years, and representing in total thirty-eight firms each of which was benefiting from the fraud, some just once, but others many times, and if they were doing that, what else were they doing? Most were to be found within fifty miles or so of Wolverton, with a sprinkling outside, plus a couple of rogue items from the west of England. Jack wondered what on earth the link might be there.

With the initial analysis work completed, Jack sent out requests to borrow all thirty-eight files from the tax districts, plus a thirty-ninth request all of his own to have the Campion tax file on loan. When this was received he immediately locked it away in his briefcase,

91

and took it home with him at the end of the day. Having made his examination he returned it to the district the following morning with nothing but a brief note of thanks. As the other files were received they were parcelled out around the group for scrutiny. Three were identified as large enough and serious enough to be registered for investigation by the group and retained.

All the others were returned to the districts with a note of the information obtained from the Stevens' papers and photocopies of the incriminating invoices and supporting documents. All would be investigated as time and resources permitted. And as they went their way Jack was increasingly intrigued that Stevens had singled out the Campion papers for special treatment. Would he have had his own private list of those firms who enjoyed his special arrangement, Jack wondered, and if so would he have been on the phone to all or some of them as soon as, or even before, Jack had left his office.

Amongst those returned to the districts were two files going to the District Inspector in Barlow. One contained invoices for three consecutive years for the partners in Bayley, Bayley and Bedgood, who had handled Jack's conveyancing, and he thought of Hilda Genner, and wondered how long it would be before news of any tax investigation into the firm's affairs filtered back to the hill. The other was for a Major Thompson, who with his wife ran one of the larger farms at the foot of the hill. Jack didn't know them well, but had met them on a couple of occasions, and had no doubt that they, like the solicitors, were well aware of his vocation.

It was perhaps a month after the files had been returned to the districts, and while Jack was still finalising his enquiries into Campion, that he was not altogether surprised to receive an evening telephone call at home from Bayley Senior. He apologised for disturbing Jack at home, but wondered whether it would be convenient for him to call in to the firm's office the following Saturday morning, as there was something he would like to discuss. He was reluctant to give any more details on the phone, but was sure it would all become clear when Jack called in to see him. Jack agreed to call into the offices at eleven and left it at that.

With just one very recent exception, Jack kept no professional secrets from Kate, and she was already well aware of the background to Bayley's call. As curious as Jack to find out what he was after, she insisted on travelling with him to Barlow, and phoned at once to book a table for lunch at The Parish Pump.

'You'll notice he's asked to see me on a Saturday when the office is usually closed,' said Jack. 'He's making sure that Hilda and none of the staff will be there to see me arrive.'

The following morning he phoned the District Inspector in the Barlow office to ask if anything had happened on the case, and was told that so far, pressure of work had meant that it had not been possible to take it up. Curiouser and curiouser, thought Jack.

Promptly at eleven the following Saturday, leaving Kate to her own devices, Jack rang the bell at the door of the fine Georgian house the firm occupied on Priory Hill, the best street in Barlow, where a great many of the other fine Georgian houses were similarly to be found in professional occupation. He was welcomed inside by Bayley Senior, who led him through to the principal reception room overlooking the street, where only the Bayleys, father and son, were present, Bedgood being a sleeping partner, having died many years earlier.

'Kind of you to call in Mr Manning,' said father. 'Can I offer you a sherry?'

Well this is one up on being a conveyancing customer, thought Jack, accepting a generous glass of a fine amontillado, and settling into the armchair offered, as father opened the dialogue.

'Can I say first of all that I fully understand that in your professional dealings, as with mine, there are restraints of confidence on what we can and cannot say, and I have no wish to breach those in any way.'

'I quite understand,' said Jack.

'If I were to mention that a couple of weeks ago we were in Wolverton with the intention of booking our winter break with Scott Stevens you might, perhaps, have an idea where I am going.'

Jack assumed as bland an expression as he could, and waited for Bayley to continue – he was quite enjoying the situation.

'We've been using the firm for many years, and John Stevens and I trust one another enough for him to mention that his business had recently been the subject of a revenue investigation. He mentioned your name in fact. Perhaps he shouldn't have done that, I don't know, but there you are.

He also mentioned the outcome of the investigation. Now I am not unaware of the implications of that, and to be frank have been expecting an approach either from the Barlow office or your own, but nothing has happened. I wonder whether, respecting in every way the restraints on what you can say, you could throw any light on our darkness. More sherry?'

'Thank you,' said Jack, 'An excellent amontillado.'

He waited as Bayley topped up his glass, and savoured another sip before continuing.

'Firstly I am sure you will understand that I can make no comment and respond in no way regarding any investigation the Revenue may have undertaken into the affairs of any other business. As far as your own affairs are concerned, however, I can certainly say something in general terms without breaching any confidence, and hope that will be of some help to you.'

'I think that might be very useful,' said Bayley.

'Well if you read the newspapers it will come as no surprise to you if I were to say that the Revenue is over-worked and in arrears, grossly so in some Districts. This means that it is not unusual for investigations to be deferred for some considerable time.

I can also mention, if you are not already aware of it, that the general rule with back duty investigations, criminal prosecutions excepted, is that a financial settlement is ultimately reached that embodies the tax lost, interest on that tax and a penalty element representing a percentage of the tax evaded.

Only the penalty is variable, depending on the promptness or otherwise of disclosure, the degree of cooperation and to some extent the nature of the irregularities. If a case is one of voluntary disclosure with full cooperation throughout, and the nature of the offence is not too heinous, then a maximum abatement of penalty would normally be given. I can't put a percentage on the final penalty of course, but it would usually be quite bearable. I think that's about all I can say.'

'Well I'm really most grateful to you Mr Manning. I think I can now see where to go from here. Much appreciated. My very best wishes to Mrs Manning. We hope she is enjoying the country life and her teaching post here in Barlow'

Fifteen minutes later Jack was sitting in the bar of The Pump with Kate alongside him and a half-empty pint glass on the table, looking forward to Mrs Arscott's plat du jour: steak and kidney pie, new potatoes, carrots and florets of romanesco broccoli.

'Bayley's a canny old bugger,' he told Kate. 'I'm pretty sure he knew the score, but just wanted some sort of hint where to go next. I couldn't resist slipping in a reference to prosecution though, just for the fun of it. He keeps in touch too: knew you were working in Barlow now.' He paused as he finished his pint. 'Lovely little town this. Old Thompson's got a nice cushy number here as DI. Wonder how long he's got to go.'

The following Monday he telephoned Thompson.

'I think that I ought to let you know that you are probably going to receive some sort of disclosure from the Bayleys before the end of the week.'

'Ah I did wonder. More bloody work for the already overburdened. Thanks very much. Remind me to do you a favour some time.'

'It'll still qualify as voluntary I suppose.'

'I thought your lot were the experts. I'll let you know the outcome.'

It would not be long, however, before Jack received further news about Barlow district, and when it came it would not be about the Bayleys, but something of much more interest to Jack. There was however one further outcome of his meeting a couple of weeks later, when a case of amontillado was left at the back door while they were at work. It was unattributed apart from the words 'Much appreciated' scrawled on the top.

6

Corrupting an Officer of the Crown

The Christmas and New Year celebrations that intervened before Jack was finally able to review the results of his own very private Campion enquiries and meet with Stevens again, would do nothing to diminish his general cynicism and a growing misanthropy. After a few years of finding increasingly unconvincing excuses, they could no longer avoid a duty Christmas with Jack's parents without completely upsetting the family apple-cart and Jack had no wish to go that far.

Confining their visit to three nights would, he thought, make the occasion tolerably bearable, but he arrived to find that his brother and family were also of the party. Jack had little in common with his brother and less with his wife. Their three children when young he thought had shown some promise, but five years or more of nurturing from George and his wife had put paid to that, and he now regarded them as lost beyond redemption.

The visit over, and relieved to be back in the peace of the countryside, he poured them both a drink, left Kate to her own devices in the kitchen, topped up the log-burner against the coming night, and dropped into his armchair. Much as he was looking forward to the coming New Year's Eve get-together with Jimmy and Celia he was increasingly aware that Barton was changing fast, and knew that things would never again be quite as they were in their early days.

Their first visit to a village pantomime had also been their last. The two brothers who had been the driving force behind it had accepted an offer they couldn't refuse, sold up, and left the area soon afterwards, and in the absence of their energy, enthusiasm and understanding of the locals, the one half-hearted attempts to revive it had been a total flop. Its place was taken by a disco, which suited the youngsters, but nobody else.

It had been the death of Ada Sutton, however, in the autumn just a little over a year earlier that seemed to knock the stuffing out of the older generation in the village. Much as she might have wished to emulate old Tom and make her last exit from the garden privy, it was not to be.

'Luckily for me, at any rate,' said Jimmy, who found her, and carried the news to her sons. 'That would have been embarrassing.'

He'd been with her in the afternoon doing a bit of fencing in the garden while she fussed around on the veg plot until tea-time, when she left him, saying that she was going to put a match to her first fire of autumn, and then put the kettle on for tea. Having worked on for some time but had no call from Ada, Jimmy walked up to the house to find the fire lit and burning well, tea and scones on the table, and Ada lying dead on the floor alongside her chair.

A week later, after a fifteen year separation and a service from Larry that would have delighted the old lady, Ada and Tom were reunited in the grave that Ada always said had the finest view in the county. 'I'll always be sure of visitors where I'm going,' she used to say.

But on the New Year's Eve following her death, however, there were to be no visitors for Ada, or for any other of the inhabitants of St Matthew's churchyard. Ted and Charlie had made it clear that they had only made their visits in previous years because Ada wanted it for Tom's sake. 'They're up there now together,' Ted said, 'With each other for company. No call for all of us to go up there disturbing them at this time of year.'

Next Albert, who normally presided over the Shagger's New Year's proceedings, went missing, confined to bed with flu. From then on the proceedings were doomed, and for the first time in many years the churchyard stayed silent and in darkness. That'll be the end of it, thought Jack. One break in the tradition will be enough, it won't be resurrected.

Before Ada died, however, Ted and Charlie, with some generous help from the archivists for the Shropshire Light Infantry and the Churchill papers, had researched their father's war service in South Arica pretty thoroughly. His progress through the Colony with the Shropshires had now been well documented, and was twice found to coincide on date and place with Churchill's movements. Proof that they had actually met on those occasions was not, however, forthcoming.

Not that that made any difference to the final value of the book, as contrary to most expectation *Ian Hamilton's March* was not offered for sale by Ted and Charlie, but as a tribute to Tom was passed to the Shropshires' museum together with his medal and the few newspaper cuttings that were found in the case. His regimental badge and the pincushion they placed in the coffin and buried with Ada.

Changes in the world at large had brought changes too in the public bar of the Shagger, where local gossip and market prices had now largely been replaced by heated discussion of the potential impact of the 'bloody EEC' (it was never anything else but bloody) on their subsidies and improvement grants.

Devaluation of the pound and the Act to decimalise currency they had accepted as part and parcel of the deep-laid socialist conspiracy to be expected from Wilson, and the arrival of Heath was originally welcomed as a return to the old ways, despite his want of the patrician hauteur of MacMillan which so impressed them. In the event he proved to be a sad disappointment to them when he took the country into the EEC with all that entailed for hill farmers.

There was plenty of angry discussion and resentment too at city dwellers who were increasingly favouring second homes in country areas, and pushing up prices so much that young locals were unable to buy houses or farms in the areas where their families had lived for generations.

But when Martin Golightly decided that he had had enough of the hill life, and put his house and few acres on the market, there was general derision in the bar of the Shagger at the price he was asking.

'£31,000 for nine acres of rough pasture and scrub and a house that my dad told me was built for little more than five hundred in the thirties! I thought old man Parsons had got more sense than to be telling him to ask that sort of money.'

But Parsons, one of the local estate agents, had got his finger pretty well on the pulse of the market and was doing very nicely in consequence. Within a few months their derision had turned to anger and some envy when they learned (Hilda Genner again) that Golightly had not only got his asking price, but had two buyers interested and leapfrogging, selling eventually to the one with ready money.

By now, deep in his reflections and nearing the end of his fourth glass of festive Madeira, Jack sat alone in a room in darkness apart from the flickering light of the burning logs. Kate had gone to bed to leave him brooding over his disaffection with his job in particular and the mutability of life in general. He was in that sort of mood.

He rehearsed it all again. Avoidance rife and nothing done. Lots of talk, but bugger all action. How was it Ted Sutton categorised the politicians: like a herd of cattle, full of wind and shit? Investigation frustrated by lack of powers and shortage of staff. Businessmen and the self-employed playing fast and loose with a system that leaked like a sieve. Pay what you like when you like, no one really gives a damn. Everyone on the make and looking out for number one. Sod it, he thought, I might just as well take Stevens' bait, get my cut and be damned with it. He finished his drink, went to bed, and slept like a child quite untroubled by conscience.

On his first day back in the office after the New Year break Jack, his intentions unchanged, sipped an early coffee and pondered on the legend of the taxman's incorruptibility. There was, he knew, a proven correlation between levels of offending and likelihood of detection. Was it really a case of absolute moral rectitude, he wondered, or simply the fact that anyone making a realistic appraisal of the chances of getting away with it would inevitably conclude that he was on a hiding to nothing. The tax system had been up and running for far too long. There were just too many checks, counter-checks and audits.

The Inspector might bear the opprobrium of the public for working out what they had to pay, but however much tax his toil produced, his hands were never soiled by the product of his labours. No chance for any cash to stick to his hands en route to the Exchequer: collection was dealt with by an entirely separate department.

Not that the taxman's moral rectitude was such as to inhibit many of them when it came to taking three year's training at the expense of the public at large, and then, with a little experience under their belt, buggering off to the richer pastures of the city houses, industrial companies or the many tax consultancies that helped the rich screw the Exchequer. A form of moral constipation or turpitude that never bothered their consciences, thought Jack. Why should mine be troubled?

Over the years Jack had acquired a reputation for determination, thoroughness, and a methodical approach to his work illuminated occasionally by those flashes of inspiration or strokes of luck that none could do without. It was now his intention to bring precisely those attributes to bear on the little private venture that he was planning. From his recent reading he was also deeply into the circus world of Le Carre's espionage fiction with its burrowers, ferrets and pavement artists, and was determined that in this his first operation his tradecraft would be immaculate.

If the perfect opportunity ever existed for a taxman to help himself to a little personal reward with almost negligible risk, Jack was utterly convinced that he had it before him. All that was called for was the suppression and destruction of a few documents, which at the end of the day would leave a simple vacancy: two gaps in the invoice sequence and box files with nothing to indicate to what or to whom they related. There would be no complexity, nothing on file, no paper trail to speak of. He balanced it up carefully, saw every prospect of success, was untroubled by moral scruples, and found to his surprise that despite a certain apprehension, he was quite looking forward to the challenge as a different form of intellectual exercise from his usual work, with the bonus of a substantial reward at the end of the line if he played his hand well.

From his overnight examination of the Campion file Jack had already gleaned a considerable amount of background information. The business was operated by a Vincent Martindale in partnership with his wife, although the accounts threw precious little light on the precise nature of the firm's activities. Martindale himself was forty-five years of age, married with three adult children. The holder of a substantial investment portfolio, he had also been a Lloyd's name for some ten years and seemed to have done rather well out of it. His wife was herself in enjoyment of a considerable income from a trust settlement. Together they made a very well-breached couple.

Now, taking his Campion folder from the locked drawer of his desk and assembling all his papers before him, he took stock of the position. No need to cover them up or hide what he was doing if interrupted. The material on his desk was the bread and butter of the investigator's work. If, by chance, any of his colleagues dropped in for a chat they wouldn't give it a second glance.

His starting point was the slim batch of thirteen fraudulent invoices totalling £14,744 supplied by Stevens to Campion Holdings and Investments over a period of four years. He had in addition documents from the Stevens' box files which described each holiday jaunt in detail, plus a thin folder of correspondence between Stevens and his clients and their accountants. All useful stuff as far as it went, but Jack wanted to know a lot more than this about Martindale and his background before he saw Stevens again. He was under no illusion about the step he was proposing to take. There was too much at stake, his career, pension, and possibly worse, for him to neglect any aspect that might be of use to him when he met Stevens, or later.

The following week, saying nothing to Kate, he took a day of his annual leave, and drove some forty miles south to the city of Ashburton where Campion Holdings and Investments conducted its business operations. Turning first to the enquiry desk and reference room of the central library he busied himself for a couple of hours with telephone, commercial and trade directories, and copies of the two local papers for the past year or so. Then, buying himself current copies of the papers, he settled down to a pint and a pie in one of the old pubs in the market area. He browsed through the papers as he ate, and felt lucky to find that the more substantial of the two devoted almost a half-page to the monthly report from the local MP Sir Marcus Martindale, Commercial Secretary to the Treasury in the previous administration, and as Jack had already been able to establish, father to Vincent Andrew.

Moving on from the pub Jack went first to the general office of the paper carrying the report he had just been reading, and then to office of the Constituency Association for the father. At both he lied his way to a little more background information about the Martindales Senior and Junior, before walking through to the commercial centre of town where the operations of Campion Holdings and Investments were conducted from an impressive suite of rooms in one of the latest high-rise office buildings. Learning precious little from what he saw there about the nature of the business operations, he returned to his car and drove the short distance to the part of town where Martindale lived.

Parking his car some way off, he took a leisurely stroll past the Martindale residence: a handsome, pillar-fronted, four-storey establishment in prime position at the heart of a square of fine, eighteenth century terraced houses. Top-of-the-range, immaculately maintained, and hinting discreetly of wealth and prestige, it was just what Jack had begun to expect as a result of his researches.

Satisfied that he was better prepared to meet Stevens again, he set off for home with a few photocopies made at the library, plus several pages of notes based on his researches there and his other discreet enquiries. He felt that he now had a much better understanding of the life, times and background of the local worthy who, as Jack was utterly convinced, was trying via Stevens to bribe him.

The family's wealth, which was clearly substantial, appeared to have been built up by the father mainly through a career in the city, before he expanded his interests in later life to include politics. Vincent, equally as successful as his father at making money, or perhaps more so, also had his own political agenda. Currently Leader of the Council in Ashburton he was, Jack had learned, confidently expected to proceed to the Commons at the next General Election, when his father intended to retire and bequeath to him a virtually unassailable majority.

Of the nuts and bolts of Martindale's business operations and the precise nature of the financial and advisory services rendered, Jack learned little from his researches. It was, however, clear from a couple of laudatory articles in the local press extolling the merits of the firm as a fine example of local enterprise and entrepreneurial skill, that it had expanded and prospered since its inception some fourteen years earlier.

Of Martindale personally it was possible from the press photographs and articles to get a good idea of his political views, his standing in the community, and the fact that like his father he probably had friends and connections in high places. From his tax file it was clear that for the years Jack was looking at he would have been liable to tax at or about 75%.

Returning again to the thirteen invoices, it didn't take Jack much calculating to work out that Martindale's £14,744 holiday expenditure had in fact cost him only £3,686, leaving the Exchequer, that is everyone else honest or unfortunate enough to have to pay his full whack, to stump up the balance.

Jack had long ago ceased to be surprised at this sort of unbridled greed. He now took it for granted that everyone did it who could get away with it, and even felt a grudging respect for the novelty of the arrangement he now had before him, and the sheer bloody chutzpah of Martindale in taking the illicit favours that Stevens extended and milking them for all they were worth. As the documents showed, Martindale was not a man to stint himself when others were meeting the cost.

In December 1969 on the first of his state-funded holiday jaunts he and his wife treated themselves to a fifteen day cruise on the Canberra costing over £1000. The following year brought a week at the Hotel des Balances in Lucerne and another in a suite at the Danieli in Venice (lagoon view naturally) that concluded with a final statement of account from the hotel that was a revelation to Jack as to the style in which the really rich indulged themselves when money was no problem. A year later came a cruise on the QE2 followed by a week in Frenchman's Cove.

It was plunder on a rapacious and imperial scale, topped up with short breaks to London or the continent for the couple, and summer and winter holidays for the children. Such was the extent of their activities that each of the thirteen fraudulent invoices represented the summation of two or three little indulgences over the previous four or five months, leaving Jack even more intrigued as to the precise nature of Martindale's business, and wondering who on earth looked after it when he was away.

In was in the last of the four years, however, that Martindale excelled himself with a Mediterranean Charter Rental of L'Esperance, a yacht with a crew of seven and accommodation for ten passengers, at a cost of just over £4,500. This not only took Jack's breath away, but left him with a problem. What the hell was Martindale doing with a charter yacht, a crew of seven and accommodation for ten?

Unwilling to draw attention to his activities by discussing the matter with his colleagues, as he might otherwise have done, Jack took the papers home to do as he often did and chew things over with Kate. He handed everything to her, including those relating to the charter, and without making any reference to his personal objectives, gave her a brief outline of the case and the nature of his problem.

Kate looked through the papers, offered the comment that Martindale behaved like a pig at the trough, and then turned back to a flimsy carbon copy of a list headed simply, 'Guests.'

'What's this?' she asked.

'Well I'm assuming it's a list of the ship's passengers prepared for the benefit of the skipper. You'll see at the top the names of my man and his wife. The second name is M Martindale with wife, and although the title's missing I assume that's Sir Marcus MP, former Commercial Secretary to the Treasury and my man's father.'

'So what's the problem?'

'Well I don't know who the other people are, nor can I work out quite what's going on. I just don't see Martindale treating a load of strangers to a week's Mediterranean cruising out of his own pocket, even at a 75% discount. The rich don't get where they are by handing out charity like that to all and sundry.'

'Well can't you just ask?'

Jack shook his head, 'Not appropriate at the moment.'

Kate worked her way through the assorted invoices and papers one more time, and then returned to the list of guests.

'Have you ever considered the possibility that Martindale's killing two birds with one stone here, and that what you've got is a sort of double fiddle.'

'Sorry don't follow you.'

'Well if he's not treating them do you think that apart from his parents he's getting some sort of payment from the others: acting in a sense as an agent. For friends and family perhaps: a cut-price cruise in the Med. They'd probably jump at the chance.'

'I say, you have got a dirty mind. Not only getting the charter at a discount, but making a bloody profit out of it you mean. But Christ he's rolling in it. Surely he can't be that greedy?'

'Well it's just a suggestion.'

Despite his feeling that Kate might have come up with the answer to his problem, Jack couldn't as yet see just what it was about Martindale's tax-dodging activities that would lead him to risk bribing and suborning an officer of the Crown. The amounts were relatively large, but otherwise there was nothing special about the fraud. There had to be some other factor operating, so before Jack met Stevens again he embarked on yet another thorough trawl through the papers. He had absolutely no intention of leaving anything to chance.

Only when he turned to the list of passengers for the fourth or fifth time, having just browsed through his notes and the Stevens correspondence with Martindale's accountants, did the pieces fall into place. After the names of Sir Marcus and Vincent (with wives) he could now identify James Thornycroft, senior partner in the accountancy firm acting for Campion, Nigel Parkinson, Sir Marcus's agent and William Haverford Chairman of the local party, each accompanied by his wife. Now he saw that the yacht charter operation began to make sense: it was Vincent greasing the wheels of the local political machine.

Jack now felt himself to be as fully prepared as he could be, and telephoned Stevens to arrange a meeting for the following week in Jack's office, on an afternoon which he had arranged to be completely clear of other business. It was a novel situation he was in, but he didn't think it called for a radically different approach. If Martindale was this desperate, then as Jack was himself putting so much at risk he intended to take an uncompromising line and go for all he could get. And this time, he thought, the settlement at the end of the day will be money in my pocket, not the Chancellor's. With that objective in mind, and after a few initial formalities, he opened his campaign.

'I should explain Mr Stevens that the nature of my occupation has been such that I have grown accustomed to speak plainly, perhaps bluntly, if the need arises, and I thought it might save time and a certain amount of tentative manoeuvring if I were do so now.

You will, I am sure, remember what you had to say at our last meeting, but it may help if I were to refresh your memory. You asked me if I had any scope for compromise in my proceedings, explaining that there were certain copy invoices where you would rather things went no further. You wondered whether there was any way in which I could assist with that, adding that that would be worth quite a lot to you, and, if I re-

member correctly, that it would be to our mutual benefit.

My interpretation of those comments, please correct
me if I am wrong, is that you were proposing to offer
me an inducement to ensure that no subsequent action
was taken involving those invoices that you subsequently went on to identify.

Put in the starkest terms, you were proposing a little
bit of bribery and corruption of an officer of the Crown.
Am I correct?'

If Stevens was shocked by Jack's Blitzkrieg tactics he
gave no visible sign of it, but although he offered no
instant denial of Jack's interpretation of his words at
their earlier meeting, he was clearly extremely reluctant
to confirm it in such specific terms.

'Come now,' said Jack. 'This isn't MI5. The room
isn't bugged, and if I were seeking to entrap you I
wouldn't go about it this way. Perhaps it would reassure
you if I were to say that if my interpretation is correct
I'd be interested to hear what it is you are proposing,
but first I would like to ask you once again what it is
about those particular invoices that so concerns you, or
rather your client.'

From the very beginning of his career Jack had seen
his function as essentially one of role-playing, and frequent practice had schooled him to stand back to assess
his performance and its impact on his audience. His present rather unusual situation seemed to him to be no
different, and his thoughts were that for a beginner he
was playing it bloody cool.

'You certainly believe in plain words Mr Manning,
and I'd like to respond by being equally frank with you
about the invoices, but it really is a issue of confidence,
and I can only repeat that it's a personal matter.'

'Can we turn then to the heart of the affair. Speaking bluntly again, what exactly is the sweetener you have in mind to induce me to betray my trust?'

Stevens was obviously still unhappy with the directness of Jack's approach.

'I'd really prefer it if we could avoid talking in quite those terms Mr Manning . . . If that's at all possible.'

'In neutral terms then, what are you offering?'

Dear God, Jack thought, this is getting to sound more and more like a settlement interview. I'll be talking about penalties and interest next.

'I have to confess that I still don't find this easy Mr Manning. It's not a situation that I used to.'

'Nor I, I can assure you.'

'I mean, I have no idea what your interests or preferences are, but I could lay on, shall we say, a very attractive cruise. Two weeks, all expenses met. Yourself and Mrs Manning, if you are married. Or perhaps a two week tour in India. Golden triangle: that sort of thing with top of the market hotels.'

'Mr Stevens I quite appreciate that we are both feeling our way here, but I don't think you fully understand my position. God forbid that what we are now considering should ever come to the knowledge of anyone but ourselves and your client, but if it did my job, pension and possibly worse would be in the balance. It wouldn't go too well for you either, I should add.

I couldn't possibly consider a holiday or anything else that might link me in any way with you or the activities of your business, however remotely. It would be utter madness and inviting disaster. Nor do I think you have considered, nor perhaps understand, what the cost would be to your client were the fraudulent invoices to be investigated in the district.'

'How do you mean Mr Manning?'

Jack held up the thirteen copy sales invoices.

'These fraudulent invoices total £14,744, and from the enquiries I have made I can tell you that the evaded tax alone on this little dodge would almost certainly amount to £11,058 . . . I see that you are surprised, or perhaps have not thought the thing through sufficiently. That I imagine is one of the risks of acting as a go-between as you so obviously are.'

'But what amounts are we going to be talking about then Mr Manning?'

'Mr Stevens, I have no idea how much you know of Martindale or what binds you so closely together, the same public school perhaps, but the present circumstances are such that, unlike yourself, I do not feel myself bound by any constraints of confidentiality, so let me put you in the picture on a few matters.'

Here Jack gave Stevens an appropriately edited version of the facts he had established concerning the activities and interests of the Martindales, father and son, as a result of his enquiries in Ashburton, and his review of the invoices and other papers, with particular reference to the identities of the other guests on the yacht.

'Now as my information seems to indicate that Martindale is a millionaire or better, I know that he would have no difficulty whatsoever in funding a cash settlement with the Revenue in the usual way, even if these invoices are not, as I suspect, his only frauds. So there must be some very special reason why he would want to take the extreme action, via the offices of a friend, of attempting to bribe a taxman

I already know that shortly after our last meeting you informed at least one of your clients, other than Martindale, of my enquiries concerning these fraudulent invoices. I believe that immediately after we first discussed these at our last meeting you telephoned Martindale, and told him what was going on. He then asked you to sound me out and make me an offer . . . I should, by the way, point out that as things stand, if anything went wrong, he could easily deny any personal involvement leaving you to carry the can.

I believe his reasons for wishing to avoid a revenue investigation are essentially social and political. Were such an investigation to take place it would inevitably involve Martindale's accountants, and so would come to the attention of the senior partner who was one of the guests on the charter cruise. I imagine he would look on that entertainment and Martindale rather differently were he to know that it was part of an elaborate and substantial tax fraud.

Confidential as such investigations are, income tax offices and accountants' chambers in a provincial city can be embarrassingly leaky places, and the word can get around in informed circles to those who need to know. This would I imagine include Sir Magnus, his political agent, and the chairman of the local party who were also guests on the cruise. With Sir Magnus a former junior minister at the Treasury and Vincent himself seeking adoption to stand at the next General Election there would, all in all, seem to be plenty of reasons, other than financial, for him to wish to keep the lid on this particular can of worms.'

Of all this Stevens was evidently ignorant, and he paused for a moment as he took it all in.

'So where do we go from here Mr Manning? I made a proposal earlier on, but you do this sort of thing more than I do . . . Sorry that's not right, but you know what I mean.'

'No apologies called for. We're both feeling our way. But let me take you back to my starting point. The invoices total £14,744. The tax on that at Martindale's rate amounts to £11,058. It's a pretty calculated and deliberate sort of fraud, so even with generous abatement an investigator would be talking about a penalty of around £2,500. Add interest to that and the total amount is pushing £15,000. And that isn't taking into account the possibility of any other frauds in Martindale's affairs that an investigation might unearth.

But in addition to that, I also have to consider and put a value upon the risk that I am taking in acceding to your client's request. In brief I'm putting at risk my career, my pension and possibly prison. I would assess that at an equal amount of £15,000.

So to wrap the whole thing up we'd be talking about £30,000. The social and political benefits to Mr Martindale and any other frauds that he may have engaged in are a bonus, I'll throw them in for free.'

There was a long pause before Stevens replied.

'I'll have to be frank Mr Manning, and admit that I'm now entirely outside my brief. I can't possibly negotiate at this time around that sort of figure.'

'I must confess I'm not surprised, but I have to say that proceeding in this way with you acting as broker means further delays, and the longer this affair is drawn out, the more frequently we meet, the greater the risk to me. So when you go back to Martindale tell him that the £30,000 I am proposing is not negotiable: in my opinion it's a bargain. If he's not happy with that then I'm quite prepared to let the Revenue enquiries follow their usual course.

Finally as it will be known that you have called here today I will leave on file a note of our meeting. It will not of course record our actual discussions, but will simply be a brief memo to say that I have been questioning you again concerning your part in supplying invoices to your clients in such irregular terms. It will indicate that I made no further progress.

I am, however, prepared to have no further meetings with you on the Martindale matter, although we will have to meet again to conclude the investigation into your own affairs in the usual way. I would ask you to let Mr Martindale know this, and that if he wishes to proceed any further the meeting must be with him, and be confined to the two of us only. For obvious reasons it cannot take place here or at the offices of Campion Holdings and Investments, so I would suggest, at least initially, that it take place at Mr Martindale's home at a time and place to suit his convenience in the near future.'

Despite his composure during the meeting Jack had from the outset been obsessed with the risk factor in the project he was pursuing, and despite agonising endlessly over the way in which it might be carried forward from this point had not arrived at what he considered to be a completely risk-free solution.

He was determined not to proceed further without meeting and involving Martindale directly, but unlike the operatives in Le Carre's fiction Jack did not have the luxury of a safe house for his encounter with Martindale. A meeting at Barton was out of the question, booking a hotel room was equally unacceptable as it would mean giving a name and address. As he saw things at that time Martindale's home was the only option left to him, and he would have to take the chance that Martindale, even more than himself, and for his own reasons, would be anxious to keep those final stages strictly between the two of them. Overall he felt that the risks of this arrangement would be minimal.

'And if Mr Martindale wishes to proceed as you propose, how is any future meeting to be arranged?'

'Either you or he can telephone. Say it is personal, but do not give your name. When I answer, simply give the date and time that will be convenient for a meeting and I will be there.'

'Understood Mr Manning. I hope that it will be possible for you to hear something very soon. I have to confess that this whole business has given me a few sleepless nights.'

The meeting over Jack found it quite impossible to settle to any other work, and finished early for the day. If he had handled the matter coolly during the meeting, he now felt rather more tense than he had expected. In circus terms had he used all the right tradecraft, covered all the angles, kept his hands clean? Was the emotion he felt elation at a workmanlike bit of skulduggery or nervousness at the path to which he was now committed. In either event he needed a drink before he left for home.

7

A Sort of Secular Absolution

To all of Jack's professional ills, life with Kate and their friends on Barton Hill provided the perfect antidote. They met frequently with Jimmy and Celia either at one of the houses, at the Shagger, or on rare occasions at The Parish Pump for a drink and a meal. For Jack and Kate, with two regular monthly cheques going into their bank account, such little indulgences presented no problem. But from the occasional hints that Jack received he was made aware that trips to The Pump had to be limited as Jimmy and Celia operated on a pretty tight, if untaxed, cash budget.

Having fallen below the Taxman's radar when they went up to North Uist, their income, said Jimmy, would never be such as to trouble him again. Poor in cash, rich in living, was the way in which he described their life style, and it was this one deficiency that was Jack's only regret in the relationship, as for him neither Jimmy's home brews nor the Shagger's anomalous ales were an adequate substitute for The Pump's best bitter and Mrs Arscott's cooking.

Not that the Gillans lived like hermits. They may have been without TV and car, but if the need arose they could always run to a taxi, and if Jimmy wanted a new LP or book he always seemed to get it. Celia too, when off-duty from the smallholding, liked to keep up appearances. It couldn't all have been barter thought Jack, who wondered if there might have been rather more coming in than they liked to admit, or perhaps a little bit of help from Daddy to Celia.

For many years following their arrival in the mid-fifties, with Celia getting stuck in to the hard graft just as much as Jimmy, they had applied themselves and the small nest-egg of money provided by Daddy to restoring and renovating the range of amenity buildings that lay to the side of the house, and getting the perimeter of their little estate securely fenced.

Despite a methodical and determined approach to their life of smallholding self-sufficiency, however, it hadn't taken more than a couple of years for their starting pot of cash to run dry. By then, however, the quality of Jim's work had been seen by the locals, and he was never without a cash commission when he needed one to top up their funds.

From the day of their arrival they had taken the locals as they found them, accepting and entering enthusiastically into the local ways and customs. On their part, wary as they were of incomers, the locals respected both this and their hard graft and honest workmanship, and within ten years or so the Gillans were as well entrenched in the community as anyone could be who had not actually been born there.

With a holding of less than six acres Jimmy had kept things simple: no sheep or cattle. Far too much trouble, he said. So they started off with a dozen or so general-purpose hens, half-a-dozen ducks, a couple of Roman geese, and a goat. To these, when he had restored the old pig sty in the outbuildings, he added a handsome Gloucester Old Spot sow, who helped as much in digging and rooting up the land as Jimmy's ancient rotovator.

Well aware of the dangers of emotional entanglement with their sow, for pigs are loyal and friendly creatures, they decided at the outset that Sadie would live out her life with them as the one family fast breeder (like

Jack and Kate they had no children), but that they would harden their hearts against the piglets when they arrived.

A couple of acres was assigned to intensive cultivation, and on an acre at the head of the smallholding, on a south-facing slope with soil conditions which Jimmy found to be perfect for the crop, he planted the Croft's crowning glory, a field of fragrant lavender, at the edge of which a year later Celia set up her bee hives.

By the time Jack and Kate came to the Croft all these operations were well established and running smoothly, and the mature Sadie had been tamed and trained to the extent that, short of being allowed on to the living room settee, she was regarded as one of the family.

By the end of their third or fourth visit to the Croft, Jack and Kate had been given an introduction to all (or all but one as Jack would later discover) of the activities that enabled Jimmy and Celia to lead what seemed to be the ideal life of self-sufficiency. Jimmy brought in cash and produce from electrical or carpentry work, for which he was in such demand that he could afford to pick and choose. Celia had an outlet in the local market for her weaving and lavender products, but also accepted special commissions for her painting: portraits, pets, properties or views. She seemed competent at them all.

And for Jack there was an intimate and detailed introduction to Jimmy's final re-cycling triumph: an elegantly crafted version of the Reverend Moule's dry earth -closet, over which he waxed lyrical, in terms better suited to a work of art than a privy.

'Approved and adopted in the best of circles in their time Jack. Even the old Queen, as Ada always calls her, had one at Windsor. Give it a trial. Be my guest.'

'Difficult to resist the strength of such a royal commendation,' said Jack, 'But I think I'll give it a miss. There is a time in the affairs of men which taken at the flood etc, and this isn't mine. First thing after breakfast for me: regular as clockwork.'

'Right,' said Jimmy, 'But isn't it perfection: clean, odourless, and no waste of water. Then into the heap and on to the garden: bloody marvellous compost. Cauliflowers thrive on it. Old Tom knew a thing or two about that.'

Jack and Kate had enjoyed quite a few of the fruits of Jimmy's vegetable garden before Jack belatedly learned what it was that nourished them, but he forced that thought to the back of his mind: better if Kate were kept in blissful ignorance.

'Didn't catch on though, it seems,' said Jack. 'Why not?'

'Ignorance and laziness. No sooner had Moule set up a company to manufacture them, than along came Thomas Crapper . . . no jokes please . . . with his water-closet. Might not have caught on, but Prince Edward got to hear of it, and had them installed at Sandringham – one in the eye, so to speak, for Mama. Once that news got out Crapper's fortune was made, and apart from cognoscenti like me, poor old Moule faded into history.'

In time Jack also came to hear a little more of Jimmy's contact with his family following his abrupt wartime departure from home. Of his mother he had seen nothing in almost thirty years, nor in all that time had he returned to the area of his childhood where his parents now lived in a rambling turn-of-the-century house with Sorcha, his younger sister, and her husband.

His father and his older brother Kevin he did, however, see regularly on half-yearly visits, when all three made a pilgrimage to Anfield for a Liverpool home game, and then stayed overnight with Kevin, before Jimmy returned home the following day. If his mother knew that they met in this way she either didn't care, or thought it politic not to ask.

It was late on the Thursday less than a week after one such visit when Kevin phoned Jimmy with the news that his father had suffered a heart attack from which he died almost immediately, leaving no time for them to call Jimmy up to see him.

Jack and Kate heard nothing of this until they returned from work on the Friday after Jack's meeting with Stevens, when Celia phoned to give them the news.

'He seems more like his old self now Jack,' she said, 'but although I've seen him drunk before, I've never seen him quite as bad as this. Kevin called him with the news in the early evening, and he'd hardly put the phone down before he was drinking hard, and ranting and raving non-stop about his bitch of a mother, and the tough time she'd given the old man in the early years. It seemed I just couldn't get through to him or help in any way.

I had had an hour or more of that before he walked out taking the bottle with him, and locked himself in the barn. He wouldn't speak or open up, so by then I was in floods of tears because he was shutting himself away from me. Eventually I wrapped myself up in a blanket, took out a chair and told him I'd be sitting outside the door until he opened up. By now it was bloody cold I can tell you, and I was getting angry. We really wouldn't have been a pretty sight.

He eventually opened up just after midnight, but only I think because he'd emptied the bottle. He was on his way to starting all over again when he came back in to the house, but by then he'd had more than enough, and somehow, around about two, I managed to get him upstairs and into bed. He came round about lunchtime, had a shower, and now he's sleeping again in his arm-chair, but before he dozed off he said he'd like to see you, so if you could both come over tomorrow evening I'd be very grateful.'

'I'm so sorry to hear that,' said Jack. 'I knew well enough from what he's told me that despite the old woman's best endeavours he remained very close to his father, but I'd no idea the news would take him that badly. Not at all like the Jimmy I've known, but of course we'll come over tomorrow.

I don't recall that he's ever mentioned you when he talked about his trips up to see his father and Kevin. Have you ever had the chance to meet any of the family?'

'Never, although I've told him several times that I'd be quite happy to go up with him. This time though he wants me with him at the funeral, and I think that's why he's asked to see you. Come about five-thirty,' she added. 'I'll have a meal ready for later, but that will give us time for a drink and a good old chat before we eat.'

As they set off across the fields for the Croft the fol-lowing day they saw Jimmy sitting on the style by the quarry waiting for them. He came towards them with a sheepish smile, but with a finger to his lips enjoining silence.

'Nothing to say. Nothing to say,' he said, giving each of them a hug. 'I know how you feel well enough. Let me do this my own way.'

They walked on in silence for a couple of minutes before he spoke again.

'Seems I went over the top rather,' he said. 'Been a bloody nuisance and gave Celia a bit of a fright until I opened up and let her in, and then she was almost as bad as I'd been because I'd shut her out. All over now though, so we can just have a quiet drink and a meal together. Glad to have your company for a few hours.'

Settled comfortably with a glass of wine in front of the blazing stove they listened as Jimmy, now quite composed, talked a little about his early childhood with his father, before moving on to the arrangements for the funeral.

'I've spoken to Kevin again since Celia phoned you,' he said, 'He told me that Michael, Seamus and my Aunt Mary are coming over, probably with a couple of cousins or more. The funeral will be from my sister's house where the Da was living, and is fixed for week from now. I'm told they'll be bringing him home on the morning of the day before the funeral, so it looks as though they're planning to send him off in the old style, which I like, but not the Catholic circus that goes with it, but I can't do anything about that.

As the Irish contingent plan on staying over for a few days I'd like to be up there on the day the old boy comes home, and stay at least two or three nights myself. This time Celia will be coming with me, so I'll need someone to keep things ticking over with the livestock while we're away. Think you could help with that Jack?'

'Just show me what to do Jimmy, and take all the time you need.'

Leaving the women to themselves as Celia busied herself with the final preparations for their meal, Jimmy and Jack stepped outside into the fading light to make a round of the livestock and the few simple chores that would need to be done.

'No problem with any of that Jim,' said Jack. 'Weather's starting to ease now, birds coming back into song, and it'll be a pleasure to be up and about before I head for the office. I'll let them know I'll be late in for a few days.'

'Before we go back in there's one other thing I want to show you Jack,' said Jimmy. 'And a confession of sorts I have to make.'

Saying no more he led Jack to the end of the range of outbuildings and a door that had always remained firmly padlocked on Jack's earlier rounds of the holding.

'Don't want to leave you in charge with one door locked against you,' he said. 'Show's a lack of trust, and I don't like that.'

Holding the door open, he motioned Jack to enter what might once have been a stable with two windows in the far wall, both of which had been boarded up, either for privacy or to exclude light for other reasons. In the fading glow of sunset the shadowy interior received little illumination from the open door, but in such as there was Jack could see against the far wall what in the gloom looked disconcertingly like a small scale guillotine.

'A cider press: all my own design and construction,' Jimmy said proudly, inserting juice tray and pressing boards and giving the process a dry run to demonstrate to Jack his pressing technique which employed the pressure from a cleverly adapted car jack.

'Very workmanlike: just as I'd expect.' said Jack. 'But we never drink cider, and why all the secrecy?'

'Now you're a man of taste and discernment when it comes to the booze, aren't you Jack? Think back to all those after-dinner brandies, or calvados as you like to call them, that you've enjoyed. Good stuff were they? Professional touch and all that?'

As he spoke Jimmy nodded, pointedly directing Jack's attention to the corner behind the door. Jack turned, and with a hint like that immediately recognised the function of the two polished copper cylinders and piping glowing dully in the half-light behind the door.

'Oh you cheeky bugger Jimmy, you're distilling.'

'Absolutely. Old Irish tradition.' he replied. 'Simplicity itself, although it takes a bit of time and care. Apples from a neighbour to the press. Pulp to Sadie who loves it, but not too much or it gives her the squits, then a few hours work with the still. I favour the old pot still myself. Doesn't give so high an alcohol content, but keeps more flavour of the fruit. Then three years in the barrels before I tap and bottle.'

'I say again, you cheeky bugger. It's illegal of course, but you're not bothered I take it.'

'Of course it's illegal, that's half the fun, but from what little I've read I don't think it's a criminal offence. It's a bit like your tax fiddles, just a civil matter with fines and confiscation of equipment. Bit embarrassing if the Customs caught me, but when did you last hear of a prosecution for home distilling? Customs and Excise have got bigger fish to fry than chasing after small-time operators like me.'

'I'd always thought there was something rather distinctive about the Armagnac you'd managed to get your hands on, and now you tell me that it's all moonshine. Me, a loyal servant of the Crown and employee of the Revenue, I really must say Jim, I'm shocked, shocked.'

'You'll take a bottle with you though?' asked Jim.

'I'll take two,' said Jack, 'Or I'll shop you.'

'A glass and a smoke then, before we go in,' said Jimmy, bringing a couple of glasses down from a shelf, and turning to a bottle that was already open.

On a couple of upturned boxes they sat in silence for a while, watching the last of the day fade away through the open door, and quietly savouring their drinks as the smoke from their cigarettes curled slowly upwards to lose itself among the tangle of beams and the cobwebs and dust of ages.

Then, passing the bottle to Jack to top up, Jimmy began softly to sing:

'At the foot of the hill there's a neat little still,
Where the smoke curls up to the sky.
By the whiff of the smell you can plainly tell
That there's poteen brewing nearby.
Oh it fills the air with a perfume rare,
And betwixt both me and you,
As home we roll, we can take a bowl
Or a bucket of the mountain dew.'

'Beautifully expressed Jimmy,' said Jack. 'Very poetical. One of the wild songs of your dear native land is it?'

Jimmy just smiled, and fell silent again before starting off on a new tack that rather took Jack by surprise.

'As a lifelong atheist Jack, what are your thoughts about the concept and merits of the confessional?'

'Bloody hell, this is a bit sudden and serious Jimmy. What's brought this on?'

'Well apart from my younger brother, which wasn't quite the same, I suppose it's my father's death. You know: the first real personal loss. Oh I'm not talking about the bloody priest and a clutch of Hail Marys, but don't you ever feel that there are some memories, events and actions from the past, that sort of thing, that you'd like to share with someone, get off your chest if you like, but for a variety of reasons not with those nearest to you? A sort of secular absolution.'

'You're not going wobbly on me are you Jimmy? Feel the need to clear your conscience on the distilling do you? Don't tell me I've been chumming up with a closet Catholic all these years.'

'No I'm being serious Jack. Let me just tell you a story before we go back in. It won't take long.'

'Sorry Jim – fire away.'

'Well you already know how Celia and I came together, but before I burned my bridges with the family by walking out on that God-awful mass for poor young Danny, I had what I suppose you'd call a childhood sweetheart. We were much the same age, went to the same school, and had known each other from the early days.

She was a lovely girl, Caireen. Just like the legend, *Caireen of the Dark and Curly Hair*, that was her. Quite different from Celia: brown eyes, about five foot and a bit, and if not self-effacing, then very quiet. But she'd a voice so soft and sweet, and a trick with her talking, a sort of defect of speech I suppose, that quite caught my heart. She was a Catholic like the rest of them of course, but unlike many she stuck with me after I walked out on the mass and all that, and for almost three years we exchanged letters when I was away, and whenever I was back in port I got up there to see her if I could.

I wouldn't say that there was ever any spoken understanding between us, but other things being equal it would probably have gone that way. I know that apart from the odd dance and social she wasn't seeing anyone when I was away.

Then I met Celia, and that was it. It was quite different: I was bowled over, and knew right away it was for good. For a few months I dodged the issue with Caireen. But eventually I tried to find the right words to let her know how things stood, and wrote to her. Unsurprisingly I got no reply. That would have been late on in 1944, and with all the commotion and uncertainty that came with the end of the war and my new life with Celia, I pretty well forgot about it.'

When Jimmy paused here, Jack thought that he'd said all that was on his mind.

'Well that's something that's bound to happen from time to time Jim. No call for a confessional there surely?'

'No that's not it Jack, it's what happened years later. In 1963 I'd been up with Kevin for a couple of nights for the local derby, and we were walking back to the station when, out of the blue, he turns to me and says, "You won't have heard, I suppose, that young Caireen Moore died a month or so ago. I remember the two of you were quite close for a while in your younger days."'

'Christ, Jack, I don't think I'd given Caireen a thought for ten years or more, and yet I felt as though someone had punched me in the chest. She'd only have been thirty-nine.

I don't think Kevin would have said anything more if I hadn't pressed him, but I couldn't help myself, and what little there was he knew. Although Caireen had apparently taken the end of our affair much worse than I might have supposed, she recovered well enough in time it seems, and couple of years later married another local lad: and so it would end you'd think.

But I was grieving as though I'd only seen her yesterday, and I couldn't get over the fact that she'd died so young: felt it as though in some strange way it had something to do with me. I didn't say much to Kevin, but all the way home on the train I could think of nothing but Caireen.

I could see her again quite clearly, just as I'd left her when I caught the train back to join the ship. It was early August, and we'd had two glorious days together. She came to the station to see me off, and I remember her standing there bare-headed in a summery lemon-yellow dress that shone out like a beacon in the crowd. I thought it looked like new, but knowing the times, it must have been something handed down from her sister from before the war, but she really did look lovely. And as we left, she just gave one long wave of goodbye, and then stood there smiling until I passed out of sight, but not out of mind for a long time it seems.

Even now I still think of it as a deeply personal loss. Just can't quite work out why. I feel better for telling the story to someone else, but you can probably understand why I couldn't say anything to Celia.'

Finished at last, he drained what was left from his glass and turned to Jack, perhaps in hope of consolation, certainly in expectation of comment. Jack emptied the remains of the bottle into their glasses before replying.

'Jimmy,' he said. 'It's sad that your Caireen had to die so young, and perhaps you loved her more than you realised, but the circumstances hardly call for absolution or penance.

I apologise profusely for ever calling you a soulless bugger, for now I see that deep at heart you're just another melancholy, sentimental old Celt, dreaming sad, nostalgic dreams of what might have been, but never was. You're like Yeats' Sad Shepherd, full of self-pity and looking for comfort from the stars. Stop wallowing in a reverie of your lost romance. Shed a few tears for Caireen if you have to, and then forget her. Don't ever mention it to Celia, and for God's sake read a little of your nation's poetry.'

Jimmy response was first a searching, hard and uncertain look directly into Jack's face, and then a long, loud roar of laughter.

'By Christ, Jack, you're a bloody hard man, but you're better for the soul than a dozen confessionals and canting Jesuits. Come on, they'll be ready for us by now. Let's go and eat.'

As they walked back to the house in the last of the fading light Jim returned for the last time to his original theme.

'So you've never felt the need yourself Jack for the comfort of a secular confessional. Been a spotless life of moral rectitude has it?'

'Nothing I can't live with Jimmy. Minor misdemeanours, little meannesses that I regret, a bit of schoolboy pilfering at Woolworths, and of course a professional life of perfidious venality: all rather small beer – no calvados.'

When Jack looked at Celia as she left with Jimmy to travel up for the funeral, he could see why Caireen would have had to be quite a girl to stand up to the competition. Fifty next birthday, she could have been ten years younger. Tall and athletic of build, clear-eyed, lithe and vigorous, with scarcely a trace of grey in her dark auburn hair, she looked and moved as she might have done when she caught Jim's eye in her service days.

From a shopping trip to Wolverton she had returned with a formal two-piece suit in a deep midnight blue (no problem with cash there either, thought Jack), and as Kate said afterwards, left for her first encounter with Jimmy's mother looking every inch a thoroughbred from the Roedean stables.

8

It Takes it out of a Man This Life Everlasting

In Liverpool the door was opened to them by Sorcha, Jimmy's younger sister.

'Ah Jimmy, Jimmy, it's been a long, long time, but I'd still have known you if I we'd met on the street . . . and you must be Celia. It's lovely to meet you at last.' She gave them each a kiss and a warm handshake.

'Too long Sorcha, too long,' said Jim, returning her greeting with a kiss and a bear-hug. 'Shouldn't have left it for this to meet up again should we, but better now than never. A chance for things to be different in the future.'

'Please God they will,' said Sorcha. 'Celia, you come through with me to the back and meet the rest of them. Jimmy, you'll find Dad in the front room if you'd like a few quiet moments with him by yourself, then come through and join us. Just follow the sound of the chat and you'll find us alright.'

Jimmy opened the door to a room in near darkness, with heavy curtains drawn, and the only brightness the light from a single candle burning on the mantelpiece alongside a crucifix.

'Dear God who's that?'

He paused in the doorway, startled to see a figure sitting quietly in an easy chair beside the empty fireplace. And then, on looking more closely, 'Is that you Uncle Michael? For just a moment I thought it was the Da come back. I'd forgotten just how much alike the two of you were.'

'So we were, so we were Jimmy, and the older we got, the more alike we got, but he's laid out there behind you, and I, for my sins, am sitting here mourning him, and thinking of the grand old times we had together as boys. How are you Jim, how are you?'

'Oh I'm fine Uncle Michael. Sad, as we all are at the occasion, but pleased, as he would be, that it's brought us all back together.'

'Now or never wasn't it Jim? Do you mind how long ago it was? Thirty-six long years and a war, and you were still a boy. I can see you now sitting in the shadows when we got together at the farm, and helping yourself to a sip from a glass here and a pull on a glass there. Do you still have a taste for the stuff?'

'Sweet and fragrant from my own still uncle, just like yours.'

'Then we'll take the chance to have a few together before we go, and now I'll leave the two of you by yourselves for a while. We'll have plenty of time for chat later.'

Alone with his father Jim switched on a light and turned to the open coffin where the old man lay handsomely dressed in white shirt, dark tie and a fine grey suit: and by now he found that he was well over his grieving, and could look at his father composedly, if not entirely without emotion.

A bloody sight better dressed than I ever saw you in life. I suppose that's for the neighbours, and as usual you could do with a shave. Why the hell do they say that anyone makes a lovely corpse? There's nothing less lovely than death, but by and large you don't look too bad Da. Pity life couldn't have been happier when I was young, but over the years we shared a few good times on the terraces, and at Kevin's with a jar or two afterwards. Could have been worse I suppose. And now they'll be sending you off with the usual jamboree tomorrow, but this time I'll just sit at the back and keep my thoughts to myself. It'll make bugger all difference to you Da, will it? And I'm past caring. All passion spent. Is that what they say?

Had he been thinking all that, or standing there talking to a corpse? He wasn't sure, and didn't care. He felt easier in his mind now and ready after thirty-five years to meet his mother again. Switching out the light, he took one last look at his father by the flickering light of the candle, and then turned towards the noise of the others gathered in the room at the back.

As he opened the door to the babble of chatter and laughter, he took in the scene at a glance: all family obviously. Michael, Seamus and his aunt Mary over from Ireland with three of the cousins he'd met at the farm all those years ago: now middle-aged men like himself. Sorcha and her husband, Kevin with his wife, but still a few to come.

His mother he saw sitting alongside Celia, and apparently won over, if that had been necessary, as she had her hand on Celia's knee and was engrossed in whatever they were talking about. He knew from Kevin that she was off the booze, doctor's orders a few years earlier, and he wondered whether that had done anything to sweeten her disposition.

As Jim moved into the room she caught sight of him and stood up. An old woman now, she looked smaller and diminished in stature from the heavy-handed, overbearing mother he remembered, and not so sour-faced. Ah well, we all change with the years, he thought, and as he moved towards her he was sure that he could detect a mute entreaty for reconciliation in her eyes, and he welcomed it.

'This is a sad way to be meeting after all these years Ma,' he said, and for the first time since his early childhood, bent to give her a kiss.

'So it is son, so it is. But it's good to see you Jimmy boy. I'm sorry things went the way they did.'

'So am I Ma, but that's behind us now. You've been having a good chat with Celia have you.'

'I have, and now I'll go back to it, and leave you to catch up with the Cork and Dublin brigades.'

And that was how the rest of the day was passed: filling in the gaps left by the years, not only with those over from Ireland, but with others of the family as they arrived, until Jimmy and Celia left to spend the night in the nearest hotel, Sorcha's accommodation being fully occupied.

Jimmy passed the following morning giving Celia a conducted tour of the dockland area that he remembered from his childhood and the war years, ending up at the Albert Dock, now empty and deserted, where all the talk was of revitalising the area by turning the dockside and buildings into a new maritime museum.

Moving on to the snug bar of the Baltic Fleet they snacked on a bite and a beer before returning to Sorcha's in good time before the coffin was closed, and this time Celia joined Jimmy for a final farewell. For Celia this was an entirely novel experience of death's last rites. At the few family funerals she had attended things had been much more sanitised and at arms' length: the deceased, if seen at all, viewed in the muzac-enhanced solemnity of the undertaker's parlour, and certainly no open coffins at home with their very real reminders of mortality.

'He must have been a fine-looking man when he was young,' she whispered to Jimmy, who took one last, long look at his father before nodding silently and turning away.

As the cortege slowly made its way through the neighbouring streets on its short journey to the church where Jimmy had turned his back on religion half-a-lifetime earlier, he looked out without recognition, interest or emotion at a neighbourhood that had been utterly transformed since the days of his childhood. Of all that he remembered only the church, as if to mock him for the rejection, stood untouched and unaltered by war or the years.

Slipping with Celia on to a seat at the very back of the nave, he watched and listened with detachment to a ritual which, although it had a faintly familiar feel to it, seemed to have changed a good deal from that mass on which he had turned his back so long ago.

'Still all pray and display,' he whispered to Celia, 'but a touch less chilling and devoid of humanity than I remember it.'

On their return to the house after the interment, they found it transformed in their absence by Sorcha's neighbours and Kevin's wife who had stayed behind. In both rooms, now completely cleared of all trace of mourning, cloth-covered trestle tables had appeared laden with all the food and drink calculated to be necessary to take the mourners through the evening, and beyond into the following dawn, if that was wanted. The curtains were now drawn back, the house fully lit, and the front door left open for all who might wish to call.

For three or four hours they came to offer their sympathies, friends from the church, from the neighbouring streets and from the Anfield terraces: to enjoy a bite and a drink or two, and then move on to be replaced by others. But by ten-thirty or thereabouts there was only the family left, and Jimmy and Celia found themselves swept off by Seamus to a corner where Michael, Mary and the cousins were waiting.

'Sit down now then the two of you,' said Michael, 'And tell us all about the desperate time you had up there on your Scottish island, and what you've been about since. But before you start . . .'

He walked from the table and returned with a bottle of Bushmills and some glasses, which he filled and passed around.

'Now I know you take it neat Mary, but what about you Celia?'

Approving of her nodding acceptance, he handed her the whisky undiluted.

'Sláinte,' he said, raising his glass and taking a pull at the whisky before turning to Jimmy expectantly.

Then, for more than an hour, with diversions for laughter, argument, debate and near disbelief, Jimmy and Celia regaled them with a rambling account not only of the shambles on North Uist and their early days at Barton, but of old Tom Sutton's undignified passing, of Jack's fruit cage and barren ewes, and the finding of the Churchill book. It was the St Matthew's graveside vigil at New Year's Eve, however, that most caught the fancy of their audience and of Seamus in particular.

'Now I'd have to be honest Celia, at risk of offending, and say that offhand I can't think of many English customs that I'd be inclined to adopt, but by God I like the sound of that. There's humanity and love for you, both for those who have gone and those left behind to mourn them.'

And the priests would be down on you like a ton of bricks for your paganism, thought Jimmy, but he said nothing.

'Back home,' said Michael, 'we might perhaps have had a bit of music by now: a fiddle or a squeezebox to give us a bit of life, and it's a devil of a disgrace that none of us was taught to play. But what about you Jim? Celia was telling me earlier how you gave them all a song at the New Year gathering. Do you know any of the old songs from home?'

'I do, and I know the traditions, so you whet my whistle and pour me a Guinness, and I'll give you your song.'

He was scarcely into the first verse of *Whisky You're the Devil* before the rest of the room had joined with him and carried it though to the end, and from then on, with Seamus and Michael leading the way they drifted into a hazy, drink-fuelled evening that carried Jimmy back to that pre-war hoolie at the farm when he was tucked away to sleep at midnight and his father, uncle and neighbours carried it through to the dawn.

Reminiscences of the old times, laughter at Mary's tales of her days in the convent school (less funny to her then than now she said), reflections on the changing way of things in Ireland, stories (some tall ones from Seamus, Jim was sure) from the life of the old man and a few more memories of Barton Hill were all punctuated by songs that Jim had absorbed at his father's knee: *Rosin the Bow, Finnigan's Wake* and *The Maid of the Sweet Brown Knowe*.

In the momentary silence that followed the striking of midnight young Danny, the baby of the cousins, started up with that achingly beautiful song of separation *The Parting Glass*. He had a sweet tenor voice, and was left to a solo performance which was much applauded, but Michael clearly wasn't ready for the song's note of melancholy and finality just then: the evening was still young.

'Ah come on now Sorcha, time for some tea and cake I think, and you Jimmy, did you know what a fine, sharp lad your father was when he was young. Did he ever tell you the story of his Puck Fair triumph?'

'To be honest uncle, he wasn't a great one at all for stories of the time before he left. Didn't seem to want to talk about those days much.'

'Well that's probably as much our fault as his, but it's water long under the bridge now, and any differences forgotten and forgiven, so fill your glasses and let me wind the clock back some sixty years or so.

I'd say Liam would have been about fifteen at the time, and making his first trip to the fair with a whole crowd of the boys. Now when the fair was on the town was so busy and lively that for most of the lads it was sleep when your could and where you could, but we were lucky with an aunty on my mother's side just outside Killorglin who was glad to see us with the family news, and give us a bed on the floor for the night.

At the horse fair on the first day we always looked and lingered longingly, but it wasn't often that anyone from home was able to buy. But this time it was different, as Jamey Brennan from the big house over the hill had joined us, and he was after a hunter. You'll know what it was like in the country in those days with never a car to be seen apart from the RIC, so we all knew our horses, and were more than free with advice as Jamey worked his way through five or six of the sad looking nags brought to him by some of the knackers.

Then Jamey spots this handsome bay gelding standing a way off to the side: five years old he was told, which we all thought looked about right. For half-an-hour Jamey puts him through his paces, and then with a spit and a slap the deal was done. So we all set off for a jar to celebrate, and then stayed on at the fair for the rest of that day and the morning of the second.

We'd gone by train, but as Jamey was going to take the bay back at the walk, four of us decided to keep him company. That meant we'd a fair few miles to cover before we were home, and as the end of the day came on we stopped off at a farm by the way, with a neat little goirtin for the bay, a fine barn for us to bed down in for the night, and some milk, rashers and a couple of slices of pan from the house to keep us going.

By afternoon the next day we were back in Millstreet, and I can tell you the bay had been admired all along the way. Pleased as punch with himself and the bay Jamey was, and showed him off to all and sundry as we took a final jar before heading off, we back to the farm and Jamey up to the big house.

It was less than a week later when Jamey turns up at the farm in a state fit to top himself. Two days earlier, he said, he'd gone out to the stable to feed the bay only to find it missing. Worse than that, as though to mock poor Jamey, the maggots who took the bay had left in its place some poor spavined beast fit for nothing but the knacker's yard. For a while Jamey thought it might be a joke, and that the bay would be returned, but now there seemed no hope of that.

So we all troop up to the big house with Jamey, and to be honest we couldn't help a laugh or two ourselves when we saw the poor sad creature that stood looking at us as though all it wanted was to be put out of its misery.

As things were at the time no one was for calling in the RIC, and Jamey and the lads were going wild for something to do when young Liam spoke up.

"Why don't we just turn him out, and follow him?"

"Dear God," says Jamey, after a moment's thought. "The boy's right. Just look at the state of the beast — he can't have come far."

And that's what we did. So the poor thing staggers out, moons around the yard for a while, and then stumbles off up the boreen that runs round the back of the hill. We follow, and from there he crawls along until we're back on to the Killarney road, the way we'd come in, before turning off up a little bogway. By now the news had got round and we must have been a couple of dozen strong, and then one of them pipes up, "He's on his way to the Kennedy place."

Well the Kennedys were a poor feckless crowd for sure: no real harm in them, but just thick enough for such a stupid trick. And we're barely in sight of the place when we hear one of the youngsters hollering out to his Da that a crowd of the lads were bringing him back his old nag.

Next thing we know there's him at the door white as a sheet, and his wife clinging on to his arm and bawling her head off that he didn't mean it, and that he and one of the boys had been out on the tear and were near-legless when they staggered back with the bay, and meant to take it back, but hadn't the courage when sober. Kennedy, the while, just stands there with his mouth open, and finally waves his arm in the direction of a wreck of a cabin that stood just across the field, and there we found the bay.

Some of the boys were for giving him a good shallacking, but Jamey wouldn't have it: said that the man looked worse than his beast, and had half the sense. The bay looked to be fine, so there we left Kennedy with his wife foul-mouthing him, the kids howling and the old mare looking fit to drop, while we, with your Da in triumph on the bay's back, made our way back for a few jars on Jamey to celebrate. I'm surprised he never told you that Jim.'

'It's sad that you all came to fall out later,' said Celia, who knew as much as Jimmy did about his father's early days, 'But that's politics, and if you hadn't I wouldn't have Jimmy now nor the pleasure of your company.'

'I'll take a final drink to that,' said Michael, 'but sadly I'm not the man I was. There was a time when I'd have danced you through to the morning, but now I'm for my bed, and as the song says, goodnight and joy be with you all.'

With Michael gone most of the rest were more than ready to follow, but Celia, intrigued by the absence at any time of a reference to the one great issue that should have divorced Jimmy from the rest of his family (religion, the Catholic church and Jimmy's standing with the Lord), took the opportunity to steal a few quiet words with Seamus before he went up to bed. She chose Seamus because of all the family he'd clearly taken something of a fancy to her, and from a few comments here and there seemed to be less imbued with unthinking respect for the faith than the others.

'Uncle Seamus,' she said, always careful to respect the old folk's titles. 'I hope you won't mind me asking this, but the family all know about Jimmy's break from his mother and the church all those years ago, and everyone saw him sitting apart with me at the back of the church and ignoring the mass. I can see you all still love him though, and can't help wondering how everyone feels my Jimmy's going to be placed when his own time comes.'

'Well I know what the priest would say, but you'd have been best placed to ask Mary, for she don't agree with the priest, and has it all nicely worked out. Jim had the sacraments of initiation when young, she says, he's loved his Da and lived a decent life despite all the happened in the past, so when the great call comes, the good Lord will look into his heart, know that he repents, and in his infinite mercy He will understand. All will be well, and Jim will join us all with the blessed, says Mary. Don't know about you though Celia.'

He gave her a wink and a kiss before leaving them to sleep out what was left of the night in a couple of armchairs, it being far too late to return to the hotel. As they settled down together in the darkness Celia heaved a long, exaggerated sigh of longing.

'Oh Jimmy, did you ever hear anything like those lovely soft Irish brogues of your cousins. My God, but they're sexy. Why on earth was I cursed to spend my days listening to sweet nothings from a Scouser. Oh I could . . .'

If Jimmy's throw was blind, it was accurate, and the cushion silenced her mid-sentence.

'God bless, please God, thanks be to God, God be praised.' For three days, and the first time in more than thirty years, those phrases had punctuated the conversations with Jimmy and around him, and as he said his farewells, and shook hands with the elderly uncles and aunt so close now to the end of their lives, he struggled once again to understand just what the factors were that distinguished their irrational and lifelong acceptance of the faith from his rejection of it. They'd all endured the same steady drip, drip, drip of indoctrination when young, and yet a lifetime later they stood in opposite camps, and on each side the certainty was absolute. Religion meant everything to them, and nothing to him.

It wasn't that the prospect of an afterlife didn't have its appeal. There were many he would love to see again, but also quite a few he'd rather not, and here his thoughts turned to his mother. What would she be like 'on the other side,' the hard-hearted scolding bitch of his youth, or the benign, almost amiable old lady of the last few days? Would there be booze, or some celestial equivalent, and would Uncle Michael be allowed the pleasure of his still? Would there be football and sex, or just cerebral pleasures? He could think of a few of the faithful on the Anfield terraces who'd soon be bloody tired of that.

And they all seemed to be so happy to accept that at the end of the day it would all be sweetness and light, without getting into the detail, but then that's where the devil is, isn't it, in the detail. And it would go on, and on, and on, and on.

'It takes it out of a man, this life everlasting.' Now where the devil had he heard that?

9

Ah Take the Cash in Hand

Four weeks had elapsed since the meeting with Stevens, but Jack had heard nothing from Martindale, and he was starting to feel uneasy. Now, for the first time, he saw his objective as something more than the abstract intellectual challenge that his day-to-day investigation work presented, and as he dwelt on his prospects should things go wrong he began to falter, his usual assurance and decisiveness being replaced by increasing doubt and uncertainty as each day passed. Had he overplayed his hand with Stevens? Was his original analysis of the weakness of Martindale's position valid? Had his certainty that Martindale would immediately be ready to stump up been misplaced?

He found himself increasingly troubled by such doubts, and in particular the thought that perhaps Martindale might in some way be able to turn the tables on him, and get away scot-free leaving him to carry the can. He went over the ground time and time again, and simply couldn't see how that would be possible. But Martindale clearly had friends in high places, and who knew what strings he might be able to pull behind the scenes. Visions of the Board's Investigating Officer, or worse, arose with each unexpected knock at his door: or perhaps such callers wouldn't even bother to knock.

Distracted from his current work-in-hand by such troubling visions, he was suddenly struck by the chilling thought that locked away in the drawer of his desk he had the very evidence that could be used to destroy him: his Campion folder containing not only the invoices, but the notes and photocopies from his Ashburton researches.

All the other Stevens' invoices had long ago been acted on and registered for investigation, either by the group or in the district. If allegations of corruption were being prepared against him, the inference that could be drawn from the documents in his Campion folder and his failure to act on them was all too clear: that he was holding them for his own nefarious purposes.

Jack, normally so calm and collected in pursuing his investigation work, was panicked into action. Taking the folder from the drawer, he sealed the contents into a large envelope, wrote a prominent note on the back, 'To be held for JM until collected,' and addressed it to Jimmy. He would telephone him when he got home to let him know that it would be arriving, and to ask him to keep it safe until he asked for it. He left the office at once, and despatched the envelope by registered post.

Access to revenue buildings during Jack's early days in the late fifties and throughout the sixties had been fairly relaxed, and people came and went without too much attention being paid to them, but such easygoing attitudes came to an end in 1973 with the arrival of the IRA bombing campaign in England. Security checks were imposed; combination locks fitted to doors, and in the Midlands immediately following the Birmingham bombings in 1974 tension was high. False alarms leading to building evacuations were not uncommon then, and Jack had not long returned from half-an-hour's absence following such an evacuation when his telephone rang.

'Sorry to trouble you Mr Manning,' said the receptionist, 'I have a caller who says it is personal, but declines to give his name. Are you willing to take his call?'

At that moment Martindale was the last thing on Jack's mind, and he'd been on the point of refusing the call when recollection of his little private enterprise flooded back, and his heart sank as it did so. He was getting cold feet, and could he have turned back the clock to Stevens' first tentative enquiry about his scope for discretion he would have done so, but forward or back, the risks were much the same now.

'Put the call through please.'

'Am I speaking to Mr Manning?'

'You are.'

'Next Wednesday the 15th at eleven o'clock, if that is convenient.'

'It is, and I will be there.'

It hadn't taken many words, he thought, to set up his little conspiracy, for that he now realised would be one of the charges should the affair ever come to light. Conspiracy to defraud: more serious than the simple offence of fraud, he knew, and punishable by up to ten years' imprisonment.

Despite the fact that contact had at last been made, his misgivings, once they had arisen, could not be shaken off. Was all now well, or was he walking into a trap by proceeding with his meeting with Martindale? And in particular had he been wise to meet him at his home? Memories of his reading of the latest Le Carre came flooding back to him. Now he was worried whether the room they met in would be bugged. If it was then surely he'd be handing Martindale the opportunity for a stalemate: to record their discussions, and then simply say, 'If I don't pay and you act on the invoices, then I'll reveal the recording, and you'll be clobbered too.' But would he? That would implicate him too in the bribery. It was all getting far too bloody complicated, thought Jack, but he could see no other option than to press on.

The meeting, in any event, was only the first part of a two-stage operation. If things went as planned and Martindale agreed to pay the £30,000, the problem then arose as to how that might be safely and securely achieved, although Jack felt reasonably content with the plan he had in mind to resolve that particular difficulty.

On the appointed day, and well in advance of the agreed time to allow him an opportunity to relax with a coffee and his paper, Jack was in Ashburton and ready for his assignation, but with no intention of proceeding with the meeting in Martindale's house as originally proposed.

He'd found in his early days in the job that as the time for any particularly demanding or confrontational encounter drew close, he was sometimes troubled by a form of nervous indigestion that at its worst could be almost disabling, and as he walked towards the front door of Martindale's impressive establishment, he was disturbed to feel an incipient stirring of his gut below his belt.

Beneath the front portico he paused, took a deep breath, reminded himself that Martindale had as much to be nervous about as he did, and rang the bell. Its summons was answered immediately by the sound of footsteps approaching from the back of the house.

Jack had no difficulty in recognising Martindale from the photographs he had seen: not tall, but a little above average height, clean-shaven, with fair hair combed sleekly back, good-looking, but with slightly fleshy features that suggested a possible overindulgence with the good things of life. There was the briefest of pauses as each made his initial assessment of the other.

'Mr Manning I assume. Please come in.'

His tone was not hostile, but neither was it welcoming, and he did not offer his hand.

'I won't if you don't mind . . . I don't wish to offend, and I'm reluctant to alter what has already been arranged for our meeting, but I would prefer our discussions to take place outside the house. I noticed some pleasant public gardens with seats just a little way off, or if you prefer there is a quiet coffee house a couple of streets away.'

'I can assure you that we will be quite alone in the house and will not be disturbed, if that is what is troubling you Mr Manning.'

'Understood, but my occupation has taught me to take nothing for granted, and the subject of our discussions is such that I feel I need to be ultra cautious. Absolutely no reflection on yourself, I would add, and no great inconvenience either I assume.'

From Martindale's delay in replying, Jack had the feeling that he might be going to take exception to the proposal, so he quickly added, 'I assume you do still wish to proceed on the basis of my discussions with Mr Stevens, and would add that I will not be in a position to make myself available at any other time. It's all a matter of the degree of risk I can afford to take to oblige you in this matter.'

Jack was already beginning to feel a little more relaxed, and not merely relaxed, but quite pleased with the calm, but positive and direct nature of his opening gambit.

'Very well, if that is how you want it. Give me a moment to fetch a coat, and I'll be with you.'

Returning with his coat, he closed the door behind him, took a look at the sky, and said, 'I think we'll make it the coffee house.'

The five minutes it took them to get to the coffee house they walked in silence. Martindale had evidently decided that it was not an occasion that called for the conventional pleasantries or small talk, and Jack was indifferent whether they spoke or not. He'd played the game too long not to have developed a hide quite thick enough to shrug off awkward silences or any hostility that Martindale might be nursing.

The coffee house was not busy, and they had no difficulty in finding a table towards the back where they could talk without being overheard. Ordering two cups of the same indifferent coffee that he had left almost untouched earlier in the morning, Jack sat facing Martindale, and felt that the onus was probably on him to open the discussion.

'I assume that Mr Stevens will have given you a full account of my last meeting with him, which as you will know was inconclusive for reasons he will have made clear to you. If, however, there are any aspects of our discussions that you would like me to explain further I will be happy to do so, otherwise I think the ball is in your court.'

'Thank you Mr Manning. I gather from Mr Stevens that you pride yourself on your plain speaking, so perhaps you will understand if I am equally blunt, and say that I feel very strongly that you have been pretty free in the assumptions you make about my personal circumstances and political intentions.

Putting that to one side, however, it seems to me that you are demanding an inordinately large amount to resolve this matter. £30,000 is a sum that I could not make readily available, and seems to be quite out of proportion to the circumstances: significantly more than your gross annual salary for a couple of years or more, if my few researches are correct.'

Jack listened to this with a certain amount of satisfaction, and a feeling that perhaps he had the measure of his man: public school no doubt. He had that air of smug self-assurance the privilege bought, but seemed not to be very sharp. A lower second at best if he went to university, and unlikely to advance very far in the Westminster arena where subtlety and crafty tact were at a premium.

His position was weak, and the initial bit of bluster served only to weaken it, and should have been resisted. It was inevitable that he had to offer some show of resistance to the amount proposed, and his financial position certainly had to be given some consideration, but a reference to Jack's 'demands' and salary simply handed the initiative to Jack to make the most of what was already a strong position.

'Mr Martindale, let me make one thing absolutely clear. I am demanding nothing. May I remind you that it was you yourself, through your go-between, who approached me and asked if anything could be done to assist you in what seems to me to have the potential to be a very embarrassing situation financially, socially and politically. If I have got that wrong, just say so and I will leave now. It's no skin off my nose.

As far as the amount of £30,000 is concerned my gross salary is of absolutely no relevance, but yours certainly is, and from what I have seen of your taxation file I can't believe that you're likely to be too hard-pressed financially. Mr Stevens will, I hope, have explained to you how I arrived at half of that figure, based upon tax on the fraudulent invoices, plus interest and penalties. The other half reflects the value of the very real risks that I am taking in assisting you in this way. As I said to Mr Stevens, the social and political advantages I throw in as a bonus.

I would emphasise too that it is only the fraudulent invoices that have been taken into account in my calculations, whereas long experience has led me to conclude that where this type of fraud exists there will almost certainly be others. Only you know the answer to that, and whether the accounts of your business would stand up to the scrutiny of a detailed investigation, which would of course include an investigation into your own personal finances and those of your wife.

I repeat, it's a matter of indifference to me whether we proceed or not. If we do, then I'm looking for a return that is commensurate with the risk I am taking and the amount you are saving. If we don't, then the investigation of the fraud and your business affairs will proceed. You can take your chance either in the district or in my branch, and you will see then what the demands of the Revenue might be when it is over.'

Jack knew he was playing a more aggressive game here than his position warranted. The delay in pursuing the Campion fraud was now such that if an investigation was belatedly undertaken it was not beyond the bounds of possibility that an explanation for his procrastination might be sought, something that he would rather avoid.

In the event, as was clear from Martindale's next comment, Jack would have nothing to worry about on that score. Martindale had realised his mistake in trying to challenge the size of the settlement (for that was how Jack now saw it – a settlement as in every other investigation, but this time to his benefit) and thrown in the towel.

'And if I agree to proceed on the basis of your £30,000, what are your views on timing for payment. I don't tend to keep an amount like £30,000 available in loose change at any time.'

'Look Mr Martindale,' said Jack. 'Any delay and all contact with yourself increases the risk to me, and in that sense to you also. You may not have the ability to write a personal cheque for £30,000 right now, but I can't believe that you can't arrange it pretty rapidly. Let's get it over with. We'll both sleep the better for it.'

'And how would you wish payment to be made, and what guarantee would I have that those invoices will never again see the light of day?'

Jack had identified the dangers associated with payment as the nub of the matter from the very outset, and given them considerable thought. His overriding objective, as it had always been, was to distance himself as far as possible from any provable connection with Martindale and his affairs. Accepting payment by cheque would therefore be utter folly.

Payment by cash was equally unacceptable. Notes could be marked and so traced, but it was not so much that, as the corrosive effect on money of the country's roaring inflation. True it had fallen below its peak of over twenty percent, but it was still well into double figures. If that continued £30,000 stashed away would be worth precious little in ten or fifteen years' time.

Jack thought in such bourgeois terms because the truth of the matter was that he did not need the money, did not want the money: at least not to spend at that time. Cars, fast or slow, bored him: nor was he interested in the flashy, louche world of the fleshpots. His disillusion with his work aside, what he had and the life he led suited him very well. He and Kate managed quite nicely and to spare on what they earned, and he'd seen and read of more than enough crime capers that came to grief from a lack of restraint in handling the ill-gotten gains to resist any temptations in that direction.

He was also realistic enough to know that the present opportunity would almost certainly be a one-off, and what Jack was looking for was a safe inflation-proofed home for his £30,000, where he could tuck it away for the ten or fifteen years that might have to be endured before he could tell the Revenue to stuff their job, and turn full-time to the things that really mattered in life, when his nest-egg really would be of use, and could be gradually utilised without attracting attention.

Other things being equal he'd have added a couple of thousand of his own, and put the money into a property, where market prices were racing away well ahead of inflation, but like fast cars and flashy living that was a little too open to public scrutiny, and questions might be asked to which he could offer no answer.

Only after much searching and thought did Jack find what he was looking for: Krugerrands. He'd seen an article tucked away in a financial column *Fancy a Flutter on the Price of Gold,* and by the time he'd read through to the end his mind was made up. In most respects the one-ounce coins offered all that he was looking for. They were compact, easily portable in the quantity he had in mind, incorruptible should he be eccentric enough to bury them, and recommended as a reasonable hedge against inflation.

They would indeed have been the perfect solution for Jack had he not been obsessed almost to the point of paranoia with the technicalities of handover, and ensuring that he could not be observed, and certainly not photographed, in the act of receiving or collecting his booty. His fixation on this one aspect came in part from recollections of real and fictional accounts of ransom demands that went awry at just that point, and in part from his recent absorption in the espionage world with its tradecraft, lamplighters and dead letter boxes.

Ever since the prospect of payment became a reality he had worried away at the problem without finding an answer which wouldn't either have him exposed and identified collecting the Krugerrands, or leave the Krugerrands, albeit for a brief period of time, unsupervised and insecure. Not until the false bomb alert, when the building had been evacuated using all emergency exits, did he find a solution: an elegant solution, he thought, that entailed just one more brief meeting with Martindale, kept the Krugerrands secure, and totally eliminated any risk that Jack might be observed as he collected and slipped away with them. Now he was ready to answer Martindale's question.

'The method of payment, if I can deal with that first, has given me a great deal of thought. For obvious reasons a cheque is a non-starter, and I'm equally unenthusiastic about the idea of a bag stuffed with notes.

The solution I've arrived at may sound a little long-winded and cloak-and-dagger in approach, but it will be slightly less costly for you, and eliminates any need for us to meet again except briefly, so may I ask you to bear with me while I explain.

I would like payment to be in Krugerrands. You may have seen references to a ban on their import, but you will still find advertisements for their sale. Prices fluctuate, but of late they seem not to have topped £90 per coin. If I were to suggest a payment of three hundred one-ounce coins to conclude the matter that would come to say £27,000, possibly less, which might be some compensation for my rather unorthodox arrangements for the handover.

I have in fact prepared a brief aide-memoire to cover this aspect of our arrangement which also includes the names of a couple of Krugerrand dealers.'

At this point Jack handed to Martindale a typed sheet containing the following details:

Payment to be made in Krugerrands.
Dealers:
David Owen Edmunds (Gold and Diamonds Division),
31A Sloane Street, SW1. Tel: 01 235 9744
Roberts Wilkie Ltd of Windsor

There are others.

300 one ounce coins in 30 packs of ten coins each wrapped in clear plastic, and placed in the holdall supplied.

Delivery to be made to Wolverton on a date to be agreed.

When coins are ready for delivery telephone to agree a date.

On agreed date come unaccompanied to the telephone box outside Wolverton Town Hall at 12.30 to take telephone call giving details for delivery – this will take no more than ten minutes.

Taking the paper Martindale read it carefully a couple of times before commenting.

'An abatement, I think that is the term you use, of ten percent is certainly welcome Mr Manning, and I see what you mean by cloak and dagger. I've no great objection to proceeding as you indicate, but is all this fuss really necessary?'

'I can see that you might not think so, but I'm chiefly concerned with keeping my own position absolutely secure, and this will do so.

Turning to the invoices, the arrangements for delivery to be given in the telephone call will include the exchange of the Krugerrands for all the incriminating documents. I appreciate that you will need to be satisfied that you are given everything, and to that end have brought with me photocopies of everything that I hold. It will give you an opportunity to familiarise yourself with what you will be receiving, and I am sure that should you feel the need to ask him Mr Stevens will confirm that they are complete. Oh and you'll need this to bring the coins in.'

He handed to Martindale the holdall he had been carrying with him.

'So now it's just for me to get the coins, and then telephone you with a date for delivery. Is that correct?'

'Yes, but you'd better have a couple of dates available in case I can't fit in with the first you propose.'

'And apart from that brief meeting that will be the end of the matter will it?'

'Absolutely, and come the election I will watch the results for this division with particular interest.'

'Goodbye Mr Manning. I can't say it's been a pleasure to do business with you, but I suppose we might say that we have reached an outcome to our mutual satisfaction.'

'More so for each of us perhaps, than if had been across the desk in my office. Goodbye Mr Martindale.'

Jack offered his hand which Martindale shook without another word, and went on his way.

Jack had fully expected that there might be further delay at this point, but Martindale's connections were evidently such that he was able to obtain the Krugerrands promptly, and little more than two weeks had elapsed before Jack received another personal telephone call.

'Is next Thursday 13th convenient for our arrangement Mr Manning?'

'It is. I will expect you to be ready at the telephone box at 12.30. Have you got everything quite clear?'

'Quite clear.'

'Then thank you for calling.'

Later that evening, leaving Kate to her TV, Jack strolled over to Jimmy's where he collected his envelope with the invoices and stopped for a drink and a chat.

'Code books?' asked Jimmy, nodding at the envelope.

'Sort of,' Jack replied. 'Something for the confessional perhaps, but not at this time.'

In Wolverton the Revenue occupied the whole of the seventh floor of their office block, and a little before 12.30 on the 13th Jack left his desk, and walked to the store room on the corner of the office building, from where he could readily overlook the telephone box which stood at the foot of the steps to the Town Hall. Martindale, unaccompanied, was already there waiting, holdall in hand, and the telephone booth was empty.

Returning to his room Jack stopped off to let the general office know that he would be taking a longer lunch break than usual, then locking his door to ensure a few moments of privacy, lifted the telephone and dialled the number of the Town Hall telephone box. Martindale must have been standing with the door half-open for he answered almost immediately.

'Martindale here.'

'If you stand with the Town Hall at your back, you will be looking along the High Street. Walk down the High Street and take the first turn left. A short way along it, just beyond the Boots store, turn left again into the entrance to a private car park. Directly opposite, on the far side of the car park, you will see some emergency exit doors at the rear of the offices and shops. One of them will be slightly ajar. Open the door and step inside. I will be there to meet you.

Hand me the holdall with the Krugerrands, and I will hand you the papers. When we are each satisfied with what we receive you may leave as you came, shutting the door firmly behind you.

Have I made things clear, or is there anything you want to ask me?'

'No that's fine. I understand.'

Apart from its one entry and exit the car park was a quadrangle totally enclosed by the well-secured backs of four ranges of tall offices and shops, and so reproduced in the cheapest possible provincial and commercial terms the configuration of the Somerset House court-yard, the very heart of the Inland Revenue: an aspect of his final arrangements that gave Jack particular satisfaction. He also considered it a deliciously ironic touch that Martindale, a stranger to the town, would be totally unaware that in following his instructions to the letter, he would be delivering the Krugerrands to the very doors of an Inland Revenue Enquiry Branch office.

In the time it would take Martindale to walk to and through the car park Jack took the back staircase, used only as an emergency fire exit, to the ground floor which contained the boiler room, a couple of store-rooms and the emergency exits which opened to the car park. It was as usual deserted.

Opening an emergency exit door slightly, Jack waited until he saw Martindale entering the car park. He was unaccompanied and remained so as he crossed towards the emergency exit, opened the door and stepped inside. Handing an envelope of documents to Martindale, Jack took the holdall and tipped the contents on to the floor. They took little time to check: thirty packs with ten Krugerrands in each, all neatly wrapped in clear plastic as requested. Everything seemed to be in order.

'Satisfied?' asked Jack. Martindale merely nodded and stepping outside gave the door a firm push. It closed with a reassuring click, but Jack tested it just to make sure. Access from the car park to the building was now impossible.

Placing the Krugerrands in a different holdall brought with him from his office (he really was carrying his tradecraft to extremes) he left the delivery holdall on the floor, walked through to the main entrance at the front of the building, and out into the bustle of the lunchtime crowds in less time than it would have taken Martindale to leave the car park.

That morning, abandoning his usual allocated space behind the office, Jack had parked on one of the little side-streets just a short distance away on his usual route out of town, and it took him a few minutes to walk to the car. Placing the holdall with the Krugerrands on the passenger seat, he resisted the urge to take one more look at them, and set off for home. With Kate at school in Barlow, he would have plenty of time to do what was needed, and return to the office without occasioning any comment.

His mood as he drove the twenty miles to Barton was a strange mixture of elation and anti-climax. Elation that he had carried off his little bit of private enterprise with meticulous attention to detail and in a thoroughly professional manner. Anti-climax, in part because he realised that for several months his disillusion with the daily round at the office had been lightened by the excitement of the affair which was now over, and in part because it was a triumph he could share with no one. The fact that, as Martindale had correctly stated, he had considerably more than double his gross annual salary sitting on the seat beside him seemed not of itself to be important.

At home he transferred the packs, each reassuringly weighty despite being so small, to a secure cash box which (his final precaution against the worst possible scenario) he concealed in a secure place in the barn, where he would leave them for a few years until it was absolutely clear that there would be no repercussions.

10

Poisoning the Wells

In the weeks that followed the settlement of the Campion affair Jack applied himself to his work with a vigour that stemmed more from a search for a modest degree of self-satisfaction than any sense of loyalty to a department which left him and his colleagues to nail the small fry, while the avoidance sharks swam free and flourished.

It was with no expectation of any immediate change in his position that he faced the future, and he was therefore surprised when he received, on the same day and addressed to him personally, two of the buff-coloured Head Office envelopes that were almost invariably the harbingers of change, generally unwelcome. His initial reaction before he opened them was that something must have gone horribly awry with his recent private venture, and that nemesis awaited him. He couldn't have been more wrong.

In the first he found notification of the promotion that he thought had probably passed him by. In the second he was informed that in eight weeks time his tenure at Enquiry Branch would cease, and that he would then take up the position of District Inspector at Barlow. There was also enclosed a note from his immediate superior congratulating him on the effective way in which he closed down the Scott Stevens fraud which had become a centre of infection for the whole area.

He gazed at the documents with a mixture of delight and incredulity. If he'd ever given any credit to the notion that the arc of the moral universe tended towards justice, it would have been destroyed by the perverse timing of this reward so soon after such a calculated act of malfeasance in office. As a card-carrying atheist he attributed neither good nor bad luck to the hand of fortune or the supernatural, but at such a time he found it hard to resist the thought that the Lord helped those who helped themselves.

At lunchtime he celebrated his good fortune with his colleagues in the nearby Marquis of Granby, and feeling that he could afford to spread himself a little, drove home with two bottles of the best the nearby off-licence had to offer for his evening with Kate when, hugging the knowledge of his transfer to himself, he told her only of the promotion. The following Saturday over lunch at The Parish Pump he repeated the exercise with the Gillans, again mentioning only his promotion.

With the meal over, coffee taken and a leisurely smoke, he turned to Jimmy.

'Never been up the church tower have you Jim? Well I think now's the time. Leave the brandy – you'll need a clear head.'

Despite Jimmy's reluctance, Jack was insistent in a way the surprised Jimmy, and stubbornly refused to take no for an answer. Leaving the ladies to linger over a second coffee they made their way to the church, and started the ascent.

Jack knew of old that it was not an easy climb. Two hundred and fifteen worn stone steps, and a narrow winding stairway, built to accommodate the frame of a medieval ascetic, not a twentieth century epicurean. They took it at a speed appropriate to their age, the lunch, and the quantity of beer consumed, but by the time they surfaced on to the leads and into the sunshine they were both short of breath, and Jim was short of temper.

'Now that we're here Jack, perhaps you'll tell me what the hell this is all about. Why spoil an excellent lunch, and why did it have to be now?'

Jack said nothing, but motioned Jimmy to join him where he stood leaning against the west parapet, and then spread his arms wide as if to grasp the whole town in his embrace.

'Just look at it. I mean really look.'

Before them the uneven roofscape of Barlow's oldest and best houses fell away down Priory Hill to Packhorse Bridge (the original replaced by a modern structure in 1530) and the river, with the age-ravaged remains of Barlow Priory on the far bank, and beyond the wooded heights through which the road ran towards Wales. Diagonally to their right, the courts and narrow lanes of the old town led to the ancient church of St Botolph and the castle (substantial ruins, but some parts still in use), and behind them lay the market square, and the Georgian solidity of the old town hall. Overall it was a picture of the best of small town living that England in the twentieth century had to offer.

'Isn't it bloody marvellous?'

Jimmy cast a jaundiced eye on the panoramic view of Barlow town laid out below them, and gave a grudging acceptance to Jack's proposition that it was indeed 'bloody marvellous.'

'And what would you say if I were to tell you that all these things will soon be given unto me?'

'Well Jack, like any chap that's endured a broad Catholic education, I'd say that you've been communing with the powers of darkness.'

'Very close to the mark Jim: communing with Head Office actually, which is pretty much the same.'

As he spoke he passed his transfer notice to Jimmy for him to read, but Jim was still feeling too fractious after his climb to offer his congratulations.

'And this is what you wanted, is it?'

'Lusted after Jim. I'd thought I must have mentioned what a cushy little number the present DI has got, and how much I hoped to follow him, but perhaps that was just with Kate.'

'Well congratulations then Jack. You're a lucky lad, and now if you don't mind, I'd rather like to get down to earth.'

'Keep it under your hat when we get down Jim. I haven't told Kate yet.'

As they sat at the table with the final round of drinks that Jim felt was essential if he was to recover his composure, Jack asked Kate if she could remember their Parish Pump lunch with Roger, after they had just seen the house up on the hill for the first time. He was surprised when she affected, as it seemed to him, to have no recollection of it.

'Oh surely you must. We'd been up on the top of Midden Hill, and you and Rog had been niggling away at one another as usual for most of the morning. Then we came in for lunch, and Rog was banging on about The Pump, and telling me what a lucky chap I was. You said you were only too glad it wasn't just round the corner or I'd be in here all the time. Don't you recall?'

'Oh vaguely: something on those lines.'

Jack began to feel that he wasn't handling the announcement of his second piece of good news at all well. He'd obviously irritated Jimmy by dragging him up the tower, and now Kate, for reasons he couldn't understand, was being distinctly off-hand. He remembered too, that she didn't seem quite as elated at his promotion as he had expected.

'Well I thought I'd mention it before I showed you this.'

He handed her the transfer note, and continued as she read it.

'We stayed in Barlow for a couple of nights when we were touring on our honeymoon Jim, and fell for it then. It satisfied our joint nostalgia for old, forgotten, far-off things and battles long ago, and that's Barlow to a T. We've always wanted to get in here, but commuting distance has always been the problem. Now this transfer has come we've got the chance at last. What do you think love?'

'Well we can talk it over later. I've got a bit of a head right now so perhaps we could have a little stroll down to the river and get some fresh air.'

Jack returned home with the feeling that his celebration lunch had not turned out quite as he had intended, and after one more attempt to engage with Kate on the matter of a move to Barlow, he let the matter drop when she still seemed to be quite unreceptive to the idea. Plenty of time to sort something out, he thought, best not to rush her.

At the office, where the Stevens case was almost ripe for the final interview, Jack decided to drag his feet and leave it for his successor. He would be cursed for the delay he knew, but he had no wish for any further contact with Stevens if it could be avoided. He was altogether too close to the Martindale affair, and Jack would have no idea just how much he knew of its conclusion. As far as the rest of his investigations were concerned, he spent his time simply treading water or tidying up the casework for whoever was to follow him.

At home in Barton, both before and during his negotiations with Stevens and Martindale, Jack had been frequently entertained and occasionally involved and assisted by Jimmy, in Ted Sutton's dispute with his immediate neighbours Geoffrey and Karen Pratt, who had arrived in the village from Barlow some two years or so earlier, trailing a reputation for trouble that spread rapidly through the village as soon as the family appeared for their first viewing of a Barton property.

As the sons Shane and Jason (now eleven and fifteen) had progressed through the junior school at which Kate worked, their names had become a byword for bullying and disruptive behaviour, just two of the many less desirable characteristics exhibited by their virago of a mother, whose arrival at the school gates was viewed with trepidation by even the stoutest, most experienced stalwarts on the staff. The father was a cipher, neither seen nor heard, and of whom nothing was known except that it was by virtue of his employment on a large estate near Barlow that the family occupied a tied cottage there.

Their translation from a modest tied cottage near Barlow to owner-occupation of the house on an acre of land next to Ted's smallholding had been achieved courtesy of a substantial inheritance which had mysteriously accrued to Mrs Pratt. Large enough for them to buy the property without a mortgage, said Hilda Genner, although she could not put a figure to the precise amount or name the source. This signal failure of Hilda's intelligence, which cost her a few points in her rating with the local gossips, led to much interesting speculation, especially when Mr Pratt arrived in a brand new four-by-four, and a local firm with a reputation as jerry-builders proceeded to adorn the house (late nineteenth century) with timber facing and rendering with a result that was variously described as interesting, eccentric, grotesque, aberrant, gross etc, but seldom identified as mock Tudor, the original intention.

Jack first saw the family when Kate pointed them out to him in the village as they passed, the mother in the van and the husband alongside her, but seeming physically always to be half a deferential pace behind, with the two sons scuffling sulkily along in their wake. To be fair to the woman, thought Jack, like the coral snake, she carries her warning colours for all to see.

Despite a seductively attractive head of Titian hair, one look at Karen's face was enough to make it clear that what you saw was what you'd get if you tangled with her. At any time of day, whatever the circumstances, as all in the village would soon be aware, Karen's feature's would be firmly set in the aggressive scowl of one who had already suffered a reverse at the hands of fate that day, and was looking for confrontation to redress the balance; and physically she was probably capable of holding her own with most men if the need arose.

Geoffrey, on the other hand, was in all respects unremarkable. Of average height, average build, average looks, and average (to be generous) intelligence, he was distinguished only by the fact that, flower-power style, he wore a moustache, beard and long hair tied in with a colourful bandana headband: his one bid, it seemed, to stamp some sort of character on the very indifferent blank provided by nature. If his passive features carried any sort of expression when he was encountered, it might have been described as one of baffled melancholy: a cloak for his infuriating readiness to see the world as he would like it to be, rather than as it was.

So it happened that it was Geoffrey, rather than Karen, who initiated the breach in relations with Ted less than six months after his arrival when, during Ted's absence at work, and without consulting either him or the deeds to the property, he applied his newly acquired chain saw to a flourishing mixed boundary hedge of field maple, hawthorn, hazel and flowering wild and guelder roses (all lovingly planted by Ted some six years earlier) and reduced it from a nicely maturing six or seven feet to a line of three-foot stumps.

That evening, as Jack and Jimmy, sat in the Shagger listening to Ted as he reported his encounter with Geoffrey; it seemed to them that initially he had been remarkably restrained.

'I mean Jack,' he said. 'It wasn't as if the deeds didn't clearly show that the hedge was mine. I'm no legal expert and I could see it, and all he had to do was look or ask, but no, he thought it was his, and that was enough. Karen had said it was interfering too much with their view. So he'd cut it down, and then left half the bloody traff from the cuttings on my side for me to clear up.'

'Did he say he was sorry, or offer to make things good in any way?' asked Jimmy.

'Not a word of apology, and what the hell could he offer anyway? Money's no good. It's six years of waiting that's gone to waste, and it was looking lovely last spring.'

'Well what else did he say?'

'Next to nothing Jack. All I got from then on was "Oh dear; right, I see, I suppose so." I might as well have been talking to the side of the barn, and then she appears. Must have been listening I think. Oh I got plenty of old lip from then on. Never mind the hedge, what about all the problems I'd caused her since they moved in. Turned out all she was referring to was the security light which she said was coming on in the small hours and blaring in, as she put it, the bedroom window: all of thirty yards from the light that is, by the way.

When I asked why she didn't mention it she had the bloody cheek to tell me that they didn't complain, but just put up with things to make the place a nice neighbourhood.

Put up with having your hedge cut down, I asked her, but I might as well have kept my mouth shut. I got a load of stuff then about people always picking on the boys, and me keeping them waiting for their football when it came over into the garden.

No hope at all of talking to her sensibly Jack, and in the end I was so disgusted I just turned on my heels and went back home.'

From that point relations deteriorated rapidly. Rubbish began to appear in Ted's front garden overnight which he was sure the boys were throwing there. Their two dogs (night-time barkers according to Ted) produced a litter of puppies that scrambled through the hedge and regularly shat in his garden until they were old enough to be sold off, but the final breach could probably be marked by the occasion when Ted, within their hearing and obviously overheard by them, referred loudly to 'those Pratts who live next door.' Unintentional, said Ted, but few believed him.

Not until Jason's departure from school (unqualified and unlamented) and his immediate engagement in the punk rock scene, coincided with an offer from the water company to provide main sewage connections to those isolated village properties that had missed out thirty years earlier, which included Ted's, did the situation degenerate into farce.

For more than six months Ted and his wife had endured disturbance from puck rock sessions from Jason and his associates in an outbuilding much closer to Ted than to the Pratts. Over-indulgent and totally uncritical of her son as always: Karen had provided funds and encouragement. They were producing a tape for their agents, she told those who were inclined to listen.

Personal contact having long been abandoned, communications were being conducted by increasingly acrimonious correspondence, when Ted received two letters on the same day the contents of which led him to seek the opinions of Jimmy, and particularly Jack, who still basked in the glow of his success with the Churchill book.

Tucked away in a corner of the Shagger, Jack and Jimmy read the two brief letters.

Letter 1.

Dear Mr Sutton,

This letter is in response to your deadline for a reply concerning the band practice. In the spirit of good neighbours we have done the best we can following your comments to us and your subsequent letters. This has obviously been in vain judging by your responses.

Having taken legal advice we do not feel there is anything more we can say on this matter.

Letter 2.

Dear Mr Sutton,

On a completely separate matter from our previous correspondence, can you confirm your time scale to connect to the main sewer.

We purchased our house with the intention of using the water from both of our wells but have been unable to do so due to the water contamination from the outflow from your septic tank, as confirmed by the County Council's Health Officer when we first moved in.

We have not raised this matter before as we knew there would be no easy or cost effective solution for you but now the main sewers are being installed we are looking forward to having the well waters retested and using them as intended.

We look forward to your response.

As he read the second letter Jack roared with laughter.

'Oh Christ Ted, you are in trouble. You've been poisoning the man's wells. Shades of *Lawrence of Arabia*: Geoffrey astride his camel riding out of the Barton mists. Have you no fear Ted?'

But Ted just looked puzzled and shook his head.

'Ah. You haven't seen the film. You should. It's bloody good, and your line is, "My fear is my concern." Sorry though Ted; I shouldn't joke. You're a bit worried about how to respond. Is that it?'

'Not my field Jack, and Sarah said I should have a word with you before I reply.' Sarah was his wife.

'Well you can simply disregard the first letter. The reference to legal advice is just the sort of ignorant bluster that uninformed people like the Pratts think will impress and deter.

The second letter's much more interesting, and what a considerate and model neighbour you've got, thinking of your costs and difficulties. And it's all confirmed by the County Council Health Officer it seems. From your dealings with Geoffrey would you say he's a big enough arsehole to make that up?'

'Oh he's stupid enough Jack, but she'd probably have put him up to it. She's an absolute bloody monster. We can often hear them at it hammer and tongs at the top of their voices – no that's not fair. She's hammer and tongs together, and he just puts up with it. I was right down at the end of the garden the other day, and with windows closed I could still hear her at it, "It's my bloody money, and I'll spend it how I like." Oh they are a happy couple I can tell you.'

'So what do you think Jimmy? I mean with your Reverend Moule and Thomas Crapper connections you must be an expert on this sort of thing, if anyone is.'

'Well to my certain knowledge, half a dozen of the properties around Ted are still using septic tanks or cesspits, so if I can be permitted a few scatalogical speculations, I wonder how it is that this genius of a health officer has been able to distinguish the Sutton shit from the Pratt shit, or that of any other of the immediate neighbours, and how and when he obtained a control sample of undoubted Sutton shit to compare with the contamination in the wells.'

By now Ted was relaxed enough to allow himself a laugh, and over another pint they drafted a couple of letters for him: one to Geoffrey, asking for copies of the councils' report on his well water, the other to the council enclosing a copy of Geoffrey's letter. To the first Geoffrey ventured no reply. To the second the council replied promptly. They had no record of tests of any sort being carried out at Geoffrey's, Ted's or anywhere else in the vicinity and beyond that had no comment to make on the letter.

The next letter from Ted brought all communication between the parties to an end.

Dear Geoffrey,
You have provided none of the supporting documentation requested in my last letter, and the council have stated that they have no record of any tests being carried out.

What, or perhaps who, may have led you to make such a ludicrous allegation I have no idea, but you clearly have no legitimate interest in any matters relating to my connection to the main sewer.

The Pratts had been exposed as liars and fools, but it was a pyrrhic victory for Ted. True, the punk sessions diminished and the outbuilding fell silent when the pop world failed to recognise Jason's genius, but the dogs still barked at night, a new litter of pups arrived to shit on Ted's lawn, and whenever and wherever they could the Pratts conducted a campaign of overt hostility.

Ted and Sarah had had enough, and just about the time that Jack was celebrating his good news at the office he and Kate received an invitation to join them at a little evening get-together in the upstairs room at the Shagger devoted to such occasions. Similar invitations were sent to Jim and Celia, and as they subsequently learned, to a few of the senior member of other old Barton families.

As Jack arrived with Kate and the Gillans, he looked around at the two dozen or more assembled, and was at a loss to know what was going on. Albert was there presiding over a little bar at the end, while his wife fussed around over the buffet that had been set out at the side of the room.

Larry Breakwell was there, minus his clerical collar, and professing as much ignorance of the event as Jack and Jimmy. Davey Bache and Martin Ellis (Snr) were there with wives, as was Charlie Genner and wife, plus a couple of other senior folk whose faces Jack knew, but not the names.

'Any idea what this is all about?' said Jack to Albert, but without learning anything further. Albert professed total ignorance of the affair beyond the request he had received from Ted and Charlie Sutton to set up the refreshments and drink.

Finally when all the guests had been assembled with time to get a drink or two under their belt, Ted, Charlie and their wives made their appearance, and stood rather hesitantly just inside the doorway, until the room fell silent when it became clear that Ted wanted to say a few words.

'First of all Charlie and me would like to say a big welcome to all of you, and if you'll help yourself to some food and another drink, and then get sat down around the tables we'll let you know what it's all about.'

The quality and quantity of the refreshments provided meant that getting provisioned and 'sat down' as Ted requested took quite some time, but eventually they were all seated and waiting for Ted to put them out of their suspense.

'Well it's lovely to see you all, and I know you're all wondering what this is all about, so as I'm not used to this sort of thing I hope you won't mind if I read from a few notes that Charlie and me have put together.

Now you'll all have heard a bit I expect about the trouble that Sarah and me have been having with those Pratts next door.'

He was expecting a laugh, and he got one.

'Well we're getting on a bit now, and we're not prepared to have the rest of our days buggered about, if you'll excuse my French, by that lot. From what we've learned from our talks with Jack and Jimmy there, and a few other people, trying the law will only mean more aggravation and cost, so that won't do.

But it's not just that. Many of you will already know well enough just how bloody hard it is to make a living here on the hill. Charlie and me both started at it when we were fourteen, and we've been at it seven days a week with few breaks ever since. I'll soon be pushing seventy and Charlie's not far behind and now we reckon that's enough. Time for a change.

So Sarah and me got together with Charlie and Lorna and we talked things over. And I don't know quite how to say this, so I'd better just come right out and say that we're all going to be leaving you.'

Ted paused here, perhaps aware how this would be received by people he'd lived and worked with all his life, or perhaps because he himself was suddenly struck by the implications of their decision.

In the silence that followed nobody said a word apart from a soft, 'Oh Ted,' from Albert's wife.

'No, no, no,' said Ted, 'mustn't take it like that. No cause for anyone to get upset. We're all going to be alright, so let me tell you. On Monday morning Charlie and me will be going in to Barlow to see Mr Parsons and Mr Bayley to put our properties on the market. . . . Sorry to steal Hilda's thunder there Charlie.'

That earned him a laugh too, and lightened the atmosphere a little.

'Most of you know we've been letting Mum's place since she died, and that will be going too, plus the few acres we've bought around the hill over the years. So if any of you are interested, now you know, and now's your chance.

Like most of you, we've been careful over the years: had to be very often. And by being careful we've got a little bit saved here and there. . . You didn't hear that Jack.'

Another laugh there: his audience now beginning to relax and quite enjoy Ted's performance.

'So now we're going to enjoy ourselves a bit. You'll all remember about Dad's book I know. Well since we started looking into that with the Shropshires we've got quite interested, and now we're going to be following in Dad's footsteps.

A few months ago I got myself a little booklet on discovering South Africa, and then we all went in to Wolverton and had a word with one of the travel agents there.'

Hopefully not Scott Stevens (Wolverton) Ltd, thought Jack.

'And come next September we'll all four of us be on board the Windsor Castle leaving Southampton for the Cape. First a few weeks on a bit of a tour around, and then we're going off to a place called Houtnek near Bloemfontein. That's where Uncle William got killed in the Boer War. The Shropshires can't tell us if the graves are marked, but now that we've learned so much about those days we'd like to see what we can find, and pay our respects. We'll be taking a bit of Barton stone with us to leave with him.'

'Drummer Hodge plus eh Jack?' whispered Jimmy.

'Well that's about it. After the cruise is back, Charlie's off to New Zealand to stay with his son for a few months. Reckons he might stay out there if they'll let him. Sarah and me will be back in the area, but somewhere like Mordiford Wells down in the valley where life's a bit softer, or perhaps a little place in Barlow. But you won't be getting rid of us altogether. We'll be up in the Shagger or at the church from time to time to keep in touch.

Anyway all that's a bit in the future, we're not off right now, but we wanted to scotch any rumours that might start up and let you have all our plans straight from the horse's mouth. Well that's about it. Eat up, drink up, and have a good evening.'

Jack looked across at Jimmy questioningly. 'Well Ted certainly kept his cards close to his chest. Sure he didn't even give you a hint Jim?'

'Honour bright Jack. Not a word, although I was only having a drink with him a couple of nights ago. Good for them though I say. Did you ever mention Hardy's Drummer Hodge to Ted, by the way? I thought that might have put the idea into his head.'

'Never thought to, but now I will. From what he's decided to do I think he might like that. Never does to pre-judge people does it? When I remember how tongue-tied and awkward Ted once was I wouldn't have thought he had it in him.

Strange, by the way, the connections life makes. Hardy when young had a tutor who became a very close friend. Name of Horace Moule, and would you believe, the son of your Rev Moule, inventor of the earth closet. Sad chap though, ended up cutting his throat.'

'Talking of connections,' said Larry Breakwell, who'd been listening in on their conversation, 'If you thought that Ted was playing his cards very close to his chest by not letting you know, perhaps I should mention now, that in just over six months time I too will be retiring and moving on.'

'Well that is further sad news Larry,' said Jack. 'The old order changeth, yielding place to new, And God fulfils himself in many ways.'

'Lest one good custom should corrupt the world,' continued Larry. 'Oh dear! I never saw myself in that light. Perhaps it's as well that I'll soon be on my way. Wouldn't want to be a corrupting influence.'

'Not you Larry,' said Jimmy, 'But we'll miss you greatly when you do go. Never thought I could enjoy the company of a man of the cloth again until I met you.'

'Seconded,' said Jack. 'Kate and I have really enjoyed our evenings together with you all at Jimmy's. You'll be much missed. Any idea who'll be following you?'

'Some bright young spark I suppose, full of new ideas for getting bums on pews. It seems to be the way now.'

'Ah!'

That sigh breathed by the two men as one, was brief but pregnant with meaning, and Larry seemed to understand and sympathise.

Knowing that there would be plenty of time to speak to Ted and Charlie the three men spent the rest of their time talking together while Kate and Celia wandered off to have a chat with Sarah and Lorna.

It would be almost two weeks before Jack had a chance to talk over the changes with anyone other than Kate, and the more he mulled them over the more he felt the old restlessness. The Suttons almost gone. Larry soon to go. Jimmy and Celia still going strong, but Celia losing some of her enthusiasm for their remoteness and the good life. Her mother had died suddenly, and her father was failing. She had to leave Jimmy for the south more frequently now, and from the few comments that Jim had made Jack gathered that when the father died and the estate was distributed Celia, in Jim's words, would be a very warm woman. When that happened Jack couldn't see them staying on, and if they went there would be nothing to hold him. But still whenever he tried to advance the idea of a move to Barlow he found Kate completely unresponsive. He couldn't understand why.

When Jimmy next called in to see Jack there was much more to be told about Ted's affairs.

'My word they're canny folk these countrymen, but they keep it well hidden. It seems that old Tom Sutton's father was a builder. He built Ada's house and those Ted and Charlie own. He also built a couple of houses down in Mordiford Wells which the two own between them and from which they've always received rents. When he wasn't building he was doing a bit of farming and buying up a few acres here and there whenever the

177

price was right, all of which passed on down the line to Ted and Charlie.

The upshot is that by the time everything has been sold, legals, tax and all the rest of it paid, they are likely to be worth, wait for it, close to three quarters of a million each.'

Well that puts my Krugerrands into perspective, thought Jack, before expressing the view that it couldn't have happened to a nicer family. A little later, less than three weeks before he was due to start at Barlow and one week into Kate's school holidays, Jack returned home to find the house empty, and Kate and her car missing.

Assuming she had gone into Barlow and would soon be back, he poured himself a drink and settled down with *Call for the Dead* which he was reading to catch up on the early history of George Smiley. Not until the clock struck six did he realise how late it was, and still Kate had not returned.

Thinking she might possibly have gone out with Celia who had no car of her own, he telephoned the Gillans, but they could tell him nothing. It was only when he went back to top up his drink while he waited for her that he noticed the envelope propped up on top of the cupboard where he kept his whisky. Kate knew him well enough to guess where he would turn when she failed to appear.

The front of the envelope was noted simply 'Dear Jack.' Putting down his glass he opened the envelope to find a long letter written in Kate's neat schoolgirl hand.

11

Kate's 'Dear John' Letter

Dearest Jack,

I wonder if you can remember the circumstances of our first meeting as well as I do. It was at that wonderfully boozy party that Jenny Roding threw to celebrate getting that producer's job at the BBC. I was there because I'd known her from our time at school together, and you tagged along with your sister, although as I remember it you hadn't got an invite. Roger was also there, and it was then that the two of you found that you had quite a lot in common, and became rather chummy for the time you were in London together.

I was wearing a long peasant-style skirt and that bottle-green sweater that you told me later you liked so much because it showed my breasts off to perfection, but we didn't really have very much to say to one another then, indeed you, as usual, had little to say to anyone, but spent most of your time alone, systematically tippling while listening and judging. Just as you did when you took me along to meet the 'bloody Commons' (as you called your political family) and left me to make all the running while you looked on.

I'm sure you will remember that you came away from that first meeting with a less than flattering opinion of me: 'stuck-up little bitch' were the words reported and to which you eventually confessed, and we laughed about it often afterwards when chance threw us together again with rather a different outcome. But I wonder what sort of a bitch you are going to think of me now.

I know you've always been a great advocate for dealing with a difficult situation face to face, and I never had anything but contempt for those girls during the war who dumped their far-away boy-friends or husbands with nothing more than a half-page 'Dear John' letter, but I know Jack that if I try to deal with this situation face to face I won't go through with it, and so a letter it has to be, and that is going to be difficult enough, for in many ways I haven't stopped loving you, but I owe you as much of an explanation as I can put into words for what I am doing.

If I've seemed a little distracted in recent months it's because I've been trying to get my thoughts together: to filter out all the emotional stuff, and say what I have to say about our relationship in a rational and reasonable way, as you seem to do so easily. That's always been a puzzle to me too Jack. On face-to-face family and personal issues you're always so cool and self-possessed, and yet give you a nostalgic reference to the 'old days,' the right theme from Schubert, or a moving piece of theatre, and you're always ready to 'pipe your eye', as you put it. Unfortunately I'm inclined rather the other way, so I fear this may end up as a pretty rambling affair.

You've often said that in your daily work you always proceed with half-an-eye on what you call the worst possible scenario, and if only you'd been able to carry the same practice into private life we might not be where we are now, for when it comes to the state of our marriage you seem at times to have been completely blind.

There's such a delicious uncertainty, isn't there Jack, about what it is that leads two people to fall in love: from the all-consuming physical passion through to the marriage of two minds, or anywhere in between. I'm not at all sure where we fitted into that spectrum, except that for you it certainly wasn't at the all-consuming physical end. Even in our early days, when all was new and a whole world of love there to be explored, I always had the feeling that there was something semi-detached (the besetting sin of your family you tell me) about your lovemaking.

Perhaps I should have been warned by the frequency with which you used to entertain our friends with that bloody quote about sex from Lord Chesterfield's letter. How did it go: the cost damnable, the pleasure transitory and the position ludicrous? Well you can't complain about the cost with me Jack, and although I can't speak for your enjoyment, I'd have been very willing to be experimental when it came to the position, but for someone so radical in most other aspects of life you seem to have been singularly conservative when it came to sex. Has it never struck you that there was something fundamentally inconsistent about a card carrying atheist (as you love to call yourself) being hooked on the missionary position? You see Jack, I've even been infected by your sardonic view of the world and all its ways – can't resist making a joke about the problem.

You used to do exactly the same. Do you remember? Whenever I tried to talk seriously about it we always seemed to end up with jokes or quotes from your extensive reading – sorry does that sound a bit bitchy? It was either 'the King's Great Matter' or like Feydeau's Victor you had 'nothing to declare.' Even on that German holiday a few years ago, when just for once you stirred from your long slumber and for a few nights it seemed like a second honeymoon (that was such a lovely time Jack) you had to make a joke about it, and attribute the quality of your performance to the high specific gravity of the Stuttgart beer.

But if you'd extended your reading a little, wasn't it Freud who said that we joke and laugh to relieve anxiety? Were you ever anxious Jack, or was it only me?

Perhaps it was my mistake (if not my fault) from the start. It's always been big men who have appealed to me. Even as a child it was my Uncle Dick who was my favourite. A mountain of a man, he'd sweep me up as though I was a feather, but I always felt so safe and comfortable when he held me. And then you came along Jack, built by the same firm on much the same lines. My big, brown bear: that was what I called you, another hangover from my childhood love for teddy bears.

But I'd chosen the wrong metaphor, hadn't I Jack? I know well enough what it is that bears do in the woods, and it certainly isn't sex: at least not with any sort of regularity. They're solitary creatures, aren't they, living apart most of the time, and coming together only occasionally to mate. Well as a couple we fitted one half of that equation perfectly, and I don't need to tell you which. You were the bear who could take it or leave it alone, and generally you left it alone. And it isn't as though I could ever accuse you of looking at any other woman 'in that way' as the soaps put it. But then you didn't often look at me in that way either did you Jack? Sorry, that paragraph was bitchy and crude, but I know from experience that bears have got broad shoulders.

So there we were Jack, me tending to one end of the spectrum, and you to the other, but although it sounds clichéd to say it, I did also love you for your mind: and for our hugs, and for our cuddles, and for the way you were always so careful to look after me. And I do believe that if the call had ever come you would in truth have died for me, so was I being an ingrate in looking for something more: for some passion, excitement and adventure in our sex life, for instance?

So am I right to blame you if you can't change? Isn't it rather the stamp of that one defect in which you are not guilty, since nature cannot choose his origin. . . As one more quoted at than quoting it took me a long time to tease that one out, and I think it works rather well, so perhaps I'm not doing too badly in keeping emotion out of this. Maybe that's a sign that our relationship had indeed become more of a habit than anything else.

I've taken all of the clothing that I need to last me for some time, but there will of course be lots of practical matters to be resolved. As a civil servant of impeccable integrity, efficiency and thoroughness you will, I am sure, have all our affairs at your fingertips, and I trust you absolutely to let me know how things stand when the dust has settle a little.

As there were no children (that was one thing we absolutely agreed on) there are no hostages to fortune. Indeed if there had been I think I would probably have gone off and had a few affairs when the urge was on me, and let things run on as they are, but as things stand there's no need for that. We've always said, haven't we, that with no one to think of but ourselves we were always free to act in a thoroughly irresponsible way, so that's what I intend to do.

There'll be the property to be sorted out of course, but seeing the way prices for attractive country livings have rocketed since we came here the house, nine acres and outbuildings should fetch more than we could ever have dreamed of when we started out. With that plus whatever our savings amount to divided between us it should leave me quite independent and you with enough to find yourself some snug little den inside the walls of Barlow. Perhaps you'll find someone else to share it with, although I suspect you'll carry on quite happily as a solitary, fulminating at your job and the world and becoming increasingly familiar as one of the regulars at The Pump.

Finally there's my confession. You knew it had to come of course, and I've left it to last as it's the part I find most difficult to write. Despite your demonstrated capacity to remain detached and controlled on these matters it will also, I think, be the hardest part for you to read.

Try as I might I have been unable to find any way of saying this other than bluntly, so I might as well just get on with it and tell you that I am going to live with Roger. I'm absolutely sure you had no suspicion that anything like this was going on, but that as I've said is because you're not really very intuitive when it comes to personal relationships, are you Jack? I think you've always seen the sniping between us as a sign of some underlying antipathy, whereas I've known all along that it was quite the opposite: a recognition that there was an attraction there, and an acknowledgement of its dangers.

We'd probably just have carried on with the sniping whenever we all met up together, but just over a year ago when I went down on one of my solo trips to see mum and dad during the summer break I also called in to have coffee with Jenny Roding as was, only to find that Roger was also there. We left together. He asked me to lunch, and I happened to be on the re-bound from one of our not-altogether-successful nights together. I'll just leave it at that Jack.

We've only been together a few times since, but it's been enough to make me realise that this is what I want, and that I'm of an age when either I do it now or resign myself to carrying on with you as I have into a sunset of carpet slippers and bedtime cocoa.

You'll soon settle down into your Barlow niche Jack. Your last port of call in the Revenue I think you said it would be before you chucked it in for good. I'm hoping that the county won't make too much fuss over the short notice I've given them, and I'll certainly have no problem finding a job down here.

And now I'm really stuck knowing how to wind this up. Firstly don't be too upset Jack. Does it help or make it worse to know that that 'one defect' aside our years together have been happy, entertaining, interesting and, in one sense, full of love. And if the epithet 'bitch' applies there must be many women who would say that I'm an ungrateful one – but they're them and I'm me. There's no other way I can explain it.

I suppose that's it, so there isn't any secondly after all, except that you may find that this doesn't come as a surprise to Celia. I've never said anything, but from one or two oblique comments she's made I have the feeling that she sensed my restlessness: female intuition perhaps.

I can be contacted at Roger's when you're ready. There's a casserole in the fridge. All you need to do is heat it up.

Take care. Still love you.

Kate.

Standing at the window Jack read the letter as he read all documents, paragraph by paragraph, with his customary civil service thoroughness and care, but before he'd got to the bottom of the first page he had no doubt where Kate was leading, and as he progressed was puzzled to find that he felt no growing sense of anger or resentment. He was saddened, but objective enough to acknowledge that there was little that she had to say about their relationship that he could honestly challenge. Not until he got to her final disclosure did he pause in his steady, methodical analysis of what was being said, and stand for a few moments gazing fixedly, but unseeing, at the hills in the far distance.

Dragging himself back from a reverie that had resolved absolutely nothing in his mind, he finished the letter, and was turning to pick up his glass when his eye caught the photograph standing on a nearby table. Himself, Kate and Roger taken by a helpful market trader on that golden day almost seven years earlier when they had first seen what was to be their future home on the hill.

It showed them after their lunch at The Pump, standing together beneath one of the arches of the old market hall. Kate in the middle with him one side and Roger the other, their arms linked around her waist, and all of them smiling happily together. He recalled then, how on their last visit to The Pump with Jimmy and Celia, Kate had avoided, studiously avoided he now felt, all his references to that earlier day together, and the constant sniping between Roger and herself. A troubled conscience at her recent behaviour he now realised, but what about those earlier days? Had it all been as innocent then as he was led to believe?

But what the hell did it matter now anyway, he thought, and filling his glass to within an inch of the brim, he took in a generous mouthful and walked slowly though the hall and upstairs towards their bedroom, slightly unnerved by a deeper silence around the place than he was accustomed to at that time of day. It wasn't that Kate made a lot of noise about the house, but often she would have the radio playing softly in the kitchen, or he could hear the sound of her movements there or the hum of kitchen equipment. Now all was utterly still around him.

At the foot of the door into the little spare bedroom Kate used as a workplace he notice Felix, one of her larger teddy bears that she used to hold open an ill-hung door. He swung his leg and kicked it violently across the room, and then feeling angry with himself at his own

186

lack of control followed it to the far corner where it had landed, picked it up, smoothed its fur, and sat it down in one of the chairs.

'Sorry Felix,' he murmured. 'Mustn't take it out on you. You aren't the one who's been shagging around.'

As he turned to leave he spotted Cynthia, one of Kate's few dolls, lying on the bed. Fond as he was of Kate's bears he'd taken against Cynthia from the outset. A po-faced, sniffy piece he'd called her, and despite the stress of his situation couldn't help a smile when he remembered an earlier occasion when he'd spread Cynthia's legs wide and left Felix lying on top of her. He recalled that Kate, usually ready to give him at least a smile in response to his cruder jokes, had not been particularly amused when she found them. Too near the mark perhaps, he thought.

When he moved on to the bedroom he was puzzled to see that all of Kate's bears still seemed to be in place. It had been the same in the spare room: the bamboo étagère in the corner packed with the many that Kate had made or bought over the years. He couldn't see that any had been taken. Roger not an enthusiast perhaps: that certainly wouldn't please Kate. Hot sex or the bears: now that would be a tough call.

By this time it was almost seven. He'd already drunk far too much on an empty stomach, and needed something to eat before he walked over to have a word with Jimmy and Celia. Back in the kitchen he opened the fridge to find that Kate had left not one but two casseroles, and sellotaped a note to the door that there were four other prepared meals in the freezer. All very caring and solicitous Kate, he thought, but it doesn't bloody help in the long run does it? Ignoring the casseroles he cut himself a couple of slices of bread and a hunk of cheese, and sat at the kitchen table gazing morosely into vacancy as he munched and sipped more whisky.

Eventually, when he knew that Jimmy and Celia would have finished their meal and be free for the evening, he locked the house and set off for the Croft. Already the worse for the whisky, and feeling very sorry for himself, he found himself thinking back to that bitter winter evening, now seeming so far away, when he and Kate had wandered across the fields to the Croft for an evening with the Gillans. The first of many very happy times together.

'When to the sessions of sweet silent thought
I summon up remembrance of things past . . .'

Oh Christ, he thought, as the lines came to him unbidden. Right on the button Kate: yet another bloody quotation dredged up from my ragbag golden treasury. And is this how it's going to be from now on: a constant looking back at the good times? And with that thought he suddenly realised just how much he was going to miss Kate. Like one of his own limbs, he'd taken her for granted, and the loss was going to be the greater for that.

As he approached the Croft he saw that Jimmy was already outside, hanging over the pig pen and scratching Sadie's back as she grunted her way through her evening meal, building up her reserves for yet another litter of piglets.

'Lovely evening Jack', said Jimmy looking up, and then returning to his back-scratching.

Giving him a half-hearted reply Jack joined him in his reflective activity, and happy as they were together with periods of silence they stood unspeaking, side by side in the calm of the evening watching Sadie lick the last of her swill from the sides of the trough, before withdrawing to gaze up at them questioningly from her litter of straw.

'Everything OK Jack?' asked Jim, who despite the competition from Sadie had no difficulty in detecting the strong aroma of whisky drifting to him on Jack's breath, and was wondering why he'd been at the bottle so early. 'Is Kate coming over?'

Jack, who continued to gaze fixedly at Sadie as though she might offer him some solace in his hour of need, ventured no reply, but simply shook his head, leaving Jim in some uncertainty whether the negative applied to both his questions, or just one, and if so which.

Jim endured the silence for another long minute or two, and then tried again.

'Smoke?'

For the first time Jack turned to Jim and it needed no more than one look at his face for Jim to know that this was no ordinary or casual visit.

'Bad news?'

'You could say that.'

Jim waited for Jack to continue, but he merely paused to light up, returned to his contemplation of Sadie, and relapsed once more into a moody silence. Unused to such taciturnity from Jack, Jim waited a few minutes and then tried again.

'Fancy a drink then, or have you already had more than enough?'

'Let's go in Jim. Celia's got to hear this some time, so it may as well be at first hand. And no, I've not had more than enough.'

Celia had been upstairs while they were talking, but she heard them in the passage-way as they came in, and was back down in the sitting room before Jim had finished pouring the drinks. Unobservant of Jack's demeanour, and believing it to be just another of his not infrequent visits, she greeted him with her customary peck on the cheek.

'Hello Jack. This is a nice surprise. Where's Kate?'

'Not a casual call love,' said Jim. 'Jack's got something he wants to say, and I think we should let him say it in his own way and his own time.'

Unseen by Jack he also managed with a very brief dumb show to advise her that Jack had already taken a good deal of booze on board.

'About ten years ago,' said Jack, having taken a good pull at his glass of Calvados, 'I was working with a chap called George Pennington: knew him well, we were quite close for a while. And one morning George comes into my office and sits down with a face as long as a kite. He'd been out with his wife the previous night, he said. A bit of a celebratory bash with some friends on their anniversary, he said, and on the way home, just a few moments before they arrived, she turned to him and said, "I do hope we aren't going to fall out over the division of the spoils."'

Having delivered himself of what he seemed to feel was a comprehensive and crystal-clear explanation of his condition and the reason for his call, Jack once again fell silent and turned to an abstracted contemplation of the empty wood burner. Celia looked at Jim with a frown of puzzlement, but Jimmy simply shrugged his shoulders to indicate that he was equally confused.

When, after a long and awkward silence, Jack returned to them it seemed that he had been expecting something other than silence on their part.

'Well?' he asked.

'Well what Jack?' said Celia.

'Well that was it, see? It was her way of telling him she was leaving him.'

That at last was enough: the meaning of Jack's anecdote and the explanation of his condition now seemed to be clear, although Jimmy was still unbelieving.

'Are you telling us that Kate . . .?' said Jimmy.

'That Kate . . .? Absolutely Jimmy boy. Right on the bloody nail. Gone. Skedaddled. Touch more class about Kate though. Left me a really stylish "Dear John" letter to find when I got home today. Wasn't that thoughtful?'

From his pocket he pulled and held up the half-dozen or so handwritten sheets that constituted Kate's letter.

'Won't embarrass either you or myself by suggesting you read it, but to put it briefly, she's buggered off to live with Roger. You'll remember Roger, you met him once. Personable sort of chap. One of my oldest friends Roger, from way back in the old days. What would we do without them eh, old friends?'

He paused, but both Celia and Jim had decided that it was best to say nothing yet: just let him run on and get it out of his system. They were surprised, however, when the next thing they heard was a drunken giggle.

'Greater love hath no man than this, than that he lay down with the wife of his friend . . . Gospel of St Jack, that Jim. Newly minted too. Not bad for a chap in my condition eh?'

Deciding now that in Jack's drunken and emotional state he was heading either for tears or laughter Celia stepped in, not with sympathy, which she felt Jack was not looking for, but with the very obvious question.

'But did she say why in her letter Jack, or give any sort of reason for what she was doing?'

'Bit tricky that one Celia. Rather embarrassing, but I can't say nothing, can I? Could lie, rather good at it in fact, but not with friends. Well if I can put it in the rather tasteful language of the agony columns, she thinks that I'm not attentive enough to her physical needs as a woman. So there you go! Sex or rather the insufficiency thereof.'

'Ah!' said Celia. Jim was silent.

'Ah!' echoed Jack, now not quite so drunk it seemed. 'Ah what? Ah sympathetic? Ah understanding? Ah, I can't think what to say? Or Ah, I'm not the least bit surprised? Did Kate talk to you about it then Celia?' His voice now had a sharper edge to it.

'Hold on a bit Jack.' Jimmy wasn't happy with the way things were going, and thought it time to chip in.

'No it's alright Jim,' said Celia. 'No of course she didn't talk to me about it Jack, any more than I'd talk about that sort of thing if it were me, although some do, and seem to enjoy it. But some while ago when I was laughing with her about our long, dark nights on North Uist, she made a few odd comments. I thought they were meant to be jokes. Never anything specific, and I certainly didn't attach any great significance to it.'

'Talked to me though, or at least tried to, if I'm honest. My fault I suppose. Too fond of voicing other people's thoughts and feelings instead of my own. She called herself more quoted at than quoting . . . Nice one that. Described our years together as happy, interesting, and in one sense full of love, and ended her letter by saying that she still loved me. . . Know anything about the works of the Blessed Augustine Jimmy?'

Accustomed as they were by now to Jack's non-sequiturs, this nevertheless took them by surprise.

'Only what little was crammed into me by the Catholic Fathers Jack: original sin, that sort of stuff. Can't say he'd be my bedside reading, if I ever did any.'

'Some good stuff here and there though if you know where to look. There's one lovely passage in the Confessions, one of my quotes that Kate actually enjoyed, where he's writing about friendship, "to talk and joke together, to do kind offices by turns; to read together honied books, (honied books, isn't that lovely) to play the fool or be earnest together, and to dissent at times without discontent."

Kate's turn of phrase brought it to mind, and I'd always thought that it was a pretty fair description of our marriage. Spot the missing ingredient – no prizes though.

And don't look so bloody woebegone for Christ's sake. I feel the better for having a talk, and perhaps Kate was right. I'm too semi-detached to be eaten up with jealousy or die of a broken heart, so let's go for a wander through the parish. I don't suppose I'll be here much longer, and we can end up with a nightcap at the Shagger.'

A couple of hours later when Albert had called time in the Shagger, and Celia and Jimmy were struggling towards the end of their third nightcap, Jack downed his drink with a flourish, fixed them with a glazed eye and a drunken smirk, and declaimed far too loudly, "His Grace returned from the wars today and pleasured me twice in his top-boots . . ." Duchess of Marlborough that, full of praise for the Duke. . . That was my big problem: no top-boots and never twice. It's a funny old life.'

'Come on Jack,' said Jim. 'Now you have had enough. Home and bed, and come over for a meal tomorrow evening. . . If you're in a fit state to remember.'

12

Barlow Scandals of 1493

When Jack's move to Barlow was being considered following the breakup with Kate, both he and everyone else assumed it would be to something small and compact. 'Bachelor pad' was the description most favoured, but having spent some time researching price movements in the town and discussing the matter with Parsons (only too happy to provide a little helpful advice to his District Inspector) Jack decided to stretch himself and take on something rather more substantial.

Secure in the knowledge that at the end of the day he had his Krugerrands to fall back on, Jack took up the largest possible mortgage offer he could find, and entered into solitary occupation of a late Victorian, four-bedroomed house at the bottom of Withy Lane. The garden was modest, but there were open views across the extensive graveyard of St Botolph's to the ancient stonework of the church itself, and Jack regarded it as a very satisfactory exchange for his nine acres up on the hill. If there was an urban equivalent of the good life, then Jack was beginning to feel that he had found it.

Situated on the opposite bank of the river from the remains of the priory and a little to the north, the area was not seen as a particularly fashionable part of town, and the houses on the little Victorian development of Riverside lacked the grandeur and status of the older, larger houses on Priory Hill and to a lesser extent the High Street. But, said Parsons, it was an up and coming area increasingly attracting the attention of those incomers whose pockets were not quite deep enough for the houses on Priory Hill. It's a good place to buy before prices there get out of hand, he said, and he was right.

Although scantily furnished at first, Jack continued and intensified the hobby he and Kate had shared of frequenting the local auction rooms and house sales. In this way over the course of almost three years he had not only furnished much of the house, but come to realise that he seemed to have a good eye for spotting a bargain, which meant that he had been able to sell on three or four items at a very decent profit, and was beginning to wonder whether he might perhaps give the game a try himself, to make a little money when he left the department.

His decision not to downsize also meant that he had been able to resolve without any difficulty the one aspect of his separation from Kate that had been troubling him, the teddy bears which she had left behind, for she had taken with her only Wilfred, a battered, old family bear from her childhood. She was over that phase of her life, she reported, now that she had all that London had to offer to occupy her. Was that an oblique reference to Roger's services Jack wondered, or was Kate spreading her wings as well as her legs? He wasn't usually that spiteful when thinking about her, but he wondered whether she really was now indifferent to the collection so lovingly built up over the years, or whether it was simply Roger's resistance to having a house stuffed full of bears.

As a few in the collection were known to be of some value (she had a couple of early Steiff and Merrythought, a Shuco, a Gebruder Bing and an early Ideal) Kate had asked that he sell them for her through a decent auction room. Instead Jack got a valuation, choked at the total, took out a loan to cover it, as he was hard pressed for ready cash at the time, and sent a cheque off to Kate in an envelope enclosing a 'With Sympathy' card. He saw no reason why he should make things easy for her.

For a couple of years the bears had simply been carefully wrapped and stored away, but as the rooms were furnished, so they came into their own again until the overall impression created by the house while undoubtedly masculine, was coloured with what Celia described as a delicious, sexual ambiguity.

Jimmy's comment was more direct.

'For Christ's sake don't let the story get noised abroad Jack. A taxman with a Teddy Bear collection! You'll lose all credibility.'

Both thought, but did not say, that for those who knew the background, the place looked a little bit like a shrine.

'He's not taken up with anyone else,' said Celia. 'Do you think he still has hopes?'

'Your guess is as good as mine love. Do you think she'd be likely to come given the chance?'

'Same answer I'm afraid.'

Far from regretting his departure from the hill as Jack had expected, Jimmy and Celia had been quite delighted with his move to Barlow. They still met regularly, and the occasional overnight accommodation that Jack provided meant that Jimmy could now indulge himself in the liquid and solid delights of The Parish Pump without stinting. And to Jack's surprise he was also displaying a newly awakened interest in ecclesiastical architecture. Although utterly dismissive of Jack's enthusiastic introduction to the masonic skills exhibited in the stone tower of All Saint's, Jimmy had now become ecstatic to the point of boredom on the constructional wonders of St Botolph's wooden spire.

'Just under one hundred and fifty feet Jack. Almost the highest, and possibly the oldest, timber-framed spire in the country. I got talking to Bill Thomas the church-warden soon after we first stayed with you. Found we'd got a common link in our wartime service. Shared the same convoys once or twice, and possibly even the same ship, although we never met up. He couldn't do enough for me then. Got to have a look at the spire from the inside. Got almost halfway up in fact. I tell you Jack, it's a bloody marvel.'

'Oh do tell me more Jim,' said Jack, but his sarcasm was lost on Jimmy, who took a deep draught of his second pint, cool from The Pump's dark cellars, and continued.

'Well it's late thirteenth century, lead-covered on oak timbers throughout, and all sitting snug on top of the tower masonry, not tied to it mind you, just sitting there, and it's straight as a die. You could drop a plumb-line from top to bottom, and it would be dead centre.'

Jack suspected that he was now being paid in his own coin for the number of times he had teased Jimmy with literary references, but he was vaguely interested in the subject and quite happy to indulge his enthusiasm.

'And that's unusual is it Jim?'

'Oh come on Jack. Think about it a bit. That stuff's been sitting up there some seven hundred years. Don't you think you might have sagged a bit in that time? And it's not just the years. This chap really knew his stuff. He'd got his hands on good seasoned timber to start with. He'd cross-braced it properly, and he'd set it on footing timbers clear of the wet. Too many of them got the construction right, but started off with green, unseasoned timber: others mixed their wood or were careless with the footings. Starting like that they didn't give the spires a chance: they either twisted, or rotted and dropped at the base. But not this chap.'

'And is this paragon anonymous, like most of his kind in those days, or do we know anything about him?'

'Yes, Bill made the same point, but he said that unusually we do know just a little. He said that much of the funding for the church came from the Barlow Merchants' Guild, and apparently a few guild records survive for the time which show payments to a Ricardus Willeson, Master Carpenter at two shillings a week. When I laughed at that Bill said that two bob a week was in fact something above the going rate for the time: only about threepence a day it seems. So our man must have had quite a reputation.'

'Two bob a week,' said Jack. 'Dear God and he probably kept a wife and family on that, and enjoyed a pint like us. Well here's to Dick Wilson, Master Carpenter, wherever his dust lies buried.'

The morning after what had proved to be a heavier than usual evening session in The Pump, Jack closed the door behind him leaving Jimmy and Celia to breakfast at leisure and then let themselves out. He'd be seeing them again at the weekend when he went back to the Croft to stay for a night or two. He'd said nothing to them, but they probably remembered as well as he did that it was three years to the day since Kate had departed. That trauma apart, however, he reckoned that things had gone pretty well: Krugerrands, promotion, the posting he wanted and even a commendatory letter from his boss at head office. Somebody up there liked him he decided.

His daily journey, diametrically across town from northwest to southeast, allowed him a variety of routes, all very pleasant walking, soured only by the final destination: his office. Leaving the river behind him he turned first into Withy Lane, an area which for many years was characterised as one of the least desirable in town. Despite later changes some taint of that earlier reputation lingered on, and was one of the reasons why the prices there and at nearby Riverside had remained so attractive for a few years.

Originally two rows of artisans' cottages interspersed with simple workshops and a couple of coach-houses, the area had slid steadily down the social scale to reach its nadir in the closing years of the war, when the activities in two or three of the houses brought accusations that the area was little more than a red light district servicing the Americans, who had arrived at the end of 1943 to set up camp on Barlow Common.

'There were two or three houses in particular,' said Elsie. 'I could point them out to you now, and the madams that were running them. Board and lodgings they called them – well that's a nice way of putting it. And they did very nicely out of it too, and now to see them about town you'd think butter wouldn't melt in their mouths.

Owned by the old Barlow gentry too, but they didn't turn down the rent did they? Nor it wasn't just the Yanks who they obliged I can tell you. I could name a few names if I'd a mind.

Mind you times were hard then, and there were a few young widows with families to bring up that I wouldn't blame for taking a pound or two from the Yanks. They always had more than enough to spare.'

Elsie was Jack's cleaner, Barlow born and bred, and highly recommended to him by Mrs Arscott for her honesty and discretion. But having heard Elsie in full spate on the red light district and other local gems after a strong gin and tonic had loosened her tongue at Christmas at the end of his first year in Barlow, Jack always took particular pains to ensure that any sensitive papers were well secured when Elsie made her weekly visit. He was not, however, above priming her from time to time to learn a little more of the local gossip.

With the coming of the housing boom Withy Lane gradually began to lose its unsavoury reputation. The old Barlow families, those who had their own houses on Priory Hill or the High Street, while content to screw what rent they could from the run-down properties, were not slow to recognise their potential as prices began to rise, and over ten years or so the cramped little artisans' houses, workshops and coach-houses were transformed and gentrified into compact, but 'deceptively spacious', cottages or mews houses.

Former knocking-shops were occupied by respectable widows, coach-houses by middle-aged divorcees, and the remaining two-up, two-down slums where Barlow's workers had once raised their families, were now bijou residences occupied by middle or upper-middle class singles. Artisans, coachmen and children may have been conspicuous by their absence, but with those who now formed the residents of Withy Lane Jack, by virtue of his regular passage up and down the lane, was soon on friendly terms. His relationship with Angela, however, a divorcee a couple of years younger than himself, had matured rapidly into a more particular and intimate affair.

Although Jack's sexual fires were more inclined to slumber than rage, he had missed his occasional comforts since Kate left, and would not have been averse to fanning the flames a little with Angela. A petite, vivacious and attractive brunette, she must have been in her late thirties, and Jack, now well into his forties, neither expected nor desired anyone younger. With Kate's comments still fresh in his mind he had no wish to be entangled with anyone too demanding.

Their recent histories meant that the relationship was exploratory on both sides: walks, coffees, a meal together at The Pump, and a trip to the theatre at Wolverton. Following the theatre Jack asked Angela to dinner at Riverside. Her thank-you kiss when she left was markedly more than friendly.

Angela returned his hospitality a couple of weeks later. She lived upstairs in one of the converted coach-houses, and as Jack passed through to her living room overlooking the walls of the castle, the door to her bedroom stood half-open. The curtains were already drawn although it was only early evening, and from one corner a table lamp threw a soft light over the bed and the negligee casually spread across its foot. It all looked very inviting.

The meal and wine were enjoyed over inconsequential chat, holidays, books, the theatre, that sort of thing; all of which Jack was certain concealed a more inviting sub-text. And with the meal over he helped to clear the table, for which he received a kiss presented with a much closer body contact than the occasion strictly required. Then they had coffee and a liqueur, and as darkness fell over the walls of the castle sat together listening to vintage Sinatra: *Maybe You'll Be There*, *Where Is the One*, and *I'm a Fool to Want You*. Familiar ballads of loneliness and longing, as the record sleeve said.

The evening, like the record, had been beautifully orchestrated, and Jack was in no doubt that Angela was only waiting for him to take the initiative, but the longer they sat, the more inhibited he became. He was increasingly haunted both by the memory of Kate's missionary position jibe, and by the dawning awareness that the familiarity he had always felt when with Angela was occasioned by her resemblance to his much loved and long deceased maiden aunt Betty, as she had been in her younger days: a resemblance that once he was aware of it seemed to strengthen each time he looked at Angela.

A second record went on to the player, some romantic ballads sung by Roberto Murolo: mementos of one of Angela's Italian holidays. In any other circumstances the songs and the voice would have been impossibly seductive, but before the record came to an end Jack realised that his situation was quite impossible. He sat there utterly incapable of action, paralysed by a vision of himself as the missionary lying naked between Angela's welcoming legs and pulling back from a kiss to see his dear, dead aunt Betty's face gazing back at him flushed with passion and wanting more. He'd feel like a bloody necrophiliac.

It was no good, he had to get away, and the sooner the better: before he let poor Angela commit herself any further. Mumbling a few pathetic thanks for a wonderful evening, he made his excuses, and leaving with a kiss which even he recognised as semi-detached, he stumbled from Angela's door into the lane.

'Arsehole. Arsehole. You stupid, fucking arsehole.'

Flushed with shame and embarrassment, he kept up the same refrain all the way back to Riverside, where he drank himself to sleep with whisky.

The memory of that sexual misadventure was still fresh enough in Jack's mind for him to look studiously ahead as he made his way up Withy Lane before turning into the abandoned churchyard of St Botolph. Glancing up at Dick Wilson's spire he smiled at the memory of his friend's new-found enthusiasm.

After the castle, St Botolph's was the oldest establishment in town. Older by almost a century than All Saints', it had at one time been the principal church of the town, but as the centre of gravity and wealth had shifted from the castle end of town towards Priory Hill and the streets around The Parish Pump, St Botolph's had entered into a slow, but irreversible decline, and it now looked as though it would not be long before it joined those other redundant churches that were to be found here and there throughout the county.

For those like Jack, however, whose taste was for the time-worn, unimproved and contemplative it had much to offer. Its graveyard, extending over more than an acre, had not, unlike All Saints', suffered a latterday equivalent of the Highland Clearances, but offered its own monumental commentary on the ravages of time and the slow movement of earth. Table tombs sagged and drooped; coffin tombs pitched and yawed, and everywhere headstones, inclining to or recoiling from their neighbours, hinted at the attachments or antipathies over three centuries of those bearing the names to be read on them, Gowring, Oseland, Boweswell and Adams: names that were still to be found every Thursday in the births, deaths and news columns of the local journal.

Nodding a morning greeting to them all as he passed, Jack moved on into the lanes of the old town, and out into Church Street to pass The Parish Pump and All Saints' church before dropping down into the Shambles, an area of small industrial enterprises where, in the thirties, the authorities had taken it into their head to build the local tax office on the site of the town's demolished abattoir.

It was a decision seized upon by the leader writer of the local rag, a man of little invention and less wit, as an excuse to take firm hold of the conceit of lambs being led to the slaughter, and systematically wring every drop of humour out of it. A framed and yellowing copy of this atrocity had been gracing a wall of Jack's office when he arrived: having been placed there in the thirties, he was told, by one of his predecessors. His first executive action had been to consign it to the rubbish bin. His second had been to ensure that an early coffee was on his desk to cheer him just as soon as he arrived each morning. This he now sat sipping as he reflected, not for the first time, on the changes recent years had brought.

Kate's departure from his life had, if anything, served only to strengthen Jack's determination to move to Barlow, as his long-held suspicion that he might after all be a town, if not a city dweller at heart was rapidly reinforced when he found himself in solitary 'enjoyment' of the house and its nine acres. Even if a sale hadn't been inevitable as part of a settlement with Kate, he was tired of responsibility for the land, had had his fill of the rural good life, and was sure that after another year or so there would be little to hold him in Barton.

Their separation, and all that it entailed, had been formalised with a divorce and settlement that had proceeded entirely without acrimony. They had met several times, mainly at Jack's request, as he was determined to keep any costs to a minimum, viewing the performance and fees of all professional men with the jaundiced eye of one who had to work with them on a day-to-day basis. Twice Roger had been of the party, but it had, nevertheless, all advanced to a conclusion on a very civilised, if not chummy basis.

Jack and Kate, having decided what they thought was an appropriate valuation for the house and land, were told by Parsons the estate agent (once again with his finger on the pulse of the market) to increase the figure by ten percent. He was proved to be right, and they were delighted when they got their asking price. With that divided equally there had indeed been no falling out over the division of the spoils, as poor old George Pennington had put it.

Why Jack always thought of George as 'poor old' George he could never quite understand, as he himself was in precisely the same boat. Like being semi-detached, it was a tendency that ran in the family perhaps, a failure to recognise in themselves what they saw all too clearly in others, and he'd frequently heard the same sort of thing from his grandmother when he saw her on his visits home, which he had made more frequently now that Kate had left him.

Much preferring his grandmother's company to that of his parents, especially as she had always regarded the political activity of her family with a faint air of distaste, he had, whenever he went home, always made a point of taking her out to the edge of the heath for a lunch at the Spaniards, where she could satisfy her taste for a good draft guinness, an indulgence not readily available to her at other times

'I mean it really wouldn't do for me to be popping into the local by myself would it darling, and your father wouldn't be seen dead near draught beer. Except for those occasions when he was out on the stump of course, and had to down one or two with potential voters. What was it you used to call them: his cloth cap days? Some of your political sarcasm I suppose. He really was upset though when it all fell through, and I did feel sorry for him.'

'Did you honestly gran? I thought it saved us all from a slow death by political pontification.'

'Yes, I can believe you did. And what about Kate, Jack? I was very fond of her. Have you heard anything of her lately, and are you seeing anyone else now in Barlow?'

'Yes to the first gran. She seems to be well and happy, but I suppose I'd be unlikely to know if it were otherwise. No to the second, but Barlow's a very comfortable barrel from which to rail at the world.'

The final part of his reply was, however, only a half-truth. He had in fact been 'seeing someone', as his gran liked to put it, but at that time found some difficulty in deciding for himself the precise nature of his association with Josie. Was it one with potential for the future, or just another semi-detached affair: even he wasn't sure.

It was on such home visits that he noticed his grandmother's habit of referring to any women who might possibly be taken as over seventy and marginally decrepit as 'poor old dears.' A strange affectation for a wrinkled and white-haired old lady who admitted to ninety, was almost certainly more, and walked with a stick.

Despite Jack's undoubted love for his granny, he would have been honest enough to admit that as her favourite he was also mercenary enough to hope for some little acknowledgment in her will when the time came. He knew the bulk of the estate would almost certainly be split between his father and his siblings (seven in all, which even at Hampstead house prices wouldn't leave much to go round) but he had for many years expressed much admiration for a matching pair of Frank Moss Bennett paintings he'd known and loved since he was a boy. His mother and sister, the only ones in the family to pretend to any understanding of painting, scoffed at his taste. Naive, sentimental stuff they called it, but he'd noticed that taste was slowly changing, the market was strengthening, and he was quite hopeful that there was an unspoken understanding between them which meant that they would in due course come his way.

Jack had, however, delayed any further return to Hampstead for a few months to allow passions to cool a little in the corridors and committee rooms of the Manning tribe. A little earlier in the year a General Election had seen Labour consigned to the political wilderness, and he simply could not summon up the resolution to submit himself to the weeping, wailing and gnashing of teeth that would await him at home.

His general alienation from the political classes had not been such, however, that he was willing to forgo the pleasures of election night: the half-concealed shock on the faces of the defeated, the ill-concealed smugness of the victors, and the platitudes ponderously trotted out by each when interviewed. Election after election they were the same, and election after election just as meaningless.

Jim and Celia had been his drinking companions through the results of a long election night, when at about three in the morning he had watched, with almost a proprietary interest, as David Butler brought him the results from Ashburton, where Labour came close to losing its deposit, and Vincent Anstruther Crispin Martindale increased the Conservative majority substantially, and assured his electorate that he would serve them diligently and honestly to the best of his ability. A couple of days after the election Jack selected what he thought was an appropriate congratulation card and sent it anonymously to Martindale at the House of Commons. 'With best wishes for the future,' he wrote. 'We once had a common interest in the cruise of L'Esperance.'

The reasons for Jack's attachment to Barlow were certainly not hard to find as its relative remoteness and insignificance in the world of the twentieth century had enabled it to escape the ravages of post-war redevelopment that had blighted so many market towns in the

Home Counties. Certainly there had been changes, but not such as to diminish the seductive charm of its ancient streets and narrow lanes, the sense of former purpose and resolve evoked by the remaining walls and battlements of the castle, its two historic churches, or the discreet aura of gracious, civilized town living that hung about the grand houses of Priory Hill.

Compared with other more ancient settlements in the county the history of the town began comparatively recently, in that there was apparently no evidence for anything further back than its foundation by the Normans in the late eleventh century. There had been a flutter of excitement among local historians when a few Roman tiles and bricks were identified in the walls of St Botolph's, but renewed efforts to carry things back a little further led nowhere.

In the immediate post-conquest years life in the Marches went a fair way towards satisfying all of the Hobbesian criteria in being nasty, brutish and short, and not even the castle could withstand the Welsh when they besieged and burnt it in 1191, leaving it and most of the town around it in ruins. But before the end of the century what was left of town and castle, together with much of the surrounding area, passed to Edmund Fitz-Alan, Earl of Arundel under whose directions both castle and town walls were re-built and massively reinforced. The Welsh, looking for easier pickings than Barlow now had to offer, turned their attention to the richer valleys to the south, and at that point Barlow castle and town effectively passed out of history.

A window of medieval glass fragments in St Botolph's was said to support the local legend that in 1403 Henry IV, weary and oppressed by the heat of July, had stopped at the priory for rest and refreshment on his way south from the battle of Shrewsbury. But that was as close as battles got to Barlow, and the ensuing Wars of the Roses passed it by, leaving the burghers of Barlow free to develop, expand and enrich themselves from the profits of its market for which the town had received a charter from King Edward I in 1301, and from the wool trade, which reached its height in the late middle ages. Just about the time, as Jack invariably added when he told the tale to visiting friends, that money-grubbing Harri Tudur (he of the bastard line) usurped the throne at Bosworth.

From the prospering citizens of the town, quite as concerned then for the future of their souls as for the weight of their purses, money flowed not only to the church, but also to the priory outside the town. This institution, however, a holy and dedicated body of thirty -five monks and fifty lay brothers at its peak in the mid-thirteenth century, had been so reduced in size by the passing years and the depredations of the Black Death that by Tudor times it amounted to no more than fifteen monks and even fewer lay brothers.

And hand in hand with that decline in numbers had come a gradual but accelerating departure from the piety and sobriety that marked the intentions of its founders, into a concupiscent life of 'such carnal and abominable abuses and manifest sin that it was an abomination.' Such had been the enormity of Barlow's clerical scandal that it had been whispered down the centuries, until finally full details were unearthed in the 1930s by a diligent researcher from the Barlow History Group who published his findings in the group's local journal. There they had languished until in 1969 a parish councillor, browsing through the journal to while away the tedium of a council meeting, stumbled upon them, and immediately recognised the tourist value of such titillating gossip.

'Carry on up the Priory' proclaimed one local rag, while its competitor's headline was 'Barlow Scandals of 1493.' Both also printed an abbreviated and journalistically enhanced version of the researcher's findings. The headlines of the two nationals that picked up the story were less inhibited. 'Priapic Prior in Passion Parlour' screamed one. 'Monks in C15 Sex Romp' was the choice in the other, with a reference to its page three, where the story was more fully and vividly reported, together with the in-house cartoonist's vision of the affair. Copies of these (the local, more restrained versions) plus a full report in the researcher's original words were in due course hung in both churches. The little local museum and most of the pubs in the town chose to display both local and national versions in anticipation of the interest likely to be shown by visitors to the town.

The evidence for this fragmentary look behind the arras in a medieval priory was to be found in the 'Comperta' or 'Things Discovered' as a result of the ecclesiastical visitation made by Bishop Robert of Hereford into the reported abuses at the Priory below Barlow. The Comperta, as reported in the two papers, was as follows:

> When Bishop Robert visited Barlow Priory in 1493 he found nothing but a deplorable state of immorality, ineptitude and disgraceful disrespect. The prior himself did not even put in an appearance, nor was any excuse offered for his absence. The sub-prior, already denounced as a profligate in reports to the Bishop, when told by one of the accompanying visitors that he was accused by the Bishop of keeping company with suspected women, replied that the Bishop and his own lumpen strumpet should be told that he cared not a turd for such suspicions, and that the Bishop should look to his own hypocrisy.

Other monks were reported as wearing strange dresses, and of being in the habit of dancing drunkenly in the guest hall at night. Women were said to enter into and out of the priory at pleasure, and when accused of unchastity the monks openly confessed it, and responded to the reforms proposed by the Bishop by blaspheming his name in public places outside the priory, and continuing as before.

Services were conducted in a slovenly and negligent manner and a litany of other religious crimes were said to have been noted, but not itemised.

The Comperta also recorded the instructions given by the Bishop following his visit: 'The Lord Bishop enjoined that henceforth no layman should be admitted to any office within the aforesaid priory until he had first pledged himself to keep faithfully the secrets of the priory.'

It was, perhaps unsurprisingly, the obscure and ambivalent nature of the Bishop's final judgment that occasioned more debate and comment in the visitors' books than any of the more salacious aspects of the affair.

Little more than forty years later, with the priory reduced to nine monks, there was little obscure or ambivalent about the judgment of Henry VIII's commissioners, Dr Layton and John ap Rice when they came calling. Whatever the truth of the matter, the old charges were resurrected by those in the town ill-disposed towards the priory. The commissioners found the monks to be 'filthy dreamers, who defiled the flesh, despised ecclesiastical dominion, and spake evil of dignities in the very spirit of the evil one.'

The muniments, plate, jewellery, vestments and other goods and property of the house were seized. The lead was stripped from the roof and melted into profits on fires made from the timber of the stalls, screen-work and fabric, and the estates were sold into the hands of

Henry's supporters. In brief anything that could be rendered into cash was. The monks were probably relieved to escape with their lives and what they had on their backs. Only Rupert Coventry the prior, on being turned out of what had been his home for almost sixty years, was granted the generous sum of Six Pounds Eight Shilling and Fourpence per annum 'because he is sick and decrepid.'

With the departure of the monks and the commissioners, the good citizens of the town moved in to mine the structure and finish the job, so that throughout the town many a fine piece of priory stonework or tracery could still be found in its walls, houses and gardens. And with that and the assistance of natural forces over the centuries the bare, ruined choirs declined gracefully into the mossy, ivy-covered, romantic haunts that attracted artists and poets in the nineteenth century and the casual tourists of the twentieth: in noticeably increased numbers following the 'Sex Romp' publicity.

But it wasn't just visitors, salacious or earnest, that were increasingly showing an interest in the unassuming delights of the town in which Jack found so much to please him. Others were coming with more serious intent.

For those like Jack who already owned their home when the madness began it was, by and large, a free ride as property values raced away, and wages piggy-backed upwards on soaring inflation, but other factors were also operating to put an additional premium on country properties with a bit of land, and on fine houses in the more desirable towns of the Border Counties.

The arrival of colour TV and the roving reporters of *Twenty Four Hours* and *Nationwide* had added a new dimension to the seeming delights of the countryside and its county towns. Fyfe Robertson canoed down the Severn extolling its delights. In *The Good Life* Tom and Barbara Goode quit the rat-race for the joys and hazards of self-sufficiency. In *One Man and His Dog*, Phil Drabble's voice and style fed peoples' nostalgia for what he called 'the deep values of true country folk,' and for those in a position to take their money and run from London and the Home Counties, where property inflation led the charge, there were dainty pickings to be found in the delights beyond the Severn, where Barlow was featuring increasingly in property magazines as a place where the living was easy.

The result was that it was not only the smallholders of Barton Hill and the countryside who were resentful of city dwellers moving in to buy up second homes, or retire from the south and push up local prices in doing so. The same was even more true in Barlow, where over the years not only did they arrive to buy, but also to settle and engage in local affairs in sufficient numbers to effect what was regarded by many locals as a sort of revolution in an accepted way of doing things that they and their fathers, and their fathers before them, had found more than satisfactory, and in so doing disturb the placid waters of Barlow society, unruffled for so many centuries: the 'us' and 'them' syndrome had arrived in Barlow.

13

The Old Adam Still Stirs the Loins

Jack had just turned forty-two when he made his move to Barlow: a time in his affairs when he was reluctantly forced to take a hard look at himself, and accept that as far as his private and professional life was concerned the tide was certainly past the flood. On the personal side he was saddened but phlegmatic at the break-up of his marriage, and uncertain whether or not he really wanted to commit himself again to any long-term relationship. His occupation was such that he'd never looked for fame or fortune, but he'd enjoyed an unexpected promotion, and was quite pleased to see how nicely the value of his Krugerrands was increasing. Now at least he could feel confident that whatever Head Office might think about the matter, Barlow would be his last posting. He could see the light at the end of his revenue tunnel, and if Head Office felt differently about it he'd tell them they could stuff the job, and freelance. He'd already been approached.

In total contrast to his chilly reception on the hill, his neighbours in Withy Lane and the little Victorian enclave by the river had been friendly and welcoming, and within a few months he had felt quite at home there. At first, despite knowing himself to be essentially non-clubbable, and not wishing to appear too distant or unforthcoming, he had accepted invitations to attend the meetings of some of the town's societies: the Music Society, the History Society, the Art Society and the Barlow Players.

He put in enough appearances at the meetings of each of these to extend his circle, and sound out those individuals he felt he would like to know better, and then one by one he let his attendances fall away with the exception of the Barlow Players, where the attractions were twofold: his lifelong passion for the theatre, and an increasing interest in Josie, the society's stage manager.

Born in nineteen sixty as the Barlow Amateur Dramatic Society, the name was changed even before the first production as soon as one of the more astute members pointed out the negative publicity value of the acronym. Born in nineteen forty as Josephine Imogen Adams, there was nothing about Josie that any but a fool would want to change, and even in her mature years most of the men who met Josie considered her to be just about as perfect a production as they come.

The Barlow Players was an active and adventurous society presenting three, sometimes even four, productions in a year under the guidance and direction of a triumvirate of the original founders, but at its heart were Brandy and Dorothy Woodvine, a couple of old pros from the days when professional repertory theatres were still just about managing to cling on to life in a few smaller towns around the country. The third of the originals was Josie, who for the first two years or so had played many of the female leads, before moving on to stage management.

Under the direction and control of Brandy and Dorothy the Players had become one of the few groups in the Midlands dedicating itself to plays from the classical repertoire, and surviving by building a loyal and enthusiastic audience for them. Jack had seen two or three of the Players' productions with Kate, and been impressed with the quality of the work. He had in his early years been an enthusiastic acting member of the local Hampstead group, where a number of romantic juvenile leads had led to some intimate and enjoyable offstage moments with his opposite numbers, but in Hampstead it had been very much a light-hearted social activity with audiences of family and friends. In Barlow with Brandy as the guiding force, however, it was a much more serious affair.

For almost three years he'd been content simply to assist the Players backstage and with routine administration work wherever and whenever he was wanted, but he resisted all Brandy's blandishments to return to the boards, even in a minor walk-on role.

'Not good for the image, Brandy,' he said. 'But anything else that I can do and I'm your man.'

Eventually, with the departure of one of the old brigade, he was asked to take over as treasurer and financial director, which would be dull and unrewarding, and as assistant stage manager to Josie, which would be neither. In fact, despite the memory of his humiliating evening with Angela, he had for some time been thinking about Josie in ways that were anything other than semi-detached. Curious and a little wary, however, of a woman so beautiful and physically attractive who had remained unmarried, he was hesitant in seeking to advance their relationship without knowing a little more about her.

The opportunity came when he ran into Brandy on the rebound from one of his regular arguments with Dorothy about the merits of the Stanislavski method, and lured him into The Pump for an evening on Prior's Pride: 5.2% abv and Charlie Arscott's strongest, guaranteed to loosen tongues much tighter than Brandy's.

'Bless you Jack,' said Brandy, having taken a long pull at his first pint. 'Dear God, my wife can be such an unbelievably infuriating woman at times. I wonder sometimes how we stayed together all these years. There I am trying to have a sensible discussion with her about a script, and all I get from her is motivation, motivation, motivation. Well eventually I said to her, "Look darling, it's really quite simple. You open the bloody door, walk on to the bloody stage, and you bloody act. I've been doing it for years, and there's absolutely nothing to it." She threw the script at me and told me to bugger off, so I did. And you my love, picked me up, dusted me down and soothed my savage breast. Bless you.'

Jack invested another pint and half-an-hour or so indulgently prompting Brandy on his favourite theme: Brandy's professional career and his theatrical philosophy, before turning the talk to the amateur stage, the history of the Barlow Players and then, subtly as he thought, to Josie.

'There's absolutely no need to be devious darling, just tell me what it is you would like to know about the lady, and as far as it is within my purview I will be only too happy to oblige.'

'Oh my God Brandy. Have I really been that obvious?'

'Well it's not just this evening Jack. I'm not the only one who's noticed how much time you spend looking at her at rehearsals. Despite your age it's really quite love's young dream, and Dot tells me that she suspects that our Josie has a reciprocal interest. That's a purely female insight though: don't want to dishearten you, but I can't see it myself, to be honest.'

'Well I'm not exactly past it you know Brandy. The old Adam still stirs the loins from time to time, and Josie's a stunningly beautiful woman. For her age there's not another in town to touch her, and even the younger ones struggle. Surely you're not surprised?'

'Oh not at all dear boy. We've all been smitten by our Josie in our time, but you should have seen her in her twenties Jack. Have a look at some of the photos of productions in the first couple of years. She was absolutely ravishing, lovely voice and she moved like a gazelle, on stage and off. Really professional in many ways, and wonderful publicity value: filled a couple of extra rows in the house when she was playing I always reckoned, and I don't mean just the men.'

'So why did she finish with acting?'

'Never really got to the bottom of that. Onstage playing a part she was totally uninhibited, a joy to watch, but off-stage she's a bit of an enigma: keeps herself very much to herself. She was determined though: nothing I said could change her mind.'

'And never married?'

'Unmarried, but not unmanned Jack. Dot and I reckon there have been two, perhaps three, over the years, but nothing permanent, and she's never said a word about them. Strictly business at rehearsals with Josie, and we don't see much of her outside. On the personal side she's tight as a clam. We bumped into her with one of her consorts a few years ago in the crush bar at the Royal Opera House. We stood and talked for three or four minutes. Would you believe it if I told you that she never once glanced at him or referred to him, and he just stood there sucking his glass the while. She's a very close lady.'

'And is she local?'

'Absolutely. One of the Barlow aristocracy. Family part of the town for centuries: literally. Have a look at the monuments in All Saints'. Her father was joint partner in Adams and Oseland, the estate agents. She took over when he died. Both parents dead now, leaving Josie the house and pretty well breached I'd say. Have you seen where she lives on the High Street, and the way she dresses?'

Jack certainly had, and there would have been few heads, male or female, that didn't turn when Josie walked by. Whether formally or casually dressed, the cloth, cut and line of her outfits bespoke the best of the fashion houses: Hardy Amies, Burberry, Jaeger, Edelstein, Charles Jourdan, with shoes by Edward Rayne, and the air around her fragrant with the scent of L'Air du Temps.

'Indeed I have Brandy, and it's a joy to follow her through town just to watch the way she moves. I like to think of her as Barlow's own immaculate conception.'

'That's very ungodly and naughty of you Jack, but I do see what you mean. Well you're a big boy now, and should be able to look after yourself, so I wish you luck in the chase.'

Of Josie, Jack learned little more, but the beer was good and Brandy was never a bore. Full of theatrical and town gossip, and delighting in name-dropping from the two seasons when he'd landed a bit-part in a West End production, it needed only a little prompting to keep him happily chatting away till closing time when they each set off for home: Jack wistfully comparing his own drab and colourless professional career with the fascination of life in the theatre, and Brandy to make his peace with Dot, and wondering how it was they had achieved so little prefessionally, and ended up running a group of amateurs in a provincial backwater.

For a few meetings of the group after his evening with Brandy, Jack looked hopefully for any indication in Josie's attitude of the reciprocal interest that Dot's intuition had detected, but without success. He determined nevertheless to press forward, and as they were winding up at the end of the next meeting asked Josie whether she would care to join him for lunch some time. To his surprise she not only agreed, but seemed quite pleased to do so.

'That would be lovely Jack. Look, I'm out on valuations over the next two lunchtimes, so shall we make it Friday at Bosewell's. That where I usually lunch, and they always have an interesting menu. Shall we say one o'clock.'

'One o'clock will be fine: looking forward to it.'

In addition to the town's more celebrated attractions, Bosewell's was also one of its landmarks. A coffee house and restaurant for over a century, it had always been Kate's choice in Barlow when Jack could be weaned away from his bitter. Although not as old as The Pump it displayed its age more overtly and enticingly, and was well patronised accordingly.

Approached beneath a pillared walkway supporting the floor and overhanging jetties of the black and white facade above, its doors opened into a deep but rather narrow room of ancient beams, half-panelled walls, curious alcoves, and immediately inside the entrance a broad, antique dresser with old plate and copper above and newspapers and country magazines below for the enjoyment of the customers. And should the weather be at all inclement there would always be a welcoming fire blazing just halfway inside, alongside a table that always seemed to be reserved for regulars whenever Jack and Kate called in. The building had an ancient staff to match the structure: grey-haired bustling old ladies, each in formal bib and tucker, who took and delivered the orders with an efficiency that belied their appearance.

Snug and comfortable it was, but not the most intimate of places for a romantic assignation, thought Jack. Farmers' wives in for a day's shopping, tourists ticking all the boxes, and those of the business fraternity who were not to be found in The Pump all combined to fill it at lunchtimes, especially on a Friday, when it could be quite a hubbub. At least he knew that Josie was reserving a table.

'I'm with Miss Adams,' said Jack, waylaid by one of Bosewell's ancient retainers assigned to intercept anyone optimistic enough to think that any of the empty tables might in fact be available.

'Oh yes sir. Would you come this way please?'

Jack eased his way past those diners already well into an early lunch, and found himself directed to a seat at the table by the fireplace: occupied by a floral display on this occasion as the weather was mild. As he sat waiting he was puzzled to find that he was apparently the object of a few curious glances from those at the tables nearby, until he saw Josie making her way from the entrance, heard how frequently she was greeted by those he took to be regulars, and realised that she was one of them and he was sitting at her table: Josie clearly had clout at Bosewell's.

'Hello Jack. Are they looking after you, and am I very late?'

'Oh well within the tolerance for a busy woman of affairs, and may I say how very elegant and attractive you look – as always.'

'Thank you Jack. Now what have they got on offer? I've had a difficult morning, and I'm ravenous.'

Jack ordered a bottle of wine, of which Josie took little more than half-a-glass, and for the next hour or so, over one of Bosewell's indifferent steaks followed by an excellent pudding, he kept up his end of their conversation while delighting in the chance just to sit there, look at Josie, and speculate on his chances in the long run. As he had said to Brandy, he felt a stirring in his loins at the very thought, but realised as their lunch drew to an end that things hadn't advanced very far, with each just learning a little more about the other, and Jack giving a heavily edited account of the break-up of his marriage. Never mind, he thought, plenty of time. Mustn't rush things, and he called for the bill.

'That was lovely Jack. Thank you. I'm going to be pretty busy with work and the production coming up in two weeks time, but after that we must do it again some time.'

Was that positive or negative? Jack spent the next three weeks alongside Josie at final rehearsals and throughout performance, but at the end was none the wiser.

Several months earlier Fate and Brandy had perversely decreed that the Players next production would be *A Flea in her Ear*, Feydeau's wonderfully farcical exploration of sexual mores and masculine inadequacy, but the very play that Kate had referred to in her final letter.

For Brandy, with the acting resources at his disposal, it was a bold choice. Farce can be difficult and demanding stuff for amateurs, but with a lot of hard work he and the group pulled it off. The houses were good. The reviews in the local papers were almost wildly enthusiastic, and at the end of the week the Barlow Players were better off in funds than they had been for years. For Jack, on the other hand, it was an agonising nightly reminder of the jibe in Kate's letter, and he was glad to see the back of it.

Things improved immediately, however, when only half-an-hour or so into the after-show party he saw Josie preparing to leave. Grasping the moment, Jack asked her if she would like to go back to the house for a quiet drink or a coffee. To his surprise she accepted, and they would have slipped away without fuss had Brandy not spotted them.

'Goodnight, goodnight my darlings,' he said. 'Wonderful work by both of you. Couldn't have done it without you. Now off you go and enjoy yourselves.'

'Oh do shut up Brandy,' said Josie as they left and set off together across the town towards Withy Lane and Riverside.

'Not keen on post-show celebrations Josie?' asked Jack.

'Not really Jack. I went to one or two in the early days, and they tended to get rather silly as the evening wore on. Not quite my style I felt.'

They walked on through the dark and silent streets of the old town without talking, and Josie offered no objection when Jack slipped a supporting arm around her waist after she stumbled, and left it there all the way back to the house.

'Just a white wine for me please Jack, and a dry biscuit to nibble if you have one please.'

For more than two hours they sat and talked together, much more relaxed and intimate now than at lunch or with the group. Jack's anecdotes of life on Barton Hill earned him some laughter from Josie, and the bear collection an unwelcome renewed interest in Kate.

'She sounds rather nice to me Jack. I think I'd like her. So what went wrong?'

'She was, and I think you would, but as for what went wrong, perhaps some other time when we know and understand each other a little better. And if we're talking about puzzles, what happened with the acting Josie? Don't want to make you blush, but Brandy's comment was that you looked ravishing, had a lovely voice and moved like a gazelle. I'd second all that by the way, but he couldn't understand why you'd chucked it.'

'Oh I don't blush easily Jack, and Brandy talks a load of rubbish sometimes. He's altogether too much of a gossip for me, but can I trust you with a confidence Jack? You come to town with a certain amount of notoriety attached: you know, your specialist activities before you came here. All the businessmen have been a bit nervous since you arrived.'

'But not you Josie?'

'Oh no Jack! I think you're a lovely man. Not pushy and shovey like some of the others.'

'Well as for trusting me, my old friend the Rev Larry Breakwell up on the hill always said that unlikely as it is, taxmen and priests have one thing in common: the secrets of the confessional. There's a recommendation for you. So what happened with the acting?'

'Oh I'm well aware Jack that men think I'm ravishing, as Brandy puts it, but doesn't the very word say it all? And I know full well what most of them are thinking when they look at me. Not that I mind the thought: complimentary I suppose, if I can be objective about it. But in the group I always got lumbered with the young romantic leads, and I just got tired of all the kissing and close-contact stuff that came with them. Too many of the men seemed to feel it gave them some sort of licence backstage. Too much hugging, touching and sticking heads round the door when they knew I was changing. All very tiresome. Best to drop it altogether, and keep them at arm's length.'

'And I'm arm's length am I Josie: sort of semi-detached?'

'Now why on earth do you say that? No that's not what I mean at all. But you don't come on at me as some of the others did. I like that.'

'Sorry. A rather poor in-joke with Kate. Forget it. Nothing to do with us.'

'Good, now that's out of the way. Well it's getting late, and I have to go soon, but now that we know one another a little better I wondered whether you'd like to go with me to the opera in the next month or so. I know you're a straight theatre man at heart, but it's Domingo in *Otello* at Covent Garden, and I have a London contact who tells me he has tickets. I'm sure you'd be converted.'

'Well I'd love to hear Domingo, but that's a hell of a long haul for a night at the opera Josie. Over three hours each way.'

'Oh I wasn't thinking we'd come back the same night Jack. In fact I thought we might go up the day before, and have the two nights in town together . . . Well don't just sit there silent. You do want to sleep with me don't you?'

After what she'd said only a few moments earlier Jack looked at her speechless, half in amazement and half in admiration at the calm way in which she had dropped her bombshell. Then he burst into laughter.

'Oh Josie, you're priceless. After all you said about men earlier. Of course I want to sleep with you. In fact I thought and hoped we might adventure a little beyond sleeping.'

'Good, now we've got that settled. I'll organise the tickets tomorrow, and book a room at a really lovely little hotel I know. You will be able to get time off in the week will you? I hate London at weekends.'

'Josie, for this I'd go AWOL.'

'Of course you would. And we go Dutch on this Jack. No arguments. I'll arrange everything, and we'll sort it out later. Now kiss me goodnight.'

Josie telephoned him the following evening.

'Thursday week for the opera Jack. We're almost central in the Grand Tier: excellent view and pretty good sound. We'll go up in the morning and stay over that night and Friday, returning on Saturday. Will that suit?'

'Anything would suit Josie. Can we meet before then?'

'Not sure about that Jack. I think it might spoil things. . . . No I think not. Pick me up at home about ten on the Thursday. We'll get the next train up, and that will give us time to drop our things off at the hotel and have just a light snack before the performance. That's all I ever want before a show. Is that OK?'

'A torment to wait, but otherwise absolutely perfect.'

'Love you. Bye.'

Love you: Jack didn't allow himself to attach too much significance to that. He understood that his relationship with Josie was going to be altogether different from that with Kate, and was intrigued at the prospect before him.

With Josie making the arrangements they travelled First Class to Paddington and took a taxi to Le Rendezvous, a little hotel in Montague Street, just behind the British Museum, where Josie seemed to be quite well known.

'So nice to see you again Miss Adams. Quite a while now since you were last with us. It's the same little suite that you said you liked so much on your previous visit. Let me take your cases for you.'

'Thank you George. Not retired yet then?'

'Oh no miss. Can't afford to.'

Jack wasn't by nature a parsimonious man, but even before he saw the suite he'd got the measure of Josie's 'lovely little hotel' from the decor and furnishing of the hall, and was making some rough calculations of his share of the probable final cost. First class on the train, taxi to hotel, mini-suite in a 'Boutique Hotel' and Grand Tier at the opera: just about as much as he'd paid a few years earlier for an extended weekend for two when he took Kate to Venice. For a moment he felt a twinge of regret at the thought of that, but he kept his eyes on Josie's shapely legs leading the way up the stairs ahead of him, and it didn't trouble him for long.

Pressing a generous acknowledgment into George's hand as he closed the door, Jack looked around at a modest-sized sitting-room very comfortably furnished which opened into a spacious bedroom with en-suite facilities that Jack could only have described as sumptuous: he added ten percent to his rough calculations. Both rooms overlooked a well-maintained area of common gardens shaded by trees.

'Now it will take me a while to unpack and take a shower before we leave for the ROH, but if you want to come in to shave or freshen up don't be embarrassed.'

Jack held that thought in his mind for a while with some pleasure. He found the prospect immensely attractive but ultimately rather voyeuristic, as he knew that he had more than enough time to freshen up while Josie unpacked. This he did, and then returned to the sitting-room leaving Josie to proceed at leisure.

Opening the window he let in the incessant background hum of London's traffic, and lighting a cigarette looked out across the trees to the parallel terrace of house, and wondered how things were with the family. The last time he'd spoken with his sister she'd told him that their grandmother seemed to be failing at last, but on this occasion he didn't really want to get tangled up with a family visit, even if it was only a few miles up the road.

Disturbed by a noise, he looked round to catch a glimpse of Josie, only half-covered by her bath robe, slipping into the bedroom to get dressed. It was enough for him to realise that had he then been told that Domingo had let them down and the performance been cancelled he would not have been overwhelmed by disappointment, but there was nothing for it: he would just have to be patient.

Allowing Josie enough time to dress, he then returned to sit and watch her putting the final touches to her presentation for the evening, and had to admire the skill with which she applied her cosmetics.

'It's always been a mystery to me how women do that with such skill,' he said. 'It's a bit like the master-painter adding that final touch of red to a composition of blues and greys that brings the whole scene to life. Very skilful.'

She smiled, looked hard at her reflection in the mirror, and then stood up in front of him.

'Will I do?' she asked.

'Absolutely bloody gorgeous Josie.'

'Very delicately put Jack. . . . No, not a kiss before we leave. Mustn't spoil the wet paint. Now we'll order a taxi to go, but stroll back afterwards. It's only about fifteen minutes from here. I'd better give you the tickets. I don't want to be fiddling about with them in the theatre.'

It had been an unspoken understanding that Jack paid for taxis, tips and all other cash outgoings of their time in town. It was all very discreetly done, no divvying up in public, but he had no doubt that when Josie said they were going Dutch she meant it, and that she would insist on a strict final accounting.

Arriving in the crush bar in good time to find seats at one of the small side tables, they sat each with a glass of wine and a couple of smoked salmon sandwiches, the cost of which had been an utter revelation to Jack. Did people actually come here regularly, he wondered, and then realised that Josie, if not a regular, obviously knew her way around. As Brandy had once put it, she must be a very warm woman in her own right.

He noticed too, how frequently other men seemed to let their looks linger on Josie just a little too long, and recalled Josie's earlier comment about that. Well he thought, as Josie said, let them enjoy their dreams: I'm the chap with the reality ahead of me. And at the thought of that reality he wondered whether he really was going to be able to keep his mind on a performance which he knew had received rave reviews, rather than the later part of the evening. He knew he could be totally involved and easily moved by a piece of good theatre: to tears at times, something that Kate had always found embarrassing. He had no idea, though, how he might respond to the operatic format.

Throughout the first act he enjoyed the music and appreciated the quality of the singing, but felt that on the whole he really would rather be watching the Shakespeare. At the end of second act, however, as the lights came up for the interval, Josie turned to him with a smile and the simple question, 'Well?' And Jack found that he was so choked with excitement that for a few moments he was unable to speak, and could only shake his head.

'Are you alright Jack?'

'Oh absolutely. Totally overwhelming though. I could feel my heart pounding.'

'I thought you were breathing a bit heavily.'

'Oh, I thought the heavy breathing came later.'

'That's enough Jack. You're in the Grand Tier remember. Now buy me a drink.'

They returned to the crush bar, now rather a noisy scrum, where Jack, with a glass in each hand, turned from the counter to find himself face to face with Martindale and almost tipping the wine on to his shirt front. The recognition was instant and mutual.

'My apologies,' said Martindale.

'No, my fault,' said Jack. 'Breathtaking performance!'

'Quite outstanding.'

Jack squeezed his way back to Josie who stood sipping her drink for a few moments looking around the crowded room.

'Who was it you spoke to at the bar Jack? He seems to have been looking this way ever since.'

'Oh just another opera enthusiast Josie. Quite a few other men have been looking this way too, and I can't say I blame then.'

It was a mild, still night when they left after more curtain calls than Jack had ever heard in straight theatre. Once away from the throng of taxis at the entrance the roads were quieter, but the pavements still busy with theatre-goers on their way home. Up Drury Lane and Museum Street they strolled hand in hand into the silent streets leading to the hotel, where George was still on duty to open the door and welcome them.

'Good performance Miss Adams?'

'Wonderful George. Goodnight.'

'Goodnight miss. Goodnight sir.'

Jack rather hoped that it would be.

14

A Little Touch of Josie in the Night

The suite was softly lit by two bedside lamps. On a side-table in the sitting-room stood two glasses and a covered plate of sandwiches. A bottle of Champagne was chilling in a bucket of ice alongside. Jack added another percentage to his total, but considered that the return was going to be worth it. Josie lifted the bottle from the bucket and inspected the ice.

'I think we can afford to leave this for quite a while yet,' she said, and walked through into the bathroom.

Wondering what on earth that remark signified, Jack followed her into the bedroom, hung up his jacket, removed his tie, and slipped on the bedroom slippers provide courtesy of the management.

He had recognised for some time that he had been assigned the principal male lead in an elegantly designed, romantic French farce: plot, costumes, direction and management all by Josie Adams. It was one of that popular, but totally unrealistic genre where everything ends in blissfully happy reconciliation, despite the many serious marital misdemeanours along the way.

They were midway through the last act Jack decided, and he was in the wings, straining upon the start of the seduction scene: the scene that takes place off-stage prior to the denouement, and is only reported, can only be reported, as the seduction (his seduction) will be carried to consummation. Dialogue and action, as throughout, would be improvisational, with Josie leading the way. Jack was very happy with his role, and had absolutely no uncertainty about his motivation.

After a few minutes Josie reappeared from the bathroom trailing a slightly heavier, more provocative fragrance behind her.

'It's all yours Jack,' she said, and sat down at the vanity unit to brush her hair.

When Jack returned Josie was already half-undressed, and stood placing a neatly-folded slip with her other clothes on the bedside chair. He could see no sign of a nightdress, and had his first uncertainty about the action. Apart from two misconceived undergraduate encounters, Jack had always been a one-woman man. With Kate, apart from a few occasions which all seemed to have occurred when they were on holiday, there had always been what they saw as respect for the other's privacy. Nightclothes were worn, and sex took place between the sheets, with nightclothes removed or not, as the occasion demanded or their inclination took them. Sex en plein air, so to speak, had not featured in his calculations, but his pyjama trousers, which fortunately he had not taken from his case, clearly did not feature in Josie's scenario.

These thoughts led him instinctively to half-turn away as he undressed, and his inability to take his eyes off Josie had slowed him down rather, so that he was only starting to unbutton his shirt as Josie stepped out of her last, lacy stitch with a little movement of her legs that Jack found desperately provocative.

Despite exercising regularly he knew that since giving up sport more than ten years earlier he had accumulated a little slack around the waist. If Josie has any slack, he thought, it's in the right places, in precisely the right amounts and looks delightful. Everywhere else is firm, smooth, youthful and utterly seductive. She was rising forty, looked less than thirty, and could be as fascinatingly irritating as an over-confident undergraduate.

He was irredeemably besotted, and wondered, not for the first time, why me?

Meanwhile Josie stood quietly smiling at him, and without thinking he had paused in his unbuttoning.

'Why Jack Manning, I do believe you're shy. You're not worried about your image are you?'

'Oh God,' groaned Jack. 'So Brandy told you about that!'

'Here let me do that,' she said, as he fumbled with the last few buttons. With the shirt removed, she took his hands, and holding him at arm's length looked him over approvingly, but in such a way that despite his best endeavour he couldn't withhold a blush. Dear God, he thought, I haven't blushed since I was a teenager.

'No problem at all about your image Jack,' she said. 'A fine, upstanding figure of a taxman, if I may say so. Now come with me Mr Inspector.' And pulling him towards her, they toppled over onto the bed.

Now Jack understood completely. This was sex as a saucy bedroom romp, with no strings attached. The game was entirely new to him, but Josie seemed to know the rules, and he was eager to learn.

'Some refreshment now I think Jack. Will you open the champagne while I pop into the bathroom?'

As Josie slipped from his arms Jack rolled over to look at his watch. About forty-five minutes had passed since they dropped together onto the bed. It seemed longer to Jack, but even that was about three times longer than his occasional engagements with Kate had been taking. He suspected that had been his fault, as Josie, with the greatest of tact, had managed to restrain his enthusiasm until she was ready to join him.

The affair had opened conventionally enough, but as far as Jack was concerned, Josie seemed to imbue even the conventional with a new and exciting dimension, and as the conventional evolved into something beyond Jack's previous experience he might perhaps have understood what Kate meant in her letter. But Jack was far too involved with the matter in hand, Josie, to give a thought to anything but the enjoyment of the moment.

Slipping into his robe, he walked through to the sitting-room, where he opened and poured the champagne. He was sitting gazing dreamily at the bubbles in his glass and reflecting, with some satisfaction, on the way the evening had proceeded, when Josie walked through, naked as she had left the bed, picked up her glass, and stood before him slowly sipping the champagne.

'Josie!'

'Jack?'

'If we're going to have time to enjoy our refreshments please, please slip into the robe provided.'

As she pouted and turned towards the bedroom for her robe, Jack gazed in admiration at the seductive movements of her retreating buttocks, but overwhelmed by another thought, was unable to suppress a giggle.

'And what was the giggle about,' she asked when she returned. 'You weren't laughing at my bum were you?'

'Perish the thought Josie. I think it's a lovely bum – classical perfection in fact, just like the rest of you. No it was another thought. One of my apparent failings: quotation incontinence. An inclination to live my life through the thoughts of others.'

'And what was the quotation that came to mind as you sat admiring my classical perfection Jack?'

'A little later perhaps Josie. When I can turn it to my advantage.'

'All right then. What about opera? Are you now sold on it?'

'Was tonight typical?'

'Sadly not Jack. Tonight was perhaps the best of the best, performed by the best. You don't get many nights like tonight – I mean the opera. I don't really see you as a Wagner man, but perhaps we could try some Puccini or Mozart later on.'

Jack liked the implications of 'we.'

With an appetite sharpened by opera and exercise they did a pretty fair demolition job on the sandwiches, and the champagne bottle was empty when Josie came over to Jack and sat on his lap.

'Now Jack. I'm going to bite your ear lobes until you let me hear that quotation.'

'Very well, then listen carefully. It's seventeenth century, and anonymous.

My love in her attire doth show her wit,

It doth so well become her.'

Jack kissed the back of her neck.

'For every season she hath dressings fit,

For winter, spring and summer.'

He slipped a hand under the top of her robe, which Josie removed.

'No beauty she doth miss

When all her robes are on;'

Jack slipped a hand onto her thigh, and this time encountered no resistance.

'But Beauty's self she is

When all her robes are gone.'

Jack's hand slipped a little further, and Josie's robe fell from her shoulders on to the floor, as she settled herself more comfortably on his lap.

Almost half-an-hour elapsed before Josie led Jack back to the bedroom.

'Mr Manning,' she said. 'You're a very remarkable man and full of surprises. And now bed, and sleep. But before we do, you told me earlier that quotation incontinence, as you put it, was alleged to be one of your failings. Well that hardly seems to me to be grounds for divorce, so now that we know one another a little better,' (what a lovely understatement thought Jack) 'perhaps you'll tell me about the others.'

'Ah,' said Jack. 'There was a time when I would have found that question a little too embarrassing to answer, but after our evening together I think I can tell you. It was alleged, now how can I put it? It was alleged that I was not attentive enough as a husband.'

'I don't believe you Jack, not after tonight.'

'I think it was the frequency of my attentions that was the particular ground of complaint Josie, or rather the lack of it.'

She thought about that for a moment or two.

'I've always believed that with clothes and shoes it was always the quality not the quantity that counted, and I think it's the same with sex. I've decided that Kate, after all, must have been a very silly woman.'

Slipping into a bed which was described in the hotel literature as 'California King – Special Import,' Jack negotiated his way across a wasteland of sheet to slip his arm around Josie, and cuddle up to sleep his way through what was left of the night – that had been standard procedure with Kate.

'Jack darling,' said Josie. 'I don't want you to feel rejected, but I do like to have plenty of my own space when I'm sleeping. It's just the habit of many years I'm afraid.'

Jack regretted the loss of his cuddles, but giving Josie a goodnight kiss between the shoulder blades he made his retreat to the other side of the bed, where he began to sing softly.

'Jesus bids us shine with a pure clear light,
Like a little candle burning in the night.

In this world of darkness, so let us shine,
You in my small corner, and I in mine.'

He hadn't quite completed the final line before Josie's leg reached out across the bed and delivered a firm kick to his rump.

'Well you just remember to keep to your small corner until morning young man – and no marauding.'

For the rest of the night Jack slept the dreamless sleep of a man who had already seen all his dreams come true, and would have slept longer had he not been shaken gently by Josie.

'This is your early morning call sir, and I'm just about to take a shower. It'll be a tight squeeze, but I wondered whether you would like to join me.'

'Can't think of a better way to start the day than another tight squeeze with you Josie, but isn't it rather early for that.'

'That's enough Jack. This is strictly showering only, although I might allow you to soap me down a little if you can control yourself.'

With the events of the previous night in mind, and his own performance in particular, the Duke of Marlborough was very much in Jack's mind that morning, and he couldn't resist telling Josie the story, as he indulged himself, as far as he was allowed, during the soaping operation. But her permissiveness had its limits, and willy-nilly Jack had to curb his enthusiasm, and he was eventually left alone in the shower when Josie slipped out to dry. He was still towelling down when she returned wrapped in her bathrobe.

'I'm just going to ring down for breakfast Jack. After last night will it be the high energy breakfast you're wanting, or just toast and water to do penance for an evening of such gross self-indulgence?'

'Oh Josie, but that was just foreplay. We have another whole day ahead of us.'

'Now you're bragging.'

The whole of the morning was devoted to shopping, as Josie led Jack on a trail around her favoured sources for clothes and shoes, an experience which surprisingly did not induce the onset of deep boredom as was usually the case. He was quite content to sit, admire Josie, and smile approvingly at whatever she paraded in front of him. But by the end of the morning, having applied her quality controls for clothes, shoes and sex strictly throughout, she sat in the taxi with just two outfits, one pair of shoes and two sets of underwear. Giving the taxi driver an address she turned to Jack.

'And now Jack you're taking me to my favourite Turkish restaurant for lunch. It's very select, and it was difficult to get a reservation at short notice, so best table manners please, and no outrageous flirting.'

'Yes miss. Understood miss, and rewards for good behaviour later in the day please miss.'

The Caravanserai was an intimate little place tucked away in a courtyard off Shepherd Street. Not more than fifty covers Jack estimated, and despite its cuisine more French than Turkish in style. Unfamiliar with the dishes, he suggested that Josie give a lead.

'Well, we have the whole of the afternoon ahead of us, so I think just a light lunch and a glass of wine. The desserts are too sweet for me, so I'm just going to pick at an anchovy pilaf and start with my favourite, Imam Bayildi.'

'Translation please.'

'It means the Imam fainted, the dish was so delicious. And it really is: eggplant stuffed with all sorts of goodies and simmered in olive oil.'

'The pilaf sounds fine, but not the aubergine: can't stand them.'

'Try the grilled koftes then: meat based, very spicy and tasty.'

They finished with Turkish coffee: new to Jack who was an instant convert. The bill he paid by card, the tip in cash. It was accepted with a discretion which left him uncertain whether it had been too much or too little. On the way back to the hotel he reflected on the implications of their light lunch with the whole of the afternoon ahead of them.

With her shopping safely put away Josie turned to Jack and gave him a little kiss.

'Now Jack. We have the whole of the afternoon before us, and we are going to have a very leisurely time. Very leisurely Jack. To start with you will undress me, and then I will undress you. Are you happy with that?'

'Blissfully,' said Jack.

As Josie was wearing only a light dress and her underclothes, Jack could think of little he could do to comply with the order to proceed leisurely other than to kiss each newly exposed area of Josie as he proceeded. This he did lovingly and lingeringly to Josie's smiling but unspoken approval.

Even so it was not long before he eased the final flimsy garment from Josie's feet, when he was seized with a sudden and quite untypical flash of erotic imagination. Dropping to one knee he lifted a foot and kissed it, moved on to instep, next ankle, then calf and knee, and so upward and upward to conclude at the last with a light kiss on Josie's lips.

'Why Jack, you are full of surprises. I liked that, very exciting. Now give me a proper kiss before I do my bit.'

Things had moved so rapidly after their return from lunch, however, that Jack had removed only his Jacket,

239

and hardly had Josie started than she was struggling with the knot on his tie.

'For heaven's sake Jack! Why do men wear these stupid things? Give me a hand to get it started. . . . And don't laugh. Surprising as it might seem to you I haven't done this before.'

Jack loosened the tie enough for Josie to pull it over his head, and then stood smiling as she unbuttoned his shirt and struggled to drag it free from his trousers.

'I can't say that I speak with the voice of experience Josie,' he said. 'But I really do feel that I made a better fist of this little exercise than you're managing.'

She gave him a slap on the chest, and then mumbled sorry and kissed him. Anticipating the next problem he lifted his foot so that she would have an easier time with his shoes, and eventually her task was done. Jack felt rather relieved that she made no attempt to emulate his finishing touch.

'Now we'll just lie down together and enjoy a few minutes of kissing, touching and stroking.'

'You lead, and I'll follow,' said Jack.

And then began a leisurely, lingering afternoon of kissing and caressing; of twisting and turning and broken murmurs of delight; of touching and stroking and sinuous intertwinings; and of frontal, flanking and rearward assaults in which Jack was constantly frustrated by Josie's determined evasive action, until delighted and frustrated with the game in equal measure, he fell back onto his pillow alongside her.

'Oh Jack surely you aren't giving up yet? But perhaps you're right: we'll just lie quietly for a while, and then start again from the beginning. That would be nice.'

By now the afternoon sun was shining full across the bed where Josie lay, eyelids briefly closed, and Jack, close alongside was content to lie and admire the soft haze of illuminated body-hair and the gentle flexing of breasts and body to her soft breathing. Then the pattern of breathing changed and he saw her, eyes wide open, smiling at him.

'No quotations for this afternoon Jack?'

He thought her question over for a few moments, and then easing across her body, insinuated himself between her thighs.

'Once more into the breach, dear friend, once more?'

'My God Jack you really can be impossibly crude. . . but I like it,' saying which she embraced him with legs and arms.

'No quarter given or taken,' she added.

'And no prisoners,' said Jack. 'Prenez garde.'

After that final vigorous and extended assault of the afternoon they dozed for an hour or so, and Josie offered no objected when Jack draped his arm around her.

'You know Mr Manning,' said Josie as they drowsily roused themselves to shower. 'I think I know now that we are going to be very good friends.'

'Just friends is it Josie?'

'Oh yes Jack, just friends, but very special friends.'

'Special friends like these two days you mean do you Josie?'

'I do indeed Jack – just like these two days. We will pleasure one another, as the Duchess so delightfully put it, whenever we feel so inclined, but you're excused the top-boots, and I don't think we'll need to leave Barlow again. Not unless we want to that is.'

'And will there be other special friends too Josie?'

'Of course not Jack; not while you're my special friend.' Jack didn't feel inclined to pursue it any further than that.

Friday was late opening at the British Museum, so when they had showered and dressed, Jack took Josie for a preprandial stroll around his favourite gallery, that for Medieval Europe. He wasn't sure that Josie found the exhibits as breathtaking as he did until he called her back to a display which included a small collection of reliquary busts.

'Well I'm damned,' he said. 'I remember on my first visit to the Players I had this strange feeling that you and I had already met somewhere at some time in the past. I fell for that little lady on my first visit here,' He pointed to one of the busts. 'Look. There. The colourful one with the golden hair: unknown female saint.'

'Nothing very saintly about me for the last couple of days Jack.'

'No, thank God, but braid and plait your hair, and dress you for the period, and you could be her sister. Same high forehead, same fine cheekbones and classic nose, and the same come-to-bed eyes. Odd that in a saint.'

'But she's beautiful Jack, and you think I look like her. . . . Well thank you for the compliment, and have a kiss.'

They slummed it that evening in a Pizza House nearby, with a bottle of wine and after-coffee liqueurs. Following the extended and energetic encounters of the afternoon that soon had them drowsy, and by a little after eleven they were in bed and settling down to sleep, each on their own side of the hotel's enormous special import. Almost like an old married couple, thought Jack, were it not for the acres of bed between us, and the fact that Josie clearly isn't thinking along those lines.

In Barlow they walked up from the station together and parted at Josie's front door in the High Street.

'Gorgeous couple of days Jack, but remember strictly business between us when we are back with the group. Next time we must get together here. Love you.' She gave him a peck on the cheek, and had half-turned to enter when she turned again.

'Oh to hell with the bloody neighbours: they can think what they like. Come here Mr Manning, and kiss me goodbye properly.'

It was a long and lingering goodbye that Jack was still relishing as he made his way through the lanes of the old town, into Withy Lane and past the door of the lonely Angela, completely forgetful now of his earlier, embarrassing assignation with that loving lady.

15

We're All Bloody Plutocrats Now

It was a quiet time with the Barlow Players after the success of *A Flea In Her Ear*, with no meetings scheduled for six weeks, when Brandy was planning to start rehearsals for a production of *Uncle Vanya*. During those six weeks Jack and Josie met and pleasured themselves several times, but they were brief evening or afternoon communions at one or the other of their houses, and they never quite re-captured the first, fine careless rapture of their London revels. They were discussing the prospect of a long spell together, perhaps a week's holiday early the following summer, but neither seemed inclined to move into permanent residence with the other.

As Josie had requested, Jack kept their relationship very much at arm's length and businesslike whenever they met at the group for rehearsals, but as he had always believed, it was an utterly pointless exercise.

'Lucky chap Jack,' said Brandy, when they came together for a few moments during a coffee break. 'Much envied by all the chaps I'm sure, a few of the girls too perhaps, but I can't understand why the dear lady insists on this charade within the group. The town's far too small, and you were of course seen departing and returning.'

'And I'm still wondering why me, Brandy. Wouldn't have any views on that would you?'

'When it comes to Josie I wouldn't dare to speculate Jack, but enjoy it while it lasts.'

Jack might have thought that a strange remark, had he not remembered Brandy's earlier reference to Josie having two or three men over the years, but nothing permanent.

'But back to business,' continued Brandy. 'Dot and I have been talking over the casting for *Vanya*, and feel that despite her age, Josie still looks so young she'd be perfect for Yelena. Now that you know her a little better, if I can put it like that, do you think I could tempt her back?'

'You mean you'd like me to use my good offices to persuade her, do you Brandy?'

'Your good offices! Oh what a lovely euphemism Jack. Yes, use your good offices by all means, and anything else that comes to hand, if only you can persuade the lady to return.'

They were interrupted by a howl from Dot, who had been sitting nearby reading the latest edition of the Barlow Recorder.

'Bloody hell Brandy, I do believe the buggers are at it again: just have a look at this.'

'Her voice was ever soft, gentle and low Jack, an excellent thing in woman. . . . Oh speak again bright angel.'

Dodging the swipe she aimed at him, he took the paper and quietly looked over the offending article, a letter on the local arts scene signed by Neophilist (Name and address supplied).

'Oh dear,' he said. 'I do believe our Dorothy is right. The buggers are indeed at it again. Gather round gentles all: perpend and give ear.'

'Oh my God!' said Dot to Jack. 'I wish I hadn't started this. He simply can't resist the chance to wrap his tonsils round his vowels in public. He can be such a bloody bore at times. . . . Do you have to Brandy?'

He ignored her.

> I understand that the next production of the Barlow
> Players is to be *Uncle Vanya*, which, despite the un-
> doubted success of the Barlow Player's last production
> leads me to ask just how much longer the people of Bar-
> low must accept the tired old diet of traditional 'classic'
> drama presented to them by what appears to be a little
> clique determined to foist their narrow and elitist
> agenda on a town which I am sure would be only too
> pleased to see something with a little more appeal to
> the population at large.
>
> We've had plays from France, from Russia, from Italy,
> Norway, America, Ireland and from Timbuktu for all I
> know. What about a few plays from England (and I don't
> mean Shakespeare) like those filling the theatres in the
> West End. Isn't it time there was a little fresh thinking
> from the Players?

'Timbuktu? Don't know anything from Timbuktu do
we Dot?' said Brandy. 'Some interesting stuff from
Kenya and South Africa, but not for Barlow I think.
Well let Mr Neophilist huff and puff all he likes, if the
needs arises we'll see them off as we did last time.'

'So what's it all about Brandy? What happened last
time?'

'Oh it's all a part of the them-and-us syndrome Jack.
Been going on for years now, ever since the property
boom brought the first buyers up from the south with
wallets fat enough to freeze those with old Barlow blood
out of the market. Trouble was though that they froze
out old Barlow influence too, getting seats on the council, and positions on local committees and clubs.

Since then it's always been there, simmering away
below the surface: local resentment against newcomers
who all too often were better breached, better informed
and had more strings to pull than the locals.

It gets a bit heated at times, but as far as I'm concerned I can't think of a more thoroughly entertaining

sight than that of the respectable, churchgoing burghers of a fine old English country town busily trying to cut each other's throats through the columns of the local rag. Beats the *News of the World* any time.'

'And although you're not exactly old Barlow yourself, you fell foul of the newcomers too did you Brandy?'

'Nothing we couldn't handle Jack, nor do I always object to what they're after. If it hadn't been for them in the late sixties the Mayor and the business cronies who supported him, bloody vandals, would have moved the old market cross and torn up the cobble-stones for a car park extension. Got more than they bargained for though: ended up with a national campaign and a camera crew from the Tonight programme down here to report on the potential atrocity. Nothing more heard then about taking up the cobbles.

Now that I agreed with, but then the Bloody Philistines had a go at the Barlow Players. Same whinge as now: thought our programme was too elitist. Well of course we're elitist I told them. If we weren't, who would be: elitist and bloody proud of it.

Then they infiltrated the group over the course of a year or two and tried their hand at a take-over. Wanted a diet of *Quiet Weekend, Not Now Darling* social evenings and cocktails. We soon saw the buggers off though Dot, didn't we? Leafleted and organised our regular supporters, called a general meeting, and overwhelmed them. Then I had a quiet word with our few dissidents. Explained what the group was all about, and in brief told them they could fit in or fuck off. Most did the latter, but a few stayed on to do some bloody good work. And now I suppose we'd better get down to some.'

Jack passed on Brandy's thoughts to Josie the next time they were in bed together, which was where they seemed to do most of their talking.

'I don't think there's any doubt the chaps will be as keen as ever to stick their heads round the door when you're changing, but in the circumstances I think I could offer you my protection if you feel like having a run at Yelena.'

'That's very gallant of you Jack, and typically devious of Brandy. Did he actually suggest that you should make the offer while we were in flangrante delicto? I wouldn't put it past him. He's quite without shame when it comes to a production.'

'Not quite, but everyone knows about us of course, and is puzzled that we keep up the arm's length charade at the group.'

'Of course they are, and that's the way I like to keep them: puzzled. They're all far too interested in other people's affairs. And you can tell Brandy bloody Wood-vine that he can look elsewhere for his Yelena.'

Although Jack hadn't been back to Barton for some months, he and Jimmy spoke regularly on the phone. He knew that Celia's father had died, and that changes were in the offing on the hill, so he was not surprised when Celia telephoned him, and asked him to join them over the coming weekend.

'Come on the Friday and stay overnight. Stay two if you can, and bring Josie with you if she'd like to come. We'll have Larry staying with us, by the way. A few surprising changes there and elsewhere that we need some time to talk over. I've had a word with the Simpsons who bought your old place and they're quite happy for you to park there and walk over to us whenever you like. Looking forward to seeing you and hopefully to meeting Josie.'

Jack had told Jimmy about Josie shortly after their London weekend together, and he understood that the call came from Celia just to make it absolutely clear to him that she, as well as Jimmy, was very happy to welcome Josie despite her own closeness to Kate, with whom Jack knew she had kept in touch, meeting her from time to time when she passed through London on her visits to her father.

Josie knew the area well by virtue of her profession, and Jack had told her a little about the Gillans and his own years on the hill, but she was surprised when Jack mentioned Gollins Croft in passing on Celia's invitation.

'Why I know it Jack. It was the very first time Daddy took me on a valuation with him. Owned by a strange old couple then. Very ancient and romantic, but terribly tumbledown if I remember correctly. The building that is, not the couple, and in other circumstances I'd be interested to meet the Gillans and see what they did with it, but there would always be an elephant in the room wouldn't there? Not a polite way to refer to Kate, but you know what I mean. No, all in all, I think it would be better if I passed on this one.'

It was almost dark, and late autumn mists were beginning to settle in the valley below when Jack parked on his old drive, gave a wave to the new occupants, and set off over the fields to the Croft. On this occasion there was no hoar frost, and he needed no lantern, but as he made his way across the fields it was impossible for him not to recall that earlier visit with Kate clinging to his arm to avoid stumbling in the rough grass, and the whole of their time on the hill ahead of them.

It was a melancholy thought and it left him uncharacteristically subdued. So much so, that even as Jimmy welcomed him into the passageway he seemed to detect his wistfulness.

'Are you alright Jack? Nothing wrong is there?'

'No nothing wrong Jimmy. Everything absolutely fine. Just a few shades of the past lingering on the meadows as I came across. Nothing a good drink won't put to rights.'

'Just before we go in,' said Jimmy. 'I should mention that our Larry has found himself a partner since he left Barton. Been living together for a couple of years in fact. I'll leave him to make the introductions though.'

Before Jack could make any response the door was flung open, and Larry came through not just to shake his hand, but to give him a bear-hug and whisper in his ear before they went in.

'Much saddened to hear how things are with you and Kate. Talk about it later.'

The Croft sitting-room was as welcoming as ever: log-burner glowing brightly, a side-table well charged with bottles and glasses, and the smell of something homely cooking in the kitchen, from where a cry of greeting came from Celia.

'Out in a minute Jack. Jimmy, give him a drink and top mine up too. This isn't a bloody temperance house you know.'

'Can't think why I always feel so very much at home amongst these publicans and sinners Jack,' said Larry. 'But let me introduce you to Robert Tanner, he's already heard a great deal about you.'

The few seconds that had elapsed since Jack stepped into the room had been long enough for him take in the situation, but not altogether to suppress an air of surprise in the glance he gave at Larry.

'Yes, that's right,' was Larry's only comment as Robert grasped Jack by the hand.

'Good to meet you Jack. You'll have to excuse Larry though. He did so want to surprise you. He's so much like a little boy at times. Needs someone like me to keep an eye on him.'

'Well I'm absolutely delighted,' said Jack. 'I'd always thought that it must have been a lonely life rattling around in that great barn of a vicarage, and did wonder how he would manage when he left, but I can see he's in good hands.'

'Dead right I am Jack,' said Larry, 'but it's not something that's happened recently. We've known each other for many years: corresponded a bit, telephoned a lot and had one or two holidays together, so when we'd both retired it seemed only sensible to set up together, and we're very happy.'

They were interrupted by Celia's summons to dinner.

'Come on through now all of you. And Jimmy open two bottles of the red that Larry brought with him. Fetch some fresh glasses too. The best ones I mean. A good wine deserves a good glass.'

Before opening the bottles Jimmy held one up for Jack's inspection.

'Larry's indulging us: Chateauneuf du Pape '62. Never tasted it myself, but apparently it's something special.'

'Where on earth did you develop such expensive tastes Larry?' asked Jack. 'I remember having some at a celebration dinner many years ago: very smooth, rich and fruity, but a bit beyond my pocket then.'

'Special occasion Jack,' said Larry. 'Don't know any friends with whom I feel more at ease than you, Jimmy and Celia.'

'Strange company for an erstwhile man of the cloth, but I think I know what you mean.'

Meals at Gollins Croft were taken in a spacious dining-kitchen where, at a table large enough for twice their number, the three guests sat under the soft illumination of a couple of hanging oil lamps while Celia and Jimmy busied themselves around them.

'Main course courtesy of Mr Just-mention-my-name-Davey,' said Jimmy. 'You'll remember him I'm sure Jack. Wonderful evening that. Greatly enjoyed by all eh Larry?'

When by themselves the Gillans lived a quiet life and dined simply, but Celia had not forgotten her Roedean training in the domestic sciences. For several hours prior to Jack's arrival she had devoted herself to the preparation of a dinner appropriate to what she saw as a special occasion, and over a couple of hours her guests applied themselves to it and the wines with the dedication and appreciation they deserved.

With a slow-roast pork gleaming succulently under a cranberry glaze, the two bottles of Larry's Cotes du Rhone proved to be an ideal but insufficient accompaniment, and a third bottle would have been opened had Jimmy not suggested that it would be best left for the cheese. For the dessert (Celia's upper-crust version of the humble bread and butter pudding made with goat's milk custard and brandy-soaked dried fruit) Jimmy left the room, and returned with a galvanised bucket full of ice containing one bottle which he lifted, dried with a cloth, and placed on the table with some reverence. Its label was faded, hand-written and peeling back from the edges.

'Apologies for the container,' he said. 'Now I'm sure you've all heard of the last of the summer wine. Well tonight you can savour it. To the best of my knowledge this is the last unopened bottle of home-brew in Barton from the hands of dear old Ada Sutton. Elderflower 1972, the year before she died. It's almost eight years old so it might be past its best, but I've kept it for a special occasion, and Larry's return seems to be as good as any.'

They sat in silence as Jimmy drew the cork, and the soft, delicate bouquet of the wine filled the air as he passed with the bottle from glass to glass.

'Just look at it,' said Larry, holding his glass up to the mellow light of the lamp above him. 'For me there's something about the colour and scent of Elderflower that delivers up summer sunshine and lifts the spirits even in the depth of autumn. It's newly cut meadows, flowering hedgerows and lazy, golden evenings, and I never thought I'd taste it again: certainly not Ada's. Sorry you never had the chance to meet her Bob. She was a lovely lady, God bless her.'

'She was indeed,' said Jimmy. 'So here's to her, and to Ted, and to the many absent friends.'

'So many changes,' said Larry after the toast. 'And yet in my early years here it sometimes seemed to me that the old way of life on Barton Hill was immutable. Silly really when even then I had the burying of so many . . . But that's enough of that. Come on now Jack, I've already had the Barton news from Jimmy, so fill me in on all the gossip from Barlow.'

They lingered long at the table over cheese, wine, gossip and (contrary to his promise to Celia) Jimmy's colourful exposition of his opinions concerning the political philosophy and policies of 'that bitch of a woman and her cohorts.' But as there was no serious disagreement it proved to be more of a soliloquy, a long one, than a debate.

Finally, however, they moved back to the warmth of the glowing log-burner, and settled down for what was left of the evening, each nursing a generous glass of the local Armagnac.

'Never ceases to astonish and surprise me, our Mr Gillan,' said Larry holding up his glass. 'I enjoyed many a sup of this over the years without ever suspecting its origins. Shortly after we arrived, however, he finally confessed, and gave us an introduction to the operation before you arrived Jack. Very workmanlike and professional. Bob and I were most impressed.'

'Jimmy's not the only one springing the surprises though, is he Larry?' said Jack. 'You've been a bit of a dark horse yourself haven't you? And over dinner I've been thinking back to that sermon you very kindly preached shortly after my arrival in Barton. Your theme, if I remember correctly, was mercy, tolerance and understanding. Were you only thinking then of your local taxman, or perhaps yourself as well?'

'Well I certainly understood your position as an outsider Jack, not that it compared in any way with mine. I think my bishop suspected, but he was liberal-minded, and said nothing as it presented no ecclesiastical problems for him. As far as the church at large and my Barton congregation was concerned, however, I'd long since learned that being gay meant that I had to be discreet. I could never be sure how people would react to that: you for instance. As for my God, I never had any doubt about his understanding.'

'Well not much of my youthful, force-fed diet of politics stayed with me Larry, but I can still give you one quote, "Liberty consists in the freedom to do everything which injures no one else." Article Four, Declaration of the Rights of Man 1789, if I remember aright, and that pretty much represents how I feel.

As for your God Larry, I think that, like yourself, he's a rather special sort of chap. Might quite take to him myself if the concept meant anything to me at all.'

'I'm sure he'll be very reassured to hear that,' said Larry.

'Sorry to break in,' said Celia. 'But before we all turn in for the night Jimmy and I have something we want to say. First, it's been lovely to have you all with us this evening, but we have to confess that as well as being a lovely reunion with old friends this is a farewell party. After more than twenty-three years Jimmy and I will soon be leaving the hill . . . Sorry Jim, I'm going to get a bit tearful so can you take over.'

'Everyone OK for drinks?' asked Jimmy after giving her a hug, and they all nodded. 'Well as Celia said, it's twenty-three years since we came to the hill: March '57 in fact. Tom Sutton only just dead, and despite a bit of modernising, life going on pretty much as it did before the war, almost unchanging, like Larry said. Well that couldn't last of course, and over recent years we've gradually found that those we were closest to have died or sold up and moved on, and to be honest we don't really take to those who've replaced them. I'm getting back problems, and Celia shows signs of the arthritis that crippled her mother – God don't we sound a pair of old crocks? So much as we love the Croft we think we've reached the stage when it would be sensible to move on.

Now you'll all know that Celia's father died earlier in the year, and Celia's been left the house. It's her child-hood home, and she's very attached to it, which is more than I could ever say for mine. So the upshot is that we're going to sell the Croft and move south. In fact, subject to the legal shenanigans I can tell you that we have sold.

Sorry I didn't mention it Jack, but for reasons you'll understand we didn't want to use Adams and Oseland so we went to Gowrings. We'd no sooner mentioned the place, than they said they thought they had someone who'd be interested. He came, looked and made us a suitable offer: didn't even have to advertise. Well that's about it. Sorry to spring it on you like this, but it's all been so fast it's taken our breath away.'

'An evening of surprises with a vengeance,' said Jack. 'And I wish I could say I'm not going to miss you both, but you're my only real soulmates in the area. It's going to feel pretty lonely without you.'

'Oh we'll still get to see each other Jack,' said Celia. 'Plenty of room for visitors in both our houses. Perhaps you'll be able to make it for Christmas and bring Josie this time.'

Although she included Josie in her invitation, Jack's comment that he would be lonely without them had set Celia wondering about the precise nature of their relationship. She'd also met with Kate a few times since the separation, and as a result was hoping for a quiet word with Jack before he left.

'Well I think that calls for a final nightcap before bed,' said Larry, holding up an empty glass.

Jimmy obliged, but somehow after their announcement the joy seemed to have gone out of the evening, and Jack soon found an opportunity to thank Celia for a handsome dinner, make his excuses and set off for bed. And as he lay in the darkness, still wide awake despite the amount of drink he'd consumed, he wondered why on earth Celia would have suggested that he might bring Josie with him. Hardly the time, place or circumstances for an introduction he thought, but perhaps Celia felt she had to go through the motions and was expecting a refusal.

From that he drifted into a dreamy, half-sleeping reverie on Josie with the recollection that the only time they went to bed together was for sex. No, not quite, there had been that one night at Josie's boutique hotel, but that was only because they were so shagged out after their afternoon exertions, and even then there'd been no cuddles.

As for tonight he thought, after the amount of booze I've shifted, and with the ghost of Kate hovering round every corner, I really wouldn't have been of much use to her even if she'd come. A flea in your ear my love! Nothing to declare my darling! And special friend! Now what the hell did that and the antipathy to cuddles mean for any sort of long-term relationship? That was his last muddled thought before he was awakened by the clamour of Jimmy's rooster.

He pulled back his curtains to one of those rare halcyon dawns that he remembered well from his days on the hill with Kate. A dawn when those who knew their local weather threw open their windows, forgot their coats, and went about their business secure in the knowledge that for that one day the old gods of the hill would be kind to them. An acknowledgment perhaps of those midsummer pipes and twists of tobacco left to them over the years.

Such days came only rarely, with one of those strange inversions of temperature (an 'inversion aloft' in technical terms, Jack had been told) that left those in the valleys shivering under a shroud of cold, grey autumnal skies, but transformed the tops of Barton and Midden hills into sun-drenched islands afloat in a drifting, swirling sea of cloud, from which the tops of trees and wooded copses on the tumps and hummocks of the valleys below appeared as ghostly, insubstantial things, briefly materialising and assuming shape and form, before slowly fading and dissolving into nothingness as wave after wave of mist and cloud rolled almost imperceptibly across the landscape, and on into the distance where, high above Barlow, the needle-point spire of St Botolph's might be seen piercing the cloud, the only visible token of the world below, its weathervane glinting in the sun, as a wayward breath of air nudged it this way or that.

So stable was the sea of cloud that the height at which it broke against the flanks of the hill would scarcely vary throughout the day. Only at sunset, as the day darkened and the breeze freshened, did an increased restlessness disturb the surface, and give notice that overnight all would be gone, and Barton Hill would once again turn its customary, uncharitable face to the world below.

Surprisingly Jack's head was clear, a tribute to the quality of the drink he supposed, and opening the window he leaned out, breathing deeply, and savouring the morning sunlight and crisp air. He thought again of Kate, and the delight she took in such mornings, and then cursed himself for the thought. It was being back on the hill in the old familiar surroundings he supposed. Hearing a noise below he looked down to see Jimmy stepping out into the yard, and gave him a call.

'Morning Jim. I'll be down with you in a moment or two.'

He got a wave in response as Jimmy wandered across the yard.

'Jimmy's outside,' called Celia as he passed the kitchen. 'Grab a mug of tea and join him. I've given Larry and Bob a call. Breakfast in about half-an-hour.'

He found Jimmy hanging over the empty pig sty, mug of tea in one hand, a cigarette in the other.

'Wouldn't think you could grieve for a pig would you Jack? But Sadie used to follow me around like a child, and when she died a year ago I hadn't the heart to replace her, and I think that was when I finally lost my enthusiasm for this place. There was no way we could bring ourselves to send her to the kennels for the hounds of course, so I got Davey to bring his excavator in over the fields, and we buried her up below the lavender. Bloody silly isn't it.'

'Oh I don't know,' said Jack. 'I can remember seeing my father in tears when my gran's old parrot died. He'd known it since he was a child. He said it was like losing one of the family.'

'Ah well,' said Jim. 'That's the way it goes. They're all in the Happy Land now though eh?'

'The Happy Land Jim?'

'Don't tell me you don't know the Happy Land Jack, you a literary man. Didn't your daddy ever bounce you on his knee and sing it to you?'

'Not my father's style, knee bouncing. Singing either.'

'Haven't thought of it for years. Funny thing memory. How these little fragments of the past come sneaking up unbidden.'

Then he began to sing softly.

'There is a Happy Land, far, far away.

Where little piggies run, three times a day.

Oh you ought to see them run,

When they see the butcher come,

To cut three slices of their rum tum tum,

Three times a day.'

'Very moving Jim,' said Jack. 'But not a literary classic perhaps.'

They sipped their tea and smoked in silence for a while before Jimmy spoke again.

'I didn't want to say too much about things in front of the others last night,' said Jimmy. 'But when everything was settled Celia's father cut up rather warmer than my old dad, if I can put it like that. Quite a sizeable estate, and she gets half of it as well as the house. She doesn't quite know how to respond to that, and now willy-nilly I find that I'm a bloody capitalist. Have to make a return of her income to my local tax man. Any idea who that might be?'

'Oh dear,' said Jack. 'What a dilemma. One of the idle rich now and all the angst of managing a small fortune is it? It'll be tough alright, but one way and another I expect you'll muddle through. Never knew a rich man who didn't.

As far as the return goes, if you've already sold you'll be long gone from here before it's due, and I imagine Celia's father would have had accountants to look after all that sort of thing anyway. But if you do run into any snags give me a ring. We mustn't lose touch. As I said last night you're my only real soulmates in the area.'

Jack paused uncertain whether to continue with what he had in mind, but then having resolved his momentary doubts, gave what Jimmy thought was a strange sort of smile, and invited him to make the most of the morning, and take a short stroll before breakfast.

'You'll remember Jim that you spent a few years getting to know me before you told me about your little distilling operation. A confession of sorts you called it. And then you told me about Caireen, something you'd mentioned to no one else: another confession you said, something that you wanted to get off your chest.'

'I remember Jack, and you said you'd no need of any bloody confessor. Done nothing you couldn't live with, you said.'

'I did, and I think that jokingly I also referred to a professional life of perfidious venality. Well I'm going to tell you a little story, a valedictory confession if you like, that might make it easier for you to square your socialist principles with the size of Celia's bank balance.'

260

And as they strolled slowly from Sadie's empty sty to the site of her last resting place below the lavender beds, Jack gave Jimmy a blow-by-blow account of his little bit of private enterprise with Martindale.

For a few moments Jimmy stood in silence just looking at Jack: waiting for a smile perhaps, or some other suggestion that he was spinning a yarn.

'Christ, you're in earnest aren't you Jack?'

'Deadly,' replied Jack, 'and so it would have been for me had anything gone wrong.'

'But I thought you always said the Revenue was watertight.'

'It is, but this was an exceptional set of circumstances as I've explained, and remember I was approached. I didn't start the ball rolling myself. That made things much easier.'

'And no repercussions? No questions asked? No knocks on the door in the small hours of the night?'

'None: rewarded in fact. Promotion, Barlow transfer, and to cap it all, the price of gold hit a new high this year. In fact it's more than trebled since I made my modest investment. Krugerrands at less than ninety then were selling at two hundred and ninety plus a week or so ago. Beats the stock market any day. So sleep easy Jim, we're all bloody plutocrats now.'

'I must say though I never really saw you as that sort of risk-taker Jack. Did you need the money for the separation?

'Not a bit. It was all over and done with a few months before Kate left. I never mentioned it of course, and haven't spent any. Don't expect to in the immediate future. In fact the more I look back on it the more I think that what I really wanted was the satisfaction of challenging the system and getting away with it.'

'Martindale. The name sounds familiar. Is that the little shit of a junior minister who was on the box so much when the Housing Act was going through?'

'The very same. Didn't rate him much myself, and he's done rather better than I expected. Learned the fine art of brown-nosing from Dad perhaps, or friends in high places.'

'Well it certainly puts my little distilling operation into perspective, and I'm tickled pink to hear that you screwed one of the buggers into the bargain.'

They were interrupted by a call to breakfast from Celia.

'And Celia?' asked Jimmy.

'No objection at all,' said Jack. 'If you think she'd enjoy the story.'

After breakfast Jack found himself alone in the kitchen with Celia, helping with the washing up while Larry and Bob went off for a walk to the village and church, and Jimmy was engaged in a telephone call to the solicitors concerning the sale.

'Sorry Josie couldn't come Jack. You're still seeing her are you?'

'Oh you know, on and off.'

He could have bitten his tongue out to recall the phrase when he realised just how very appropriately the words described the circumstances of his meetings with Josie, but happily Celia seemed preoccupied with another line of thought, and the moment passed.

'I met up with Kate for lunch a few months ago when I was on my way down to home. I wondered whether you knew that she'd left Roger.'

'No, I've heard nothing for almost a year. When was that?'

'About eight or nine months ago. She went back to live with her parents.'

'Is she well?'

'Seemed to be, but not terribly happy I think. She got quite upset when I told her you still had the bears. I'd no idea of course that you'd paid for them.'

Jack made no response to this, but busied himself stowing away the dishes and cutlery.

'She didn't say so, but I think she misses you Jack. She sent her love.'

She might have added that she was sure that Kate would have loved to have things back the way they were, but felt that if Jack was in any way so inclined he would do something about it himself without anything further being said.

'Not to worry about the bears Celia,' said Jack. 'I knew you were seeing Kate occasionally, and should have told you what I'd done. It looks as though life has got a bit complicated for both of us at the moment. Give her my love though if you see her again.'

Jimmy's return brought the conversation to an end, and then the three of them set off for the village to find Larry and Bob, and drop in at the Shagger after making a few farewell calls.

Larry and Bob had to leave after lunch, but Jack stayed on for another drink-fuelled evening with the Gillans and a few old neighbours before returning to Barlow cursing the personal complexities that life could bring even when fortune seemed otherwise to be smiling.

16

A Debacle in Venice

Before the end of the year Jimmy and Celia had completed their sale and made the move south, and early the following summer Jack and Josie left Barlow for the holiday they had been planning for some time. Jack had initially resisted Josie's wish to spend the week in Venice. He still looked back on his time there with Kate with much affection, and had no wish to reawaken old memories. He did not feel that this was an argument he could readily advance with Josie, however, so he said nothing, and having no other had reluctantly to agree.

Josie's passionate desire for Venice, he soon learned, had been engendered by an evening of photographs and chat with Mandy, a friend who had been there the previous year and, said Josie, knew an absolutely fabulous hotel where they had been looked after like royalty. Jack, with his memory of Martindale's bill in mind, was greatly relieved to learn that it was not the Danieli. Having agreed some financial guidelines with Josie, however, he was content to let her do the organising, which she seemed to enjoy.

From the airport they took a private water-taxi into the city. Expensive, but faster and more comfortable he would have had to admit than the crowded water-bus he'd taken with Kate, which had deposited them some distance from the hotel, laden with luggage and trying to make sense of the directions to the hotel. In the water-taxi they travelled via a confusing maze of narrow waterways to the very door of their canal-side hotel where a porter appeared to carry in the luggage. They were, Jack realised, just a short walk from the Campo Santa Maria Formosa

It was a location he would have been happy to avoid, as he and Kate had passed through the square regularly on the way to and from their hotel in Cannaregio, and adopted one of its little restaurants for their evening meals. It did not seem an auspicious start, but if Jack had any fears that he would be retracing their earlier footsteps with Josie by his side they would prove to be unfounded.

Having been once to the city already, he decided that on the first day at least he would give no lead, but let Josie set the pace. It was soon evident then that Josie had her own programme for Venice, and it would not be one that troubled Jack with memories of his earlier visit. Sex played its part, but was confined to night-time encounters sometimes so cursory as to leave Jack wondering whether his novelty was wearing off, but to be honest he wasn't unduly worried about that. Not for nothing had Kate described him as the bear who could take it or leave it alone.

Sex aside, it seemed to Jack that Josie must be taking her lead from her Barlow friend. She rose late, showered leisurely, dressed and made up with fastidious care, and then took a lingering but light breakfast on the hotel roof-terrace which had attractive views across the rooftops to San Giovanni e Paolo. Following breakfast, taking in a shop or two on the way, she strolled leisurely through to San Marco where they took a seat outside Florian's.

Seducing the waiter with a smile and tucking a note into his top pocket as he took their order, she made her cappuccino and water last an hour or more, and was content to sit and give herself up to people-watching, with perhaps an occasional glance around her at the more celebrated attractions of the Campo.

Bemused and a little puzzled at the way Josie was choosing to spend the morning of her first day in Venice, Jack nevertheless had so far been happy to play the devoted escort, admiring her looks and dress, the easy elegance with which she moved and sat, and not unpleased with the covert glances she attracted from other men nearby. But with lunchtime approaching he felt that she might now like to play the part of the conventional tourist, and suggested that they take the lift to the top of the campanile.

'You mean squeeze in with all of them, do you Jack?' she said with a look of distaste, nodding towards the crowd pressing around the door at the base of the tower.

'That's how it's going to be at most of the major sights I'm afraid Josie. That's the way it is most of the year in Venice, unless you chose to come in the depth of winter.'

'Well if that's the case I don't think I'll bother: at least not at the moment. Perhaps they'll be less crowded some other time. And now I'd like to have a little browse around the shops under the arcades, and then you can take me to Harry's Bar for a drink and a snack.'

Seated in Harry's bar Josie ordered a Bellini and a club sandwich. This must be bloody Mandy, thought Jack – 'and of course you simply have to go to Harry's and have a Bellini.' He sipped a beer, and looked around him. He'd glanced in at the door on his earlier visit and hadn't been impressed. He was even less so now. Soulless, totally without character, rip-off prices, and not particularly clean (the table was sticky and the waiter's jacket stained) he wondered how it managed to retain its reputation. Time for a little discussion with Josie about the rest of the week he thought. If she found the tourist crowds at the main sites daunting, he said, perhaps she would enjoy some of the city's other, but less popular attractions.

More than fifteen years had elapsed since his earlier visit with Kate, but he remembered it as though it were yesterday. Up early and out into the half-light for Venice at sunrise, with Piazza San Marco hushed and deserted, and dawn breaking behind the domes of the basilica. Strolling the empty streets to linger in the strengthening sunlight on the Rialto bridge. Then an early coffee and croissant amid the bustle of trading at the fish market before an hour or so on vaporetti busy with Venetians, not tourists. And after breakfast, as the crowds began to arrive, they would lose themselves in the outer reaches of the sestieri, where a maze of narrow, winding alleys had led them via silent stretches of waterway, secluded campos and little-visited churches to lunch at a canalside bacaro where the fried sardines came crisp from the kitchen and the wine cool from a barrel behind the bar.

Jack hadn't mentioned that earlier visit with Kate, but he restrained his enthusiastic recital of the city's minor delights when he saw Josie smiling slightly as she listened to him, and realised that she must understand very well the reason for his intimate knowledge of the byways of Venice.

She didn't exactly reject his proposals out of hand, but somehow none of them quite fitted into her idea of a week in Venice. She wasn't in the least a morning person, she said, and would be a poor companion for Jack on a dawn vigil, lovely as it sounded. At his mention of the fish market she said nothing, but wrinkled up her nose dismissively. Those little churches and quiet campos sounded charming, she thought, but she'd read that there were over four hundred bridges in Venice, and with one around every corner would be too utterly exhausted to enjoy those distant attractions long before she got to them.

The unfortunate truth was that quite apart from Mandy's misreporting, Josie's dream of Venice was born out of vague and romantic teenage memories of Katie Hepburn in *Summertime*, where the city, quite untouched by tourist hordes, shimmered and glowed under the loving direction of David Lean. The reality, unfortunately, didn't live up to her expectations.

'It's a wonderful film set,' she said. 'But I have to confess that it isn't quite what I expected. It's smelly. It's too hot, and it's far too crowded. I'd no idea it would be overrun with day trippers like this. It might as well be Blackpool.

But we mustn't spoil it for each other Jack. I know there's a lot here that you'd like to see again and introduce me to, but if I'm honest old masters, crowded palaces and dusty museums really aren't my cup of tea.'

'And if I were honest I'd have to say that Harry's bar isn't exactly mine.'

'I realise that Jack. It is rather nasty isn't it, and I've got a proposal. . . . Now you mustn't be offended, but I think we should go our separate ways during the day and then meet up later in the afternoon. We could have afternoon tea at Florian's or somewhere on the waterfront, and then saunter back together to freshen up for the evening: a gondola ride perhaps, and then a leisurely dinner together.'

Far from being offended, Jack was more receptive to Josie's proposals than might perhaps have pleased her had she known. He'd already been envisaging a pretty barren week ahead if he was confined to acting as Josie's escort.

'And you'll be quite alright by yourself?'

'Of course I will. I'm a big girl now. Then, if you really want to, you can slip away for your Venice sunrise without disturbing me, and I'll make a nice leisurely start to the day. But now, if you really want to, and while we're together, you can give me a conducted tour of the Piazza, and show me Venice from the top of the campanile.'

Although Jack had no enthusiasm for a solitary dawn vigil, he was nevertheless up and away the following morning while Josie was still lingering in the shower, and in avoiding those places where the tourists clustered most thickly, found himself treading the paths of that earlier visit. But even Venice changes, and after bemoaning the closure of their little canal-side bacaro he struck off in search of some new but minor delights; never difficult to find in Venice.

Josie, as he learned in the course of the week, utterly determined to indulge herself to the full despite her initial disappointment, had started each day in much the same leisurely way as her first, but rang the changes for her morning coffee between Florian's, Gran Caffe Quadri and the Danieli Terrazza. Beautiful, immaculately dressed and solitary, she inevitably attracted attention, but politely declined all advances save one, that of a middle-aged Italian who assured her that he sought nothing but the pleasure of her company while he showed her the splendours of his city from the water: he had a launch at his disposal. He was as good as his word, she said, and after a late lunch together, returned her to the door of the hotel having conducted himself throughout with perfect propriety.

She bought jewellery from Missiaglia beneath the Procuratie Vecchie, and lace from Burano, travelling by private launch. Guided by the hotel porter to La Fenice, she was disappointed to find no opera in production at that time, but procured for herself (part charm, part financial consideration she said) a tour of the theatre including back-stage, and came away with a poster of the latest production.

In fact, as Jack later reported in a letter to Jimmy, Josie achieved the seemingly impossible by staying a week in Venice without stepping inside a palace, museum or gallery, or viewing any form of artistic expression other than the facades of the 'film set.' Just once, having fallen in with a family of American Hemingway devotees, she joined with them in the cost of a private launch to Torcello for lunch at Cipriani's, and subsequently, almost incidentally, went with them into her one and only church, the basilica of Santa Maria Assunta. God knows what it all cost her, he wrote, but I can assure you Jim, we did not go Dutch on that little bout of extravagance.

On the flight home he gazed bemusedly at Josie sleeping quietly alongside him, and managing to do so with grace, even in an aircraft seat. Shaped to perfection, exquisitely decorated and enticingly tactile, she was almost a form of artistic expression herself, he thought, but she was, alas, a hollow, empty vessel. Their week together had been enough to confirm what he had for some time suspected: Josie was a bit of a film set herself, all surface, no substance.

Apart from such drama as Brandy had introduced her to she knew next to nothing about literature at large. Most of his quotes passed her by unnoticed; that had seldom been the case with Kate. Her passion for opera seemed to be no more than a purely visceral response to the thrill of a tenor in full flow. Of music beyond the opera she was almost entirely ignorant. She hadn't a political bone in her body, or an original thought in her head. Despite the many pleasures Josie offered, Jack was beginning to suspect that for him, as well as for her, the novelty might be wearing off.

On the Monday following their return Jack bent himself once again to the demands of the office, but after almost nine years of specialist investigation work he would have had to admit that grateful as he was for the transfer to Barlow, he found the routine of district life tedious. He'd made sure that the concluding stages of the investigation into the affairs of Bayley, Bayley and Bedgood were conducted by someone other than himself, and left his casually acquired knowledge of the evasion activities of Jackson's Agricultural tucked securely under his hat marked private. If they came under scrutiny for any other reason, well that would be a different matter.

He did his best with the increasingly inadequate resources, and was generally successful in avoiding any unwanted Head Office attention, but by and large he found his work dull and unrewarding until he met again with Mrs Davenport. Of Noddy Davenport, her husband, Jack had seen a little and heard much during his years on the hill, where Noddy had become a legend for self-improvement and success, and was accordingly commended, or envied and denigrated in equal measure.

Born on the hill in the winter of 1930 with flat feet that would earn him a Grade Four exemption from Military Service, and the taunts of his childhood companions for his clumsiness, Noddy took refuge by withdrawing from the world. The upshot was that at school his innate intelligence and remarkable ability with figures went unnoticed. Escaping his rustic education at the age of fourteen, he was accepted into the Civil Service as a trainee clerical assistant, and assigned to Barlow Tax Office. There, as junior lowest of the low, he made the tea, shuffled files, and occasionally received some basic instruction.

In Barlow, however, Noddy was neither impressed with what he saw, nor with the pay and promotion prospects. But for three years he looked, learned and applied himself with such success to evening classes that his application for a vacancy at Batesons, a large Wolverton accountancy practice, was accepted, and brought with it the prospect of professional training. He said goodbye to the hill, moved to Wolverton, and apart from occasional return visits to his parents, nothing more was seen of him.

A little more than six year later M W Davenport ACCA surprised the village by returning with his professional qualifications, the first in the community to achieve such heights. Even more surprising was his newly acquired, but passionate love affair with the glory that was Greece, inculcated in him by one of the Bateson seniors, a Balliol classics man, who saw more in Noddy than was seen by the common eye, and took him under his wing.

Hanging his handsomely framed certificate on the wall of the office he opened in Mordiford Wells, a small market town at the foot of the hill, Noddy buckled down to making his way in the world, commuting each day from the Barton house which he occupied with his mother, now widowed.

Noddy had left for Wolverton a diffident, shaggy-looking country boy encumbered with flat feet and a broad local accent. He returned, still with his flat feet, but now confident, trim and well-dressed, with his accent suppressed for all except the men from the hill who came to him for their accounts, and to whom he could talk in a way and in terms that they understood.

To Noddy, invariably belatedly as far as the taxman was concerned, the boys who had mocked him at school now came as young men with their cardboard boxes packed with farmyard-soiled scraps of paper, a few books and an assorted collection of invoices. From these, on two quality sheets of A3 and by that magic alchemy that only accountants can work, Noddy and his one very attractive lady assistant, produced one neat and tidy Balance Sheet and an accompanying Profit and Loss Account, all rounded off with a fine-sounding certificate to the effect that the accounts now produced were in accordance with the books and records of the business and the explanations and information supplied by his client.

The accounts that Noddy submitted to the Inspector on behalf of his clients were, of course, absolutely kosher, and indeed prepared strictly in accordance with the transactions appearing in the books and records, but without any embarrassing enquiries or probing into any that might be outside them. When, however, he had no alternative but to seek some further information from his clients, he accepted all but the most outrageous explanations with a few grave nods of the head, and so acquired his nickname with the locals.

Amongst his clients, and in the few local tax offices to which he worked, Noddy soon became well known both for a prompt and businesslike approach to his work, and for the distinctive nature of his stationery all of which was headed with the legend:

'And each shall give an account of himself to God'
Romans 14:12

Neither his clients, nor the taxmen could ever quite satisfy themselves whether, in addition to his qualifications, Noddy had acquired religion during his time in Wolverton, or simply a very dry sense of humour. Cynics watching his progress in the world were, however, of the view that he had rightly identified the Church (orthodox C of E of course) as one of the establishment clubs to which it might be useful to attach himself to further his advancement socially, and in his business career.

Four years of judiciously expanding his practice in the business community, whilst at the same time retaining its rustic base, saw Noddy flourishing to such an extent that he took on a partner, and together they moved the base of their operations into Barlow, where the opportunities for further expansion were seen to be proliferating on the back of commercial growth in the 'you've never had it so good' years. In Barlow with the same determination to further his career and social standing that he had shown throughout, and despite the inherent disadvantage of his flat feet on the golf course, he procured membership of the local club, which had a reputation for being rather select, and sent off his application for membership of the Rotary Club. And in Barlow, 'Noddy' was no more: there he was spoken of as Mr Davenport by the world at large, and Maurice by his familiars.

At home in Barton, after nine years basking in the reflected glory of her son's renaissance, Mrs Davenport Snr went to join her dear, departed Albert in the graveyard of St Matthew's, and Noddy lived on alone in the house that Albert had worked himself to death to pay for.

Devoted to his widowed mother while she was alive, Noddy, throughout the years following his triumphal return from Wolverton, seemed to have been unaware that more than one of the unmarried women of the village, who would have joined enthusiastically in mocking him when he was young, now regarded him as an eminently suitable catch. And with his mother dead, and Noddy a property owner with a flourishing practice in nearby Barlow, his appeal to those women was compounded. Of this, however, he remained seemingly ignorant, content to cook, wash and clean for himself, and pass a couple of evenings a week in the Shagger where the drinks were usually on his grateful clients, and Noddy seldom had to put his hand in his own pocket.

Seen within the community as an exemplar for steady, devoted application to business and a sober, no-nonsense life-style (or as Jimmy said, as a bloody, dull dog) Noddy shattered all such preconceptions within a year of his mother's death. Leaving the affairs of the practice in the hands of his partner and a locum, and giving little notice of his intentions within the village, Noddy embarked on a solitary pilgrimage to Greece.

There, following in the steps his Bateson tutor had taken in the years before the war, he relived the Athenian Golden Age as well as time and his financial resources would allow him. At the end of three months he returned leaner, suntanned, dreamy-eyed and with a Grecian beauty on his arm that he introduced as Mrs Davenport. Sceptics of the legality of the union were silenced by the knock-down argument that they had to be married or she wouldn't be allowed to stay in the country.

Golden-haired, blue-eyed, of slender waist and with long shapely legs, Marilita Davenport (nee Kanakaredes) was a light-skinned exception to the Mediterranean norm, and a beauty. The consensus of opinion within the village was that she had to be at least ten, possibly fifteen years younger than Noddy.

'But what does a woman like that see in someone like Noddy?' asked Charlie Genner in the Shagger.

'She sees escape from the shambles that's been Greece since the end of the war,' said Jimmy. 'She sees security, a successful business man and the prospect of a life that she could only dream of in the Piraeus. If you think Noddy's lucky, so is she, and good luck to her.'

Jack's social acquaintance of Noddy and his wife was confined to the dozen or so occasions when they met at the Shagger or village functions in the two years after he and Kate settled on the hill. By then Marilita had worked so hard at her English that she was left with little more to indicate her origin than a rather fetching catch to an already huskily seductive voice, and Jack was intrigued to note the confidence she showed in a society that must still have been in many ways alien to her. She struck him as shrewd, personable and sexually extremely alluring. Did Noddy really make the most of that, he asked himself.

Their two years' acquaintance was brought to an end when Noddy sold his old home in the village, and moved into Barlow to a house which he saw as better reflecting his improved circumstances. There, for a couple of years, he took every opportunity of furthering his social and business connections, and began to set out his stall for a seat on the town council. At the end of his first year in Barlow he made one return to the village for New Year in the Shagger, and joined with the others in visiting the grave of his parents in what was to be the last of the churchyard vigils, but from then on the village saw him no more.

A couple of years after their move to Barlow, Noddy and Marilita returned from a social function at the Golf Club, enjoyed a final nightcap together, and while Noddy watched a little late night television, Marilita completed what Noddy regarded as her unduly elaborate preparations for bed. Joining her half-an-hour later he kissed her goodnight, went to sleep, and never woke up. At a stroke and totally unexpectedly Marilita, still a youthful thirty-three year old, was left a widow.

'A serious, but undetected heart condition,' said the coroner.

'Just like his father before him,' they said in the village when the news reached them. And both in Barton and Barlow there were a few mature, but unattached gentlemen who indulged themselves in the thought that in due course, when things had settled down, Marilita might be looking for a companion.

Noddy with his customary foresight in life had put in place provisions which ensured that after his death Marilita inherited the house free of any mortgage. She would also be in receipt of a modest annuity in perpetuity, and she received in addition the lump sum due under the partnership agreement for Noddy's share of the practice. On these funds Marilita would have to manage through her long years of widowhood. Surprisingly composed and competent in the face of such a blow, she took such advice as seemed to her to be sensible, and rejected much that wasn't.

For forty days, following the Greek tradition, she honoured Noddy's memory by wearing black and eschewing all social gatherings except for the Sunday services at All Saints.' Then, putting her widow's weeds aside, she accepted all the invitations that came her way, and as she was popular both with the men and the women they were many. She was seen again at the Golf Club and Rotary functions, accepted invitations to sit on some of the ladies' committees, and so allowed herself to be absorbed into a Barlow society which, in a favoured retirement town, was already rich with widows. To the disappointment of the unattached gentlemen, however, she declined to entertain any further permanent relationship.

In the seven years that had elapsed since Noddy's premature decease Jack had seen nothing and heard little of the attractive widow, until he saw her name again a few weeks before he departed for his week in Venice with Josie. Ned Potter, a junior inspector, had been transferred out without replacement, and Jack had taken a hand in disposing of a share of some low-grade hack work he had left unfinished.

In working his way through this Jack had come across a newly opened file for Mrs Marilita Davenport from which he could see that following Noddy's death, his widow had apparently slipped below the revenue radar. There was nothing particularly surprising in that, as the annuity she received and such income as arose from the investment of her lump sum would not have given rise to any liability to tax.

In recent years, however, information slips had been received from banks showing that she had been in receipt of increasing amounts of interest on deposit accounts. General arrears of work meant that these had been allowed to accumulate, until eventually Ned Potter had made enquiries, asked to see her deposit account books and then the bank statements for her current account. So surprised had he been when he examined these that he had written asking her to call in to see him. His letter had been ignored, as had two follow-ups.

Such was the state of play in Mrs Davenport's affairs when Jack took them up and issued a letter couched in such terms as to elicit a response. A meeting was agreed, and now shortly after his return from Venice Jack sat waiting for Mrs Davenport's arrival.

17

Known to all Posterity For
Amorous Dexterity

'Mrs Davenport, sir,' said Jack's secretary showing her into his office.

She was a little taller than Jack remembered. Slightly thicker in the waist and fuller in the bosom too, but if anything it suited her. Still the same open beauty though that dazzled all the men when Noddy first brought her back to Barton, even if the first delicate bloom of youth had faded. She must now be what, late thirties or thereabouts. Such were the thoughts that flitted through his mind as he stepped forward to meet her and offer her a chair.

She gave no hint that she recognised him, and waited until he'd returned to the seat on his side of the desk before slowly crossing her legs. It was discreetly done, but not without exposing rather more thigh than might have been necessary. Knowing the effectiveness of the Barlow gossip mill Jack wondered whether she knew of his affair with Josie, and whether there might have been a subtle signal there. That was the effect of his time with Josie, he decided: his first thoughts were of sex. And then he realised that it was the first time in his career that he had found himself conducting an interview alone with a sexually attractive woman. It was an intriguing experience. Assuming his professional persona, he turned to the matter in hand.

'You may remember Mrs Davenport, that when Mr Potter asked you to call he suggested that you might like to bring an advisor with you, but you come alone.'

'I do Mr Manning.'

'And you're quite content to proceed with this meeting without any other guidance.'

'Oh yes, quite content. In fact, as it might touch on confidential and rather intimate matters, I much prefer it that way. I'm quite sure you will proceed absolutely fairly and take no advantage of me.'

Jack thought that an odd expression to use, and wondered what he was supposed to make of it. It also crossed his mind that it might be prudent for him to ask another member of staff to sit in with him for the rest of the meeting, but there was too much loss of face in that idea for him to pursue it further. He did though feel that before proceeding it might seem strange if he didn't mention the fact that they had met before, and that he had known and had dealings with her late husband.

'You may remember that I met you and the late Mr Davenport a few times while you were living in Barton, and of course I had business dealings with your husband on several occasions.'

'Oh yes, I remember you very well Mr Manning, and Mrs Manning, and you mustn't let the fact that we once met socially inhibit you in any way in your enquiries.'

Dear God, he thought, she's being cheeky and putting me at my ease. But he couldn't help admiring her confident composure and the seductively husky voice that he remembered so well. So far the interview was certainly not proceeding by the book.

'Well I'd like in due course to turn to the details disclosed by your current bank account for the three years that I have before me, but first of all could I ask how you supported yourself in the earlier years following the death of your husband?'

'How do you mean, supported myself?' She re-crossed her legs with perhaps a little less discretion than before: a hint perhaps that in that department at least, she could hardly be more satisfactorily supported.

Think eyes not thighs damn you, hissed his other self, but even the eyes were a problem: limpid blue, perhaps slightly amused, and deeply alluring. He recalled Kate's comment that he really didn't know how to respond to women very well.

'I mean where did the money come from that you lived on. You have a large house to keep up, you run a car, and I can see that you dress very well.'

'Why thank you Mr Manning, you're very kind.'

Oh this was getting out of hand. He hadn't intended a compliment at all, but fortunately she continued.

'Well how can I best put this . . . For most of the years since Maurice died I've been in receipt of little testimonials from appreciative friends.'

'Little testimonials from appreciative friends?' Even as he repeated her words his heart sank. He couldn't believe he'd made such a stupid blunder.

'I just said that.' That's what she'd reply, bound to, and then the whole bloody interview would topple over into an Eric and Ernie comedy exchange. But fortunately she didn't.

'Yes, from gentleman friends who enjoy my company, and like to leave me little gifts to show their appreciation.'

Now Jack could see with utter clarity just where this was going, and he was casting about for a way in which he might press forward in the most neutral of terms, when she continued.

'You must understand what I mean surely Mr Manning. You're a mature gentleman, and all gentleman have their physical desires don't they? And so do the ladies, and if they find one another pleasant and attractive, well . . . .'

'Well they pleasure one another!' Things were getting so far into the surreal now, that Jack felt he might as well finish the sentence for her and be damned. He resisted the temptation, but in his increasing desperation and embarrassment, reverted to the sort of conventional response which he might have adopted had she just told him that she lived on betting winnings: which was just as witless.

'And you can produce evidence of that, can you?'

She smiled and re-arranged her legs yet again.

'Mr Manning, I'm finding it rather stuffy in here. Do you think you could open a window, and let me have a glass of water from your decanter?'

He poured her some water, and walked to the window with the feeling that somehow the meeting wasn't proceeding quite as he had intended.

'Thank you, that's so much better,' she said. 'As for providing evidence, I really think that with the best will in the world it can't be done. You surely can't be suggesting that I should go to one of my friends, perhaps a married man, and ask him to let me have signed statement that on a certain night he slept with me, and subsequently made me a gift? And why should I be asked to provide evidence Mr Manning? I'm not running a business.'

Well at least it's out in the open now, thought Jack: no more beating around the bush. But he also realised that Marilita had picked up a thing or two about taxes in her time with Noddy. Source: that was the crux of the problem. In every other case he'd worked on, unexplained money could be attached to some other known and taxable source, almost invariably a business, and when he picked up her file he'd assumed it would possibly be disposed of as a little bit of bed and breakfasting on the side. Well in Marilita's case he'd certainly got the bed: but was she taxable on the proceeds of her activities there: that was the issue.

He thought it best to defer an answer to her question for the moment, and turned instead to the bank statements obtained by Ned Potter.

'Can I return to your question later Mrs Davenport, and ask you instead to look with me at the transactions on your bank statements which cover the three years to 31st December 1980, concentrating on the last three months.

You will note the frequency and amount of the deposits in that account during those three months. Are you seriously telling me that they are all in respect of your favours to your gentleman friends?'

'Mr Manning please. I'm flesh and blood, not superhuman. No, of course they aren't. And "favours" what a sweet old-fashioned expression.'

'Then where do they come from?'

'They are in respect of my lady friends.'

Oh Christ thought Jack. Lady friends too; I'm getting out of my depth here, but he had no alternative other than to plough on.

'You mean you receive payments for favours to ladies as well as gentlemen?'

'No, of course not. What were you thinking? They are gifts to my lady friends in respect of their favours to their gentleman friends, as you so delicately put it.'

She smiled and re-crossed her legs to provide a more generous display of thigh, as though to drive home the strictly heterosexual nature of her activities.

Bloody hell, she's telling me she's running a knocking shop, and she sits there smiling sweetly and apparently giving me the come-on. Well if she thinks this is a game, it's a game two can play, and then we'll see where we get to. His problem was that his instructions were a bit vague when it came to the taxation of profits from prostitution. It might be the world's oldest profession, but so far it seemed no one had tried to tax it, or if they had Jack hadn't heard about it. No case law, so no guid-ance.

He recalled that the issue had been given a brief air-ing in the House of Lords some six or seven years ear-lier, when although their Lordships were reassured that such profits were in principle taxable, the difficulty of finding, assessing and collecting the tax from such ladies was much emphasised. Well it seemed that Jack had per-haps found one, and so from now on he'd just have to wing it, and see what turned up.

He smiled back at his charming adversary.

'If they are gifts to your lady friends, as you put it, why are they being banked in your personal account?'

'Oh of course: I see what you mean. Well if I tell you that some of the ladies are married, you may perhaps understand that they wouldn't want to pay those sorts of cheques into their own accounts: too much possibility of embarrassment should a husband notice it. So all the gentlemen understand that if they want to leave a little cheque as a gift to the lady it has to be in my name, and then I give the lady the equivalent in cash.'

Jack considered this for a moment or two.

'Mrs Davenport, if I understand what you are saying correctly you are telling me that you are running . . . How can I put this in the least old-fashioned way . . . you are running a brothel, a bordello. I could think of other ways of saying the same thing, but perhaps those will do.'

'Oh Mr Manning, how could you, and I thought you were such a nice gentleman.' She imbued her words with such a grotesquely theatrical air of pathos that Jack, despite his admiration for the game she was playing, found it difficult not to laugh.

'No, I am not a madam,' she continued. 'My house is not a brothel, and our visitors are real Barlow gentlemen, not the boys from Piraeus. You have it all wrong.'

The boys from Piraeus: of course. Mercouri: that was who she looked like. Did she know it, and had she seen the film? No wonder her gentlemen came calling. He allowed himself a momentary vision of Marilita swaying enticingly in front of him, snapping her fingers to that wonderful Greek music, and then reaching out to draw him slowly towards her.

He dragged himself back to the matter in hand.

'Well if I have it all wrong, please tell me what the truth of the matter is, and put it all right.'

'I think that might take some time Mr Manning, so do you think I could have some coffee before I begin.'

Jack picked up the phone to ask for some coffee to be brought through, but then was struck with a different thought, and spoke instead to his secretary.

'Joan. I'm going to be out of the office for a while with Mrs Davenport. Should anyone call, take a message and say I'll phone them back.'

'I feel I really can't subject you to civil service coffee Mrs Davenport, and thought we might perhaps slip up to Bosewell's. They won't be busy this early in the morning, and we'll be able to find a corner to talk quietly.'

Not strictly in accordance with the accepted rules of engagement, thought Jack, but what the hell. Inspectors were always being enjoined to obtain a thorough understanding of the businesses they were examining, and within the bounds of discretion Jack intended to do just that with Mrs Davenport's activities. He was in any event past the stage in his career where he was concerned how Head Office might respond, and was now more interested in hearing her story for its own sake than for any other reason.

She turned to him as they made their way towards Priory Hill and Bosewell's.

'If you wished to, I'd be quite happy if you dropped the Mrs Davenport and called me Marilita.'

'That's very kind of you, but I think we ought perhaps to preserve some degree of formality.'

In Bosewell's they settled themselves into a corner, and after coffee had arrived she began.

'You must understand to start with Mr Manning that none of this was happening while Maurice was alive. Although he was so much older, he was always very kind and considerate, and I respected that. And of course he introduced me to lots of people in Barlow, where I made, and still have, many friends.

Then, perhaps six months or so after his death, one of his friends, a charming man, shall I call him Mr X, asked me if he could take me to dinner. Afterwards we went back to the house and . . . Is this what you want to hear Mr Manning?'

'Well there's no need to dwell in detail of any of your own early liaisons, I think. I'm more interested to hear about the time when the other lady friends became involved.'

'I understand. Well Mr X told me that he had a friend who would like to meet me if I had no objection, and one thing led to another so that within about two years, and by personal recommendation, if I can put it that way, I had four or five others calling to see me quite regularly. All of them perfect gentlemen, but not all of them unmarried I have to confess.

Mr Manning, can you please not smile like that. You're making me blush, and I haven't done that since I was a teenager.'

'My apologies, but just tell yourself all this is purely business, nothing more: a bit like a visit to the doctor.'

'Well, just like Mr X, each of the gentlemen had the custom of leaving me a little something when he left, and as it was sometimes a cheque I had to put it through my bank account.'

Now what would the gentleman's cheque stub have shown, wondered Jack, and did it go through his business accounts? At least Martindale didn't charge his whores to the firm: not to my knowledge anyway.

'And the other ladies?' he asked.

'As I said at the office, many ladies get just as much pleasure from sex as gentlemen, and like the gentlemen, they sometimes talk about it, as I did with one of my friends, who was not long divorced. She was a little taken aback at first, but then she called and was introduced to one of the gentlemen. They seemed to like and be very happy with each other. It was spoken of confidentially to other ladies, and now there are five of us including myself.'

For one sickening moment Jack thought of Josie, but then realised that this just wasn't her style. Josie was very much a one-man woman on a medium term basis: until the next special friend came along, that is.

'Five of you at it . . . My apologies. Five of you? In a town the size of Barlow? That's unbelievable.'

'Look Mr Manning. It's not a brothel as you seem to be thinking, and it isn't open nightly. Men can't just drop in, and the ladies don't charge. Couples meet by mutual arrangement and understanding, and if the gentlemen wish to leave a little token of appreciation, well that's fine. But to be frank, all the ladies participate because they enjoy it, and are either divorced or have husbands who aren't quite as interested in that sort of thing as their wives. And it's all arranged by word of mouth: by personal recommendation and mutual agreement only, mainly through the Golf Club, Rotary or the ladies' circles in the town, but very discreetly of course.'

'You say they leave a little token of appreciation, but looking at the bank statements it seems that some of the gentlemen can be very generous indeed.'

'The ladies are very attractive and obliging, and some of the gentlemen are not only rich, but extremely grateful that they can be entertained in circumstances that guarantee their pleasure and utter confidentiality.'

'And how many men?'

'That's really very difficult to say. Some are regulars, almost old friends, but others may come and go. And there are quite a few now from beyond Barlow itself.'

'And all this sexual activity bubbling away beneath the unruffled, respectable surface of this fine old county town: I am surprised.'

'Oh come now Mr Manning: surely not. It's as old as the hills. The Greek gods were always at it, to use your own words. Just think of Zeus. How does that little jingle go: 'Known to all posterity for amorous dexterity?' Haven't you read about wife-swapping and car keys in the fruit bowl?'

He had, of course, but had naively imagined that all that sort of thing took place in the swinging south, not the quiet border counties.

'And if, as you say it isn't a brothel, how would you describe it?'

She thought about that for a while.

'Shall we say a sexual cooperative? I think that would be a fair description.'

Jack found it quite difficult to conceal his admiration for Marilita. She now spoke idiomatic English like a native, and had probably handled their little confrontation better than any advisor that she might have cared to bring with her. He felt sure that at the end of it all there would be little prospect of attaching any liability to tax to her activities or those of her friends. Indeed he had no wish to do so, but the situation was so rich in its possibilities for information and understanding, that he decided he would carry it forward a little further. It was also true that he was now enjoying the experience immensely.

'Mrs Davenport, as you may have gathered, the purpose of this meeting is for me to establish whether or not the money that you and your friends received for the entertainment you provide to the gentlemen is taxable.'

'Yes, I had assumed that Mr Manning.'

'We find that it can sometimes be helpful in reaching a decision if the inspector makes a visit to the premises where the activities in question take place. Do you think that would be possible?'

'Why certainly Mr Manning, but I have to tell you that I am returning to Greece for six weeks or so very shortly, so I will have to telephone you when I am back to arrange a date and time that will be convenient.'

'Well thank you very much for your time Mrs Davenport. I look forward to hearing from you again soon.'

Marilita rose with a smile to shake his hand, but retained a firm grip upon it as she spoke.

'And that will be just a business visit, will it Mr Manning?'

'Oh yes Mrs Davenport: strictly business.'

'You've been entertaining strange ladies in Bosewell's they tell me.'

Jack hadn't been so naive as to believe that his assignation with the beautiful Marilita would go unnoticed and unreported, and in truth he was singularly indifferent whether it was or not. If Josie said nothing, but suspected everything, so much the better: perhaps she wouldn't take him quite so much for granted. If she asked, well he'd tell her the truth.

'Yes, I thought they might. Strictly business though. We'd started in the office, but when it came to coffee time I really couldn't offer her our standard sludge, so we walked up to Bosewell's. Do you know the lady?'

'I've certainly seen her about town, and I've a feeling we may have met at some time in the past, but we don't seem to move in the same circles.'

When it comes to the men though, you've probably got rather more in common than you might suppose, thought Jack.

'Name of Davenport, and born in Greece. Came over . . . Oh it must be almost twenty years ago now. She married a local lad from Barton who went on to do well in the accountancy line and eventually moved here. Died young though, and she's been a widow for six or seven years now. She lives in that handsome old Edwardian place just outside Eastgate. God knows though what she does alone down there with all those rooms.'

He'd thrown in the final comment as a bit of bait to see whether Josie perhaps knew more than she let on. But she didn't rise to the bait, which seemed to indicate just how discreet and confidential Mrs Davenport's services were. If Josie had no suspicion what was going on just outside Eastgate few others would.

'It's nothing you can tell me about I suppose, your business with the lady.'

'Wouldn't do Josie. Priests and taxmen: secrets of the confessional. All that sort of stuff.'

'Isn't it fascinating though: knowing so much about everybody in town?'

'But I don't. It's all mainly finance, accountancy and technical matters: dull routine stuff. It's in the private lives that you find the smut and all the interesting gossip. Think of us Josie.'

He stretched out his hand to stroke her thigh, but she slipped out of bed before he could go any further.

'That's enough Jack: time to get dressed and go about our business now. And I do wish you would move that great lump of a bear out to some other room. I have the feeling that he's always watching us when we're together like this. It's most off-putting.'

'Move Buckingham? My other self. Oh I couldn't do that Josie. He's the very soul of discretion. I tell him everything, and we talk over my problems when I can't sleep at night.'

'I really don't know how you can be so silly about a collection of old bears Jack.'

It was the first time they'd been together since his meeting with Mrs Davenport, and Josie's question had come when they woke up from an overlong post-coital slumber with barely time to shower and dress before going to The Pump, where Josie had booked a table for dinner. Dinner at The Pump with Josie was not a choice Jack would have made: it had too many memories. When they'd eaten out on previous occasions he'd made the booking, but this time he'd been pre-empted. Josie had said that she wanted to give him a treat for a change, so there was nothing he could do about it.

After coffee, when he was relaxing with a brandy and a cigarette, Josie sprung her surprise.

'I thought we might perhaps pop up to London again and take in a show. I've got tickets for *Cats* at the New Theatre. It only opened a few weeks ago, and its getting pretty good reviews.'

Jack knew Josie well enough to understand that it was only their meal at The Pump that was the treat. She wasn't including the London trip, when they would be going Dutch, as they did for *Otello* and Venice. He didn't know the show, and now that he was sleeping regularly with Josie in Barlow, he didn't fancy stumping up for his share of another two nights in Le Rendezvous, if that was what she had in mind. She seemed to understand his hesitancy and perhaps the reason for it, and spoke again before he answered.

'I thought we'd make it just the night after the show this time. Perhaps Arran House in Gower Street. It's a simple little place, but comfortable and clean.'

'And what's the show about. It's an odd title. Not a modern opera is it?'

Beyond the fact that it was a new musical about cats and by Lloyd Webber, Josie couldn't tell him much, and that was enough to give him pause. He'd once gone with Kate to see a production of *Jesus Christ Superstar* at the Wolverton Hippodrome, and they'd left at the interval unimpressed with the production and blasted out of their seats by gross over-amplification. He wasn't eager to expose himself to another dose of the same, but he didn't want to disappoint Josie either, and after satisfying himself on the dates it was agreed.

At least Josie was right about Arran House. Clean, simple and comfortable, their double room (not even a King Size bed he noted) wasn't going to break the bank, and the Turkish restaurant around the corner looked reasonably priced. For someone whose Krugerrands were now worth almost £70,000 Jack was still a remarkably careful man, but he had stuck religiously to his resolve not to attempt any encashment until he was well clear of the Revenue.

They ate lightly before the theatre, where they had good seats towards the front of the second block of stalls with easy access to the bar at the interval, where Jack topped up a glass of champagne (Josie's treat she said) with a large whisky, which after the first half, he felt he needed. They exited to a fine night, and a short stroll back to the Turkish restaurant for a late supper.

'Wasn't that wonderful Jack?' said Josie, giving him a squeeze around the waist.

'You enjoyed it did you Josie?'

'Why didn't you?'

'Not really my cup of tea, and I'm wondering what they thought poor old Elliot had done to deserve that.'

'Elliot?' said Josie, clearly puzzled by the name.

'Yes T S,' said Jack.

'What's he got to do with it?'

Jack stopped walking and looked at her, before giving her a hug and a kiss.

'Josie, you're absolutely priceless. You haven't even read the programme notes.'

She bridled a bit at that.

'Well what's that got to do with enjoying it?'

'Absolutely nothing. You're quite right. I was being tedious. Forget it. I'm glad you enjoyed the evening: now let's have a nice pleasant supper together.'

As it was late they contented themselves with a selection of mezes and a dessert, and were enjoying a coffee and liqueur when Josie, clearly not content to let the matter drop, took up the cudgels once again on behalf of *Cats*.

'But why didn't you enjoy it Jack. Everybody else there seemed to think it was terrific.'

'But that's hardly an argument. Perhaps they all went knowing what to expect and looking forward to it. If you were to take me to a football match, though God forbid that you ever should, you'd find forty-odd thousand roaring their heads off, and me bored to tears. It's horses for courses Josie. Can't we just leave it at that and not spoil the rest of the evening.'

She pouted and sipped at her liqueur for a few moments before speaking again.

'But you must have your reasons.'

'I do, but are you sure you want to hear them.'

'I can't see why not.'

'Well then overall I thought that it was ghastly, meretricious poshlost. The plot line was almost non-existent. The melodies, if you can call them that, were a cheap, naive and sentimental tug at the heart strings which even Puccini would have been ashamed of. And it was all epitomised by the ghastly, tear-jerking caterwauling in *Memories*. I was bored silly.'

'Well to be honest Jack, I felt much the same when you insisted that I should sit down and listen to . . . Oh what was it called? Winter something or the other.'

'Josie. You mean *Winterreise*! How could you? You're a bloody Philistine, a lovely one, but still a Philistine.'

Their conversations from then on were fairly terse and matter-of-fact, and had it not been for the fact that nightclothes had never featured in their preparation for bed, and that the bed was only a standard double, things might have stayed that way until morning.

But inevitably flesh touched on flesh, and in Jack flesh began to stir, but he remained on his side of the bed with his back to Josie, until he felt her arm stealing round his chest, and heard her singing softly into his ear. She'd chosen *Memories*.

'If you touch me,
You'll understand what happiness is,
Look, a new day has begun.'

By then Jack wasn't at all reluctant to surrender once again to Josie and the old imperative, but when they turned aside to sleep he found himself remembering that when he'd first played Schubert to Kate, she had cried.

18

Eastgate Villa: Im Chambre Séparée

Early visitors to Barlow's open market were already out on the streets as Jack set off from his office for Eastgate and his meeting with Mrs Davenport, who had now returned from Athens. The town was busier than usual, it being one of only two days in the month devoted to a genuine local market, when fresh produce brought in from the countryside and villages around drew shoppers from all over the county for a day out: a wander around the town, an early lunch at Bosewell's or The Pump, and then a visit to the ranks of stalls before returning home laden with pies and cakes, fresh fruit and vegetables, dairy produce and perhaps a couple of bottles of local wine or cider.

To avoid the crowds he turned into the gates of All Saints' and worked his way diagonally across the churchyard and on to the cobbles of Shady Lane that ran parallel to the market square, and then dropped down to Eastgate, the only surviving postern gate in one of the best preserved sections of the town walls.

If Noddy had set out to find a safe and secluded location from which Marilita and Barlow's frail sisters could pleasure their gentlemen friends, after his untimely departure from such earthly delights himself, he could hardly have chosen a house in a better location. Tucked away from common view outside the town walls, and overlooked by only one other property, Eastgate Villa could be approached by car along a winding drive off a country lane, and yet was easy of access on foot from the town through the old postern gate and a secluded side entrance, through which Jack now made his way to the front door.

Stepping back a little to get a better overall view of the house, it stuck Jack that in buying such a property not only must Noddy have been very conscious of the sort of social status to which he ultimately aspired, but also hoping that Marilita might perhaps give him one or even two little Noddies to follow in his footsteps. It would have been the perfect house in a perfect location for a large family. Built around the eighteen-nineties, he would have guessed: large, solid and well-proportioned, but not particularly handsome.

His ring at the door bell was answered by Marilita looking as elegant and beautiful as ever, but now lightly tanned after six weeks of Mediterranean sunshine.

'Do come in Mr Manning,' she said, stepping back into a roomy entrance vestibule, where the patterned tiles of the floor were faintly coloured by the last of the morning light through two stained glass side windows.

Even in the vestibule Jack was impressed by the quality of workmanship and materials employed, but much more so as Marilita led him through double stained-glass doors into a spacious high-ceilinged inner hall, where a handsome staircase led up to a galleried landing, and off which three doors gave access to the rooms of the ground floor. The quality of the few pieces of furniture, of the prints on the walls and the decoration he took in at a glance. My word, Noddy did it in style, he thought. Must have had a hell of a mortgage.

'Mr Manning,' said Marilita. 'I'd just like to be absolutely clear on one thing before we go any further. Anything you hear today will be held in absolute confidence, will it?'

'I can give you my complete assurance on that,' said Jack.

'Very well. Would you follow me please?'

She opened a door from the hall and led him into a large sitting room comfortably, almost certainly expensively, furnished and full of light. At one end an arched bay window looked out on to the front garden, at the other double doors opened into a old-fashioned, vine-shaded conservatory where a dark-haired young lady stood alone gazing into the garden. As soon as she was aware of their presence she turned and came towards them.

'This is Marilyn, one of the other ladies, who I should add are always known only by their first names,' said Marilita. 'I asked her to join us in case you wished to have anything I say confirmed. I'll just go and pour the coffee, and then be right with you again.'

With that she departed for the kitchen leaving Jack and Marilyn standing a few feet apart. A deliberate ploy, to embarrass him he suspected, just to show him that she was now on her patch and held all the cards. What the hell did he say now? 'Do you come her often?' His technical training had never prepared him for this.

'I suppose we might as well sit down.' That was all he was able to muster.

Marilyn said nothing, but with a smile eased herself into a chair, and crossed her legs with the same discreet exposure of thigh that Marilita had employed in his office: standard operating procedure he imagined. What next? 'Lovely weather for it?' Fortunately Marilyn came to his relief.

'I understand that Marilita has told you all about us?'

He nodded in reply, and was a little taken aback at the ladies' willingness to talk about their activities quite openly.

'And what do you think about it?'

He needed to give some consideration to his answer to that.

'Well, if you are asking for a personal opinion.' He paused, thinking ahead a little, 'I should say that I see it as a very useful social service, and one for which there is quite a demand I understand.'

'Well we enjoy it,' she said. 'And professionally?'

'Oh I think it's a little too early for me to express an opinion on that. Ask me again when I'm leaving.'

Their conversation was interrupted when Marilita returned with the coffee and took up the baton.

'Firstly Mr Manning, can I take it that you will not be embarrassed as we go around the house if we speak absolutely frankly on these matters?'

'Well I hope I'm broad-minded enough not to be shocked, but you do have the advantage of me remember, in that you know where we are going.'

'Perhaps I should deal first with the housekeeping arrangements which may be of more interest to you from a professional point of view. This room and the rest of the ground floor is mine alone, and quite private. If one of my gentlemen calls then we go to one of the upstairs rooms to which we all have access. When I'm away, as I was recently, the ground floor can be closed off, but as all the ladies have a key to the front door the upper part of the house is always open to them.

Contributions to the overhead expenses of that part of the house are made by all of us on a pro rata basis, and we keep a separate floating fund for what I could call operational expenses: laundry bills, oils and sex aids, costumes and make-up, wine and little tit-bits.'

'She means eatables Mr Manning,' said Marilyn with a smile.

'Don't be a tease Marilyn,' said Marilita, and continued. 'Well, as I said when we met last, we are all quite experienced ladies of course, married or formerly married, and looking for a little something extra in our sex lives that we might otherwise be missing.

And if I can turn to the pleasures that we enjoy, and of course the gentlemen with us, well I think I can say that although we all have our own little specialities and preferences, I don't believe that any of us go in for anything too bizarre, do we Marilyn?'

Marilyn pursed her lips and shook her head, but gave Jack such a meaningful look that he was left with the very firm impression that she might be offering her visitors a rather more extensive menu of fare than Marilita.

'More the conventional ways of enjoying sex, if I can put it that way,' continued Marilita. 'Although I do realise that conventions have varied in time and place. Certainly none of us would entertain any of the nastier perversions. Not that any of our gentlemen would be interested in that sort of thing, although we do offer role playing, a little spanking if wanted and perhaps some modest bondage if they insist. I suppose it's really a question of how far the lady is happy to go.'

Dear God, thought Jack, once again taken aback at the uninhibited way in which they thought and spoke about their activities, she might just as well be describing the lost wax process, she's that bloody cool about it.

'And now, unless you've anything you want to clarify with Marilyn, I think I should show you around our little love nest.'

'Always very happy to oblige with anything Mr Manning,' teased Marilyn. 'You only have to ask.'

'Most generous of you,' he replied, at last feeling a little more at ease. 'It's an offer which in other circumstances I might find it difficult to refuse, but for the present I must say no.'

'Then now I must sadly leave you in the very capable hands of Marilita, and return to town,' said Marilyn. 'And perhaps we will meet again in those other circumstances some time. I'm sure we'd both enjoy that . . . And you're so right Marilita: he's a lovely man.'

Her final words, a blatant stage whisper ostensibly to Marilita, were primarily, and very obviously, for Jack's benefit.

'I'll see you out,' said Marilita, walking with her to the hall, where Jack could hear them talking softly.

Jack had been called many things in the course of his career, but 'lovely man' was a first. What on earth was it that appealed to these libidinous ladies? The fact that he didn't 'come on' at them, as Josie chose to put it? Well that certainly hadn't worked with Kate, quite the reverse in fact. It was all very puzzling.

As he waited for Marilita to return he wandered round the room looking at the paintings and prints that she favoured, and generally doing what investigators do when they are left alone with the opportunity: nosing around where he shouldn't. His interest was quite superficial, however, until he noticed a Guildhall appointments book alongside the telephone on a side table.

His resistance to temptation was short-lived. At first he contented himself with a quick peek inside, but then intrigued he picked it up, and looked through the pages in more detail: few morning assignations, he noted, many afternoon, but mostly evening and some even overnight. How on earth did that work out for the married ones? Astonished at the few names that he saw that he recognised, he was still methodically working his way through the book several minutes later when Marilita returned, and saw him with it in his hands.

'Mr Manning. You should be ashamed of yourself!'

He ignored the reproof, and returned to the book.

'These,' he said. 'All of these? T Bayley, that would be Bayley Jnr from the solicitors, I suppose. T W Evershed, presumably the managing director of Eversheds Ltd. Major Thompson from out at Barton Hill. I could go on. You've really have got admirers from the great and . . . the good I was going to say, but perhaps not.

But my apologies. I shouldn't have peeked. No part of my brief. All instantly forgotten.'

'You'll excuse me Mr Manning if I say that this seems to me to be a rather strange sort of income tax investigation.'

'Mrs Davenport, it's been strange to me from the outset, and it gets stranger by the minute, so please carry on as you intended before Marilyn left us.'

From the hall she led him up to the galleried landing on the first floor, off which there were four rooms, and a staircase leading to the top floor.

'We do have two attic rooms,' she said. 'But as the four on this floor are usually quite sufficient for us, we very rarely have occasion to use them, so unless you particularly want to look up there we'll just keep to this floor.'

'This floor will be fine.'

She opened the first door inviting Jack to enter, and then followed him, closing it after her. As she did so the curtains were slowly drawn across the windows, and the room darkened, only to be discreetly illuminated again by some carefully concealed lighting that left most of its space in shadow, but the bed and the simple chaise longue at its feet clearly, almost dramatically lit. And as the light softly strengthened, Jack heard the sound of a small orchestra and a warm, female voice singing. He recognised the melody at once, although he had never before heard the words in an English translation.

You may say tonight will come and go,
But you can't hide the light that's in your eyes.
And you may say my arms will only leave you cold,
But wait till they hold you and then look wise.

'We do our very best to be discerning and imaginative for our gentlemen Mr Manning. What do you think of it?'

'Very artistic,' said Jack, who had indeed been impressed. He'd no idea that covert, extra-marital sex, as it was for most of the men and some of the women, could be conducted in such style. No hugger-mugger, wham bang thank you m'am encounters here. All very creative and to be conducted at leisure. Those thoughts he kept to himself, but continued, 'I'm interested in the choice of music. Do you know it in the original German?'

'Oh no Mr Manning: I'd always thought it was English. Maurice first played it to me from an old LP, and I had it copied to tape.'

Her voice had a note of nostalgia in it, and Jack was surprised to find himself quite touched at the thought of Noddy Davenport romancing his young Greek bride to the strains of *Im Chambre Séparée*.

It struck a nostalgic note too for Jack, who'd first heard it with Kate in the early years of their marriage, on one of many visits to a little bed and breakfast establishment they used when they went to the Edinburgh festival. With only three double bedrooms, it was small enough to give the landlady Mrs Johnson enough time to indulge her favourite occupation, sitting down with her guests and talking politics over breakfast to the sound of her favourite pieces on an old record player.

On the last day of their visit she had confided to them that she only accepted return visits from those couples whose political views she found to be in accord with her own. As these could best be described as a robust, if slightly eccentric, form of socialism, return bookings would inevitably have been limited. Jack and Kate, however, found themselves amongst them, and it would have been during breakfast on the second visit when Mrs Johnson paused (a very rare event) in the middle of her fulminations against Macmillan's pay pause policy, so that they could better listen to the recording. 'Schwarzkopf,' she said. 'The ultimate song of seduction.' They went out and bought a copy immediately after breakfast. It was one of the few records Kate took with her when she left.

'No, no, not English. It's from an old German operetta, said Jack. 'And I once knew a lady who said it was the ultimate song of seduction.'

'What a lovely thought. I'll tell the other ladies,' said Marilita. 'But we have quite a range to suit the varying tastes of our gentlemen.'

As she spoke she pressed another button, and as the curtains slowly opened again Jack's ears were assaulted with the less than haunting sound of a light tenor wrapping his tonsils round a thousand and one grace notes to the strains of *Unchained Melody*.

'The Righteous Brothers,' she murmured.

'I suppose so,' said Jack.

'And as you can see, now that it's quite light, it's all very stylish and comfortable. Nice buttoned armchair for the gentleman, built-in wardrobe for the costumes, best linen on the bed, tasteful prints on the walls and always fresh flowers on the side table. Each room also has its own ensuite shower, although putting those in did tend to make it a little cramped and intimate, but nobody seems to mind that.'

Tasteful and nice, just the right words for it, thought Jack. It looked indeed to be the very essence of comfortable, conventional, middle class domesticity, which in the circumstances did seem rather odd.

'We have one other room just like this one as you can see,' said Marilita, moving on to the landing, and throwing open its door. 'But the next one along has been fitted out with a little more imagination and flair for those chaps who like that sort of thing.'

Once again Jack was impressed at the way Marilita had grasped even the subtlest conventions in her use of English. It would of course be 'chaps', who were not quite gentlemen, who liked 'that sort of thing'. Both types were busy screwing away while the little lady sat quietly at home of course, but the distinction still carried weight. And then, remembering the married ladies of Eastgate Villa, it struck him that perhaps the little lady might be hard at it too. In adjoining rooms perhaps, providing all the elements of a good French farce.

'That's a very intriguing smile Mr Manning,' said Marilita. 'Can you share the joke with me?'

'Oh just a private thought, nothing special.'

Unlike the unadorned door of the room they had just left, the door at which she now stopped was graced with a porcelain plaque embossed with a coloured portrait that was quite unambiguously that of the god Priapus. Even so Marilita made such a point of drawing it to his attention, that Jack was left with the feeling that she might now be out to test his capacity to remain unembarrassed.

'We call this room our cabinet of curiosities. It's the god Priapus on the door, of course. From the fresco in the House of the Vettii as you may know.'

She opened the door, led him into a darkened room and using a dimmer switch, slowly turned up the light to reveal what Jack would subsequently describe to Jimmy (while keeping his source completely anonymous) as a regular treasure trove of erotic curiosities.

'I really can't take any credit for this room myself,' said Marilita. 'The furniture, furnishings and colour scheme are all down to Marilyn, everything else you see, the prints, pictures and the little curiosities, are on long-term loan from a gentleman who is a collector and aficionado of this sort of thing, and would rather have it on display for our other friends than locked away at home, as it apparently was for many years.'

In contrast to the bright and tasteful pastel shades and crisp cream linen that lent an air of domestic innocence to the room Jack had just left, the furnishings and decor here were heavy with sexual innuendo. The walls were hung with soft, velvet flocked wallpaper in a deep crimson that was replicated in the heavy drapes at the window. The bed was clearly dressed for pleasure not for rest, with thin sheets of striped silk that gleamed now deep blue, now purple as Marilita brushed her hand across the surface with a smile. At its head matching pillows with a handsome old-gold trim were piled high, offering all the comfort and support that the most passionate of couplings might require.

At its foot a sofa and footstool stood out in a brighter more vibrant crimson, as though demanding more particular attention. Across bed, sofa and floor deep, yielding scatter cushions were strewn, and overall hung the exciting, seductive fragrance of some subtle, but sensual perfume.

On the wall facing the bed, in front of a floor to ceiling mirror, the god Priapus made his second appearance: this time in the form of a generous and equally unambiguous statue.

'Quarter life-size I am told, at least in most respects,' said Marilita. 'He was only a minor god you know, although you wouldn't think it to look at him would you? Protector of livestock, fruit and plants: and so the Greeks used to keep a statue of him in their gardens, and give him a little stroke as they passed by, to propitiate him, if you understand me.'

She smiled innocently at Jack, who did indeed understand her very well, but by now was well beyond showing any sign of embarrassment, and beginning seriously to question Marilita's antecedents. Where on earth had Noddy found her? Strutting the beat in Piraeus with the other poutanaki? Or had she sprung sui generis from the nubile loins of Aphrodite, and just dropped into his lap. Despairing of making any further sense of her, he directed his attention to one of the many prints that covered the walls.

'It's not a room I use much you know. My gentlemen never seem to need to be encouraged by this sort of thing. I believe though that . . . Mr X shall we call him again, did leave some sort of guide to his collection for those who might be interested.'

She opened a drawer to a side table, and soon turned to Jack again with a piece of card in her hand.

'Ah yes, here we have it. Now you must be looking at . . .' she glanced down through the list on the card, 'Yes it says here Four Japanese Shunga Prints, Edo period. Oh aren't they delicate? I wonder when that was. And next there's *The Kiss,* by Klimt of course: now that's beautiful isn't it Mr Manning, bold, bright and discreet, yet so erotic.'

As Jack said nothing, but moved on to another of the prints on the wall, she continued to read from the list.

'Two Erotic Engravings by Thomas Rowlandson:
   The Curious Wanton and *The Pasha*
Four Erotic Lithographs: Paul Avril

Two Aubrey Beardsley ink drawings: scenes from *Lysistrata*

Now there's a woman after my own heart Mr Manning. Maurice took me to see the play at the Herod Atticus before we were married. He was mad about ancient Greece you know: took me all over the place before we came back. But to continue we also have

Six C19 Erotic Lithographs: France, possibly Achille Deveria

The Sleepers: Gustave Courbet

Four prints of erotic frescos: House of the Vettii (Pompeii)

Now I saw those on holiday with Maurice. They're all a little faded, but still very evocative.

Erotic art of Khajuraho: six fine art prints

Now I don't remember those. Where are they?'

She moved along the wall until she came to a stop in front of a cluster of six small prints, which she stopped to examine more closely.

'Oh my goodness,' she exclaimed. 'That really is quite remarkably uninhibited, but I don't think any of our ladies would care to engage in that.'

Jack found it impossible not to respond to that, and had in any case long since decided on the outcome of his unusual investigation, and was now quite content just to enjoy the experience. He wandered along, and looked over her shoulder to study the print that had so engrossed her.

'Mrs Davenport,' he said. 'I don't think the issue is whether they would care to engage in it. Looking at the physical attitudes of the participants, I doubt very seriously whether they could.'

'You surely aren't questioning our athleticism are you Mr Manning? I'm quite sure that if push came to shove, such an expressive phrase in this context, we could prove you wrong.

And that leaves just two engravings from *I Modi (Or The Sixteen Pleasures)*: Jupiter and Juno, Ovid and Corinna. Oh, and they're rather unpleasant I think: great lumpish Roman creatures, not at all like our stylish Greek gods.'

While Marilita continued to study the Khajuraho prints with some interest, Jack walked across to look at the half-dozen or so books that were piled on the table by the easy chair. As he had expected they all continued, or perhaps amplified, the one and only theme of the room.

The Erotica of Pompeii (Colour Illustrated)
Fanny Hill: Memoirs of a Woman of Pleasure
The Lustful Turk or Lascivious Scenes from a Harem
Sexual Mores in the Ancient World (Illustrated)
De Figuris Veneris – English Translation (Illustrated)
Secrets of the Boudoir by a Lady
The Girls from Norton Convent
The Pearl and The Oyster – Anonymous

'I've never been able to understand why men find this sort of thing so fascinating. Art imitating life I suppose, but personally I much prefer the later,' said Marilita, who had completed her examination of the Khajuraho prints. 'But it seems to be Marilyn's gentlemen who most like this room, and from what she tells me they do have some rather strange whims.

Well, now that you've had a good chance to look around, what do you think of the contents of Marilyn's little den Mr Manning?'

Jack gave this a few moments thought before replying.

'Well as an exposition it is inevitably disadvantaged by the restricted scope of its subject matter. Within the

309

limitations that imposes, however, I would say that the Beardsley shows the masterly economy of line that we have all come to expect, as indeed does the Shunga, which also handles its colour palette remarkably well. Courbet, of course, is noted for his wonderful flesh tones, an attribute which this example demonstrates to perfection. As for the Klimt, well . . .'

He was interrupted by Marilita.

'Mr Manning, you are being very naughty and mocking us.'

'No I assure you Mrs Davenport. I'd no more dream of trying to mock you, than you would of trying to embarrass me.'

'Very well then: shall we call it quits and move on to the final room?'

Returning to the landing she opened the door to a room which Jack initially thought might have been a store room, so spartan did it seem after the excesses they had just left. Hung with drapes which enabled it to be sub-divided into three parts, its plain cream-coloured walls were relieved by just three indifferent prints. Containing no bed, its furniture included a dozen or so upright chairs ranged against the walls, two plain sofas, a table, a great pile of scatter cushions in one corner, and what looked to Jack like a rather low vaulting horse with a saddle on it.

'We call this the games room,' said Marilita. 'We keep it exclusively for our themed meetings when perhaps three or four each of our gentlemen and ladies will come together for our own rather special version of blind date, or to engage in what Marilyn likes to describe as a little group therapy.

It could be role playing: the French Maid, Little Red Riding Hood, the Passionate Policewoman, that sort of thing. Or it might be games: Blind Man's Bluff, Ride a

Cockhorse, Musical Chairs or Hunt the Thimble. They're all very popular. Oh, and of course Nymphs and Shepherds, that's the favourite. We open up the whole of the two top floors for that.'

By now Jack's mind was reeling as he tried to reconcile the list of artless children's games with the reality of what might have been taking place. Nymphs and shepherds, for God's sake: that certainly carried him back to his days of innocence. Tea in the front room at his Gran's to Purcell's *Nymphs and Shepherds*, with the piping voices of the Manchester Children's Choir singing their hearts out on the rasping old Columbia 78. He could hear it still:

Nymphs and shepherds come away, come away.
In this grove let's sport and play, let's sport and play.
For this is Flora's holiday,
Sacred to ease and happy love.

A different sort of sport and play at Eastgate Villa though. And Hunt the Thimble? He simply refused to give any thought to what that might involve, or the purposes to which the vaulting horse and saddle might be put.

'Well I think that concludes a pretty comprehensive introduction to our activities here, which is what you requested. Would you like a cup of tea before you go back to the office?'

'Tea with *Nymphs and Shepherds* perhaps?' The words tumbled out before he could stop himself: a catastrophic confusion of ideas across space and time. It could of course mean only one thing to Marilita, and it earned him a very old-fashioned and uncertain look.

'I beg your pardon Mr Manning.'

'Sorry, sorry, sorry,' said Jack. 'My mind was miles away in the past, and no tea thank you very much. I've been away much longer than I anticipated.'

'And are you able to tell me now what your final decision will be about the taxation of the little gifts that our gentlemen friends make to us.'

'Oh certainly, and I think your conception of it as a sexual cooperative comes pretty close to the mark, although for the records I think something a little more oblique might be more fitting. Shall we say a gathering together of two or three, or more, for the sharing and enjoying of a mutual interest and the exchanging of gifts? None of the indicators of trading present, and so no taxability.

My private opinion is that you are all performing a very useful social service to what seems to me to be the highest of standards, and one which I would never in my wildest dreams have expected to find in the very purlieus of a little provincial town like Barlow.'

'I'm sure that all the ladies will be very grateful for that, and I can assure them that all this will be kept absolutely confidential can I?'

'You can indeed.'

'And is it possible that we might meet you again in different circumstances some time Mr Manning? I'm sure that Marilyn would be very pleased to see you: as would I.'

'It's very kind of your to say so, but I think I would find the mix at Eastgate Villa a little too rich for my taste.'

'Oh not with me you wouldn't Mr Manning. Not with me.'

Jack smiled a response, shook her hand and returned to his office. The financial documents he held for Mrs

Davenport he returned to her by letter, and in her file he left a permanent note.

'Few, if any, of the indicators of trading are met. A satisfactory explanation for such money as Mrs Davenport has received being given, the enquiry has been closed.'

19

So Goodbye Dear and Amen

If the Barlow Players' production of *Vanya* had not been quite so enthusiastically received as their preceding farce, it had nevertheless made them a little money, and their regular supporters had been more than satisfied. Following *Vanya*, with a return to comedy, the group was now well into rehearsals for a late summer production of *The Importance of Being Earnest* where Brandy had chosen Justin Hanna to play Jack Worthing.

This was unusual as Justin had only joined the group when rehearsals for *Vanya* were starting, and apart from Brandy and Dot nobody knew much about him. Over drinks in The Pump, however, Jack had learned from Brandy that although a newcomer to Barlow, Justin had many years experience working with an Oxford group under Johnny Ford, an old pro who'd known the Woodvines well in their professional days. He'd spoken so highly of him to Brandy, that he and Dot had done a little work with him alone, and been more than satisfied with what they saw and heard.

'Very, very useful chap Jack,' said Brandy. 'Early thirties, so we can age him up or down, moves well, and has one of the best voices I've heard in years. Let's hope he stays with us.'

'Handsome bugger too,' said Jack. 'Touch of the Greek god about him: all that golden curly hair and a classic profile. The sort who appeals as much to men as to woman I would think. Have you learnt much more about him?'

'Not a lot. Tends to keep his private affairs private, but I know he's unmarried and works for a national firm of architects. He had been based in London, but when he got a move to Wolverton he preferred to live here rather than there, and so he commutes, but says he is able to do much of his work at home. That's about the measure of it.'

For the first time since he joined the group Jack had been less regular in his attendance at rehearsals for *Earnest* than he had for previous productions. Time and the weather were taking their toll on the fabric of his riverside house, and he was working all the daylight hours that were available to get his repainting finished before the autumn rains arrived. He'd also taken a spell of leave from the office so that Jimmy could come up from Rottingdean to look after the carpentry work that was needed, and give him a hand with some re-wiring.

They'd quite enjoyed having some time together entirely by themselves. Jimmy was at last able to talk Jack into joining him in his second exploration of the wonders of medieval craftsmanship that were to be found in the upper reaches of St Botolph's spire, from which Jim returned ecstatic, and Jack grazed, dirty and less than enthusiastic.

'Was that a little tit-for-tat for the climb up All Saints' tower Jim?'

'God, your daily occupation's made you a suspicious bugger Jack. How on earth can you go into raptures about so much in the arts, and not see the beauty that's up there? Go and get cleaned up, and I'll buy you dinner at The Pump.'

The Pump was where they spent their evenings tucked away in a corner, and doing their best to drink the barrel dry, after dining well on Mrs Arscott's cooking. She was still there, looking a touch older, but with the same masterly touch when it came to pastry. At The Pump, despite many long years of penny-pinching, Jim had assumed the role of a man of substance with consummate ease, and insisted on paying throughout. A return, he said, for the many occasions when Jack had stood treat.

'And what about the Krugerrands Jack,' he said, lowering his voice. 'Have you done anything with them yet?'

'Don't intend to Jim. Not till I'm well away from the Revenue, and have thought it through carefully. No need of the cash at present, and the coins are increasing in value hand over fist. They're tucked away nice and safe, and they won't rust.'

'And you and Josie? You're still together are you Jack?'

'Well "together" hardly describes it Jim, as you've probably worked out. We've enjoyed providing each other with a little R & R, as they say, but that's about the measure of it. So it's not exactly an ideal domestic scenario, and not likely to become one. She's not inclined that way, and I think I've known from the beginning it never would be like that.

To be honest Jim, apart from her very real and beautiful physical attributes, there's not very much there. Not the sort of woman you'd want to share breakfast with day after day. Oh she's brilliant at her job, and somehow she's an excellent stage manager. I say somehow, because apart from what she's picked up from Brandy, she's read nothing much since she left school. Wouldn't be a marriage of true minds if we went that far, so better left as it is. And how are things with you and Celia?'

'Fine Jack, fine. Both glad to be shot of all the bloody hard graft at the Croft. Have you heard how the new people are getting on there?'

'Haven't heard a thing from the hill since you left Jim. I really ought to pop back some time, but never get round to it.'

'Well I can give you a bit of news then. Because I was always so close to dear old Ada, Ted has kept in touch with me since he and Charlie left. Just an occasional letter you know. Well in the last one he told me that Charlie and Lorna have decided to stay out in New Zealand with their son. He says they've got a beautiful place out there at about half the cost it would be here. Spot called Akaroa: describes it as bloody gorgeous. Just like paradise after all those years slogging his guts out up on the hill. He's invited both you and me, if ever we feel like making the trip.

Ted says he and Sarah are going out for a few months next year. They never did go back to the hill by the way: settled in the West Country instead.'

They made good progress on the house while Jim was with Jack, and by the time they settled down for their final evening at The Pump, Jack told Jim that he reckoned he would be able to finish things off in a week of evenings.

'Well if that's the case, why don't you pop down and have a weekend with us as soon as you've got your painting and the next Players' production behind you? Celia would love to see you. She still sees Kate you know. Pops up fairly regularly on the train and stays overnight so they can do a theatre together. She asks me to let you know Kate keeps well, and sends her love.'

He didn't add that without telling Kate what she was up to, Celia was manoeuvring desperately to bring the two of them back together. From her recent meetings with Kate, Celia was convinced that she would like to make an approach to Jack, but feared she would be embarrassed by a rebuff. Jim had mixed views about interfering. His opinion was that they should be left to sort it out for themselves, but he had reluctantly agreed to do

317

his best to sound Jack out on the idea in the course of his visit.

'I'm pleased to hear she's well Jim. Still with her parents I suppose. Tell Celia to pass on my love when she sees her next.'

'So if it's not likely to be permanent with Josie, are you going to carry on rattling around in that great place all by yourself, or look for somewhere smaller?'

'Oh I'm staying put Jim. It gets a bit lonely at times, but I've got the bears for company. At least I can have an intelligent literary discussion with Buckingham, which is more than I can say for Josie.'

'You're going to keep them all then?'

'Too many fond memories attached to them to let them go.'

'And what about R & R if Josie moves on?'

'Well if ever things get really desperate Jim I know a couple of very attractive ladies who apparently think I'm a lovely man. So I reckon I'll be alright. Get another couple of pints, and I'll tell you all about it.'

They'd finished that pint and were well into another before Jack reached the end of his anonymised, but detailed and colourful account of the Eastgate Villa saga.

'Well that's quite a yarn Jack,' said Jim. 'And I thought life in taxes was dull. Trumps anything I saw or heard in the war, and I knocked about a bit. Nymphs and shepherds as a sex romp! Now you wouldn't find that in the Berkha, though you might the saddle. Very imaginative those ladies: classy too.

And I must say I like the sound of your little Greek widow and her friend. And that was actually what they said when you left was it, that they'd be pleased to see you?'

Jack sipped his pint, and said nothing.

'So that's Josie: and now two others throwing themselves at your feet. What's your secret Jack?'

'Oh I just play hard to get Jim. Works like a charm, but not with Kate it seems . . . Sorry Jim, shouldn't dredge that up again. It's being in The Pump. Always reminds me of the old days.'

Jim left the following morning with the understanding that Jack would be paying them a visit before the winter set in, and the belief that Celia was right after all, and that if Josie wasn't in the way Jack and Kate might well be happy back together.

Jack returned to the Players a little more than a week before the production to find that Josie's competence was such that he really hadn't been missed. Everything was proceeding smoothly, and continued to do so right through to the curtain on the final night.

Audiences had been good at the start of the week, but were even better after a mid-week review in both the local and the county paper in which an excellent production was said to be notable in particular for the outstanding performance of Justin Hanna in his first appearance with the Players.

The after-show party began, as they invariably did, with Brandy's address of compliments and constructive criticism to the company. 'Just a few words,' he said, but inevitably they went on to become many, as Dot knew they would.

'Dear God,' she whispered to Jack. 'Have you ever known a man who loves the sound of his own voice as Brandy does? He promised to be brief, and now the bugger's been at it for almost ten minutes. Be a darling please, and sneak across and top up my glass for me. I mustn't let him think he hasn't got my devoted attention, or he'll sulk for the rest of the evening.'

The after-show party, or booze-up which more accurately described it, had been an aspect of his association with the Players that Jack had particularly enjoyed, but on two earlier occasions he'd been happy to fit in with Josie's preference to leave before the serious drinking began.

This time, however, he was surprised when she not only showed no inclination to slip away, but seemed quite happy to mix it with the men, and apparently relish the attention. As Jack's enjoyment of such affairs was mainly that of an interested and entertained observer of proceedings as inhibitions fell away under the influence of drink, particularly those of one or two senior ladies, he remained attentive enough to notice that as things began to get rather silly (Josie's words at an earlier party) she was still nursing the same almost untouched glass of wine, and very easily fending off any unwanted attention from the men.

By one in the morning, when Jack was himself ready to suggest to Josie that they might leave, he noticed that she was tucked away in a corner, deeply engaged in conversation with Brandy and Dot, and so they remained for some time. Eventually, however, Brandy heaved himself to his feet with much assistance from Josie and Dot, and after a valedictory address to the assembled company that not one of them heeded, was ushered out of the room and home by Dot, who cursed him roundly under her breath the whole of the way.

Only then did Josie walk across, and for the first time that evening, devote a little time to Jack.

'Enjoyed the evening Jack?' she said, giving him a peck on the cheek and taking a sip from his glass.

'In my own quiet way Josie: on the outside looking in.'

'Is that what you meant when you called yourself semi-detached once?'

'Yes, I suppose it is in a way. Surprised to see you mixing it with the boys though. I thought you didn't like that sort of thing.'

'Now don't be jealous Jack. Just fancied a bit of a change. We mustn't let ourselves get into a rut.'

'Oh I hadn't realised we were doing that: must be careful in future.'

He took back his glass and emptied it.

'Ready for off?'

'Ready for off Jack, but you won't mind if I ask you just to walk me home tonight will you? I've got a bit of a thick head, and would really like to get some sleep, and have a long lie-in tomorrow. It's been a hectic week.'

If Jack's expressions of understanding and commiseration were touched with a hint of irony, it was only half-intended, and apparently went unnoticed by Josie, but as they sauntered back through the silent streets he was very conscious that it was the first time that Josie had made an excuse. A headache: such a cliché, but that was Josie.

Her kiss on parting was just as warm and generous as ever, but she didn't linger, and was soon gone with just a brief, 'I'll give you a ring later in the week Jack.'

A post-party Sunday would normally be a day of rest and recovery for all concerned, and as it would be at least a couple of weeks before any consideration was given to the next production, Jack was surprised to receive an early afternoon call from Dot.

'Sorry to interrupt your day of rest Jack, but I wonder if you could pop up in about half an hour and join me for afternoon tea at Bosewell's. It's ever such a genteel affair on a Sunday: altogether fitting after last night's excesses.'

'Secret assignation is it Dot? No Brandy?'

'Don't mention the bugger Jack. Even after all he put away last night he was up at The Pump at lunchtime, and now I can hear him snoring his head off in the next room. Just you and me Jack: a little tête à tête.'

'Sounds very mysterious Dot. Not a seduction scenario is it?'

'Oh I think my seducing days are past Jack, but there was a time when I might have been tempted by a fine upstanding young fellow like you. And you by me I might add. But all will become clear when we meet. Shall we say three-thirty? I'll see you inside.'

'I'll be there.'

It Is A Bosewell Tradition That Gentlemen Do
Not Smoke Pipes At Afternoon Tea On Sunday

Sunday tea at Bosewell's was a Barlow ritual that Jack was experiencing for the first time, but the sign hung prominently on one of the double doors gave notice of what he might expect within, where on the dresser by the door *The Sunday Times, Church Times* and *Barlow Briefings*, the Parish magazine, were the only reading on display.

Beyond the dresser he found a genteel (Dot had chosen her words wisely) world of jackets and ties, stylish millinery, doilies, wafer-thin sandwiches, three-tiered cake stands, subdued conversation and the soft chink of high quality epns on fine china: all of it serviced by Bosewell's long-pensionable brigade of 'nippies,' perhaps not as mobile or attractive as their predecessors of the thirties, but beloved of Bosewell's regulars, who mourned the passing of each one as that of an old friend.

'Isn't it wonderful Jack?' said Dot looking around her. 'A window on a lost world. I can remember tea in Hathaway's before the war on my early trips to Stratford: it was just like this. That was when I first caught the bug of course. It always takes me back when I come here: shades of Wolfit, who was really much better in those early years, and not the bit of a joke that he became later: but that's not it Jack.

In fact it's a bit of a long story I'm afraid, so enjoy your sandwich, listen to your aunty Dot, and perpend. For as long as Brandy's been out of the business himself and working with amateurs, he's wanted to do a *Much Ado*, but he's never yet found his Beatrice and Benedict: at least not at the same time in the same place. We played the roles together in our early days: great fun and not bad either.

Then as soon as he worked a little with Justin, he knew at once that he'd got another Benedict, but still no Beatrice: great frustration and much fuming around the house of course, until I suggested we should make one last attempt to lure Josie back on stage. We both knew she'd be perfect for the part, and that was why you may have seen us in a bit of a huddle at the party.'

'I noticed, but Josie said nothing, and I had no particular reason to ask her what was going on.'

'So she didn't mention that she had finally agreed to take the part then?'

'No she didn't. I'm surprised, but it's up to her. I'd know soon enough anyway, and surely you and Brandy are delighted aren't you? Why the urgency to tell me?'

'Well Brandy and I know pretty well how things are with you and Josie, and it wasn't so much that she'd taken the part, but that she only did so when she knew she'd by playing opposite Justin.'

Jack thought about that for a moment.

'And you both think that's significant for reasons other than the play?'

'Sorry to say we do Jack. You've been away for most rehearsal meetings until the last week or so, but from what I've seen, I feel pretty sure that Josie's rather keen on our Justin, and Brandy's inclined to agree. You'll have noticed how chummy she was with the men last night: a bit unusual that. Usually keeps them at arm's length, present company excepted of course, but last night Justin was of the party.'

'I'm greatly touched by your concern Dot, but I'm not Josie's keeper you know. We each have our own lives, and go our own way if and when we want to. Let's say we're just special friends: nothing permanent.'

'Special friends. What a lovely way of putting it Jack: very delicate. But it wasn't only you we were thinking about.'

'I'm sorry Dot, you've lost me. If Josie and Justin choose to get together who else is going to be concerned?'

'But that's just it you see.'

'Dot, please say what you want to say, and don't be so bloody opaque. What's just it?'

'He's gay Jack.'

'I don't believe it. I'd have sworn that he was absolutely straight. Why on earth do you think otherwise?'

'Oh I don't just think Jack; I know. Johnny told Brandy when he had a word with him about Justin's work with the Oxford group: said there was no doubt about it. As far as Brandy and I are concerned it's neither here nor there; chacun à son goût say we. I thought though that perhaps Josie should be told, but Brandy says it's not for us to say anything and won't hear of it.'

'Why not?'

'Think about it Jack. He might seem hail-fellow-well-met in The Pump, but when it comes to a production nothing else matters, and he's quite unforgiving of anyone causing a problem. If Josie gets to know she'll almost certainly pull out, and then he loses his Beatrice.

And he's so enthusiastic and happy at the prospect Jack that I haven't the heart to say anything to spoil it for him, but I still feel mean at not saying anything to Josie. So . . .'

'So you're putting the ball in my court to ease your conscience about fouling things up for Brandy. You think that I'll tell Josie for my own personal reasons.'

'You're being very hard Jack. Try to look at it from a woman's point of view. Brandy doesn't want her to be told. You might very well want to tell her, and I'm entirely in two minds about it. In brief it all seems to be very nicely balanced, so my female intuition tells me to leave it to the gods, whose wisdom is profound.'

'Having delivered yourself of all of this, I take it that you are paying for tea Dot.'

'My pleasure Jack. Now let's indulge ourselves in some of these scrumptious cakes, and you tell me which of these God-fearing, church-going gentlemen you see around you is fiddling his taxes.'

The end of the affair came with the same light touch and good-humoured banter with which it had started and been conducted. On the Saturday after the show Josie had telephoned Jack to ask him to drop in for a pre-lunch drink before they strolled up to The Pump for lunch together.

'It's such a lovely morning you'll find me in the garden,' she said. 'Come in through the side gate, I'll leave it open.'

The gardens of the houses on High Street and Priory Hill were generally considered to be one of the features that made life there so attractive, and enabled the properties to command such high prices. Having their origins in the long burgess plots of the medieval town, they were almost without exception high-walled, secluded and secret, apart from the one day of the Barlow Flower Show, when a dozen or so might be opened up to the common gaze for a small fee in aid of a good cause.

The gardens might at one time have been entered through their coach houses on The Narrows or Withy Lane, but as these had one by one been sold off and converted into bijou residences, the owners of the big houses had to suffer the inconvenience of their gardeners gaining access through the house: boots in hand of course. Josie, however, was one of the lucky ones with a garden gate opening to the High Street through which Jack entered to make his way up the narrow tiled side-passage into the garden.

The real work of the garden, mowing, hedge trimming and all that grubbing around in the dirt, as Josie described it, was done by Arthur, who for thirty years had earned what he regarded as a satisfactory living in the gardens of the same dozen or so houses on High Street. Josie's personal horticultural activity was never such as might be calculated to leave a lady in a glow. She gardened as she passed through life generally, with style and grace, and dressed as she would for a garden party.

As Jack passed out from the passage he was just able to catch sight of her at the far end of the garden. Half-screened by greenery and distance she seemed dryad-like to be hovering effortlessly in mid-air, until he moved forward, and was able to stand unseen behind her, silently admiring her figure posed elegantly before him, three feet above the ground on the capping stones of a raised flower bed. Poised with assurance on one attractive, nylon-clad leg, and bending gracefully forward to trim a few faded blossoms from a rambling rose, she preserved her balance by raising the other leg gracefully behind her, to expose just as much of a shapely, eye-catching calf and thigh as she might have been happy with had she been in public view. As he stood unobserved observing her, he felt a passing twinge of regret that his enjoyment of all of that he saw before him might soon be a thing of the past.

'Oh hello Jack,' she said, suddenly aware of him. 'My word you are a silent mover. Here catch me as I come down will you?'

He did so, and held her to him until he got the kiss he was waiting for.

'I've put out chairs and a table under the tree Jack. You'll find a bottle of white in the fridge. Will you bring it out with a couple of glasses while I put my gloves away and freshen up.'

He was sitting enjoying his wine and the view of the eccentric roofscape of the High Street visible above the garden walls when Josie returned, and settled not in the other chair, but on the grass beside him where she took his free hand, and sat holding it in silence as she slowly sipped her wine. Forewarned of the situation by Dot, and quite sure that this appointment had not been made with mutual pleasuring in mind as in the past, Jack sat wondering with some amusement just what her opening gambit might be.

'Jack.' Somehow, like a young child, she managed to draw out that tersest of syllables into a two-toned diphthong, and then paused. 'I've been thinking.'

'Yes, I thought perhaps you had.' He continued to be deeply absorbed by the High Street skyline, ignoring what he was sure was Josie's strange look at his reply.

'We have had a lovely time together this last year haven't we?'

'A lovely time Josie.'

'And we've both enjoyed it haven't we?'

'Well I've certainly enjoyed it, and although I'm no aficionado when it comes to the finer points of copulation and the female climax, it seems to me that you've had a pretty good time too.' He thought after he had spoken, that perhaps he might be going at it a bit strong there, but he was determined to make her work for it.

'That's not a very nice way of putting it Jack. You're in an odd mood today.'

'Sorry: just trying to be dispassionate and objective. I thought perhaps it might help.'

'Help with what?'

'Just help.'

With that Josie was silent for a while, and Jack said no more.

'It was just . . .' she began, and then paused.

'One of those things?'

'Pardon'

'Just one of those crazy flings,

One of those bells that now and then rings?'

'Oh God Jack. Cole bloody Porter: another of your quotes. You've been teasing me haven't you? That's really mean of you.'

'Why? Hasn't it been all that the song says? A trip to the moon: our London visit at least, and a few fabulous flights since then.'

'So what do I say now Jack?'

'Shall I say it for you instead? A misquote this time: Josie, I think this is the end of a beautiful friendship.'

She puzzled over that until he hummed the tune for her.

'Casablanca.'

'Right,' he said. 'And remember Josie, whatever comes along in the future, we'll always have Venice.'

'That's enough Jack. Empty your glass and take me up to Rick's for lunch.'

To Jack's surprise he enjoyed their last lunch at The Pump just as much as he had their first a year earlier at Bosewell's. Josie was her usual delightful self, and Jack was content to sit and look at her, and reflect on the fact that a year had probably been just about as long as he would have wanted to keep up her pace.

She hadn't mentioned Beatrice, but it wasn't really significant now, and as for Justin: Jack decided to let sleeping dogs lie. Brandy could have his Beatrice. Dot's conscience would have been eased. Josie's next operational endeavour would be frustrated, probably without her ever understanding why, and he would return to the quiet life.

'But we'll remain friends, won't we Jack?' said Josie as they finished their coffee.

'Oh yes indeed Josie. Good friends if not special friends from now on.'

'And a final quotation to take with me Jack?'

He paused for dramatic effect.

'Farewell thou art too dear for my possessing.

And I say that sincerely with the cost of Le Rendez-vous and Venice very much in mind.'

'A taxman first and last. Come kiss me Jack.'

Little more than a week after his meeting with Josie, and before there had been any further gathering of the Players, Jack's life was further complicated when he found that his morning delivery of mail included a letter addressed to Mr Buckingham Bear, 14 Riverside, Barlow. It was postmarked London, so he had no doubt concerning its author.

Carrying the letter unopened, he walked upstairs wondering what on earth might have prompted it, until he remembered that he'd told Jimmy that he always had the bears for company, and talked things over with Buckingham. Sitting on the end of the bed so that he was almost at face level with the bear, he waved the letter in his hand.

'Someone's written to you from London. I suppose you'd like me to read it to you, would you?'

Taking the bear's silence as tacit consent, he opened the envelope and took out the contents. He had no difficulty in recognising the neat, schoolgirl hand. Addressing the bear he began to read:

'Dear Mr Buckingham Sir,

I now take up my pen to write these few lines to you, hoping that this letter will find you quite as well as it leaves me at present. This was the way I was taught to begin a letter by my first mistress almost seventy years ago, and since then I've stuck to it, because I've always believed that the old ways are the best.

And thinking of the old ways and the old days, I've been wondering how things are with you and Felix, and all my other friends. I often think back to the fun we used to have together when the folk were out: what larks eh? Nothing like that for me though since we parted I'm sad to say. The bears down here are a pretty unsociable crowd, and keep themselves to themselves rather. To be honest I don't get a sensible literary discussion from one month's end to the next, and never a decent quote to be heard. I tell you Mr Buckingham, life in London can be jolly dull.'

So they'd worked quite quickly he thought. I'd jokingly referred to my literary discussions with Buckingham. Jimmy had told Celia, and Celia almost certainly telephoned Kate on the spot: hence the letter. He returned to his reading.

'I said that to Samuel the house cat here, and what do you think he had the nerve to say? He told me that when a bear is tired of London, he is tired of life. Sits by the fire all day and delivers himself of such pearls of wisdom as that, he does. Well I put him right on that. Give me a country house full of bears, I told him, and I'll show you what life is all about.

But I mustn't take up too much of your time, and I'm really writing to let you know that the weekend after next I'm being taken down to Rottingdean to spend a couple of nights with Mr and Mrs Gillan. I'm sure you'll remember them from the days when they used to call in on the hill. And I'm wondering whether you might be able to persuade your master to bring you down to join me, and give us a chance to talk over old times.

I hope that you and all my friends are keeping well and enjoying life in Barlow, which I understand is a very pleasant town. I hope very much that it will be possible for you to join me at Rottingdean, and remain Mr Buckingham,

Your very sincere and affectionate friend,
Wilfred Bear.'

'Well what do you make of that Buckingham?' said Jack. 'He sounds very keen, your Wilfred, so I suppose you would like me to take you down. Speak up if you don't.'

Later in the day Jack telephoned Jimmy to say that if it was convenient he would be keeping his promise to visit them, and suggesting the weekend referred to by Wilfred. He made no reference to the letter, but asked Jimmy if he would let Celia know that Buckingham would be keeping him company.

'It'll be a pleasure to see him,' said Jimmy. 'And I can't think of a weekend that would be more convenient.'

It wasn't easy accommodating Buckingham in the front passenger seat as not all bears are made to bend, but by late afternoon on the Friday Jack had him in place and strapped in by the safety belt. Then, settling

331

himself for what would be a four hour journey, he turned to the bear.

'Are you sitting comfortably Buckingham? Then we'll begin.'